TO CAST A VIOLENT SHADOW

BY

CRISTOPHER DEROSE

Whitestar Books

www.whitestarbooks.com

Copyright 2008 Cristopher DeRose

ISBN 978-0-6151-9588-9

For Jennifer

PROLOGUE

INVOCATIONS

It always starts small.

Avalanches, of any kind, begin with the tumbling of a fistful of pebbles. Then comes the roaring… and the roar becomes the unstoppable.

It always starts small, the woman with the India ink hair trailing nearly to her waist thought on the observation deck of the Nazareth Bay lighthouse. And by the time anyone notices the thundering, the pebbles have become lost, forgotten in the tumble.

It would not be the first time Rebecca Scott would think of such things as she considered allowing herself to fall over the cold guardrail from the early morning stillness and into the swirling darkness below, full of crests of water shattering itself time and time again against the rocks beneath the reaching barrel of the Fresnel lens.

It was not the thought of suicide that motivated the thoughts of Rebecca Scott, who considered such ideas to be selfish things conjured by those misguided enough to not seek any kind of enlightenment that may make it that much easier for someone to get themselves out of bed day after day.

It was because it looked like something resembling serenity underneath the swirling of the surface. There were dangers below, to be certain. Things with teeth and senses mankind had long thought fit to avoid developing in their evolution, but there was no deception. The monsters looked like the beasts they were.

An unrealistic fantasy throwing back to her years as a young girl, picturing herself as a mermaid not because of some childhood trauma, but for some innate calling of the sea and the early appreciation of the irony of many stories about mermaids and the like envying those on the shore they could never walk themselves.

The escapism factor *did* gain ground inside her as time wore on and she pressed into puberty, recognizing not only the cruelty that her classmates visited upon the outsiders but also the cruelty she would come to understanding a capacity for, herself.

But the world was worth fighting for, no matter how hard its occupants appeared to not care one way or the other.

Which was why she found herself in Nazareth Bay, a little once-forgotten fishing town on the California coast a handful of miles above the wine country, now remembered as a bed and breakfast town that had the innate properties of being able to make it virtually impossible for Rebecca's mind to race with any uneasy thoughts. It was a place to unplug long enough to allow her metaphorical (and metaphysical) batteries to recharge to face the real world in Los Angeles and wherever else her research and love of travel would take her.

In Nazareth Bay, they did not hide their secrets in tall spires made of great panes of smoked mirror and steel gleaming warmly in the sunlight fighting its way to the concrete and pavement below. The Bay's secrets (and there were always secrets and those who would harbor them, regardless of where one went) were enshrouded in fog from the Pacific, making them as important and material as so much sugar-thread, to be lessened, lifted away, and forgotten about.

At least that's how she came to think of it as an outsider. She didn't wish to live there, not really. There had to be magick somewhere, and to live in a stream that afforded her such ability as to be able to live in the world in her own kind of sanity was to soften its own focus and value, as well as showing more than a bit of disrespect to the powers that generated it in the first place, marking herself as someone with a profound sense of self-interest and therefore opening up a part of her that would very much enjoy it and never see the ground coming up to hit her as the power changed, dissipated, or turned on her.

That way led to wither.

She began the climb back down the spiral staircase that led back to the ground floor, casting one more glance out across the early morning that was clear enough to let her see the lighthouse on Chatham Island a few unknown miles further west, answering the illumination of the Nazareth Bay light. Her fingers dragged themselves through the waist-length rat's nest her hair had become, trying to get the worst out. She was at the door before she remembered to leave a thank-you note to Darrell for letting her spend a few hours on her last day in Nazareth Bay. She scribbled a few lines about how she enjoyed her stay as usual, hated to leave, blah, blah, blah. And that, as usual, she owed him for extending the Coast Guard's courtesy on his own behalf, because it always paid off to have an ex-husband in the service.

Rebecca slipped behind the wheel of her Mustang, keying the engine to life and trying to push away the thought that was gaining a more authoritative voice that she was not going to be enough in the avalanche that was beginning to roar in the distance.

She dropped the parking brake and nosed the car into the morning.

PART ONE

A QUESTION OF FAITH

CHAPTER ONE

There is a devil, there is no doubt.

But is he trying to get in us,

Or trying to get out?

Unknown

It wasn't the trips to Italy Gavin Fox minded, it was one particular client, Tony Calarco, that was the thorn in the paw. While he had great taste in the arcane items he collected simply to have them, the measure of his knowledge of the background of the pieces and history in general of the occult was beyond admirable.

But for all that, the man was, in the words of the lovely and understanding woman beside him before the door to Calarco's sprawling villa, 'High maintenance.'

Gavin would've settled for 'Pain in the ass,' but Simone had always been the more patient of the two of them. Gavin knew instinctively that was why he would fall in love with her before he actually did. She provided balance and unconditional support to his admittedly rough edges retained through the years despite being cushioned from too many financial problems due to his parent's inheritance, which came complete with what Simone referred to as The Manor, a two-story house in the Hollywood Hills that had been in the family before the hills had that name. He had his grandfather's cynicism, a trait that some considered charming in its way seeing how ol' gramps could temper what could be considered the negative opinion of an embittered old man had gramps actually been mean-spirited or spitting-tacks mad at the world. Instead, his opinions would find themselves couched in humor Gavin would spend his life appreciating and trying to emulate. On more than one occasion, Gavin would find himself saying 'Insert laugh track here' to let the listener know he was kidding. Such flippancy often only ended in making the situation worse. Therefore, Simone would step in when needed.

When the door opened soundlessly, Calarco stood behind it, a big man in a white linen shirt and khaki slacks. As usual, he wore no shoes in the house and encouraged his guests to do the same. Gavin and Simone did so as the collector handed them each a glass of chianti. As usual, their entire conversation was in Italian, a language Simone spoke better than Gavin, but the

5

latter seemed to be better at translating the properties of the items Calarco was interested in. As Simone often pointed out, while Gavin was the one with a long bloodline with regards to the occult and its sundry trappings while Simone considered herself was more a sideline enthusiast who made the right decisions in finding a man who didn't find her collection of rare athames or dusty manuscripts written in dead or 'Esoteric' languages at all unusual. If it hadn't been for Gavin, she had said, her own talents in the occult may have never been awakened much past idle curiosity.

"A new vineyard," Calarco said with a grin. "Please, tell me what you think!"

The two sipped. Simone enjoyed Chianti to the point of being an armchair expert at it and its properties, so Calarco watched her with enthusiasm rather than waiting for Gavin's admittedly more pedestrian opinions. It wasn't that Chianti wasn't enjoyable to him, he just would have preferred a good single malt scotch, or if he felt particularly exotic, a sip or two of sabra. As the Chianti passed his lips, it only reinforced the fact that terms like 'Good finish' and the like meant nothing to him. It tasted fine, that was all, and he nodded appreciatively.

Simone was able to exchange a few words with Calarco on the subject, complimenting the finer points and Simone going so far as to telling him that if he hadn't bought the vineyard in question already, she would have, something that made Calarco chuckle in that way he had that made it difficult to stay mad or frustrated at him.

"But this is not why you've come," Calarco said, pouring himself another glass. "Please, come with me to the library."

This was always something Gavin could look forward to; Calarco's collection of rare books and manuscripts, many handwritten, was amongst the most comprehensive Gavin had seen in his travels. The Calarco Collection, as it was referred to in collector's catalogues and related publications, was the envy not only of collectors of arcane things, but also to those who found them on the collector's behalf.

The scent of well-preserved pages and binding glues pervaded the room that sported ceiling-high libraries on each wall. The single window had, to the best of Gavin's knowledge, always been curtained lest harmful light and heat enter the room, which was equipped with a humidifier and state-of-the-art thermostat with more buttons than Gavin could figure a use for. He hazarded a guess that Calarco had someone in charge of such things, although he was a man of some consequence who would answer his own door, something Gavin gave a good measure of respect for.

Gavin didn't recognize the slight, uncomfortable-looking man seated on the overstuffed leather chair that was set among other pieces of furniture that seemed designed in long ago times to provide the optimum in comfort while one spent his or her time in a good read. There were no doubt more comfortable furnishings to be had in modern times, but it would never reach the style and taste of the dark hardwoods and fine cushioning that dotted the bare polished wood of the floor.

Calaroco stretched his huge hand out to the seated man who appeared to be of the belief that if his leather briefcase left his lap, he would surely burst into flame. "This is Marco DeLucia, the man who insures my more valuable items."

The man finally made eye contact with Gavin and Simone. "Actually, I only represent my company, Findlay and Reserve. I don't personally insure Mr. Calarco."

Simone, knowing what sort of comment was currently fighting its way out of Gavin's mouth, answered first, shaking the man's hand and thanking him for his time.

"It's our understanding that the item stolen had already been appraised," Gavin said.

"That's correct," DeLucia replied. "By the man who sold him the piece, a Mr. Markab, an American."

"Yes," said Simone. "We don't know him personally, but we respect his opinion."

"I'm sure you do. I'm afraid that isn't enough. Findlay and Reserve require a second opinion on such matters. The piece in question, the *O'Barr Manuscript*, is to say the least, difficult to put a price on."

'I'm sure Markab was able to supply one," muttered Gavin.

"I'm sorry?"

"Nothing. A stupid American joke." Gavin grinned to show there was no rancor, and doubted it helped the situation very much at all.

In one swift motion, DeLucia produced a paper watermarked with his company's logo, a crown with a scroll behind it, from his briefcase and presented it to Gavin in a manner that conveyed it was not to leave his hand. On it was a figure in Lira that made Gavin's eyebrows climb.

"Would you agree that this figure, which takes into account not only the amount spent by Mr. Calarco for the piece in question in adjusted monies, but also the manuscript's appreciated value?"

"And the value would and *did* appreciate," Calarco interjected, aiming the statement at Gavin. "As you said it would, yes? I believe your words were 'It would be impossible for the *O'Barr Manuscript* to lose its value.'"

Gavin stared. "Yeah, that's what I was requested put into writing and have Notarized in Milan when you purchased the manuscript. Do you not have the original?" He spared a glance to Simone, who instead of kicking him in the shin, settled for a 'Shut the hell up' look.

The paper was turned to Simone, who managed to keep her expression unchanged despite the astronomical amount. The document was then tucked carefully back into the case, when it was replaced by another on identical paper but allowed to pass into another person's hands.

"Please sign here and here," DeLucia said, indicating spaces for both Gavin and Simone to place their signatures. Thankfully, there was a translation page stapled to it that explained in English that Gavin Fox and Simone Perfect agreed that the stolen article known as the *O'Barr Manuscript* was indeed worth the value indicated on the preceding page. Presumably, Markab had had to sign one, as well.

During what seemed like a characteristic awkward pause, DeLucia cleared his throat. "Now, I have asked Mr. Calarco, but he said he would defer to you, and this is more a matter of curiosity rather than an insurance matter, but what precisely is on this manuscript?"

Calarco turned sheepishly to Gavin and Simone. "I felt it best if you answer the question, especially since Markab came and went before it could be asked."

Gavin exchanged a look with Simone, who stepped into the question effortlessly.

"The manuscript is sought after by collectors because of its unknown use. Its sole contents are a series of items, books, to be specific, listed in what appears to be a particular order. Items that seem to convey a degree of power, although that is only a guess."

"Things having to do with the occult," it was not a question from DeLucia.

"Well, given O'Barr's history as a voice in the occult, yes."

"Although no one knows exactly what these items are meant to do, if anything."

"Correct."

DeLucia did nothing to hide his sour opinion about such things, as well as those who spend exorbitant sums on them. He muttered something in Italian Gavin didn't catch, but didn't need translated.

The agent rose and nodded to Simone before giving a weak, self-conscious shake to the hands of both men and excused himself, noting that he knew the way out.

"I'd like to think there are some things that can exist as much-needed mysteries in the world," Simone said, her voice throwing far enough to allow no doubt as to whom she was addressing.

When the shadows had grown long from the trees Gavin could not identify on Calarco's expansive patio on the west side of his villa and DeLucia's car had ceased to be even a speck on the horizon, their host led Gavin and Simone to an intimate marble-topped table with a set of four chairs. He offered up another serving from the bottle of Chianti that had appeared in his hand as if by magick and waited until they were both seated before sitting across from them.

He wasn't a bad sort, Gavin mused as he watched the sun dipping down into the ocean behind Calarco's head. The man was generous with a smile and whatever wine he had been the most proud of at the time, and certainly with his money, but his insistence on face-to-face meetings and documents upon documents requiring signatures and witnesses contributed to the mental toothache he caused Gavin every time he would call on them to help authenticate an acquisition or ask advice regarding the viability of an investment in such things. He was also the Fox's highest-paying client, a fact which came in handy despite the Manor and the land it was on being paid for generations ago and the books they had written singularly and together covering the paranormal and the antiquities connected with it were steady sellers, as were seats at any of their lectures. The occult was a sticky thing to rely on when it comes to paying bills and throwing money at the problems life insists on throwing it in everyone's face.

The thing about the man named Calarco that really stuck with Gavin was that he was the type of collector who did it simply because he wanted something no one else could have, provided his source or sources got to it first. There was no passion for it, no love of the universe's great mysteries. He saw, he wanted, he had. Simple.

In a way, Gavin was surprised that Tony Calarco hadn't spontaneously combusted when he'd discovered the theft of the *O'Barr Manuscript*, which amongst some conversant in the paranormal, was also known as the *Laundry List of Nonsense*, being a single sheet of parchment, some of which had been removed for two carbon dating tests and other methods to determine whether it was produced in the 1600s, probably between 1627 and 1633 by English occultist Stefan O'Barr, whose written works had been collected and burned by authorities as heretical. To date, the *Volume Arcanus*, the only respected guide to occult printed matter and artifacts had only O'Barr's name, approximated dates of birth and death (which was at the hands of a young Bulgar during a heated argument regarding a gambling result disputed by the Bulgar) and the three known works that O'Barr had published, *The Book of Names*, published circa 1622 which concerned the proper, true names of both demons and angels, something key in conjuring the former or petitioning the latter, although whether the volume actually described how to do such things was the stuff of heated debate.

Gargoyle's Shadow, published two years following *The Book of Names*, and the only O'Barr book on record in authoritative papers of the era to be listed with an actual year that most historians took to be as authentic as could be expected and there were no grounds for fraud to be suspected. The exact contents were in dispute.

Hand of Light, Fingers of Shadow, published circa 1625, was considered by many to be a biography of Lucifer, portrayed as victim rather than destroyer. Widely regarded to be only a translation of an anonymous French volume known as *The Red Book* that O'Barr saw fit to take credit for.

"I hope I didn't step out of place," Simone said to Calarco. "I probably just made your insurance premiums jump a few percent."

"It *was* a bit out of character," Gavin interjected, although Calarco didn't seem to think twice about it.

Calarco waved her concern away. "Please. No problem. Some people need all manner of things explained to them. It's a sad existence, to be sure. Full of bottom lines and calculators." He chuckled as he poured himself more Chianti. "But then, I'm not at all sure I'd want to be insured by someone of a different mindset."

Gavin swirled his own Chianti before taking another swallow, anxious to take a different tack with his client. After the last statement, Gavin could see how he could actually come to tolerate the man, and that wouldn't do at all. "Do the police have any idea as to who could have taken it?"

"No, they are pursing an 'inside job' angle, insisting it was one of the staff, but I know that's the wrong way to take."

"How so?" Asked Simone.

"Just an instinct. I tend to hire a superstitious lot, and that's why; When you have such things about on display, you need to make sure those around it fear it, even if there's no reason."

"Maybe they took it to rid the house of some kind of threat they perceived," Gavin put in, garnering a look from Calarco that made him think he should just sew his mouth shut and let Simone do the talking from here on out.

"No. I feel it in my gut. They didn't take it. There's someone out there who knew what they needed, and where to get it. The rain we had took away most of what the police would have had to have something to start with." The big man sighed. "No, it is gone. That is something I have to cope with." More Chianti spilled into his glass.

Gavin eased back into his chair and considered Calarco, silently grateful that magicks of most kind came harder to men like him and because of that, could not produced the results that were bragged about at tables and functions meant to elevate ones own value among those desired to be fearful. In order for magick to be effective in the slightest degree, it had to notice you, and a man who harbored thoughts like Tony Calarco was beneath such notice.

But the *O'Barr Manuscript* was now out of impotent hands and into uncertain ones.

As if she sensed this unease, Simone's slender fingers found his and entwined there, giving a reassuring squeeze that reminded him that they were in a land that was to be drunk with the eyes, and that he should at least try to enjoy the Tuscan sunset.

CHAPTER TWO

There is good in the world, this I understand.
I also understand there is great evil, and lie awake at night knowing that is entirely up to us
as human beings to perpetuate either one, for whatever reason we find justifiable at the time.

Simone Perfect, MEDITATIONS

Gavin Fox's eyes popped wide as Simone's driving took the Avalanche into a hard right leading to the ribbon of driveway leading to the Manor. He was well in the throes of jet-lag and was unable to appreciate the way his heart was left at the sidewalk by Simone's unique brand of wake-up call, which heralded a diamond splinter migraine currently gaining speed behind his eyes as he blinked them in an attempt to clear his head.

"'We're here' works better," he grumbled, uncurling his legs onto the blacktop.

"You don't make that little sound if I don't surprise you."

"What, 'indignant?'"

"No, like 'Pissy little schoolboy.' I think it's kind of cute. You used to say you loved my spontaneity."

Gavin gave a grunt as he pulled the pair of suitcases free from the SUV's hold. "I used to love pulling the wings off flies, but that passed, too."

"You're equating our undying love for one another with that? I'm angered! I'm appalled!" Simone shouldered the carry-on bag and led the way to the walkway going to the double-door entrance.

"And you're overacting. The Oscar will have to take its business elsewhere."

Simone gave him an air-kiss and shook the house keys in her fist until she located the pair needed, one for the deadbolt, the other for the lock inside the knob itself. "You okay?"

"Headache. Need to lay down and let it pass." The pain behind his eyes throbbed in time with his heartbeat. It had been over six months since his last migraine, but as they all did, this one did return after a hiatus. His prescription would knock it down, provided he lay down and let it work. An odd thing, he thought and not for the first time, that there were book to cast any given kind of spell available at a cost, many of which resided on the shelves in the Manor, and a Rolodex filled with the names of reputable witches and the like, but not a one of those things could do an inch of good against the migraines.

Simone keyed the locks and let him pass first before moving to the security keypad and punching in the code to disable the alarm.

11

"Maybe I'll just check our messages and join you," she said. "That trip took more out of me than I thought. Are you sure we have to go globe-trotting? Can't we just have an official website or something with a 'Frequently-Asked-Questions' part they have to consult before contacting us?"

Simone didn't look worn out to Gavin. Her auburn hair, darkening as she strode into her forties, fell just to her shoulderblades and didn't look at all mussed. The hazel eyes that saw through him and his human faults and loved him anyway were as bright as always. She followed him upstairs, a few paces behind, detouring into the connecting bathroom as Gavin kicked his shoes free without going to the bother of untying them and laid down on the sleigh bed Simone had insisted they buy four years before in Milan, another trip on behalf of Tony Calarco.

His meds were in the bathroom. Simone knew there were some in his bag, but she picked the easiest route. The curtains needed to be pulled, as well. According to glowing red numerals of the digital clock on his nightstand, it was nearing 3:00 in the afternoon, just in time for unforgiving sunlight to spread throughout the room. Normally a pleasant sight that lent itself to a watercolor or something as serene, but now it was only a wide-eyed threat.

Simone re-entered the bedroom, her wire-rimmed glasses back in place on her face, replacing the contacts she preferred to wear. She'd removed her burgundy top, which she held draped over one arm, affording him a view of the black lace of her bra. She came to the bedside and held her hand out to him.

"Your meds, lazybones."

Gavin accepted them gratefully from her palm and swallowed the two tablets dry.

Simone moved to the window. "I really wish you'd stop doing that, it can't possibly be good for you." The pane was blinded with a few deft flicks of Simone's wrist, darkening her small bookshelf facing her side of the bed and the canvas print of Jack Vettriano's melancholy 'In Thoughts of You' in a gold-toned frame Simone had waited until she had moved in with Gavin to add. The print she'd had since her sophomore year in college, but had never felt right in actually putting it up on a wall until Gavin.

"Thank you," said Gavin, waiting for the pain to subside.

Simone moved to her dresser and removed an oversized Notre Dame Soccer T-shirt, pulling it over her head as she made her way to the doorway leading to the hall. There were work clothes, which in their line of work meant business casual, then there was knockabout clothing, meaning jeans and in Simone's case, a shirt from her *Alma Mater*. Footwear was optional around the Manor, making it a rare sight when Simone was seen walking about in any kind of shoe.

"You're welcome. I think I'm going to go downstairs. I think I'm getting my second wind. Call me if you need anything. We'll just wing it for dinner, depending on how you're feeling. 'Kay?"

"Sounds good."

The door clicked shut behind her, giving Gavin just enough time to wonder what he'd done to deserve her before his body relaxed, and he fell into a dark, dreamless sleep.

The first thing about Fox Manor (referred to only in self-deprecating jest) that struck Simone upon descending the stairs was its inherent stillness. As long as she could remember being with Gavin, somewhere between ten and one hundred years now, she could not recall so much as a creak in the eaves. There was the occasional groan when a strong Santa Ana wind kicked up or while during a winter storm, but otherwise, it not only was without settling protests, but it simply sat unassuming in the hills. At first, Simone thought it was a sign of balance. The Fox family had a long history of spiritual connection, and of masters of stage magick, giving to the family fortune she and Gavin now enjoyed, as the natural inclinations of his father and grandfather helped in decisions regarding investments and the like, giving Gavin's father the opportunity to retire early and Gavin to pursue his own interests in the arcane unencumbered by the costs of everyday living and create the respected name for himself he'd aspired to without having to live down his surname, as the Foxes before him chose to keep their brand of luck out of the public eye and harbor it close to home. Once, Gavin had confided to Simone that he doubted very much that his mother and grandmother had any idea at all regarding their respective spouse's ability to listen to things around them that others couldn't be bothered to pay any mind.

But there were times, growing in number and frequency now, she noticed, that she got the overwhelming sense that she was not at all as comfortable with the stillness as she had been when she'd moved in an year and a half after she and Gavin began dating steady.

The house should have noises. Life within it. New laughter growing to hesitant footsteps that became the blessed thundering of running belonging to feet that had become certain of balance and placement.

It was a subject she and Gavin had talked about soon after it had become obvious they both had designs on one another, and neither were inclined to have children. It wasn't a matter of not liking them; they certainly seemed gravitate to Gavin when they would take their walks in the park, and he could enter their world willingly if not with a given degree of difficulty on account of his calling showing him things that would take the wide-eyed wonder out of anyone. And Simone herself never hesitated in the presence of her niece Eliza, all of six years old now. She even proudly passed the test of a parent's mettle known as 'A Trip to Disneyland with a Child' which she got to experience when she and her sister Sarah went with the then five-year old Eliza on a girl's day out.

Only now, as she began to see the first threads of grey making their unwelcome appearance in not only her own hair, but also Gavin's classically wavy charcoal hair, was she treated to this turn of events in her spirit and mind.

But she and Gavin both agreed at the start that children just weren't in the picture.

Namely, their rather dark business wasn't a way of life that either one of them felt justified in thrusting upon an adult, much less a child. Over the past two or three years, Simone had gotten the distinct impression Gavin had resolved himself to the course they were on: Just the two of them, glorified Ghostbusters, on their way to whatever kind of retirement such folks are allowed to have.

At that, she brought herself short and touched her fingertips to the back of her head. Glorified Ghostbusters? Where had *that* bitter little chestnut come from? Good God, they were more than that. Okay, maybe not in the eyes of her side of the family, but they weren't thrilled with Gavin getting the proverbial milk for free for as long as he had, and Simone not putting up any kind of ultimatum.

Mom and Dad didn't mind the improvements to their house the Fox stature had gotten them, though. Her sister Sarah and her husband Nicholas certainly didn't complain about the gifts that would be given to them and/or Eliza on the holidays, either. Despite their surname, her family wasn't perfect; she understood that as well how hard it must have been whenever she and Gavin were consulted for television shows that researched into the paranormal and appeared on-camera at some hotel that claimed to be haunted and her Mom and Dad's friends would see and ask if they ever worked any other day besides Halloween or that *something* must be fishy with Gavin, because there was no way anyone could be respected in such a field, much less have any real money to live on. There had been hints and allegations of scamming, taking advantage of the elderly and the ignorant, so on and so forth. It never got any easier. Nearly every time her Mom or Dad were called, it was something new. Because of it, Gavin stopped accepting offers from the shows a few years before and lowered the considerable Fox profile back to where it was before the TV shows and magazine articles he would later say he should never have had a part in because it did nothing to validate or legitimize his legacy or the world outside belief. Such things were held in better stead in their own circles, and that had always been enough before.

Simone would've been ashamed to thank him for the decision, but that didn't keep her from thinking it and being grateful for the fewer lectures from Mom and Dad who did *not* help her go to Notre Dame for her to pursue such silly things.

The fact she attended on an athletic scholarship did nothing to brighten their mood during conversations of that kind. She would only be reminded of the soccer career she threw away to be with Gavin.

She didn't care. She would've done it again. No question. World League or whomever else pounding down her door be damned. She loved the man she loved, end of sentence.

14

Resisting the urge to raid her stash of emergency pack of Marlboro Lights located in the back of the requisite kitchen junk drawer, buried beneath batteries and a Ziploc bag stuffed full of rubber bands, she stabbed the playback button on the answering machine in the living room and hoped it was something that might actually brighten her suddenly dark mood.

She got a kind of compromise from the phone message gods. It was Rebecca Scott, card-carrying witch and fellow author regarding the unknown. It wasn't that she didn't like Rebecca, in fact she was quite enamored with the woman. The thing that got stuck in the gears of her head, which she would be the first to admit were tricky and temperamental things to begin with, was the memory of the time she caught Gavin checking her out as the witch walked away from them at an occult convention. Southern California. Five years ago. Rebecca wore black pants that were painted on. Gavin wore that black button-down shirt Simone gave him as an anniversary present.

Rebecca's message was to the point and more cryptic than it needed to be, in Simone's opinion. A witch's equivalent of 'A disturbance in the Force.' She wanted to hold council with them and get their take on it.

Even concentrating, and going to the trouble of closing her eyes, Simone couldn't come up with anything. But Rebecca had been right about such things before, so it stood to reason. But she'd never had the tone she had in her message; An underlying context Simone didn't care for in the least.

She found herself digging under the baggie of rubber bands, and fishing out a cigarette. The Bic that she kept with it had long since given up its flame, leaving the stove as the most convenient lighter.

In the backyard beneath the deck of the patio, the cigarette tasted staler than she'd expected. She stubbed it out on one of the stones ringing the azalea flowerbed after two half-hearted drags. She was able to stave off the light-headedness faster than she'd expected, considering that the last cigarette she'd had was... when? Two years ago? Maybe. She couldn't remember when, much less the occasion that had prompted the action.

Defeated, she went back through the sliding glass door and waited for Gavin to wake up.

CHAPTER THREE

Certainly, there are charlatans in the world who would identify themselves as Finders, but they are beneath contempt. Those who are truly Finders understand that it is not in their best interest to go about identifying themselves, because they understand all too well that in the world of the occult, they are regarded as being no better than graverobbers or thieves.

Lucas Brady, THE OCCULT IN THE CONTEMPORARY WORLD

Daylight gave way to headlights in the city of Hollywood, a clearer evening than the one previous, but the pollution of the constant moan and throb of every light known to man blotted out most of the stars above the 8800 block of Sunset Boulevard.

Karac didn't like it. It made it too easy to forget about such things as humility in the face of vastness. But then, look where he was; it would be like arguing honest faces in Las Vegas. One didn't go to Hollywood for ethics.

It wasn't that The Wash was seedy. Far from it. The name wasn't emblazoned on the wall facing the street, but the unassuming *façade* certainly didn't suffer, and those who didn't belong there rarely frequented it, or stay for very long if they tried to visit more than once. There was a rhythm to the place, as there is in all charismatic places to hang out and drink and talk with folks. It was dark within its walls during business hours, without looking like it had something to hide, which was sometimes more than a few of its regular patrons had to offer.

Karac wouldn't have had it any other way.

He tipped an imaginary hat to the doorman, Gregor, who took time away from the two young ladies who stood rapt as he related some adventure in the way only he could to nod him through the second door that electric blues was busy squeezing through.

Karac wasn't sure which band was playing that night, but found his head nodding as he made his way to the main bar. The woman bartender he desperately wanted to remember the name of was working that night and had his bourbon rocks waiting for him by the time he made the bar.

It was still early in the evening, and a Friday to boot, so soon enough, the floor would become less and less visible, noise would increase, and lives would become (at least for a little while) less complicated. It would be during the busier times he'd feel a bit more camouflaged than usual – he wasn't particularly striking, knew it, and felt the better for it. Karac wasn't one to mind that he could go unnoticed. In fact, he relished it. He was only found when he needed to be. It was what a Finder did, lay low and relax before someone came looking for you, then something buried would rise to the surface in his body and his mind. A challenge, which was what a Finder truly lived for, despite the fact it was rare when someone wanted something of a positive nature, whether it came from this world or another better left undiscovered.

At least for the time being.

He finished his drink. The alcohol was going down quicker and easier these days, but he was still able to suppress concern to a degree past actual acknowledgement of it. He was old enough to know he should be wary of such things, and numbing himself was never a good idea, especially in his line of business.

The glass landed mouth-down on the hardwood tabletop. He had no more than leaned back in his chair when Karac saw a waitress serve up another highball. Before he could protest, the woman poked a finger in the direction of the bar.

"Compliments of the lady," she said, indicating the brunette standing at the bar, dressed in blue jeans, distressed leather jacket and a crimson closed-mouth smile. She raised her own glass in a toast before pushing away from the bar and walking slowly to him.

"Mia Baudino," Karac said. "You're the devil."

In one smooth motion, Mia grabbed a chair, spun it backwards and sat down, hands holding her drink by the edge of the rim. "Nah, I'm a much better dancer. I *will* get you to see the wisdom of the whiskey sour, though."

Karac sipped at the drink and considered the woman before him. He'd never asked, but he was pretty certain she was probably in her mid-twenties, making her about seven years his junior. He never saw her in anything but all-black ensembles of jeans complimented by either trendy t-shirts or loose blouses. Every inch of her left ear was pierced by small silver hoops curling up into her cartilage. Her right was pierced only twice.

Karac came back to her, shaken from his reverie not by her silence combined with the tilt of her head. If he didn't know any better, he would have sworn she could read his mind.

"Sorry," he said. "What was that you were saying?"

"Didn't say anything. I was just looking. You okay?"

"Long couple of weeks." It wasn't a lie, just a stretch. He'd been job-free for about five days, and that suited him just fine. But he was feeling the itch. The familiar longing for a job to find something.

It wasn't the money. Never was.

And without the hunt, the bottle beckoned, especially when the longing became wishing. Dangerous stuff, wishes. There was nothing worse than getting what you wanted. One would only have to just ask a few of his clients.

It never seemed to matter much what the two of them would talk about, just so long as the two of them were speaking, playing the game of verbal give-and-take. Sometimes, Mia had a way of using her smile almost as a punctuation. She never once looked away from him when he was talking, pinning him to where he sat, drinking in the features of this woman, who seemed to have little place in the world he first met her in, although if he concentrated, he could still see how her attractiveness was somehow tempered with a kind of darkness her eyes fought to betray.

She was bright and mighty and terrible.

She was beautiful.

"You know," she said after a time. "I still don't know your last name. You know mine. You have the advantage."

"It's just Karac."

"Just Karac? Just like Cher?"

"I hope not."

She leaned away from the chairback, cocking her head to the left slightly. The corner of her mouth curled upward. "So no last name." She considered this. "Okay. Names are important things, and I always thought you should call someone by the name they tell you, so…" She let the sentence hang between them unfinished. He could tell she knew there was more to it than just vanity, but she'd let it pass for now. She was able to convey all this without the alarm of letting someone think she was exhibiting the patience of a learned – or worse, a *natural* – predator. It was just something she'd tuck away for the present… until the person across the table from her decided otherwise.

This suited Karac fine.

He watched as she took time away from him to turn and applaud the band as they finished their first set and they excused themselves for a short break. When she turned back to him, she had what seemed to be an anxious expression on her face. The tip of her tongue pressed itself into the corner of her mouth as a smile grew. "You know, I was wondering something. Do you think I can get the answer to a very important question from you?"

He spread his hands before him. "I am at your service."

"Well, I was thinking that," in a moment, whatever happiness and momentum lived in her features fled without warning and her eyes broke away from him as she completed her sentence: "That there's some
guy coming up behind you."

Her drastic change in expression may have alarmed him at first, but the slight figure before him radiated no anger or potential trouble. Karac noticed there was no fight-or-flight mechanism in himself at all while in front of this soul in ratty corduroy jacket and face that hadn't seen a smile in a long time. Long enough, Karac wagered, for it no not be very healthy at all. In the distance, Gregor could be seen watching the table. Soon enough, he relaxed and went back to the door, but not before nodding one of his men to keep tabs on the situation.

The man's slate eyes flitted to Mia only long enough to mind the place she was occupying, nothing more before returning to Karac.

"Your name is Karac." There was no mistaking the man's tone. The words he spoke far from a question.

The switchblade was in the satchel at his feet, and Mia had actually backed up a pace.

"What's your name, friend?"

The man almost seemed surprised he was being spoken to. "Solomon. My name is Solomon Archer."

Then Karac saw it. That thing that lurked behind the eyes of another human being when all other avenues had been tried and found wanting. In this Solomon, it was almost as if that hunger or whatever you would call it was fighting for time with the ugliest kind of desperation; the type that tends to bend inward and slowly devour its host.

"Why don't you sit down?" Karac indicated Mia's vacated chair as Mia remained standing.

Solomon's eyes flicked around the room. "I... I don't... can't we go somewhere else?"

"We're talking here." Karac tempered his voice enough to where he made it clear he was in charge of the decisions. The man had found him, now Solomon was on the Finder's turf. It was up to him whether to run or sit.

"I'm just a little nervous."

Karac returned to his seat. "You're a lot nervous. Sit down."

Without removing her gaze from Solomon, Mia said, "Karac, I'll see you around. 'kay?" She did not wait for an answer.

Karac watched her retreating back, not looking at Solomon until she'd disappeared and Solomon sat down.

"That you're girlfriend?"

Karac waved the question away. "Let's just say this better be worth it."

Solomon nodded quickly. "Right.... Right... None of my business."

"Uh-huh. First, how did you find me?"

"I got desperate enough to realize there were people like you in the world. There had to be. You're name just naturally came to me when I saw you here."

Typical explanation. More importantly, it was the right one. "And what are you looking for?"

"I dunno, exactly."

"Not what my customers usually tell me."

"I just mean, I know what I need, just not what *form* it's going to be in."

Karac made no show in opening his satchel, keeping it to simple gestures and constant eye contact with Solomon. Inside the bag, and next to his worn loose-leaf leather notebook and atop the book-shaped flask filled with Bols gin sat the blade. He was able to keep it at rest on his lap without undue suspicion from Solomon. If someone would pass by, he could nudge it under his leg. For the hundredth time, he made a note to carry it on his body. The discomfort of it in a pocket would be better suited rather than submitting to the vanity. The canvas bag he purchased because it paid a passing resemblance to the one Indiana Jones used could contain the usual items he needed on the job; the reference books, catalogs, random papers, at least two-hundred dollars in cash in various denominations, the battered notebook, pen, and pencils.

For the palpable creepiness Solomon had been apparently cursed with, he seemed completely genuine and in the grasp of something Karac would probably find a challenge in. The use of the word 'Need' rather than 'Want' in his customers made him want to help them, not just hunt something down. It was something that Solomon had thought enough about to consider every possibility in getting that help in whichever guise it would make itself available in. Again, something Karac rarely saw anymore. His usual clientele knew exactly what they wanted.

But they usually didn't look like they were about to jump off a cliff if things didn't work out. Solomon did.

"What do you need it for?"

Solomon leaned forward and stared into Karac's eyes. "To get rid of a gift. I can see spirits..." here he paused, testing to see if Karac would laugh or hit him. Karac maintained his look of detached interest, and the man continued. "Everywhere. All the time."

"Go on," Karac said.

"I'm having trouble telling who are ghosts and who are real people," Solomon continued as if he hadn't heard Karac's comment. "If I kind of squint, I can sort of tell..."

"And you want it to stop."

"Like you wouldn't believe. It's only gotten worse since I was a kid."

There was no doubting the man. While Karac had dealt with only a couple of people with a penchant for dangerous curiosity and access to information only a privileged few would have, and he could sense them a mile off. This guy wasn't curious. Like he'd said earlier in their conversation, he had become desperate enough to search out a Finder.

"Can you help me?" Solomon was leaning forward again.

"Let me get back to you." Karac pushed a napkin across to him and handed him a Bic pen to write his name and phone number.

"I'll pay whatever price necessary," Solomon said.

"Yes," Karac nodded. "I'm sure you will."

Solomon scribbled his information down on the napkin and stood. He looked like he was about to shake Karac's hand, then thought it may breach some kind of protocol and pulled his hand back. "Do you know when you'll be able to tell me more?"

"Give me until tomorrow afternoon. Then we'll talk price."

Solomon nodded and thanked Karac no less than five times in various ways before taking his leave as the band took their places again.

Karac rested his chin in his hand, setting his elbow on the tabletop. Despite of the voice in his head asking for another drink, he declined a refill from the waitress. He sat there, alone, listening to the first opening notes of a song he couldn't remember the name of.

For the first time in his career as a Finder, he had no idea what to do.

CHAPTER FOUR

It is mystery; the child and the unopened box, that compels us to look even when we know we shouldn't.

Lucas Brady, STILL AND ALL

She hadn't made it halfway to Los Angeles when Rebecca Scott felt it; the expectation in a part of her that made her eyes go to the rearview mirror time and time again despite the fact there was hardly any traffic on the blacktopped ribbon of highway.

Rebecca could not immediately see them, but she was being watched, most likely from the time she left Nazareth Bay, she just didn't sense anything up until now. The reason why could be any of several; magickal cloaking that was now failing, as the most of them did, usually at the worst of times for the user, although it could have been that whomever it was was now getting closer, and therefore easier to detect for someone of Rebecca's abilities.

As the speedometer needle started its reach into the nineties, Rebecca recalled the saying, 'You should never run away from magickal things – it only gains their attention.' Whomever thought it up clearly had never had the hackles raise on the back of their neck, not because of what they knew was coming, but because they had no idea.

There was a roadside advertisement for a Denny's two exits away. She would close the gap in short order if she continued her current speed, but was not entirely sure it would be fast enough.

There were two places someone of her ilk could go in times of isolation and trouble; go to as remote an area as possible and have it out, whatever that might mean. The other was to go to the most public of places and see what happened. You couldn't very well ask for help, but public display of powers were things either heroes or villains seldom wanted to resort to, regardless of what color hat any given person considered themselves to be wearing. Those who practiced secret things, with few exceptions, wanted very badly to keep them that way, and with good reason. Because those secrets worked.

She was seated by the hostess almost as soon as she crossed into the restaurant, and kept her back to the wall with the menu in front of her while carefully peering over the laminated pages.

Whomever was coming would be able to sense her at least as easily as she could them, perhaps easier. Not a comforting thought.

Now they were close enough to tell there was more than one coming to the door. Rebecca could feel their energy, both singular and collective, before they put their feet onto the worn entryway carpet. One of them she could handle. But two... that was another story with a less than optimistic end. But they were combining their powers to boost them, and probably concentrating on finding her more than anything else, so that might mean they wouldn't be able to pool their resources in a fight.

21

It might also mean they could shift their attention to the offensive without effort and kick her into next week.

A man and a woman entered, appearing for all intents ordinary folk who hadn't the slightest of interests in power. If Rebecca allowed her eyes to unfocus, she knew she'd be able to watch the power arcing off the two of them in blue-white sparks.

Rebecca made sure she made eye-contact with the both of them as the hostess greeted them with a smile.

Get out, Rebecca sent. *Get out, or I'll call challenge.*

The confidence with which she transmitted her warning was meant to convey the effect of *I've already won this battle. It's all over but the bleeding.* All this was usually a given, but playing a bluff was certainly not unheard-of. It could also be considered a tactic to goad the enemy into action, ideally a rash one. Challenging in a public place was discouraged, but it could communicate that a party was willing to do some collateral damage if that's what it was going to take.

The woman turned to the hostess, matching the woman's wide smile, said something and gestured to where Rebecca sat. The hostess nodded, glanced over to Rebecca and moved behind the counter.

The man sent, *We're just here to talk.* He and his partner made their way past the tables and booths, never breaking eye-contact with her. As they grew closer, they sent their order's sigil; simple representations of the phases of the lunar cycle. Rebecca recognized it as the sign of the Second Order, the largest nation of witches in the US and UK.

And you usually introduce yourself by stalking?

We'd just missed you in Nazareth Bay, this came from the woman as the two of them sat across from her at the table. "We've been following your aura trail since we figured you'd be headed to Los Angeles."

"Who the hell are you two?"

"My name is Dana," the woman with the dark hair just beginning to show threads of silver said. She gestured to a man younger than she dressed in nondescript black shirt and pants. "He's Lincoln. We're from the Second Order's UK Coven."

That would explain the slight accent in the woman's voice. The man was obviously an American. "Neat. And what can I do for the top organized coven? Oh, and how do you know what I'm doing?"

"The disturbance has been felt by the members for about a week," Lincoln answered. "It's gaining speed and dimension and frankly, we have a good idea that the your friends are going to be involved. It stood to reason that you'd know about it, or at least have felt it. You're abilities are renown."

Rebecca shrugged. "And the coven is going to try to recruit me again? It's about time, you know. It's been at least six months since your last attempt."

"That's not it at all," Dana bristled. "We know that Gavin and Simone are going to be in on this in some way or another. It's got that magnitude, whatever it is, and you're friends with them, so we needed to find you."

"What for?"

"The Order, and ten others thus far, have decided to stay out of whatever it is that's happening. It does not concern us or our belief system, and is of the importance that we want to be well clear of the blast zone when it happens."

"And no one knows what that is, only that something big is afoot."

"That's right."

A waitress approached them then, but Rebecca asked for more time, which the waitress was more than happy to give them.

"If it's as big as I think," Rebecca continued. "It's not going to matter where anybody is."

"Elizabeth Danvers feels otherwise."

Rebecca and Elizabeth were about the same age, with Elizabeth in the lead by a nose. They went separate ways in their beliefs years ago, when they were just out of their teens, as friends often do. Elizabeth went on to pursue the more political climes of the Order, which suited her personality, anyway. Rebecca became a lone practitioner, the differences between the two keeping them apart by necessity rather than by design. Rebecca didn't mind the public eye her books created, and despite some sniffing among others, some being alumni in the Second Order, the roads they each took seemed best suited.

Dana and Lincoln both appeared to be waiting for Rebecca to actually say Something. When she didn't, they shared a glance and Lincoln spoke:

"We're to act as escorts to your meeting with her."

Rebecca couldn't resist an elevated eyebrow. "Really? When am I to be there? Do I bow or do I curtsey?"

The looks on their faces was priceless. It was as if their friendliness was cracked in half and they were left holding the pieces. One did not question Elizabeth when she wanted to see them.

"She asked for you to be there soonest."

"Well, I still need to eat …"

She could almost hear Dana's aorta closing. Lincoln did better to hide his horror at her pithy attitude, but not by much.

"I'm sure there would be something provided if you asked," Dana replied.

Rebecca knew that, too. She had no idea of what would be given to her, but Elizabeth treated those around her right, especially those she inconvenienced. Unless it was intentional.

Rebecca lowered her voice and eschewed any pretense. "I need bodyguards?"

"The term is 'Escort,'" corrected Lincoln.

Dana nodded. "We *are* sorry to have startled you." Dana leaned forward. "Lincoln and I are readers of your work, and we respect you and what you have done." Here she paused, seemingly afraid of keeping eye contact with Rebecca as she finished, "Or what you are *able* to do, as Elizabeth asking for an audience shows us."

"She hasn't asked anyone else to see her?"

"Not that we know of."

"Do you have access to that kind of information?"

"We are part of her administration," said Lincoln. "Even if we weren't meant to know, we'd know."

Rebecca nodded and stood, much to their pleasure. "Okay, then. I am in your hands, willingly, and with perfect confidence. I know the way. Do I follow or do I lead?"

"It may be best for you to take the lead. We'll follow momentarily."

The Interstate Rebecca had been following would've taken her past Elizabeth Danver's house, but being as it was off the road by several miles in a small section of a town called Ocala, it was too significant of a detour for her to consider on her route to see Gavin and Simone, but since Elizabeth had sent bodyguards no less to send word and basically intercept her, Rebecca allowed herself to be redirected.

It wasn't the requesting an audience part that got under her skin, it was the fact that not one but two witches had been dispatched to retrieve her, not a sign that inspired confidence when considered with the feeling she already had driving her to seek out Gavin and Simone. Rebecca was able to handle herself; this Elizabeth knew as well as anybody. Still the bodyguards.

Safety in numbers, Rebecca thought and turned into the driveway, realizing she hadn't seen the two-storey house in the daylight for at least seven years. Usually the drive would be lined on either side by votives burning bright into the night, more for aesthetics than any real ceremony. Anyone outside their circle probably would've hiked their
noses to such theatrics, but then, they would've done the same to Rebecca for not joining a coven, and even those detractors couldn't understand why she would decline an invitation to join the Order under Elizabeth's administration.

Dana and Lincoln parked a few feet away and led the way up the steps that took them to the front door. They rang the bell, which played a melody Rebecca was never able to place. After a moment, the door was opened by a young woman wearing a smoky quartz crystal around her neck. A novice in her late teens, Rebecca reckoned. Basically an intern for the house and things needed to be done to run it. Dana introduced Rebecca, who the girl clearly recognized, before leaving her to be escorted inside the house. Dana and Lincoln had business elsewhere and took their leave a few steps into the house, probably to go up to the library upstairs.

"It's a real honor to have you here," the girl said as she guided Rebecca through the large sitting room where many of the Order's rituals would usually be held. A small altar covered with a simple black cloth kept time with a glass container of salt, the same ebony-handled atheme Rebecca had always known her to have, a sterling censer, a length of cord and a chalice. At some point since their last meeting, Elizabeth had replaced her old brass bell with another, even more antique than the last. Other items were kept nearby, but stored away.

Among them would be Elizabeth's sword, which unlike her predecessor, kept his sword on display prominently in his house.

"It's always an honor to be here," Rebecca replied. "What's your name?"

The girl seemed surprised someone like Rebecca Scott would be interested in such things as the name of a novice, but answered nonetheless. "Jessica."

"How long have you been in the Order?"

"Three months, officially. My folks weren't real sure about my working for a witch, much less my being one, but it's like, an honest job, y'know? Only without the time clock."

Rebecca nodded. "I hope you find your path here."

"Thanks." Jessica led her to a sliding glass door that Rebecca remembered would lead to the back garden where Elizabeth insisted on doing her meditations and thinking. Anything indoors was usually counter-productive to her as walls kept her from the natural force of things. "Miss Scott?"

Rebecca chuckled. "Please, call me Rebecca."

"Oh. Oh. Okay." Jessica momentarily forgot how to operate the glass door. "Could I ask you to autograph one of your books for me? Just one. I promise I won't sell it or anything."

"Of course. Just catch me on the way out."

Jessica thumbed the catch and slid the door open. "Thanks. I'll do that." She then stepped aside, gesturing for Rebecca to pass through while stayed inside, more out of respect for the conversation rather than any sort of demand of Elizabeth's, Rebecca knew.

Rebecca took three steps off the porch and onto the freshly cut grass and froze.

Half the garden was gone, replaced by a stone path leading to an open concrete patio, complete with swimming pool, in which Elizabeth lay, floating on her back, giving small kicks to keep her moving from deep end to shallow.

Rebecca made her way poolside, standing at the stairs leading into the pool. Her arms crossed her chest and she waited for Elizabeth to notice her, which she did presently.

"Becca," she said, making for the side of the pool. The smile was the same, even if the garden had been decimated. Elizabeth pulled herself from the water, dressed in a black two-piece bikini. Her platinum blonde hair had been cut from mid-back to its present length well above her shoulders. Streaks of magenta were another addition. She toweled off and padded to her friend, giving a hug that crushed the air from Rebecca's chest.

"Smiles like Elizabeth," Rebecca said. "Acts like her, and yet has done away with her garden and went all postal with her hair."

Elizabeth's fine-boned features scrunched up. "I'll have you know that more than half the garden is still here," she pointed over Rebecca's shoulders. "And the pool was something I'd wanted to do for a long time. The water's very conductive to my meditation. You should give it a try."

"I'll keep that in mind."

"It's been awhile, hasn't it?"

"A little longer than I would like to think, I guess."

Elizabeth made a full turn, allowing Rebecca a view of her back. The ornate backpiece tattoo of a pentagram had now been joined by a half-border from shoulderblade to shoulderblade of the phases of the moon. After a compliment from Rebecca and some good-natured ribbing from Elizabeth about when Rebecca herself was going to get her own tattoo that she'd been bragging about getting for years and years.   Elizabeth gestured to a pair of antiqued canvas deck chairs. "I am glad you could make it."

Rebecca eased into one of the chairs. It was more comfortable than it looked. When she had to shield her eyes from the glare, Elizabeth scooted her chair to a better angle to accommodate a conversation. "How could I not when I had two of your people scaring the hell out of me?"

"I'm sorry. They did the best they could, considering everything that's happening."

"What do you know?"

"Conflict is coming. That's all I know. Stuff that's ugly and deeper than people want to be bothered with. I first noticed it about three months ago when I had trouble concentrating on my meditative state."

"But you've always had difficulty…"

"Not like this. At first, it was just like a minor distraction would pull me out of it. Then it was as if someone was watching me. Well, not so much *me*, but it was like whatever it was just went around trolling. After that, I couldn't even get into a state. That's when the pool went in. I guess it's like running back to the womb or something."

"So now you can meditate?"

Elizabeth's eyes fluttered. "Sometimes yes, sometimes no."

Rebecca nodded. "So you think this thing you're feeling is something material?"

"No. That's just it. I keep thinking it's like a precursor of some kind. Like it's like a phenomenon unto itself, just wandering around, taking a look around before everything goes to hell."

It made sense to Rebecca. And Elizabeth had always been considerably more able to give accurate theories regarding things that lurked on the horizon. She'd become known for it, and that in part became one of the reasons she was able to be elected into her position.

"What do you think is going to happen? You sound like a war is coming."

Elizabeth's eyes dropped. "Not a war. In wars, there are battles. This isn't a battle, it's just an end. Everything answered."

"What does that mean?"

"What happens when all the mysteries are solved?"

Rebecca shrugged.

"Yeah, that's just it. No one knows. The ones who say otherwise are just too bullheaded to know when to hide under the bed."

"So the Orders are going to hide."

"In a manner of speaking."

"I've never known you to run from a fight, Elizabeth."

"This isn't a duel. It's not three-on-one, or sending a Dawn Killer back to the ashes it sprang from when we were too stupid to know there are things young witches shouldn't screw with."

Rebecca nodded. "So you're going to run. You're going to listen to the collective panic and run with your Order."

Elizabeth's eyebrow snapped to attention. Rebecca could feel the shift from old friend to current politico. Distasteful and sudden. "It doesn't concern us, it can only trample us. The Craft will be collateral damage, not intended target. This the entire Nation agrees on. We stand no chance, Rebecca." The attitude remained although the expression softened. For the first time since she'd met Elizabeth, Rebecca was left without knowing where she stood with the woman. "That's why I asked you to come here."

"You're asking me to run with you and the others."

Elizabeth shifted her weight, crossed her legs. "I am offering asylum."

"Really? So far, I haven't heard how you all intend on avoiding this destruction." Elizabeth hesitated long enough for Rebecca to lunge for the heart. "You don't have the slightest idea, do you? None of you do."

"And do you, Rebecca?"

"No. But then, I'm not running."

Elizabeth's arms folded across her chest. The eyebrow declined. The conversation was over, at least to her.

"What are you planning, Elizabeth? What do you want to do to get out of the crosshairs? You can't hope to erase whatever traces you can of the Nation."

Finally, Elizabeth's eyes returned to meet her gaze, defiant.

"You can't be serious," Rebecca said. "That would mean – "

"Burning scrolls," Elizabeth finished. "Destroying records older than we truly know. Eradicating every inch of shared knowledge, and even that which is kept away from all except the highest in the Orders."

"That's impossible. Even if you had access to everything you'd need, you couldn't do it. Somebody somewhere would keep something that would tip the scales. They'd want to preserve whatever they could to keep the beliefs as pure as possible and true to history."

"This is why there is inaction in the Nation as a whole. Some want to, others don't. It is causing discord."

"Which side are you on?"

"I don't know anymore." Elizabeth veiled her eyes with the palm of her hand. "Nobody does, and we're afraid to admit it to one another. We're afraid to set any plans into action, and we're scared that somebody already has, and that centuries of records are now going up in smoke, or bathed in acid so not so much as an ash is left to lead trouble to our doors."

"And so you're going to be standing there debating with the other Priests and Priestesses when the time comes."

Elizabeth's hand fled from her face to flutter indecisively.

27

"So why do you want me here, if you have nothing to offer?"

"Because I was hoping you would. Because I'm scared and don't want to be alone when my Order finds out I have no idea of what to do."

Rebecca rose slowly to her feet, taking in her friend's overflowing eyes before reaching out and wiping away the tears with her thumbs. She kissed Elizabeth on the forehead and pressed her own head to hers, eyes focused on eyes.

"'Waste no more time arguing what a good man should be, be one.'"

"Marcus Aurelius," replied Elizabeth as Rebecca pulled away.

"It's all could think of to say," Rebecca said, taking steps away from Elizabeth. "Maybe it's time to back away from the role of politician and lead. Use the power you have or you won't have it for long."

Elizabeth nodded, chuckled as she wiped the last of her tears away and visibly composed herself. "Leave it to Becca Scott to kick my ass."

Rebecca swept her hand before herself in a grand, theatric gesture. "And with that, I leave you to your will."

"As it should be."

"Blessed be."

"Blessed be."

"I love you."

"Love you, too. Watch your back."

Rebecca spun, and made her way back into the house, where she met with Jessica. She signed the girls' copy of her first book, *Modern Practicing* and tried to shake the feeling that this was going to be the last time she'd see her friend.

CHAPTER FIVE

In order to understand the occult and its collective repercussions, one should learn the game of chess, and play it every day. This teaches us we do not see everything we think, and that we are not the only players present on the board, and that there is always somebody better at it than we are.

Gavin Fox and Lucas Brady, HOLE IN THE SKY

It was not unusual, only unlikely that during their Sunday morning backgammon games on the uncovered porch of the veranda located at the back of the Manor that Gavin Fox could be found actually winning a game by a decisive edge. Chess was more his game. But he'd long since cultivated a love for the game nonetheless, due in no small part to the company he kept.

Amid the pages of the Sunday paper he'd read, and the Sunday-Go-To-Meetin' coffee mugs (as Simone had taken to calling them) Gavin had but three stones to bear off while Simone still had four to move into position before she could begin her own process of bearing off. A live Dave Brubeck CD playing on the stereo just a few steps inside the manor, Gavin watched as Simone finished the last of her coffee and suppressed a grin at his certain victory.

The game finished, Gavin picked up a few of his own pieces and set them in their respective starting places on the board. "A rematch?"

The pink slip of Simone's tongue played at a corner of her mouth. "Actually, I was thinking of taking you upstairs and forcing myself on you."

"I understand," Gavin replied, and rose from the small table. "You'd just as soon distract me with your considerable feminine wiles and avoid another humiliating defeat." His hand reached out to hers. She accepted it, getting to her feet in one smooth motion.

They embraced, and Gavin inhaled her freshly washed hair, still a bit damp from the shower she'd taken before he awoke. The natural scent of her, the warmth of her body pressing against his forced all thoughts but those about her from his mind. His lips found hers as her fingers traced small circles on his back.

"You know," she said when they had finally parted. "I could just take you right out there on the grass." Her hand found its way past the waistband of his loose cotton lounging pants when the chime came from the door.

"She's early," said Gavin.

"No," Simone replied. "More like on time. I don't think it's a physical possibility for Becca to be anything but punctual."

Hugs were exchanged with the witch before Rebecca had gained the entryway. A few well-placed verbal jabs at Gavin's choice of drawstring pants and remarks about age before beauty, and they made their way into the backyard to clear away the backgammon set and move to the larger of two tables available to backyard visitors.

Simone asked if Rebecca had eaten, and when the reply was in the negative, offered toast and coffee, both of which were gladly accepted.

Gavin said, "I have to tell you, Rebecca, I'd rather have you over to commiserate about book deadlines or ponder over some scroll you came across at a sorcerer's estate sale rather than talk about all this dark stuff we all seem to be sensing."

Rebecca's teeth tore at the crust of her buttered toast. "I want what you want." She swallowed and poured another round of coffee for everyone, leaving herself for last. "I also want a million bucks in small unmarked bills, peace on Earth, goodwill towards men, and never to hear another Tom Petty song ever again, but like the song says, you can't always get what you want."

"What does the Coven say?" Asked Simone.

"'Big bad thing coming. Run and hide, run and hide'. That comes from the big muckety-mucks themselves, apparently."

"Scared."

"Terrified, more like. I've never seen anything like it."

"It hasn't become any clearer for me," noted Simone. "I've been trying to come up with a way to amplify it somehow, but no dice."

"Just as well," Rebecca said. "We don't know what we're dealing with. Better to not make it notice us."

"It already has," said Gavin, then exchanged glances with the ladies at the table. "I have no idea why I said that."

"One of those universal truths," this came from Simone. "I was thinking it, too."

All eyes went to Rebecca who set down her coffee cup long enough to give an effeminate little wave. "Ditto."

"So," said Simone after a time. "We sit in edgy silence."

"No," this came from Gavin.

Simone nodded. "Until Gavin says something."

Making a show of ignoring the comment, Gavin continued. "We pool our resources and until we know what's going on, conserve them."

Simone reclined in her chair as far as the metal backing would allow her to. "Works for me." She turned her attention to Rebecca. "I think it would be best if you stayed here at the Manor."

Rebecca nodded. "I've recently become a believer in safety in numbers."

"What about your house?" Asked Simone.

"I was up north when I called you guys. I haven't been back to my place since. I was too freaked."

Gavin offered that they all could go together. "There must be something you need there."

The witch's eyes dropped, studying the porcelain mosaic inset into the table top. "No. I don't want to go back there." Then her eyes snapped back up. First to Gavin, then Simone. "I just don't want to be alone right now."

30

Gavin and Simone shared a glance. If Rebecca noticed it, she gave no outward sign. There were things of strong magick in Rebecca's possession. To leave them unattended was to invite nothing but trouble.

But Rebecca knew that. All three of them did, and Rebecca had abandoned not only those items, but the very place in which she lived. Whatever she had seen or felt that had sent her to leave whatever sygils and wards she would normally have left in her absence in their places, and probably would not withstand an attack that the coming enemy would send against them when there was no constant defense or upkeep, which Rebecca or another witch of like power would have to be would need to be preset in order to maintain. There was nothing pedestrian about this threat, and Rebecca Scott had all but left her belongings to the whims of the universe.

Gavin waved Rebecca's offer of a warm up to his coffee away and managed a smile.

On any other day of the week, it would have been an hour's drive from the manor to Rebecca's home in the upwardly suburban sprawl of Casa Hills, but early Sunday it only took about thirty minutes. Not three blocks away from Rebecca's single-storey house, children played softball in the street, ran through neighbor's sprinklers in the summer and probably never checked their Halloween candy given by their neighbors.

Without any prefabrication, Simone had invited Rebecca out to the Sommersby Mall for not only new clothes to replace the ones left behind, but for a welcome distraction from the Great Big Something. It would also allow for Gavin to slip out and reconnoiter the house.

Gavin stood at the end of Birchwood Lane which wound out and away from the shadows the weeping willows and long stretches of ivy that defined its cross-street.

He didn't know what he expected to find. The only sounds around him were the click-whirr of a rainbird somewhere nearby, the sporadic call of a bluejay and the wind, calm through the ivy or dragging a dry leaf or two down the blacktopped street.

If the circumstances were different, he would've been able to enjoy it all.

He stepped around the blind bend a short hill afforded the stretch and saw the house half a block away, there at the end of the dead-end street. It was flanked by two other houses on each side, one residence sported a for sale single displayed prominently on its front lawn.

Nothing else. No, that wasn't quite right. There was none of the sound that had been around him just down the street.

The wards, or whatever it was that Rebecca left whenever she'd be away from the house, were still in place, but there was a disturbance somewhere close. The birds in the trees around him were watching, not singing. There was no wind here. It was closed, and things being what they currently were, the insulation of Rebecca's house was spreading to the outside, bleeding. People living nearby would not find themselves in heated arguments or fight with those they lived with; they would become quiet, insulated themselves, all because of what was, or what wasn't happening, inside that house. The tension wasn't going to kill anybody, but it shouldn't have been a presence there to begin with.

He became all too aware of how loud his breathing sounded to him. Gavin closed his eyes and forced his hands to relax from the fists they had subconsciously become.

He could neither see nor sense any markings on the house he and Simone had helped their friend move into... how long ago? It must have been six years. He knew that Rebecca never left physical traces of magick unless she absolutely had to. There was such a thing as a kind of reverse-engineering in the Craft, and sometimes even the slightest remnant of components to a casting could give the wrong person, usually untrained, more knowledge than they needed to have. Of course, more than one critic of Rebecca's pointed out that it also indicated that the person believed in the keeping of secrets, which was not always a good sign in what it may mean about one's instincts.

Wards were there. Uncertain, wavering things, but there. No sign of anything invasive or anything that would indicate an attempt to enter uninvited. Despite the fact Rebecca had never kept a familiar, Gavin reached out a thought to find one lurking about. He found nothing.

All told, it could have been worse.

He returned to his Mercury, uncertain as to what his next action was to be.

But that was what he had Simone for.

After Rebecca had treated them to dinner at the Japanese place Simone had suggested, they each retired to bed, Rebecca in the spacious guest room on the first floor, her hosts to the master bedroom upstairs.

Gavin tried to not let his pacing back and forth and the foot of the bed actually look like pacing as Simone, already in bed, flipped through a copy of *People.*

"What could she be thinking?" Gavin asked no one in particular.

"I know," came the reply from behind the glossy magazine covers.

"It's totally irresponsible. It's unlike her."

"Completely out of character."

"Is it just me, or should she know better?"

"I know. After what he pulled at the last movie premiere they were at?"

Gavin's foot succeeded in taking half a stride before stopping short. "Who the hell are you talking about?"

Simone's face came into view over the magazine. She turned the interior to face him, showing the face of the power couple the entertainment media was currently enamored with. "Who are *you* talking about?"

Gavin's index finger stabbed the air between him and the floor.

"Oh, for God's sake, Gavin. She's shook up. Yes, it's unlike her. And yes, it's utterly irresponsible of her to do it. But she's scared to death, and she's not thinking properly. When she gets her head cleared, she'll go back there, with or without us. I've never seen her so freaked out over something. We'll talk to her in the morning. And you said yourself that the wards are still in place."

"For now," Gavin grumbled.

"Don't underestimate Rebecca. She's doing enough of that on her own as it is. If you go all dramatic on her, she'll pull back. We'll talk to her about it tomorrow."

Gavin looked at her, seeing the certainty in her topaz eyes framed by a spill of auburn. Those eyes that served to smooth out the rough edges, as they always did. The circle of calm in the center of a vortex. Something he admired, and in his less guarded moments, would admit to being envious of. He nodded and Simone returned her attention to the pages of her magazine. Gavin moved to her side of the bed.

"What's my best feature?" He could tell by the way her voice pulled she was concealing a smile behind the magazine.

In a grand sweep, he took the magazine from her grasp. "Love of my life, where would I begin?" The magazine landed somewhere across the room as he edged onto the side of the bed.

Simone leaned into his sudden kiss and pulled him completely onto the mattress. "I dunno," she said. "Find someplace and go from there."

Somehow, he was able to manage.

CHAPTER SIX

No time is the right time for making enemies.

Lucas Brady, FOLLOWING MY PATH

Karac sat at his work desk, hands folded before him, as he tried to ignore the thick volumes he had pulled down from their shelves in his house. He was not known for being overconfident as a rule, although some may have considered him cocky, and while he would admit to being a tad jumpy, he was not known for overreacting or giving up easily.

But now, amid the books that had helped him reference both things and phenomena, he was beginning to rethink that last. None of them, not even *The Black Chronicles* or *The Mother of Songs*, the last being one of two known and catalogued legitimate editions printed and bound by hand by none other than Nathaniel Agnew himself during his stint in Europe before he was executed for heresy for printing such volumes and refusing to reveal their authors, had anything to offer in regards to Solomon Archer's request.

Karac rubbed at his eyes. The books had failed him before, so that wasn't much of a letdown, but he could usually find himself being pulled in one direction or another when it came to needing a path to follow for the benefit of a client.

He still needed to talk to Solomon, a kind of in-depth interview on Karac's terms. It was not at all unusual for him to have several ideas spring up during such conversations, as words had been known to cause the manifestation of enough of the right kind of energy and thought to provide inspiration to the listener and, on some rare occasions, the speaker.

But the Solomon Archer's specific problem was not mentioned as such in any of the books. Karac toyed with the idea of going online and searching page after page of cyberspace that promised occult knowledge only to serve up spells for *Dungeons and Dragons* campaigns or innocuous little spells that would do absolutely nothing. There was a reason archaic knowledge was bound in musty old books and half-completed manuscripts and loose pages and the like; the ones who had such things knew what they were, and what they could do if they fell into the wrong hands (an objective thing, at best) and so no copies would be made, no page would be scanned on the Internet. Not by any serious collector or practitioner, anyway. There were only two occasions Karac could think of when the Internet had been used to perpetuate a genuinely dangerous spell, and both times, the First Order was dispatched to deal with the person or persons responsible. He had never been able to find out exactly what that may have meant or what the result actually was, but understood that a spell that would grant invisibility or flight would not be one to be trifled with, and if someone was ignorant enough to think posting such a thing on the World Wide Web was a good idea, then reasoning with the person was probably out of the question, as well.

One of the biggest liabilities in the Craft was that someone who was merely curious would try something along the lines of such spells (both of which were outlawed by both First and Second Orders, and had been for a century and a half not only because of the intoxicating power such a thing would give the caster, but also for the terrible price required for such things to be granted, and then not by the whitest of powers). Such knowledge in the minds of the uninitiated would compel them to want to share the spell, spreading its darkness wherever it was cast. It was a wild clutch for power.

But then, the Craft was just like most belief systems, and were not originally designed to grant powers, but to provide illumination and faith in the world without and within. But somebody always had to spoil the party.

He stood, wincing inwardly at the popping in his knees that had not been there two years ago. Neither had been the mental fatigue that accompanied the long stretches of research time he had to put in just to find another grimore. But that's what he did; find grimores, whether they wanted to be found or not. It was his calling. The fact he was noticing he was getting along in years was irrelevant. There was a calling all people had, it was a matter of listening to it.

He'd never regretted answering, or maybe more to the point *listening*, to it, as his profession, career, whatever one wanted to call it, provided something that few people ever got to experience; a challenge and with it, the thrill of the chase and a feeling of accomplishment in a job well done, and he'd never failed in any of his endeavors of searching, even if that meant years looking for a particular volume.

It was a challenge that did not wear him down, as so many things in the world are able to do with maddening ease. His fear came from the fact that he may not find it as challenging ten years down the line as he did right that very second.

But he'd thought that before, to no bad result.

Karac moved to the kitchen and poured himself more coffee in the bootleg *Buffy, The Vampire Slayer* mug with Eliza Dushku as Faith emblazoned on it and moved to the living room, now dappled with late morning sunlight afforded by the blinds set just so. He wanted to fall into the couch and just hope the change of scenery would give him a new train of thought, but if his knees were already protesting, that meant the back would be next, and so came the decision to stand, swirling his coffee amid the decidedly un-posh interior that surrounded him; mostly shelves and five-shelf libraries containing everything from books of the more common variety (although mostly sticking to historical fiction and the works of Eco and his ilk) DVDs and VHS videotapes to CDs and their accompanying players and widescreen TV, recently purchased with the money the *Harmony Codex* sale had bought him the month previous to that kindly gentleman in Paris. It wasn't the biggest sale to date – that had been five pages of an unfinished manuscript called *The Gunn Manuscript*, named after the man who had discovered it in the Seventeenth Century and wrote the first treatise on its possible use, which had never been fully established, rather than the author (never identified) whose had it was written in.

The pages had bought him the house and provided him with a tidy sum he shared with his mother, who thought he was a dealer in print antiquities, which he was. Only the books he went about finding and selling (he never kept any volume unless it could be of use in his reference library, in which case, every Finder he ether knew or heard of had needed for research) also were renown for spells, incantations, or thoughts best not thought of by those unable to deal with the concepts and/or their consequences.

But being a Finder had a certain perk that he had never considered until he realized he enjoyed the act of domestication rather than simply having a place to hang his proverbial hat; even those who would be enemies never dared to find out where a finder lived, or to steal from one, or actually kill one. They were perceived as being simply too powerful to upset without some rather unpleasant repercussions.

Karac had no idea where such a notion had come from, but was grateful for it. Such a sort-of respect for him and his kind was indeed valuable, and he had heard numerous stories of jealous sorcerers raiding one another's abodes in search of wisdom they did not possess themselves, leading to things like the past three occult wars, the last being known alternately as The Four Days Wars, with another having a title unpronounceable to Karac although he suspected it was because it was derived from a non-human tongue, and The Dragon War (a name whose meaning eluded him as there were no dragons involved), wars that had seen things left behind such as weapons and books and beings. Worst of all, they left behind ideas those uninvolved would actively subject themselves to as well as lessons that no one wanted to learn when living in the constant shadow of their need to be right.

History, he reflected, was not only written by the winners, but sometimes the survivors were able to provide a voice, as well.

But he felt the Finders were seen not as people, but as resources. And while human nature seemed perfectly content to use any and all resources to their hearts content until they dried up, the Finders were seen a differently. No one wanted to upset them, at least not to any great extent. It was as if non-Finders viewed them like commoners would consider wizards in ancient Europe; The real wizards weren't renowned for colossal exhibitions of power and ability, they were men and women known for their wisdom, not turning people into toads. Karac kept this thought to himself, but it was getting harder not to discuss it with one of his fellows these days, and the only reason he had never broached the topic with any of them as because there was no set Finder protocol or pecking order. There was no guild, just a loose association that you could be a part of or not. It didn't seem to matter to anyone, and therefore Karac was uncertain as to whether it was a touchy subject or not.

He allowed his thoughts to wonder back to the last time he saw Mia, and the time before that, and the time before that. The woman had been making cameo appearances in his evenings for how long now? It seemed that they had always had their little meetings, had known each other since junior high school. Karac knew if he spent too much time thinking about it, he would realize it would be more like less than a year, and some illusions he liked to keep.

The paper Solomon Archer had written his name and phone number on in an almost elegant hand that betrayed the man's exterior rough edges found itself in Karac's hand. He turned it over and over in his fingertips, pushing the thoughts of Mia aside with some difficulty. He was uncertain as to what to tell the man, who was quite literally haunted in every sense of the word. Solomon was on the edge of doing something rash in an attempt to get rid of the visions. Living with the unusual, and that was putting it politely, was never easy, whether the paranormal was involved or not. Some people handled it better than others, that's all. But the great unexplained, that was something else. Hardly anyone handled that correctly, let alone well.

So the receiver to Karac's cordless phone was lifted and the numbers punched with his thumb. In two rings, the other end was lifted and Solomon's voice came to him, sounding a bit more certain than it had in the bar the night before. He agreed to Karac asking a few more questions, and didn't have a problem with doing it face-to-face on neutral ground, but he wanted it outside. Karac gave a verbal shrug and suggested a park about a mile away. Solomon agreed. In an hour? That would be fine.

Karac thumbed the phone off and tossed the receiver onto the couch. An hour would give him time to shower and try to figure out what he could ask for a start.

From there, it was anybody's guess.

The approach Gavin and Simone took to convince their friend to go back to her home and at least collect the most dangerous items was not a miserable failure in the strictest sense, but it had not resulted in anything but Rebecca avoiding the issue.

Gavin had let Simone do the talking, as usual in time like those. He was a bit surprised that she was unable to persuade the witch.

However, she was a great success at getting Gavin to agree to go to the house on his own to de-activate, if not remove, the items that could do the most harm. The witch's primary weakness was shopping, something Simone was more than able to exploit when there was still another mall to be plundered.

Gavin stared at the house, as he had less than twenty-four hours before, only this time, he had a greater sense of foreboding. De-activating magickal or enchanted items was only slightly easier than an exorcism. He didn't have a hard time table in which he needed to operate in, but he couldn't take long, just in case there were other interested parties that were going to be paying a visit to Rebecca's house at the same time.

He would have to enter the house, which involved bringing down or fooling the wards Rebecca already had in place. Then, he would have to identify the worst of the items. If he had any luck, they would be secreted away, but not impossible to find. He doubted Rebecca would dabble in the forces required to turn a thing invisible, but a few of the things she had in her possession certainly deserved the distinction.

Then, Gavin would have to try one of any number of rites that in all possibility could render the thing forever useless, which was not his aim. All he wanted to do was the magickal equivalent of putting the safety into the 'On' position on a weapon. But if he stumbled over a word, or mistranslated something as he was reading from one of the books in the canvas and leather knapsack he carried slung over his shoulder, a great many unwanted things could ensue. He could ruin the instrument, it could explode in his hands…

He had to concentrate, and letting in such thoughts would only lead down the path to distraction.

The ward at the door was more effective than a lock, but to the right person, easier to pick than a material lock requiring a different kind of skill. It was a fifth-class ward, meaning if he said the wrong command or the wrong inflection, the entire house would go into lockdown and he hadn't the slightest notion as to what sort of backup Rebecca may have had in place to deal with intruders.

He spoke the entry chant, three lines long, and hoped he had the right tongue and that Rebecca hadn't used a codex that would allow her to make the ward recognize her voice only. There was only one way to find out if voice recognition was part of the equation, despite Gavin's best efforts to find one.

He closed his eyes, more for effect than anything else. After a count of three, he opened first the right, then the left. Nothing unseemly stared back at him. A heartbeat later, the lock clicked over, a bonus he hadn't expected and spent some time considering the invitation.

Once inside, he let his fingertips close the door gently into its jamb. He could sense nothing unusual, just the high levels of power he always experienced when in Rebecca's house or with her standing close by.

The scent of candles hung heavy in the air. Gavin was unable to tell which color had been burned, but knew enough that Rebecca was enough of a candle enthusiast outside of her usual ritual burnings that if she were to burn different colors, they would be complimentary both in magickal effect as well as aesthetic scents. It struck Gavin as a trifle odd, not for the first time, for someone as appreciative of art as Rebecca had proven herself to be that the sole piece of artwork to be found in her house was the framed print of Franks' 'Angelique'. But as the dark-winged beauty in the painting attested to the passion and beauty of the spirit while perhaps hinting at something a bit darker was, so did the world she and other like her lived in. The blinds were closed against the sun, not yet at its optimum height to fight against them, but there was enough ambient light to afford a decent view of the layout of the house. Gavin didn't want to disturb anything, lamp or otherwise, if he didn't have to, so he simply made do with what he had available.

The sweep of the house began in the living room, going to the kitchen, bathroom, the bedroom that she had turned into a study, and the master bedroom. The entire house sparked with paranormal energy, but that was because of the level Rebecca was at with herself, the Craft, and the universe. There were small spikes in the areas where her personal items were located, such as the silver brush and mirror set that had belonged to her mother, who was not a practitioner, and of course the study, where there was enough magickal residue from all the rituals and studies conducted there to get a coven of intermediates utterly stoned, but the energy currents Gavin was seeking were a cut above, and just a bit more subtle. A novice would know enough to be nervous in the presence of such things, an intermediate would react without thinking, and those who were advanced enough to know better than the others would regard it as a living thing, worthy of respect.

The study had some objects of mild interest, such as Rebecca's personal atheme and sword, but they were among the more pedestrian of the things that could be expected to be found in the home of a witch on par with Rebecca Scott's abilities.

Gavin all but forced himself to relax. He was looking too hard, putting more effort into it, and therefore narrowing the field to what should come naturally to those with whatever the gift of the senses he had was called.

His eyes lidded, and he metered his breathing, deep and slow through his nose, exhaling through his mouth, allowing his body and mind to relax. Time was of the essence, but spinning his wheels in an anxious state was not going to help any.

The living room. One of the items was located somewhere on a shelf of the entertainment center, probably behind a component.

There was no way of knowing what it was until he was actually face-to-face with whatever it was. He was able to use that kind of far-sight in order to visualize exactly what it was behind a door, or in another state, on more than one occasion, but he was never able to do it at will without the luxury of time and the presence of Simone by his side. She was better at far-sight than he, but couldn't do it at will reliably, either. But together, she acted as a powerful booster that resonated on a level deeper than words could express.

Gavin sorted as quickly as he could through the shelves, drawers and the twin glass cabinet doors, searching for the item that was throwing off the strongest signature. He was rewarded with more books than movies, and a smattering of classical CDs , heavy on the Beethoven.

He scanned the back of the cabinet, looking through the mess of component wiring, for any indication of his target. It wasn't until he looked behind the DVD player something dark and seemingly out-of-place caught his eye.

Left arm stretching the scant space between the wall and the cabinet, and the right gripping the front edge of the center, he touched something of leather and hard spine with five raised bands at the top edge. He had managed to turn the volume slightly askew and tried to wedge his body further against the cabinet when the voice came, loud enough to send him windmilling away from his quarry.

"What fresh hell is this?" Rebecca Scott thundered, standing tall and sudden in the center of her living room carpet.

While he could've done without the glare the sun burned just at the top of his line of vision, Karac only had himself to blame for not only forgetting his sunglasses in the car – he'd driven the '80s Mazda where dents went to die instead of his Tucker Torpedo, which just seemed to ostentatious given the circumstances his client was in as well as where they were meeting – but also being too lazy to go back and get them despite his best intended lie to himself that he was only staying on the park bench on the west side of the entrance to the park to be sure he saw Solomon when the man came in for their meeting.

When Solomon Archer made his appearance, it was three minutes early and with a gait entirely removed from the slump he had shown in the Wash. He didn't have a spring in his step, but the light of day seemed at least motivate him to keep up appearances just a bit. His eyes were level with those walking past him, and while he hadn't shaved, his clothes were clean and he gave every outward appearance of being what he desperately needed to be: Blessedly *normal.*

It was the darkness beneath his eyes that spoiled the illusion. It, combined with the almost-half lidded eyes that made the man look exactly what he was: A man haunted, in the truest sense of the word. Karac wasn't the best judge as to how much sleep a person had been deprived of, but he had a guess that it had been about three days since Solomon had been able to get a decent night's rest, let alone a full night of sleep.

Night and its darkness changed things. In this case, it only made Solomon's problems worse. If not wholly, then at least in the man's reality, and that's the one both of them needed to deal with.

Solomon made eye contact with Karac and nodded, ambling slowly over to where the latter sat. He's trying to walk normally, Karac thought. He's trying to blend in.

A few moments passed in silence as Solomon sat down to Karac's left.

"Should we talk about my parents," Solomon asked at last. "Or something like that?"

"Does your problem have anything to do with that?"

"I don't think so."

"Then why don't we skip over all the exciting stuff and cut to the chase?"

Solomon nodded, and began. " I was six when it first started, and it's gotten stronger – worse – ever since. It got real bad right around puberty."

"Doesn't everything?"

"Sorry?"

"Bad joke. Never mind. Talk about that first ghost you saw."

Although he seemed a trifle put back by the flippant manner in which the question was presented to him, Solomon pushed on. "I saw my grandmother shortly after she died. I told my mother about it, but the look on her face made me stop before I told her that all my grandma wanted was to tell her that she was doing well, she was with grandpa again, and that her arthritis didn't hurt her anymore."

"Did your grandmother tell you why she saw appearing to you and not her daughter?"

"No. And I didn't think to ask."

"That's okay. Spirits don't usually mind how they get their message across, they just pick the path of least resistance and don't question it because their perception just takes those things as a given. Sorry. Go ahead."

"Well, I started seeing other relatives after that, mostly distant ones, one being the captain of some kind of ship. I remember that distinctly because was wearing one of those old-fashioned blue captain's hats with the black bill in front. I tried to talk to my dad about it, then my uncle, but nothing came of it. They didn't punish me or anything for saying all this stuff, they just ignored me." Solomon chuckled, a humorless thing. "I guess they figured I was just trying to make sense of death or something. When I was twenty, my mom passed away. She visited me that night, and reprimanded me for not passing along grandma's message."

"How did you react?"

"I felt it best to drop into a black depression," a small grin that held no good humor to it, spread across his lips. "I found that depression actually enhanced my power, and no matter how much of a good mood I could genuinely experience, it didn't lessen."

Karac nodded. "Depression does that to people with abilities like yours. What happened after that?"

"I started losing it. I read as many books as I could on anything like what I had, and I found out I was becoming what some writers were calling a 'Random precognitive.' Nothing I see is ever positive, only how and when the person will die."

"Are these people friends?"

Solomon seemed surprised at the question. "No. Never. I don't really hang out with anybody. I can't tolerate trying to act normal, or not be able to say anything about what my trouble is."

"What kind of stuff do you see?"

"Most of the time, it's pretty banal stuff as far as death goes."

"Do you really view death as banal?"

Solomon chuckled. "No, not really. Not for as long as I can remember." The jocularity died. "But it wears me down. I've been trying for the past five years or so to get rid of the visions of either the ghosts or the precog stuff. I've given up on getting rid of both of them."

"When you say it's wearing you down, what do you mean specifically?"

"Ghosts are as commonplace to me as living people. It's getting harder and harder for me to distinguish between the two, and that bugs me even more, because I can never be sure what I'm seeing is really what I'm seeing."

"That must be hard." It was a leading question, and the tension that grew between the two declared it as obvious.

41

"I've tried killing myself twice," Solomon finally said. "I've talked to everyone from psychics to witches, including a couple who have written books on spells regarding the dead. It's become a question as to what *haven't* I tried. I've even considered gouging my eyes out, but that won't stop the voices that I hear."

"Are the voices disembodied?"

"No, no. What I meant was that the ghost talk to me sometimes. More often these days. But what's really stopping me is that I'm afraid it might amplify my power in some way."

"Okay. So how did you come to find me?"

"I guess I must have gotten desperate enough to know there's only one last chance; find someone like you – because I knew just where to go and what you'd look like and what your name would be."

"That rings true enough. After a certain amount of need, instinct kicks in. You just come to know things." Although Karac wasn't lying, he strongly suspected a ghost that had crossed paths with Solomon or actually sought Solomon had ratted him out. Probably that New Orleans gambler Karac still owed for that Superbowl bet. Cash meant nothing to the dead, Karac had said more than once, but try telling them that.

"Yeah," said Solomon. "What's the alternative?"

Insanity, Karac thought. "Let me get back to you. I think I have a better idea of things now." He and Solomon rose simultaneously and bade their goodbyes.

Simone's feet had made six thunderous steps into Rebecca Scott's living room, just in time to see Gavin in an offensive posture asking the witch what she thought she was doing, just barging into the room like that, apparently unperturbed at the sight of some of Rebecca's flyaways lifting in static electricity as the power in her spiked. The bright popping sound that came with the smell of fast-charged power did nothing to shake him, either.

"You come into my house," Rebecca said, ignoring Simone's entrance. "To what, make sure I didn't allow my Ward of Demisyth grew legs and started doing evil about the suburbs?" At last she turned to Simone. "Oh, hi Simone. How's tricks?" Her head turned back to Gavin before she could answer.

"How the hell did you get back here so damn fast?" Simone demanded, sparing a glance behind her, making sure she'd applied the parking brake to the Avalanche. She couldn't see it from where she stood, but she tried to let the sound of the engine still running provide some reassurance that the car hadn't rolled downhill. She'd left Rebecca amidst the moderate crowd of the mall to use the restroom, and when she returned, found the pair of shopping bags Rebecca had been holding by themselves, with no sign of Rebecca. Gavin must have done something wrong. She'd run red lights and very nearly run a Honda complete with Jesus fish and soccer mom off the onramp as she struggled to beat Rebecca to her house, even while she knew she'd arrive too late.

"I teleported," came Rebecca's reply.

The sound Gavin made might have been construed as someone exclaiming, *'What?'*

"She's lying," snapped Simone. "There's no way she'd do something like that. The price is too high."

"Everything is too high, Simone." Rebecca didn't bother to turn back to her, content to let her eyes stare at Gavin.

"Calm down," Gavin asked.

"No, she's right. I am lying. I flew."

Trying to control her shaking hands, Simone balled them into fists. "Rebecca, stop it."

"No, I think I must be if you lot are so sure that I'm enough of a bumbler that you need to distract me while the other goes and what, powers down my artifacts?"

"You can hardly blame us for our concern," Simone said. "You have tons of power here, waiting to be exploited if left alone."

"And you think I wouldn't have wards and alarms?"

"Maybe sentient ones that didn't turn Gavin here into instant soup mix because they identified him as a friend and that the time sink I set into the ward would take care of him or anyone else until I was able to get here?" Her attention swung back to Simone, nearly making the latter jump a little. "If you'd like, I could crash-summon the shadowcat that would've manifested - "

"Okay," Simone muttered. "You've made your point."

"Have I? Are you sure? Because you seem to be pretty sure I need babysitting."

"No," said Simone. "We were wrong to doubt you. It was all our fault, and we're sorry."

Despite Simone's deepest wish, Rebecca's eyes wouldn't drop. Her lips wouldn't relax from the bloodless line they had become. "Yes, I'll bet you are. Out."

"Simone, please. Let's talk about this."

Rebecca's head tilted. Her eyes finally snapped away. "Am I hearing voices? Hmm. I must be as unstable as Gavin and Simone thought."

For the first time since she'd gained the room, Simone's eyes met Gavin's. He took soft steps in a wide berth from Rebecca, who was retaining the posture of idle curiosity as if frozen there. When he'd made it to Simone's side, they retreated without further ceremony, turning their backs to their friend only after they'd crossed the threshold.

The door slammed behind them with enough force to let them know their feet should know enough to carry them back to their respective cars faster than was being done.

CHAPTER SEVEN

Research is key even when one is certain they know what they are doing.

Leland Fell, STRANGE HORIZONS

Simone made no bones about going for a cigarette being the first thing to be done upon arriving back at the manor, lighting it before she'd stepped into the backyard, knitting her arms across her chest as the cigarette burned between the tips of her first and second fingers. Thankfully, Gavin had opted to not turn on any music or the television for the sake of background noise as he normally did the minute they would return from errands. Instead, he made himself scarce and said nothing about the cigarettes she'd picked up at the small liquor store a few blocks away from their home. In time, though. He came outside to join her before she was finished with her cigarette.

He stood to the far side of where the cigarette burned and said in the soft tones he could manage only when he was truly trying to make amends about something. "Are you mad at me?"

Simone sucked at the cigarette, exhaled the smoke without inhaling, the words coming out in a rush. "No, I'm sorry because Rebecca is right. We totally underestimated her, and we were the ones who should know better. What you did was just part of what we thought was the right thing to do was. Not your fault. Neither of us did a very good job at being as smart as people tell us we are."

Gavin moved behind her and held her close to his chest, something that for no particular reason Simone found infinitely comforting. His arms held her about the waist and he pressed his lips to the crown of her head and said nothing, just held her there like that and would until she needed to move.

Rebecca would calm down and speak to them again. The witch's temper, while tough to bring to the surface, was renown among their circle and those more closely associated with what the public at large would refer to as 'The occult.' But this was different. They had intruded into her domain as authority figures because they felt she couldn't handle the situation at hand.

They had each acted as they should have, Simone supposed. But the fact that it had ended as badly as it did did nothing to help what she was trying to create; a stride that would carry her through this bump in their relationship with Rebecca and into a better one where they could look one another in the eye again.

But the level of anger Rebecca exhibited was that which when encountered by anyone needed to be left to itself to repair to its own lair where it could be allowed to cool down and make the decision whether to continue to be mad or be able to put such a thing behind its bearer, and if in the case of the former, what action was to be taken for the indiscretion or trespass.

Rebecca would have to make the first move towards speaking again, and at least for the now, Simone was able to let her have it.

Later, when the sun had begun its dip behind the mountains and during discussion between Simone and Gavin of what would be a good place to go out and eat (Simone wanted Italian), the phone interrupted. A shame, because while Gavin wasn't much in the mood for the fare, he was just beginning to bend. The phone was going to break Simone's verbal stride, and now she'd have to start over again, or worse, lose ground to a left-field counter offer from her mate.

She snatched the phone from its cradle in the middle of the third ring. The voice on the other end was unfamiliar, but was even and businesslike after confirming whom he was speaking to.

"My name is Marcus Rigg. I run the Saltzman Museum in Manhattan."

"Sure. We've been there once or twice. I believe that we authenticated some parchment for you?"

"For my predecessor, yes. Mr. Hampton."

Simone nodded, making a sound acknowledging her own recollection of this. Hampton was one of those kindly folks who had to second-guess everything you told him despite the fact that he cited your credentials as the reason you were hired on.

"Right. Is he no longer with your museum?"

"I'm afraid Mr. Hampton passed away some four months ago. He had stepped down a few months before because of his health. He was... rather robust."

Simone believed Gavin had once compared the portly man to 'A bipedal pear.' "I'm sorry to hear of his passing," Simone said. "What can we do for you?"

Rigg sounded downright relieved to actually be talking business. "Well, we've suffered a theft of the piece you appraised, and require a certification from you to allow for the cost we're declaring for the insurance."

"Yes, of course. Which piece was this?"

"A page from a book called *The Book of Ranks.*"

Simone closed her eyes, searching for the memory. The museum had purchased the book to use as a sidepiece for a Yugoslavian artist she could not even begin to pronounce the name of. The painter had been interested in pursuing polytheology, something that some felt *The Book of Ranks* could help with in integrating several apparently incompatible religions into one discipline. Both Simone and Gavin thought this was a blind ambition at best, and upon inspection of what time, natural erosion in uncontrolled circumstances, and at least one ambitious bookworm had left behind of the twelfth century volume, it seemed to be nothing more than a jumble of half-formed ideas written by someone (uncredited, as usual. Even if there was a name supplied, it was highly doubtful it was indeed the real name, much less true author) who did not think the future would give way in regards to advanced doubt.

"Just one page?"

Rigg grunted. "I know. Odd, isn't it?"

"Which page, if you don't mind me asking?"

There came the sound of pages in a notebook being referenced. Then, "Page 112. The page with that fine illustration our featured artist used to inspire his work, *The Dreams We Hold.* Considered to be his masterpiece." Rigg added this last as only an impassioned enthusiast of the artist noted could manage.

"The angels called Principalities standing over the Earth" said Simone.

"An oversimplification, but that's correct."

Refraining from speaking her mind, she made her own grunt into the receiver. By and large the book was given its considerable value only by the virtue of being associated with the artist, who essentially swiped an idea from one of the book's illustrations. It was still catalogued as being the only genuine copy of what many not in the know would be considered a rather controversial topic, certainly in the time it had been written, but it was disregarded by the more serious as not containing much of anything resembling occult thought or the roots of same. It was merely a book someone who eventually became famous liked, probably because he fancied himself a bit controversial himself, or wanted to be viewed as such, for whatever reason. It was now a matter of artistic antiquity.

She walked to the small antique teak and mahogany ship captain's desk in the hallway leading to the front door and switched the phone to her opposite ear before grabbing for a pencil and pad. "Give me your address again. We'll be on the next available plane."

"Oh, I'm sure that won't be necessary."

"I really think it best for Gavin and I to see for ourselves. For our own records," she added quickly.

After a long moment, Rigg consented. "Very well. Give me a call when you get in." He then provided her with his direct extension and the address to the museum. Simone hung up and ripped the page free of its pad. She found Gavin flipping through the TV channels on the remote, blissfully unaware.

"Clap hands, honey. You're taking me to New York!" She took time to savor his confused stare before filling in the details of the conversation.

"*The Book of Ranks*? Who the hell would want that piece of crap?"

"And run the risk of getting caught," Simone was happy to add. "And going to the trouble of removing a single page."

"It's just some fan of the artist, honey. We're not really going to New York, are we?"

"Would an obsessed fan do that, go to all that trouble and risk, and then not get caught?"

"You're hearing that whisper in your ghost again, aren't you?"

"Hurry, Watson! The game's afoot!" Simone turned tail, and pounded upstairs to gather the appropriate records from the office and make sure the PDA and laptop had all the info required. As she made the door to the office, she thought she heard Gavin mutter something about not really wanting to talk her into Hawaiian pizza, anyway.

Simone had never made a secret about her love of museums or the objects they help within, and as she and Gavin made their way across the modest open plaza between the two wings of the Saltzman, she as always, felt a little giddy about their visit, despite the bag slung over her shoulder containing the laptop, PDA and small spiral notebook reminding her about the serious nature of the business at hand.

Arriving after business hours took the edge off the excitement as she could see through the glass double doors the crimson service lighting that replaced the stark white light and grew in brilliance as they approached the heavy glass doors.

The security officer – armed with what appeared to be a Glock in a holster at his hip, Simone noted – was waiting for them outside and just to the left of the entrance. He was a tall man with an open face and was clearly someone who took pride in his job and uniform whether anyone was looking at him or not.

The officer tilted an imaginary hat at their approach. Upon introducing herself and Gavin, the officer made a request of their identification, even going so far as to shine a beam from his flashlight onto them as he inspected their drivers licenses and did a rudimentary search of Simone's bag with a dowel.

Satisfied what he saw was genuine, he thanked them and spoke into a shoulder-mounted mike. "Gavin Fox and Simone Perfect here to see Mr. Rigg."

The confirmation crackled back.

In moments, Rigg arrived. On the stocky side and more than a little nervous-looking, Rigg nevertheless cut an official figure in his double-breasted suit and dark tie knotted in a Windsor. He waited at the door until the security officer had opened the door with his passkey.

Introductions were made, and while Rigg was on the rather un-impressive side, Simone thought the man shook hands not to intimidate or simply be done with a gesture her perceived as archaic at best, but to convey self-confidence and welcome, even though Simone could feel he was clearly uncomfortable about them poking around in his museum.

"I let the security chief go home about an hour ago," said Rigg. "I hope that's okay; this is being handled more as an internal matter, the police were called, but only out of protocol."

"We understand," Simone replied.

"Right. The police report will be made available to you should you need it. I'll fax you a copy in a couple of days."

Gavin's grunt told Simone he felt that Rigg would have kept that little offer from the conversation entirely had Simone disagreed with him on the grounds on which they were visiting and in what capacity.

Simone felt her enthusiasm wane as they passed through the lobby, made barren-looking by the lack of formal lighting, their footfalls echoing into the yawning darkness punctuated by red fingers of light reaching to the floor. She had spent enough time in museums and with the curators of same to know they used the red light to prevent accelerated aging to the art the museum housed and subjected to white light during business hours.

They traveled the distance to the Joyce Wing, where the semi-permanent works, primarily paintings, were kept.

Rigg directed them to the west side of the room, eyes flicking back to them every now and then, as if waiting for the to reach out and touch one of the works hanging on the walls despite the security measures in place. Between Rigg's behavior and the metallic taste the de-ionized air the museum had courtesy of the coal-filter dehumidifiers they had employed to counteract carbon dioxide brought about by human breath and would only serve to create more degradation to the art, Simone simply wanted to be done. She knew the souring of her mood was due solely to her own illusions suffering a bit of battering, but it was hard not to be disappointed at not getting the full experience of the museum.

As they were brought before the Nikolarevic-Kopnyitzki exhibit, Riggs gave them a brief in museum security measures. They employed, as many museums larger than the Saltzman, what was termed 'Containment security' that would seal off exits if a piece were moved from a wall or floor display. There were camera installations everywhere, conspicuous in their wall-brackets, and while they certainly were convincing to the layman's eye, no one had to tell Simone they were fake. The logistics of monitoring them all was nightmarish to consider, both in cost and in manpower. The Saltzman was by no means the Louvre, but it was one of the more ambitious of the smaller museums in the world that was never passed over when some of the most important pieces were toured, earning the Saltzman in a place of respect in the eyes of other, greater museums.

The tall plexiglass case that would normally be found standing beside the exhibited paintings, which remained untouched on the wall, now lay on its side with a rend in its side large enough for two arms to be inserted into it and the book within to be reached. Rigg told them what they could already puzzle out; the break had been created before the case had been pushed over, meaning that the thief had contempt for the rest of the contents. Enough to risk capture in order to make his opinion known. It was odds-on that the person responsible was an enthusiast of a given kind of art and shared the dislike for the artist that many others in the field of art criticism regardless of how one felt about the author of *The Book of Ranks,* the majority of which was left intact, although the pine and therefore the binding had suffered some significant damage in the fall it took along with its stand as the case tumbled to the floor. A pair of other sketches believed to be rough drafts, or as Simone noted on the display text, 'Early envisionings' of the artist's work that would lead to his creating *The Dreams We Hold.*

"The thief was risking getting trapped in this room just to make a point?" Simone wondered aloud. She had spoken so softly that she gave a little jump when Rigg responded.

"Yes," he said. "Odd, isn't it?"

"And the door seals closed properly?" Asked Gavin.

"That's correct. Our guards responded in less than a minute to the scene, to find nothing." Rigg's tone conveyed that he had figured that there was no other way to feel about the situation other than to suffer the loss and the subsequent punishment that would be meted out by his superiors. It was not unheard-of that a curator was kept on at a museum following such a thing, but it was a mark on ones records that those in certain circles always remembered. The passion for the art world often carried a curator through the difficult years ahead. In Rigg's case, it would be difficult to find a similar job in America following this, and impossible in Europe.

A few minutes were spent as Simone took in whatever residual energy she could as Gavin walked around the room, doing more of the same. The sound of Gavin's footsteps being the only thing in the room ticking away the time proved to be too much for Rigg, who made no small show of his exasperation at their continued presence and repeated his note regarding the police report.

Simone nodded and worked the PDA's stylus over the controls, making very few notes, but making sure she conveyed the finality of their visit when she replaced the stylus and put the PDA back into her bag. "Thank you very much for your patience with us, Mr. Rigg. I know you've had quite a day already. We'll be on our way now. But if you need us, please don't hesitate to let us know. We'll give you whatever help you need. The Saltzman has been very good to us." It was mostly empty praise, but Rigg needed to have something to cling to at this point, and if it came from niceties from Simone, and by association, Gavin, so be it. They bade Rigg goodbye and let him walk them to the door, where the guard once more tilted the imaginary hat.

"The Saltzman hasn't been *that* good to us," Gavin said when they had crossed the street to where they had parked their rented Honda Accord. "In fact, they've never given us any sign of validity, even when we authenticated that worthless book."

"Rigg doesn't know that, and is too distracted to care or check up on that. I don't like to burn bridges, and half the reason you're upset about the authentication of *The Book Of Ranks* is because it actually increased the value of the book."

As Gavin drove the car back to the main drag that would take them away from the row of galleries, he spared a glance to Simone. "I wasn't able to really get much from the room. Were you?"

"Seemed pretty strong to me."

"That's why I still hang out with you."

"I figured as much."

A few moments of silence passed before Gavin would turn to her again, mock-serious. "Well, are you going to share you findings?"

"Oh yes. I almost forgot! Well, the police are right. The person responsible hates the notoriety the illustration gave someone he feels in undeserving of such a thing, meaning the painter, not the author of the book."

"It was one person? I thought it would take at least two to get that glass display over like that."

"He knows what he's doing. There's a lot of power left back there. Just traces, but detectable."

"Yeah, I got that, too. Not really sure what to make of it, though."

"Do you think he's done?"

"Nope. Not yet. He knows what he wants to do."

"He's connected to that 'big bad thing' we've all been sensing, though."

"More than connected," Gavin grumbled. "He *is* that big bad thing."

Simone looked at him hard. "Do you really think that?"

Gavin met her gaze with one that told her that her tone of voice had been sharper than she'd meant. "Yeah."

"I didn't get that," Simone muttered, returning her eyes to the darkness punctuated by stark display lights ahead of them.

"Yeah, well, what I really want to know is how the hell this guy got out of there without being caught."

Simone's face broke into a grin. She spun on him like a taunting schoolgirl. "Really? I thought you knew."

"No. What all did you get?"

"Oh," came Simone's matter-of-fact reply. "The bastard teleported."

PART TWO

A CRISIS OF FAITH

CHAPTER EIGHT

It is unique among us that we, when villains do not identify our self as such to our within.

Stefan O'Barr, THE SMALL PLACES

Among the less than charitable, it could be believed that a priest like Father Alec Copeman had committed career suicide at a point during the years following the receipt of his holy orders that others would have given most anything to achieve themselves; a fast track to the office of archbishop-prefect.

Granted, even with that lofty title, it would most likely not have resulted in working as closely with the Pope as Alec would have once liked, but it would have allowed his becoming a cardinal in relatively short order, something that his American fellows in the clergy would never have expected to be possible, although they would never have voiced such opinions to anyone save their contemporaries, and even still, that would be couched more in what was *not* said rather than said.

His position would have placed him in the corridors of power in the Vatican, something that while in his early studies, Alec would have very much shown an interest in, but following his appointment as a parish priest, it seemed less and less important.

He could have rubbed proverbial elbows with those in the College of Cardinals, going through the rank of Cardinal, Cardinal Deacon, then lastly Cardinal Bishop, themselves second only to the Pope himself. Alec Copeman would never have become Pope, and had never held any illusions of such a thing, but he would have been amongst those behind the pontiff, and it was believed by many in both the College of Cardinals and the Pontifical Colleges that one could do just as well to lay that sort of important groundwork, as the ear of authority often became the lips and speech of same.

Alec was quite contented to let those who were more ambitious to have it. Such things led to infighting and campaigning for oneself – which of course meant against another. Alec had always felt his actions and the results were what mattered most, not his words about topics he only cared about as much as could be bothered, which was to say not a whit.

As it happened, it was not necessarily the actions of a young Jesuit that had garnered the attentions of the offices of the Vatican, but Alec Copeman's potential. If that was not reflective of how much the Holy See could use him or mold him into, Alec would never be sure. It was to be the grounds on which he would base his decision to stay where he began, generally speaking. He felt infinitely more connected to than those who had apparently read his papers on subjects ranging from whether or not Christ laughed – he'd argued that He had indulged in such a thing as humor, despite what Anthony, Pachomius, Augustine and Benedict who all condemned laughter, would have had their followers believe, as laughter had been cited in Scripture as a wonderful thing in that it was always held as precious and noted to be taken away from those unworthy. Christ had eaten with sinners, befriended the likes of prostitutes and performed miracles. It was argued by Alec that such a man would certainly know the value of humor, provided it had its place. While one could find Proverbs 10:23, 26:19, and 29:9 citing fools laughing as they headed for destruction, and The Book of Sirach (one of his favorites to re-read) noted in 21:20 that only a foolish man raises his voice in laughter, and a wise one gives a gentle smile, Alec wrote that Christ (who once warned against the mocking of a victim in Acts) was a man of great depth, and knew the difference between fool's logic and the wise even though both found room on earth to laugh, using the Old Testament passage in Ecclesiastes 8:14, and its commendation of mirth, as it is stated that there is 'Nothing good under the sun except eating and drinking and mirth: for this is the accompaniment of his toil during the limited days of his life which God gives to him under the sun.' to his essay regarding the validity of Biblical archeology and its findings to support (or disprove, at least to the scientific mind) certain events or people found in the Bible, all the while retaining that there were things that science could never explain with cold logic. Topics that were on the controversial side, to be sure, but even moreso coming from a novice.

His choice to remain in small parishes could be seen as a black mark to many, as he was essentially saying 'No,' to the College of Cardinals and, ultimately, the Pope. His decision to stay in the United States of America was also viewed as ignorant or as the nail in a coffin Alec Copeman had willfully and knowingly built around himself.

As he stood in the doorway leading to the sanctuary of the Our Lady of Sorrows church, he considered that it was not the first Sunday where Mass had gone unattended save for elderly ladies and one or two couples who seemed to be God-*fearing* rather than God-*loving*.

But such was the parish of Benjamin, California. Father Alec hadn't the foggiest notion what the population was, but knew it was modest, to say the least. Perhaps just over six hundred, if that.

The people seemed to like it that way, not looking for the glitz of Los Angeles and the troubles it would no doubt bring, although technology did seem to have a decent foothold here. Alec wondered if that would lead to the town's eventual end, but reckoned that while the population was not made up of the church-going sort, it was by no means a town of easy virtue.

He supposed part of the problem would stem from his church – a post he'd accepted no less than six years before – being well-removed from the road. When he'd arrived, the church had been so overgrown with weeds it was nearly blotted out from sight.

Alec had been able to enlist the aid of a few students of the local high school who needed summer jobs to help with the weeding and came across a case of dumb luck when one had a father who was more than willing to donate his time and materials, noting that while he was not a religious man, he was happy to have a hand in restoring one of the oldest structures in Benjamin, dating back to the 1860s, when it resembled a mission more than a church. The seven stained glass windows, supplied by a local artisan who had since found mass-market appeal with his statuary and paintings, all with inspirational themes, featured the Passion and Resurrection, beginning with Christ entering Jerusalem, palm branches spread before Him by His followers. Following this was the scene of Jesus, wounded and in rags, standing before Pilate. The next window featured Christ on the road to Golgotha, bearing the Cross. Then came the scene of the Crucifixion, St. John and Mary, and Mary Magdalene prominent in the foreground, the two thieves too detailed to be considered background despite their placement there, something Alec was especially appreciative of.

The scene that followed showed the Blessed Virgin cradling the body of her Son following his death, a compelling image in itself, and Alec realized that he had never seen an artist's rendering of the scene that he did not find moving and profound. The window glowed when the sun shone through at midday, more than any of the others. The penultimate window showed Mary and Joseph of Arimathea standing by Christ's tomb with a soldier stationed before the stone. The Holy Spirit kept watch from above in the form of a dove with wide rays of sunlight emanating behind it.

The final window featured the Resurrection, with Christ rising within the tomb. The color palette was darker and more dramatic than the others in the church, as Christ entered the Kingdom of Heaven.

The priest who had ministered at the church before Alec had been ineffectual at best, whiling away the days to exhibit his displeasure at being stationed in what he once referred to as a 'Backwater town' in a letter Alec was shown once he'd accepted the orders to go to Benjamin.

His predecessor fell ill and was finally moved from the bed in hishome (which Alec had not been forced into occupying, thankfully) to St. Francis in Los Angeles where he died shortly thereafter, leaving the church to languish for months until Alec's appointment.

Alec's thoughts shifted once again to others in the Vatican who knew something their contemporaries couldn't be bothered to consider, or eschewed altogether; Alec Copeman was a good man. One who served 'In the trenches' where good men were the most needed the most often, not clicking their fingers for an assistant as they walked the Ditta Medici marble floors of the Vatican. Men who knew that going amongst the people of his parish who did not currently attend services and trying to recruit them appeared ham-fisted at best.

Alec's practice was non-invasive. He made no secret of his profession in town or no, but he wore the collar as his uniform, and was a man proud of his achievements. Occasionally, he would wear something more casual like a simple oxford shirt, his youngish face belying his forty years.

A man like Alec, some officials knew, was one that would slip under many a notice. The fact that he had sought his own brand of self-imposed exile did nothing to elevate him.

A good man beneath notice also carried the liability of feeling conflicted within himself, Alec knew. To be unsung and unappreciated by the world at large could wear away at the spirit as well as the conviction.

Alec closed his eyes and inhaled the cold morning air through his nose deep into his lungs before exhaling it slow past his lips. His palms rubbed against each other behind his back finding him in a pose and attitude that would make passersby think – wrongly – his position of at-ease was a carryover from time spent in the military. It was simply a gesture of habit he had come to feel more and more natural doing, the results of self-discipline, a term that had been overshadowed by dark associations, particularly in the priesthood.

The spirit could never break. The conviction could never slip.

While Alec knew better than to think in absolutes like 'Never', there was no better word. He had been charged with a great responsibility by those within the Vatican who knew the value of someone like him. People like Alec, or more to the point, *enough* like him to know things and be silent and let it be enough and never – there was that word again – to be concerned with being spoken of in revered tones by cardinal bishops or whomever he would feel validated by.

And go without the notice of the Pope and those who had his ear.

But still there were times when Alec Copeman wanted very much to be rid of the thing behind the lock of his heavy oak desk drawer.

When he opened his eyes once more, he saw before he heard the black Saab rental car approaching from the east, and knew instinctively that his morning was not over.

His arms crossed his chest and watched the car grow larger.

Alec would have wagered Bishop Ashe probably would've worn his purple cincture around his waist along with the traditional black cossack, but didn't want to draw the undue attention to himself that the cincture would have doubtless attracted to those he sought to avoid, as this was indeed official business. And it was on those grounds that Alec reckoned the bishop had elected to wear his 14-karat gold bishop's ring, complete with diamonds, amethyst, and mitre-crozier appliqué despite the attention it would garner. It was pride, nothing more

For some reason, even when on clandestine business, there was an element who wished to make it known where he stood in the pecking order. Ashe most likely was going against orders. He was a man with an obvious love of rank, namely his own, and was the type of person who would use such things to whatever advantage possible. He was Alec's superior, and it was imperative Alec knew it.

It also marked him as disposable.

"Da Vinci chose to forget the Last Supper took place at night," the Bishop said.

Alec nodded. With those words came official business, to be spoken only by the Order or a representative of them.

Alec's offer to meet in the rectory was accepted while the offer of Bewley's coffee was politely declined, though Ashe did accept the offered alternative of loose, unflavored tea.

As Alec eased into his leather upholstered chair, just now beginning to show its wear, he leaned back and smiled at the bishop looking for something to rest his cup on sitting opposite him across the desk. Alec folded a paper napkin into a makeshift coaster, setting it at the corner of the desk closest to Ashe.

"You're surprised I'm an American," Ashe said, a smile playing at his features Alec guessed the man had gone grey somewhere in his twenties and had been fortunate enough to mellow rather than become embittered and condescending.

In another time, in another place, Alec and he could have been friends.

Alec had recognized the bishop's name from one or two conversations he'd had with those from the Order over the past few years. He'd never spoken to this man before, but knew that while Ashe was in a position over him, Ashe was low man on the totem pole in what would equal middle-management.

In other words, an errand boy.

Alec was not offended. More likely than not, Ashe didn't know himself; they had sent him rather than an actual dignitary (complete with guard, one would imagine) because bishop Ashe was expendable. The only value the man had was that he didn't know it.

As if reading Alec's mind, the bishop's expression widened, confirming the fact that something had so shaken the Order as to motivate them to send someone to personally contact Alec, but also know that the person sent was most likely going to be a target.

Well," Alec responded. "It wasn't what I was expecting."

"The Order excels in the unexpected, as I'm sure you'll agree."

Alec was living proof of that, but nodded silently nevertheless.

"And you're thinking, 'So what are you doing here?'" Ashe smiled and sipped at his tea. When he was presented with a duplicate of Alec's previous expression, he set the cup down and allowed his features to darken.

"The Order has reason to believe their ranks have been compromised."

Alec tried not to show any outward show of alarm. Ashe had the passcode, but if the Order had been compromised, this man could be anybody. Alec had never met bishop Ashe, and to request identification earlier would have conveyed mistrust. Now to the wrong person, suicide. The .44 Magnum was in his desk drawer, which he pulled open with careful ease. Ashe seemed not the least bit worried about the priest's actions.

Disguising his actions with some admittedly unconvincing misdirection with his free hand, Alec managed to get the gun to drop into his lap while making a show of retrieving his appointment book and placing it as an afterthought on the face of the desk.

"What leads them to think that?"

"Items have now come up as missing. Stolen, to be exact." Ashe rattled off the relatively short list of items recently reported by private parties and galleries as stolen.

"There's no mistaking that for coincidence."

"No. Whomever is doing this knows what they're looking for."

The two stared at one another for a time.

"It is safe," Alec said at last.

"Are you prepared?"

"As much as one can be."

Alec could tell by the way the older man shifted his weight that he was decided whether to ask if he could see the item he was inquiring after. In a moment, the expression was gone and the bishop had restored his calm, and practiced, demeanor.

"Is that all the Order wanted to know?" Alec asked, knowing full well that if this was indeed the genuine bishop, he would not ask to see it for two reasons; he was not allowed to know what it was specifically he was asking for and therefore was out of the loop in terms of laying eyes on it, and that the object he was inquiring about may well not be where the meeting was held.

"Yes," replied Ashe.

And no, thought Alec. A coded communication would have done it, as well. It would by no means be the first time. No, the real reason an emissary was sent to his parish was to make sure he was still alive and he was who he claimed to be, which meant Ashe had been shown a picture of Alec, with the photo being destroyed following its commitment to memory.

"And so ends our business," bishop Ashe said, rising from the chair with the decided air of one who was grateful for the charade he had been asked to participate in was at last over and he could get back on the plane and get back to Vatican City.

There was no invitation to tour the church, nor was there a request made, which suited Alec just fine, and he was certain the feeling was the same on the behalf of the bishop.

Ashe rose from his chair, leaving his cup of tea unfinished. As almost an afterthought, he cocked his head at the top of the desk, spotting the dog-eared trade paperback copy of Geoffrey Chaucer's *The Canterbury Tales*. There was a finer, leather-bound 1928 gilt edition reprinting the Riccardi Press 3 volume 1913 original with 24 color illustrations by Flint in his library, but that was more out of a love of the book rather than actually read.

The Bishop's face broke into an easy smile Alec found he believed actually genuine and off-the-record. "Which is your favorite of Chaucer's stories?" He weighed the volume in his hand as if waiting for permission to open the book.

Despite his best intentions, Alec found himself relaxing enough to smile back. "'The Parson's Tale',", he replied. "When he finally chooses to tell a story, he picks one of truth for the benefit of being clear. He has his opinion of what's important and makes no bones about wishing to remain clear throughout."

"Go on," Ashe said, now flipping through the pages.

"He cites references for his opinions," Alec continued, finding his rhythm. "Among them not only Christ and His Apostles, but Ambrose, Augustine, and Galen. The discussion of sin and the many ways one may find themselves succumbing to it is tempered with guidelines of prevention rather than rely on threats. He does not want to see anyone suffer, only to serve God."

The Bishop looked up from the fanning pages, seemingly satisfied with the answer and make Alec ask him his own favorite, which Alec did after the book was replaced almost exactly where it had been

found. "I forgot you liked to write essays," Ashe said and turned to the door. "'The Knight's Tale," Ashe shrugged. "The chivalric ideal."

Waiting for more, Alec nodded. When none was forthcoming, and the easy grin of the Bishop had turned into a condescending smile, Alec broke eye contact and was able to replace the gun.

It was only because of self-inflicted protocol that Alec showed him out.

As the Saab drove away, Alec contented himself to watch as it became nothing As it nearer the horizon. It was not the first time he had received a visitor from the Order, but it was certainly the most uncomfortable. Five years before, a Bishop had arrived sans notice, as was expected, and given the message to be wary of strangers. Nothing came of that, but Alec knew he would never see Bishop Ashe alive again. It would be a shame that one who would surely have missed the irony of 'The Monk's Tale' should perish without knowing why. A more fitting story for the Bishop to have picked might have been 'The Nun Priest's Tale,' with its moral of not believing everything that is fed to you, and the cunning of a man who can use his gift of a well-crafted phrase to get himself out of trouble.

Such things would escape the notice of a decoy, not a martyr.

Or, Alec reasoned, someone under different circumstances who had a habit of turning casual thoughts into essays.

Bishop David Ashe's ring tapped at the Saab's steering wheel in time to the Tchaikovsky playing on the sole classical station the rental's stereo could receive in this part of the coast. He would have preferred Vivaldi, or perhaps some Mozart, but any port in a storm.

Not for the first time, he considered his visit to the States an utter waste of time. To 'Maintain relations,' as he was told, which was a way of saying, "Mind your own business' and making it sound like a general business trip.

He should have been a cardinal by now, Ashe thought, not some messenger for that had all but condemned him as an overly-critical voice, and that in itself had perpetuated itself to this day, leaving him where he was, and not at all certain as to change his unenviable position.

The strip of two-lane highway was about two hours north of anywhere approaching Los Angeles and far removed from anything outside the occasional Denny's or independent gas station. He'd stopped for a light lunch about thirty minutes after his meeting, if you wanted to call it that, with Father Copeman and had decided he was not going to stop after that until he hit LAX, where he could turn in his car with the one acceptable radio station and return to Rome and perhaps draft a heated letter to the College of Cardinals.

The sudden shunt of his head and bucking of his car broke him away from the first draft he had begun to compose in his head. His eyes flicked in a scowl to the rear view mirror, coming to see the primer grey fenders and hood of a one-time muscle-car, which he believed to be a Mustang, behind him.

He regained his bearings, and his eyes returned to the rear view just in time to see the car behind him accelerate again, coming to an even greater impact with the rear of the Saab.

Mouth suddenly dry, Ashe watched as the Mustang dropped back, then bolted into the other lane, edging closer to the Saab.

In a panic, Ashe planted both feet on the brake pedal, allowing his pursuer to launch past until it came to a sliding brake, leaving behind a thick curl of smoke from the tires and black streaks on the face of the road until the driver corrected the car's attitude from across both lanes to accelerating towards Ashe going the wrong way down the lane.

Ashe's trembling hand fumbled at the gearshift, missing the stick completely first, then gaining it, banging the gears into reverse without checking his path behind. His foot slammed the accelerator into the floorboard, the rush of copper in his mouth matching the roar that erupted from the sudden strain on the engine of the Saab.

The Saab jolted backward, the needle climbing the face of the speedometer as the pursuing car grew in the windshield, its driver obscured by the gust of burning rubber and road dust.

Ashe grunted as his head snapped back at last to the rear window, his hand clawing the back of the seat opposite as he navigated the beginning of the turn he had just come out of.

The Saab bucked once more and the bishop's wet palm slid from the wheel. A terrible grinding sound belched from under the hood, followed by tendrils of pewter smoke seeping from the lines of the hood.

Ashe's attention returned forward as he tried to gain the wheel once more. The came the impact at the rear as the guardrail came up to meet the back end of the car. Both feet hit the brakes once more and he was rewarded with a screech from beneath the car and the passenger side as the guardrail ripped at the side of the car while his attacker now pushed his car toward the maw of a rend in the railing that opened behind him as the car fell through it, and for a handful of heartbeats, there was blessed silence before the resounding impact.

There was pain, and blackness. Ashe could not bear open his eyes against the throbbing blooms that soon appeared behind his eyes.

The Saab had come to a stop, but in which position, Ashe hadn't the slightest notion. He could be hanging upside down over a cliff, for all he knew.

Then came the sound of metal protesting against metal. For one fleeting moment, he entertained the notion that the two fingers pressing themselves against the side of his neck were those belonging to a paramedic, but the dismissive grunt and riffling through the contents of the car allowed him to realize that it was indeed his attacker, looking for whatever they hoped to find amongst his carry-on bag and valise.

He would be uncertain as to how long he lay there, listening to his assailant tear the interior apart as best they could, even going so far as to pry the trunk open with what had to be a crowbar.

Soon, at least it would seem to Ashe as he felt himself spiraling away, there were no more sounds of search, and his body was allowed to lay undisturbed.

His attacker had left him for dead. No assistance would come to him. He did not possess what the enemy had sought, and even as a possible carrier of whatever it might have been to have been scavenged – it hadn't been money – his purpose was that of a non-entity. His life was cast away, regardless of whether he had what they were looking for.

The weekend Parisian nightlife was a pleasant distraction when observed from a reasonable distance, like that afforded by the third floor suite veranda of the Hotel Ritz. One could watch the usually upwardly mobile suspects milling about with the tourists who were trying desperately to appear as natives. The evening was still young, and appeared to be fully prepared to pass without incident or comment.

That was why Gavin Fox preferred to stay at this particular hotel whenever the occasion allowed, which was rare enough as it was. He could go through the business of France, which he considered as busy a place as many parts of metropolitan Japan, in the comfort of his Simone, who enjoyed France quite a bit more than he could muster – he once said it was trading one metropolis for another, throwing in language shortcomings, a long flight, and jet lag just for good measure – even when business rendered their trip unable to support the time to visit the wealth of culture the city had to offer with its galleries and grand architecture that seemed to change face at night, when all things differ just so, pinned in light and marquee.

Simone sat in the oversized king bed, sheets to her left folded down on her left, his side of the bed. She wore her grey wire-rimmed reading glasses low on her nose as worked her way through one of the antique penny dreadfuls she found in the bookstore several doors down that seemed to keep only evening hours.

He stood there at the open window for some time, listening to the night sounds only Paris could share while he watched his wife read one of her beloved books, the faint scent of her musky perfume blending with the smell of the pages of Simone's antique book. "Do you think Becca really used teleportation?" He hated to spoil the scene with the question, but it was something that had not left the front of his mind since they had last seen the witch. They had tacitly avoided talking about the subject, but the impression that Simone had received at the museum had renewed the worry two-fold.

Simone looked up at him over the lenses of her glasses. She considered him for a long moment, and for a second, appeared to Gavin like she was going to actually close the book, marking her spot with an index finger, place it in her lap, and answer his question in an erudite, reassuring manner

Instead, she simply said "No," and returned to the page she was working through.

Gavin straightened away from the window, arms folded against his chest. "Well, I don't want you to rush to judgment or anything."

Simone's eyes returned to him. Her finger inserted itself into the book, but its covers did not close.

"Do you honestly think she did?" It was not a challenge, more of a clarification as to whether she had missed something in a subject she believed, rightly, she knew a great deal about, via both instinct and learning.

"No," Gavin had to say. "I'm just concerned with her judgment. She left her house – "

"Well-guarded, as it turns out."

"And her temperament – "

"Was completely understandable, given the circumstances. I kept her busy while you broke into her home."

"You took *your* car, though. The two of you."

"That's right, we did."

"And even with timeslide, or whatever spell she used, she traveled quite fast, leaving your car behind."

Now the book found its place on Simone's lap. "Gavin, I have no idea how she did it."

"Flight?"

Simone's eyes lidded in thought for a moment, then returned to him. "I don't think so, no."

"How, then? I can't come up with a single thing that does not indicate her use of a darker power."

"I don't know what to say. Maybe when we mend fences with her, she'll tell us."

Gavin's eyes studied the floor. Outside, a car horn honked. "And what if she doesn't?"

"Then we'll know a wall has risen and our friend has made a decision we can only disagree with."

"Can we trust her?"

"What do you think?"

"I think we have to for now."

Simone removed her glasses, folded them, and kept them in her hands.

"Is she someone we could confront?"

Gavin gained the bed in short strides and covered her hand in his.

"If we had to, we could. Together."

He felt her give his hand a reassuring squeeze, then release it.

"You're more concerned with what you sensed in the museum." From Gavin, not a question.

Simone snapped out of the kind of quiet fugue she had slipped into. "Yes, that does worry me. I get the impression the decision to use teleportation came very easy, just out of necessity. The casting cost is irrelevant to him. It's a mission this person is on. There is very much a target to be hit, and they know it very well."

The subject of what kind of person who not only would require the power of teleportation, but also what might indicate of why, given such a high casting cost, had come up with some degree of frequency between the two of them, but the topic had regained prominence now, and Gavin was grateful for the time they'd spent talking about it.

On the twenty-minute drive to the hotel from the museum, they had had time to mull over their individual impressions of the person responsible for the theft, which indicated involvement not only with the previous break-in, but the foreboding on the horizon.

The age of the person was unknown, although it had been discussed briefly. The use of teleportation indicated to Gavin the brashness of the relatively young and extraordinarily advanced and gifted while Simone maintained the use of higher-level magicks showed someone who had the experience that came with years of studying ancient and contemporary texts alike. Probably an older person who reasoned their way free of the ethics presented to him, or simply eschewed them altogether.

The missing part, and the most disturbing to them both, was to what end these pieces were to be used for? It was as if someone broke into a store renowned for Waterford crystal and looking for sporks instead.

CHAPTER NINE

We are flawed beasts, insisting we are able to blame the gods for our lot in life all the while blissfully ignoring our own actions, and the consequences we cause for ourselves.

Leland Fell, THE FELL BEASTS, Second Edition

Not for the first time in her life, Diana Adair lay prostrate and shivering, afraid to let her eyelids rise and pull light into her eyes.

And not for the first time, the woman with ashen hair and grey eyes prayed to a god in which she no longer believed in to just get it over with and kill her already.

She knew she alive from the pounding in her ears that, while subsiding, was thrumming a tattoo deep into the back of her skull. Her lower ribs ached with each breath. That was new. No matter how she tried to drive them into a shallow huff, the pains refused to recede.

She was unable to tell if the hard coldness in her feet and ankles was from exposure to the night time elements of the night before or if she had walked a football field's length of crushed and shattered glass, leaving curious footprints back to wherever she had ended up, and wouldn't that be a bitch?

Her sense of smell had mellowed back to normal, and her ears didn't seem to harbor the amplified mess of a spectrum they usually did, so that was a good sign.

With a curse, Diana allowed her eyes to open.

Too bright for a moment. Tempting to squeeze them shut again.

No. No. Get yourself up. It was the sound of her father's voice: *On your feet.* Some of the friends she grew up with saw the harsh disciplinarian edging higher in the ranks of the Navy. What Diana got was a lifetime's worth of love and an understanding of what it meant to rely on yourself. When she was bad, that was another story. But she never hated either of her parents.

From an early age, she understood almost too well what that word, hate, could do and mean to a person. As she grew older, it became even clearer.

Back to the pain as it washed anew over her, the soft brightness pulled into focus faster than she'd expected, but at least the influx of what came to be identified as the half-light of early morning pushing its way through the blinds of her apartment didn't increase the pain in her head. If nothing else, it actually seemed to help.

She would have no idea as to how long she lay there, or how many times she repeated her petition to die. When the latter failed, as it always did she woke up this way, tried to will herself to die. Eventually, she gathered enough energy to roll over onto her back and take stock of her condition.

The small of her back harbored the familiar ache. It was taking longer and longer these days, she had to admit to herself, but it *would* get better. Eventually. The pounding in her head was slowing, if not lessening. That too would disappear given the chance. If not, she would have to rely on bombing it with a cocktail of various over-the-counter painkillers that would make any self-respecting physician do whatever possible to keep her from continuing such actions. It almost made Diana laugh; she had tried repeatedly in the past to find the sort of irresponsible doctor that she kept hearing about on the news and from friends that would just prescribe painkillers for a mystery illness. But she was soon to learn that with perhaps one exception, she didn't feel she could trust anyone for medical grade drugs on the sly. And the few times she tried whatever pill a friend would turn her on to, it would incapacitate her to a greater degree than Diana was willing to accept.

In a place she kept to herself, she was readily able to admit that this was probably for the best. But the pain wasn't going to decrease completely. It never had before. It only got worse as time wore on, and she realized as her body got older and suffered more from the physical and mental trials she put herself through, the price would be high indeed, and sudden. This pain was only a precursor. She could sense that what would come without warning would be complete; breakdown. Mental, physical... she'd already suffered the spiritual. She wagered that was what had gotten her in this condition in the first place; spiritual breakdown leads to all sorts of interesting thought patterns and action, she thought. Freaking out the way she did once in a while was just a part of her trying to get out, and knowing that only served to scare the hell out of her.

Deep scratches on her calves. That was new. At least there's variety, she thought. She'd seen her legs get pretty mangled during her outings, but this was among the worst. She'd probably been pursued, although by what was anybody's guess, and she was certain that she had no desire to know, and was grateful for the forgetfulness her body forced upon her when she would come to. A kind of shock. Something she'd come to welcome.

The cold and wet leaves and twigs still stuck to her abused skin told her she'd probably been in the reservoir again. The only reason Diana knew she'd ever been in one at all was the one occasion she'd awoke outside of her home. A mere block and a half, but a foot and a half is a football field when you're naked and shaking and barely aware of yourself. It had been dawn last year, and she'd been able to make it home
without incident.

She'd never found blood on her that wasn't an obvious result of some wound she herself had suffered. For that, she was grateful.

But for now, her legs would have to be the issue, as had been the norm for several months now. She'd been more active lately, and that in itself was enough to keep her up and pacing the floor on more than one occasion.

It wasn't that she couldn't appreciate serenity. Far from it. In fact, it seemed like one of the few passions she had these days, short of her music.

But the *practice* of serenity; now that was something else again. It was as if no matter how hard she tried, the wiring in her brain, or whatever made her her simply wouldn't allow the manifestation of it in her life. Theory was all well and good, it was in practice she would consistently fall short.

There was too much anger inside her. She could admit that, even if she wouldn't say it to anybody. The power of prayer or positive thought or meditation would only work so well before the storm clouds would begin to gather. She'd gotten good at acting like aggravation rolled off her back, and occasionally, it actually would. But in most instances it would only build up with in her, lurking, waiting for a way out.

Until it finally did. Usually at night, when the world had finally shut its mouth long enough for her to try to sort things out in her head.

And she would wake up the next morning in much the same situation as now.

She would have to wear slacks for that night's performance. No big deal; it wouldn't be the first time she'd had the need to wear them, and it wasn't like skirts were the order of the day at Ryan's Pub on the ground floor of the Hotel McFarlane she played piano at, singing jazz standards. And there were thankfully no additional musicians to add their opinion, so slacks would do.

She broke away from this train of thought in order to perform a quick check of her hands. A couple of broken fingernails, but she'd never been one to grow them long, piano playing or no, so that wasn't much of an issue. A few minor scratches here and there, but nothing unusually noticeable. There was hardly ever any kind of mark on her hands and arms after one of her evenings out, and when there were, it was only on the rarest of occasions that they had been serious enough to either cover up or concoct a cover story for. And she had stopped wearing jewelry unless it was for an appearance at a get-together or a performance ever since she'd nearly lost her mother's garnet ring a few years before when she'd gone out at night in what she was referring to herself in those days as her 'Aggravated capacity.' Maybe she'd wear a small ring that evening for her show, maybe even a thin gold bracelet around her wrist. Jewelry tended to get in the way during her performances, but over the years, she'd been able to find a piece or two here and there that would allow her to adorn herself in a modest way with taking away from her agility at the keyboard.

For an unknown handful of time, Diana lay there, allowing her body to be still, trying to push down the pain. After a time, it worked, but she would still need to get up and go into her home's bathroom an agonizing rise to her feet and several steps away from where she currently lay. She contemplated crawling, as she often did these days after waking in the manner she was currently in, but her father's voice again commanded her to get up, and she was never one to argue with something that built on the strength you still had when you were at your worst.

Diana found her feet because this wasn't the worst. It wasn't as bad as it was going to get. She knew that. It was going to get worse. A lot worse. And it was not going to go away. Ever. She could only prepare for it. She refused to think of it as conditioning herself, even in her innermost thoughts about her predicament.

She gained the bathroom, not caring how long it took her. It wasn't that she hadn't the courage to lay her eyes on the small clock on the bathroom sink countertop, she was only beyond the caring as her head began to pound anew in time to her heartbeat.

Diana guessed at the dosage of three different painkillers, filled a Dixie cup full of water, and took the first wave of however many were in her hand. Then came the second wave. She'd need to eat something soon or her stomach would suffer the consequences from the heavy medication and the caffeine some of the tablets carried with them. Ideally, she would have eaten before she'd taken them, but this time, as so many others, she wasn't able to find it within herself to be able to choke down a slice of white bread or a handful of saltine crackers along with a few swallows of water. She needed to kill the pain, bury it. At least take the edge off it before going any further.

She sat on the lidded toilet, not caring about how cold it was on her backside or on the backs of her legs. She folded her arms on the countertop and folder herself over so that her face was resting on her forearms. After a time, she moved her head to one side, resting her cheek on her arm.

The waves of nausea hit sooner than expected. She stayed her ground, determined not to move unless she had to. The sink was directly in front of her, and although she would have preferred throwing up in the toilet for the simplicity of cleanup, in her current physical condition, the sink would do just fine.

After four dry heaves, she had gotten past the worst of it. When she opened her eyes, she felt the pain had receded just a bit. Enough to be noticed. It then fell back to a dull throbbing behind her temples and an ache that encompassed her entire body. Progress. It was enough.

Before long, she was able to clean the wounds on her legs with tissue and water. She then fished a pair of swabs from the cup they were kept in from atop the counter. The bottle of hydrogen peroxide was under the sink. Diana carefully dabbed at the scrapes on her legs, hissing through her teeth as the hydrogen peroxide ignited in the wound, foaming over the cuts. She left them unbandaged, letting the wounds breathe and hoping that was really the best way of treating them.

A slice of bread and another cupful of water were next. She stood nude in the kitchen, one hand bracing herself against the Frigidaire, the other holding the Dixie cup. The trembling of her hand subsided as she watched, and she nibbled on another slice, feeling the progression of her recovery.

Her terry robe was next. It was overdue to be replaced by something a bit less worn and more vibrant than the faded burgundy, but it was an old friend.

She sat on the sofa, legs curled up beneath her as she finished the bread and got her bearings. As per usual, she couldn't remember much at all from the night before. Just images; a reflection she couldn't bring herself to face in a pool of water lit by a three-quarters-full moonlight; the rush of air on her naked skin as she ran, her calloused feet beating faster and faster across the ground.

Probably the hills surrounding Hollywood, she mused. She'd always felt that's where she went. Back to the wilderness, or at least where she could manage to find it here.

It was just her out there on nights like that. The full lines of Diana's lips ticked into a slight smile over that.

A pure form, lighting into the dark.

A part of her had grown to like it, recognize it. And not fear it.

Before long, she padded into her bedroom and walked on her knees into the middle of the mattress of the queen bed. The digital clock on her night stand read 9:46, its numbers fading as more light filled the room.

She wouldn't have to be at Ryan's until evening came. As long as she got there by 8:00 PM, she'd be fine.

Diana let her body slump into the pillows, a rush to her temples bringing fresh pain between her ears, but it subsided in a few moments, and the pain had gotten bearable enough now to where she could actually be consciously aware of unclenching the muscles in her jawline.

She'd have to come up with a few new songs in her set list for the next few nights just to keep things new, and brush up on some of the old standards she would occasionally be asked to play by a patron. But for now, Diana Adair simply felt her body relax and ease away from the pain as best she could. Some times were harder than others, and thankfully, this was not one of those times despite the degree she had experienced upon regaining consciousness.

And again, she dashed into the dark.

CHAPTER TEN

It strikes me no one is actually interested in facts. Opinion has become more important than the facts.

Leland Fell, THE FELL BEASTS

(Second Edition)

Early afternoon brought with it not much save for a soft blue to the sky and a few scuds of clouds. There seemed to be more conversation amongst the local birds that usual, but they always appeared to be unpredictable in their behavior anyway. Nothing more to worry about than usual.

Alec Copeman continued his afternoon constitutional a few feet inside the boundaries of the church, listening to cars on the road approach, and fade. Observe the sky for the sake of the beauty nature could put to what could be considered an utterly unremarkable canvas. He preferred early morning walks after praying his morning rosary, and had made walks a habit since well before he moved to Benjamin. The still of the world at that hour gave him some distance, despite having to rise at an hour earlier than he would have preferred. It would have been easy for the years to have sewn a sort of resentment into him for the inconvenience of having to wake up at five in the morning in order to feel his own kind of balance, or as he'd come to know it, as a different kind of meditation in which one did not disconnect from the world, but instead re-connect on his own grounds, at least for a little while before he became outnumbered.

But then, that was probably why he'd come out here again in this frame of mind, he mused. Although a nagging part of his mind reminded him that he was not entirely sure as to whether the came out of his office to try to perform his meditation during a time he otherwise would not have bothered with, or that he wanted to make sure everything was still in its place out here.

He was afforded a view of a thin stretch of ocean over the hills his church overlooked in the west. Some fog still clung to the waters there, obscuring even more of the view than usual simply due to distance. But it was still there, and always would be. Something Alec found some comfort in.

Alec was just finishing his thoughts and readying himself for the trek back inside to papers and the occasional phone call, and maybe a bologna sandwich with some iced tea when the squad car drove up, trailing road dust behind it.

The big man who stood from the car and caught Alec's attention nodded. Alec found himself nodding back.

"Father."

Alec tried on a half-smile. For some reason, it actually felt like it stuck. "Chief Nedry."

The officer's own face split into a smile. "We don't need the honorifics today, do we?"

Alec shrugged. "You started it."

The big man nodded, looked off to the sea, then back to Alec. "Know why I'm here?"

Alec just looked at him.

A nervous chuckle from Nedry. "No, I wouldn't imagine you would."

"Why *are* you here?"

David Nedry's face was browned by the sun and a life led by passions outdoors. His eyes had at one time probably been a deep blue, now faded to a shadow of it. "Official business, I'm afraid. Can we go inside?"

"Would it be all right to stay out here?" Alec's attention returned to the strip of ocean. "It's such a nice day, and I've been cooped up inside."

"Sure, Alec. I wanted to know if you'd heard of a Bishop Ronald Ashe?"

Alec didn't hesitate. "Yes, of course. He's an emissary from Rome."

"You've met him?"

"Yes, just yesterday, in fact. Has something happened?"

"I'm afraid so. Roadworkers found his car wrecked off the interstate this morning. He was inside. He didn't make it. Found your name in his notes." David shrugged. "You're not a suspect of course, but we need to run a few things down before taking this any further."

"What do you mean?"

"We have reason to suspect foul play. It looks like his car was intentionally run off the road."

Alec wiped at his mouth with his palm.

"Do you know anyone who would want to cause Bishop Ashe bodily harm, Alec?"

In time, Alec moved his eyes to the Chief. "No," he replied softly. "He was a decent man."

"So you knew him pretty well?"

"No," Alec admitted. "Just a feeling, I guess. Sorry, I know you need the facts, not just the impressions."

David nodded, appearing somewhat relieved at the fact that Alec was not a close friend of the Bishop's. It would no doubt make the other questions easier.

"Did Bishop Ashe say anything that would indicate to you that he might feel his life was in jeopardy?"

"No. Not at all."

"What business did the two of you discuss?"

Alec shrugged despite his best intentions to allow for any body language at all. "Just things regarding the direction of the church, how the renovation has held up... things of that nature."

The questioning continued further, with Alec noting the questions themselves were becoming more and more (at least to a layman's ears) uninvolved and at best being recited by rote by the officer he had known since

Alec had started his stay in Benjamin. Occasionally, Benjamin police would ask for Alec's help in assigning work for whatever at-risk youth Benjamin might have at the time, which had never been that many. And while Alec had never seen David at any of his services, he understood by the simple act of several telephone pole over his knee that David Nedry was at the very least a man of principle and one who had an agreement with the universe.

In Alec's estimation, that put David well ahead of the game when compared to others, whether any of them attended a church or not.

"David, I'm not sure what I can say."

"I don't know either. I've got a dead Bishop in the morgue and car that looks like it's had some help tumbling down a hill, and absolutely no motive."

Alec sympathized with the man's frustration. David was the type of man whose only destiny was to be a cop; he had all but told Alec that in the past. He did not come from a bloodline of cops, he was just someone who wanted to protect others against the injustices of the world while making them aware that they were there.

Again, ahead of the game.

David was a man with much work ahead of him, not the least of which was going to be how to remain enthusiastic about his job as time went on.

David took a couple of steps back. "Well, I should be getting back."

"You know where to find me."

"Yep, I do. If you think of anything, even if it doesn't seem like anything at all…"

Alec smiled and nodded. "You'll be the first one I'll call."

David turned away, nodding, the soles of his feet crunching on the stone pathway leading to the car as Alec head inside, although more for effect than actual purpose. The priest was brought up short by the steps of David coming to a halt.

"Alec? One more thing."

Alec turned, shading his eyes.

"Is it standard procedure for someone from Vatican City to come talk to the priest of a small church like this one?"

Coming from anyone else, the question would have been formed as an insult. At least to Alec. But from David, it was police business couched in a sincere request for clarity.

The best Alec could come up with was, "It's not unheard of."

Satisfied, David nodded and thanked him before returning to his car.

Back inside his office, Alec sat at his desk and stared down at the papers upon it. He scanned the computer he rarely used, the telephone… searching for a distraction, which was not what he should have been doing, he knew that, but a part of himself just couldn't help it.

Ashe was dead. Killed. That meant that whomever did it thought he either had possession of the page or documents regarding its location. Best case scenario; the killer knew it was in California, but didn't know who had it. Worst case scenario: Killer assumed Ashe would have retrieved it from its keeper to safer ground, wherever that might be, discovered not only Ashe did not have it, but found evidence regarding just who might have it, and was simply biding their time before paying a visit.

Much of what he was told as a guideline when he accepted guardianship was more intimated rather than outright said, which was standard operating procedure for the Vatican, at least where he was concerned, which did strike him odd. When something as important as the item he had was in question, he would have expected greater concentration on it than the old 'Don't call us, we'll call you.' In fact, he was certain that there was no one he was able to reach who could help or offer advice. But he also knew they knew quite a bit more than they let on, and that the only thing stronger than the Vatican when it spoke was when it remained absolutely quiet.

The world outside his window was still. He would have appreciated something in the background, anything to let him know the world was still going on, that hadn't stopped dead in its tracks, waiting for him.

And that what he would do; wait.

His faith had undergone tests throughout his life, as he believed all lives did. And throughout whatever crises he was experiencing, or had witnessed in the world, his faith had remained steadfast. It could be said that it could be due in no small part to the strength of Alec's convictions. He once wrote in his journal that it was due more to his belief that there were greater things in the world than himself.

Alec opened his desk drawer to where the gun lay, closed it against with his fingertips. He had a doubt that it would be enough when the time came. There was a tiny rush within him; of a kind that not since he had helped renovate the church he had feared he wasn't going to feel again... the jolt of excitement... the charge of purpose. He was more than able to feel and welcome peace and the silence it brought with it, but there was another part of him that had longed for the same kind of inner charge that allowed him to feel another kind of purpose.

It had begun.

Diana Adair kept her face to the stinging spray of the shower, braced with her outstretched hands pressed against the smooth power blue tiles to keep her face in the heat. The hot water dried her skin out, but it loosened the kinks and the steam opened the sinuses. Without this kind of shower, she made her way through the day complaining to herself about how sleepy she felt.

The wounds were healing quickly as they usually did, but her skin remembered the phantom pain. Forcing herself out of her half-meditation, Diana pushed away from the wall and the spray and began to ball her hands into fists then relax them rhythmically. She'd never had trouble with her hands, or fear of arthritis. She used it more as a centering device, to bring her back into the world of others while living in her own. She had to ease back in, otherwise her mood would darken considerably, leaving her with a hypersensitive psyche that led to no good. A part of her that was quickly silenced tried to talk her into going in early to see Eric before the rest of the staff arrived at Ryan's Pub for the Friday dinner crowd. Eric would be there to let her in if she showed up at say, five instead of the usual six-thirty. She wouldn't be due at her piano until seven, but she always liked to arrive early and listen to the room beforehand to see what kind of crowd was gathering. The staff would begin to show until about six, when they'd be going about whatever last-minute things Eric required them to do.

And that meant she and Eric would have enough time to talk…

Shut it. Not going to happen. Talk, nothing else. It was the 'Else' part that had created the weird friction only sex between co-workers could spark.

'Dipping in the company ink,' her father called it. And also warned her against doing it under any circumstances.

Circumstances, Diana reminded herself. He never said about not doing it under the piano after everyone has gone home.

It was a lame joke, but she grinned all the same. No one was there to call her on it, so she could enjoy a laugh at one of her own jokes if she wanted.

Especially when the situation wasn't particularly funny. Not to her, not to Eric, and certainly not his wife should she find out.

But that went without saying. Each time they made love. They did it for different reasons, although she knew that neither of them would talk about what was lurking beneath the surface. Hell, it wasn't even making love, in *The World According to Diana.* Lovemaking could be a desperate thing, she knew, but not every time. At least it shouldn't be. It can be a release. It can be relied upon to erase the world for a period of time, or just to let go and not worry about a thing.

Making love was supposed to beautiful. Not because Hallmark or the romance novels told her it was so, but because that's what common sense and experience dictated to her. With Eric, it started with a kiss she provoked. From there, they took each other wherever was convenient.

Therein lay the problem. They took each other. Didn't care about the other, so much as she could tell. They never shared the glimpses those carrying on an affair might be wont to do. Didn't even make eye contact with each other unless they had to. But they shared that tension.

And neither of them wanted it, and it seemed to her, tried to push it onto the body opposite them. An interesting little footnote to all this was that neither wanted it to end.

It wasn't lovemaking, not by a long shot.

For him, she supposed, it was someone stuck in a marriage that seemed to be a good idea at the time, enough to conceive a child in sincerity rather than desperation. But somewhere along the line, the varnish had gone off the relationship to reveal the players as they really were shockingly human, complete with faults and hopes and annoying habits.

She could see it in the way his face got pinched just so when he was talking to his wife on the phone, or if he related some banal story about his home-life, occasionally he would let slip some sort of smart remark about

Heather, nothing major, but with just enough venom for one who was paying attention to wonder just how happy this man was.

So Diana knew her body had become little more than a harbor. She had actually built up enough rancor about it at one point not so long ago to think about laying into him about it, until she realized she had been doing the same thing with him, and even though it was odds-on that he not only didn't know what her motivations were, but probably didn't care, she was not about to bring that to the forefront and expose herself for what he truly was.

So instead, she had sex with him that night in the kitchen of the Pub.

But it wasn't working anymore. Not for her, and she had the sneaking suspicion that it wasn't working for him now, either. They had become too familiar with each other. The thrill of the affair was gone.

But the tension was still there. Always would be.

But she refused to think of herself as desperate. In spite of all the times she could recall clinging to Eric like she were drowning, and that she intentionally didn't plan too far ahead in much of anything save her career, she thought of her actions as handling the world as it truly was, unpredictable and largely unrewarding. That was why she had the music in her soul or whatever that part of humans is called that instructs you to be better than you are. It made the cynicism worth it. It proved her wrong.

And gave her the only escape she truly enjoyed, because while she was behind the keyboard, she was in control. She was a solo act, and it would stay that way. Too many times she had depended on other musicians or agents to help bring the music to the fore. But invariably, she couldn't stand relying on others.

Diana gave her head one last dunk beneath the spray before turning it off and opening the sliding glass door, letting the stream curl away from her skin as she reached for her usual shower towel, something from a splurge urge when she felt the time was ripe for some kind of self-spoilage. She never regretted it. Part of staying sane in a world aggressively gone mad was to treat yourself when you could. Nothing major, mind, but a larger helping of that pie, or a DVD she'd wanted forever or a couple of bath towels with a name she wasn't sure how to pronounce and was fairly sure were somehow immoral given the level of luxury it gave the user.

She hadn't been indulging in the spoiling as often, she realized. It got that way after a change sometimes. The feeling would last an hour or so or a couple days. Lately, it had been hanging around from change to change. Some might label it depression. Others malaise. Diana herself wasn't sure what to call it, and was finding it increasingly difficult to care.

No way for a future Grammy award winner to feel, she reflected, pulling on jeans and the black blouse with the long, loose sleeves. No, not at all. But then, it was also difficult to believe such a thing was going to happen. It seemed at about the same time she took the gig at Ryan's about two and a half years ago, she'd made her mind up that the road leading to the big-time limelight just wasn't for her. Again, there was that depending on others thing she couldn't abide, and she had been able to release two of her own CDs containing the songs she wanted to sing with the artwork she wanted to see, recorded at her own pace, and they did okay in their own right. Not enough to live on, but enough to feel proud about her efforts and her own popularity. By the end of the week, her own website would be up and running, of her design and approval.

Okay, she thought. Maybe things weren't bad.

Maybe.

But she was still going to talk to Eric before opening, and got behind the wheel of her black Saturn and keyed the ignition before her better reasoning could get its foot in the door.

Half an hour later, she was again behind the wheel, this time headed for home, lips pressed into a thin, bloodless line.

She made a show of laying several feet of rubber away from the Hotel McFarlane, delighting in the nasty odor the burning rubber left in the car. It was juvenile, yes. Unsightly? Certainly. Did it make her feel better? Absolutely.

She knew anything resembling a conversation revolving around the situation she and Eric had would come to no good end. Went into it willingly, just to get it off her chest. Within spitting distance of one's thirtieth birthday, it seemed only fitting to take account of what was worth keeping and what was worth dropping, and whenever possible, some kind of closure.

And that was why she'd gone to see Eric. Not for one last roll in the hay, although that wouldn't be completely out of the question, depending on his own reaction, but to just break it off. Cleanly. No mess, no muss, no fuss. Get it over with. Do the right thing and get your foot onto another path. About time, just do it now before circumstances take you down a road you *really* don't like.

He seemed surprised when she tapped at the glass of one of the double doors leading into Ryan's. But there he was, all the same, at the same table he always sat at, going through paperwork of some kind or another in his black slacks with matching shoes and socks punctuated by the same kind of white button-down he always wore. But this time, he wasn't making eye-contact with her. He'd always done that, even before they started sleeping together. Something dropped inside her, but she stood her ground.

He made some kind of sound that might have been a greeting as he opening the door and left room for her to come through. She suddenly found herself with her hands clasped in from of the fly of her jeans and taking tentative steps on the tiled floor she'd walked on a million times before. Just around the bar was *her* turf; where her rented piano kept time on the carpeted space before the wood-paneled dance floor. She wanted to get him there, away from his floor, his table. But he wasn't having any of it. He just stood there beside the table, arms folded across his chest and looking impeccably annoyed. He didn't even say anything to her, he merely arched his eyebrows while one of his hands lifted away from its resting place on his forearm. She resisted the urge to brush the dark forelock away from his eyes.

Fine, then. No problem.

"I think – "

"I'm going to tell Heather about us," Eric blurted out.

"What?"

"I can't do this anymore."

Diana nodded, motioned for him to continue.

"It isn't fair to my family, it isn't fair to me."

"And to me?"

"Yes, right. To you, either."

"But you're going to see past all this and tell Heather."

"I think it's for the best."

"The best for who, you?"

"Well, yes. And my family."

Okay, so he was doing this for the right reasons, just not giving a damn how he was putting it. "Wait. Telling your wife about our affair," at this they both looked to the door just to make sure, a habit they'd both fallen into and since cultivated. "Is going to make your life better?"

"It has to stop, Diana. Surely, even you have to see that."

Diana shook her head as if to clear it. "Even *I*? What the hell is that supposed to mean, that the other woman is dumb enough to get stuck in an affair with a married man, but isn't going to understand the dynamics of it?"

"I can't keep living like this."

"And no one's asking you to. In fact, I was coming here to tell you the same thing."

For the first time, it seemed to Diana, Eric looked at her. His gaze lay on her in such a completely different way than it ever had before that it gave her pause to wonder if he'd ever really looked at her at all, ever. Then, almost as soon as the look came over his face, it passed, giving over to a look of amusement tempered with something resembling condescension .

"Diana, you really don't have to defend yourself. It's over."

She began to sputter. It was just getting wind enough to be an indignant flurry when he waved her away.

"Look, I've made up my mind. It's what's best for all involved."

"I'm not saying it's not – "

"No, but you're saying that you were coming to break up with me."

"I was, I actually thought it was a little funny, you know, to break up the tension."

"There's no tension here except for what you're bringing in." Diana nodded. Break off now, this is just going to get messier, and it's not worth it. He's not worth it. Let it go. Now. Leave.

"Maybe it's time you found someone who didn't need to be seduced to be with you."

Time froze.

"This was a mutual thing, Eric. I didn't need to squeeze myself into a dress slit up so high you could tell what sign I was, and sing 'Peel Me A Grape' to you."

Eric's hands went up in an exaggerated gesticulation of defeat, "Okay, okay. Whatever it takes for you to get up in the morning."

All the times she'd heard muttering from the busboys, to the bartenders, to the servers, to the hostess, about what an utter prick this man who stood before her was to them, and all the times she'd endured them, knowing she knew the man beneath the business came slamming back. She almost spat out something along the lines of 'Now I understand what all your employees have been saying about you' but that would have only caused trouble for them, and that wasn't her target.

Her target was the snide-looking man with the beginnings of a paunch and a head that never quite got out of the frat house.

What made it worse was the fact that he believed what he was saying, and that this little component to his personality was buried until he felt like unleashing it.

Such a man didn't have the balls to tell his wife, much less the drive. Diana could smell this on him. He was a man driven by fear. And in some part of him he couldn't name, he had finally had enough of trying to look his wife in the eye after having been with another woman.

He was a man who that had made a mistake, but could never cotton to it for long in his own mind, so this is what took over, more or less, a liar pointing an unloaded revolver at the only one who could deny with authority all that he was saying.

This man stank of fear. She chided herself for not noticing it before, burying her own gift for the sake of the company of another to stave off her own fear.

No, not fear. Certainty.

Certainty of people like this walking the earth with the rewards of a mate and children, never to see punishment because their accusers could never say anything without making themselves a target.

"Maybe it's time you found another place to sing," Eric said at last.

Diana shook her head slowly, eyes trying to burn him to the ground in a pile of cinder and ash.

In a moment, she had pushed past him and took half the distance to her car before recognizing the same quick stride that she'd seen other women exhibit when the day has just shot from beneath their feet

She tried to slow her steps, but couldn't. It was already too late. Too late for a lot of things.

She wasn't fooling anyone. Least of all, herself. Everyone else was out for themselves, why not her? What great favor was she doing the world by trying?

CHAPTER ELEVEN

Belief, in itself, is unique in that there are more things than we care to admit that exist despite our belief in them.

Rebecca Scott, THE BASICS OF BELIEF

The Manor was beginning to feel like Gavin recognized it again, a feeling he hadn't been able to shake since just after they'd landed in France. It was a feeling unlike he'd had before; it was beginning to be like he wasn't going to see it again, even though he knew that wasn't right. Of course he'd step foot in it again, Simone beside him. Yet something still gnawed at him. It was in all likelihood that the current tumult was simply having its way with the dynamic of roof and rafter. Simply put, it wasn't feeling like home now because he wasn't enjoying it as such.

He rubbed this thumb against the glass side of the oil lamp that was lit atop the mantelpiece of the fireplace situated into the west wall and watched Simone descend the stairs.

To a man completely devoid of appreciation of the finer things in life being the simpler things, the subtle almost matter-of-fact kind of beauty of such a woman would escape them utterly.

All the better, Gavin reflected, for men like him, who had no problem seeing the wonder in the form of a woman in beat-up painter's overalls giving the wall in her office upstairs (that used to be occupied by his grandparents who used it as a bedroom) a second coat last year, all the while blissfully unaware of how sexy that lick of paint on her forehead was... or the look that came with it, following a blowing of a forelock out of her eyes. The cocking of the hip and the wry 'What?' didn't hurt, either.

Simone now finished her steps at the bottom of the stairs and took in the house, as if just making sure everything was okay before deciding what to do next. She wore faded denim jeans and a raglan shirt that sported the Disneyland *Pirates of the Caribbean* logo and played with a multicolored hair scrunchie, finally deciding to let it stay ringing her wrist for now. In a moment, he caught her eye by not moving from the spot he still stood. Her hip jutted to one side, and an eyebrow raised. "What?"

It felt good to smile. Especially at her, especially now. "Yeah, just like that," he said under his breath.

Her bare feet closed the gap between them. Her head tilted to the side and her grin widened as she wreathed his neck with her arms

"Hey you," she delivered a kiss, light and quick, and stared up into his face.

"Hey."

This was how the world began and opened for him, all those years ago, when he looked into her eyes and wondered how the hell he couldn't have

76

figured out that this was just what was missing in his life all the while as he tried to fill some void within himself that he didn't even know he had up until then.

He pulled her close just to smell her hair.

"Quit sniffin' me, you old dog," she muttered into his chest. He smiled at how he could feeling her cheeks rise in a lazy smile.

"It's not my fault I've fallen prey to your feminine musk."

Simone's fingertips traced the ridge of his backbone. "'Musk?' How politically correct of you, my love. Some would have just settled for 'Stink.'

"You don't stink."

Simone pulled away, and Gavin's arms collected her again, and lowered her in a dip more suited to a tango than casual conversation between two people who knew each other better than they probably should have

Simone stopped giggling long enough to turn to the sound of three brisk raps at the door.

"I hope that's the pizza," Gavin said, still holding her steady.

"You ordered pizza?"

"No, I just hope it's pizza."

Simone smacked the flat of her palm against his chest, the international sign for 'Let me up' and went to the door.

In the foyer, Gavin peered over Simone's should to see who was on the other side of the double doors when she opened the left one, blocking the limited edition canvas replica of Arthur Hopkins' 'The Vistor' in its floral carved hardwood frame, the famous painting of the young girl reaching up a hand to knock on an oak door was an addition to the house Simone had added during a trip abroad. He was half-surprised to find Simone's scan had found their visitor a friend.

Rebecca Scott stood in their doorway, her expression not entirely readable.

"Hi," said Simone.

"Hey," came the response.

"Want to come in?"

"Please."

Simone stepped aside to allow Rebecca passage, closing the door and following the witch into the living room, where Rebecca and Gavin exchanged chin nods.

Simone let the heavy door slip from her grasp to close as she made her way back to the living room, where eyes were flicking more to the tops of shoes or the odd detail on the fireplace rather than other eyes. Simone stood close to the two others. It was Rebecca who spoke first:

"I want you to know that I'm still mad at you two. What you did violated my trust and showed that despite my own status, you consider me someone who needs a degree of babysitting when not meeting a problem as you see fit."

"I feel it was a perfectly understandable mistake," replied Simone.

"It was indeed. A mistake. But see accompanying illustration of *Witch, Still Pissed.*" Simone was about to give a terse response about said witch's apparent fear that had been exhibited, but allowed Rebecca to continue on.

"But there are greater things going on," Rebecca went on to say. "As we all already know." Here she waited for the nods from her two rather reluctant hosts. "Now, things are getting stepped up."

"How so?" This came from Gavin.

"I got a phone call from a friend early this morning. She's with Dawn's Eclipse."

Simone knew much of her man's outward show of interest lay in the degree of eyebrow raising over his left eye; the higher the raise, the greater the interest, and conversely, the greater the amount of cynicism that had met it in his head. And at that precise moment, Gavin Fox's left eyebrow had descended so much as to nearly be in a squint.

"That satanic cult up in the Hollywood Hills?" He asked.

Rebecca nodded.

"The one with all the celebrities?"

Again the nod from the witch. "Right. They don't actually *do* anything, but it is quite the status thing."

Simone's hands went to her hips. "But they perform rituals."

"What they believe to be rituals," Rebecca said. "Yes, they do, but it's just like any other club of that sort where power and money allow you to buy everything except for the thrill of the devil."

"Power follows evil," noted Gavin.

"Evil only follows power. Man succumbs to it." Rebecca smiled.

"And giving credence to evil, whether one believes in it or not, gives it substance, which gives it belief enough, which empowers it," said Simone. "Which, ultimately, is what allows it to harbor power."

Rebecca appeared to be fighting back the urge to wave the statement away. "Yes, I know. I think we all understand that. My point is, they're not actually summoning anything, they're not performing anything involving blood. They're idiots, but they're not like those idiots who kill children in order to prove their influence. This group is harmless…"

"'The perpetuation of evil,'" Gavin began.

"'Is as bad as evil itself,'" finished Rebecca. "Yes, I've read my Leland Fell, thank you very much. Now may I get to why I came here?"

Gavin opened his hands and spread them wide, palms up. After a moment, a part of Simone wanted to stretch out a tad longer as she savored the tension gave in, and she nodded instead.

"So there they are," Rebecca started. "All naked 'neath their black robes, ready for their orgy in the great hall after the incantation the priestess is finished reading from the great little book that has no name but is called by *From the Darkness.*" Here she paused, a grin barely suppressed.

Gavin groaned, and Simone knew why. *From the Darkness* was known, amongst the most serious circles, to be by and large fraudulent. No author was ever credited, and no absolute publication date or year was ever able to be established, as none of the copies in any collection had ever been confirmed as being identical to one another, much less constructed in a fashion that would convey the age certain uneducated individuals would clasp onto as genuine simply because of the use of what the preface referred to as 'Middle English translated from the Latin.' And as Simone herself had noted in more than one college lecture, excerpts of which were published in the now-defunct *Journal of Paranormal and Occult Studies*, 'When you want something to sound like it is of the occult, make sure it's written in Latin. It's like writing music in a minor key… it's 'Spooky.'" At which point, the audience would, without fail, burst into laughter. *From the Darkness* also had the pleasure of being the primary tome of reference amongst those lured into following the ever-fashionable evil, mainly it was believed, because it told them not only what they wanted to hear, but what they expected. It was laughed at, but never corrected, as it would forever provide an indicator as to one's intentions.

Soon, Rebecca's expression disappeared, to be replaced by a distant stare Simone recognized as one that came with a terrible realization coming back to someone who had dared forget it for a moment.

"Then, someone came in. They don't know how; no one in security saw him come in, it was like he was just there, in mid-stride in the hall, quoting from the book in Latin, along with the priestess, only he was doing it in a mocking fashion." Her eyes flicked first to Simone, then to Gavin. "He then took the book from the priestess, gave her forehead a smack with it… hard… and turned to assembled and basically told them the devil would have nothing to do with them. That they were ridiculous. He overturned the altar, knocked down the candelabras. Nobody tried to stop him because as my friend said, this man radiated power beyond what they could handle. Then, poof, he was gone, as was the book."

"'Poof?'" This came from Simone.

"My friends' very words. One instant, he was there, the other, not so much."

Simone couldn't control it – she smiled despite the dread attitude of it all and nudged Gavin in the ribs with an elbow. "See?" She said proudly. "I told you he could teleport."

The witch blinked at the two of them and made little helpless motions with her hands as she spat, "Okay, could you two settle your bet or whatever it is Simone just won, and concentrate on all this? I mean, can we really think together about what this all means?"

"Sorry," Gavin said.

"Just trying to break the tension," said Simone

Rebecca nodded, obviously looking for more.

"Does this mean we're all friends again?" Asked Simone.

"It means," replied Rebecca. "That I'm still mad as the dickens with the both of you, but there are better things to worry about right now. I'm not so pissed as to watch the world crack in half over whatever was or wasn't done."

After a moment, Gavin and Simone nodded.

"Agreed," Simone said. "There's no point in working on a friendship if the world's going to end, is there?"

Rebecca closed her eyes for a moment. "Something like that."

"Okay, does this give you a better idea as to what might be happening?" Inquired Simone to Rebecca.

"'Might?'"

"Sorry, poor choice of words. *Is* happening."

"I have an idea," Rebecca said, and went off in as fast a trot as her boots could manage in the direction of the stairs.

"Where are you going?"

"Upstairs," came the reply, with the witch already making the stairs and out of sight. "What's keeping you two?"

After a shrug from Simone, they followed.

They met back up with her at the closed door to the library, moving through the hallway lined with photos of the Fox family dating back to the 1700s and up to the most recent photographs of Gavin and Simone; one from their trip to Maui just the year before, a formal portrait in which Gavin was dressed in the monochromatic suit Simone still wished for more occasions for him to wear, and a cute snapshot taken by Rebecca herself during Simone's birthday dinner held at her favorite Japanese restaurant the previous year. A few posters from the days of when some of the Foxes celebrated themselves as magicians lined the walls further down, framed with treated plexiglass to avoid undue aging from light and air.

Gavin moved between Rebecca and Simone to open the door. There was the familiar sound of a puff of air from between the door and its frame as Gavin pushed it in. Simone waited for Rebecca to move in following Gavin, but Rebecca declined, instead motioning for Simone to go in next, which she did.

The room was called the library, and for all Simone knew, had been for generations, despite the fact the title 'Archive' would probably have been better suited. Although the term library was apt enough; it looked like something Indiana Jones would have broken into, both in the degree of volumes, many incredibly rare, as well as in the décor that was straight out of the thirties; dark wood desks, shelving, and antique reading lamps with treated bulbs to provide maximum throw of light while being able to prevent any damage from exposure, one of the few things changed over the years. The others being items like the heavier curtains to block the large west-facing window and the improved weather stripping. The air treatment system and thermostat were all museum-grade pieces, and were updated, without fail, every year when the new models came out. The sole distraction from the volumes came in the form of the 'The Bookworm' by Karl Spitzweg, double matted in burgundy on white hung on the south wall in its burled hardwood frame. The anecdotal look of the man atop the ladder holding three books, and clearly distracted from the world at large never ceased to bring to mind to Gavin the irony of its placement in this room, which it had been in since he could remember, and he had never seen a reason for it to be moved.

For a time, the only sound was the soft whir of the purification, before Gavin spoke.

Rebecca was already on the move to one of the shelves against the south wall, index finger held in midair, as she aimed for the book she was looking for, scanning the spines of each.

Simone's arms crossed over her chest, and her eyes flicked to Gavin, gauging his reaction. There was a part of her that wanted everything to be okay with Rebecca, but the effects of the past few days, and granted the lack of decent sleep, left her with the feeling that she was just a tad too nervous with Rebecca nosing around one of the finest collections of rare books on the various subjects of belief systems.

Gavin spent just enough time exchanging a look with Simone to let her knew he wanted to see how this would play out. Simone made a show of rolling her eyes, but was willing to concede.

"Can we help you find anything?" Gavin asked at last.

Rebecca's teeth worried her bottom lip as her eyes still scanned the books. "Is this all you've got?"

"I'm resisting a strong urge to throw something heavy and bound in leather at you," said Simone. After a moment, Rebecca's hand reached up onto the shelf just above her head, her fingers curling around the spine that had long since suffered a short rip at the front cover seam. The gold lettering pressed into the top third of the spine was largely worm away, but Simone recognized it as the *David Codex*, a collection of notes and details regarding the veracity of certain controversial manuscripts in their field. Dating that to 1618, and having a translation in both French and English authorities (Gavin included) considered accurate and comprehensive. It was the book that provided the foundation for much of the history that surrounded, or didn't surround, other books and subsequently their veracity.

"We've looked at that," Simone noted. "It leads us to places, but doesn't really tell us anything we don't already know; that this joker is stealing seemingly unrelated texts." Rebecca's index finger swirled in the air, her other hand held the weighty volume in her open palm. "And there's the operative word; 'Seemingly.'"

"Okay, how are they related?"

"Well, that's just it… I don't think they are."

Simone blinked. Made a show of it. Gavin barely suppressed a groan.

"'S'plain, Lucy."

"Well, I just got to thinking, that maybe it's not the books themselves as a whole he's after, but maybe just something that's written in them."

"You mean like a code?" Asked Gavin.

"Yeah, maybe, or like handwritten notes in the margins, or something." The witch's aquiline nose had buried itself back in the book.

"Don't you think that's a bit of a longshot?" This came from Simone

Rebecca's shoulders formed a distracted hunch. "Yeah, it is, but I can't come up with anything better." Her eyes wandered over the top of the book, studying Simone, then Gavin, waiting for one of them to pipe up a theory.

Simone dropped her eyes, then sent a glance over to Gavin, who had nothing to say, verbal or otherwise. Rebecca's index finger thumped into the text. "See? Here it says there's at least two documented accounts where written matter was used in conjunction with two or more pieces to form a united whole."

Simone nodded. They were books that when put together and the text decoded, allowed the user to cast spells for use of power or knowledge, usually the former. It was a kind of supernatural cocktail, untested, and incredibly dangerous. Fueled mostly by rumors, or by study in single practice only.

The stories regarding the two accounts were sketchy, at best. They had both been failures, for the most part. The text was both vague and disturbing. Enough that anyone who read it would understand that such undertakings were not to be handled lightly, or better yet, not at all.

"I think whoever is doing this," Simone said. "Knows better than to try that."

"I'm not convinced of that." "Why is that?"

"Well, mainly because this person – whoever it is – knows what they're doing. They're striking targets with precise motives, knowing what they're looking for and leaving. They seem to be moving faster now, like their actions are causing the acceleration."

Gavin nodded. "I agree."

Simone's eyes narrowed "So what is it do you think he's planning to do?"

The book closed with a thump. "Well, that's where you two come in."

Simone exchanged a look with Gavin. "Yes, of course, us being omniscient, and all."

Rebecca placed the book carefully on a nearby lectern with carved eagle's talons for feet. "You two are the most sensitive people I know. There's no one else to go to." She held their eyes. "There's no one else I *want* to go to."

After a moment, Simone's expression softened, as did Gavin's.

"Okay," Gavin said at last. "Let's put our heads together, what say?"

Rebecca nodded. "What say."

The reading and open discussion about the various texts the chain of conversation and conjecture were leading continued as the grandfather clock downstairs struck seven, which was decided time for just a short break for dinner. It was understood the books didn't leave the library for atmospheric conditioning reasons, let alone damage from food or drink, and of course the unspoken part about their value.

Simone wasn't convinced any of the books were going to lead them anywhere in particular, and the conversations were veering into ground more closely resembling the annoying rather than going into the realm of revelation. Not only were they researching from their own point of view, but also that of someone trying to harness something that they all admitted should be left free of reigns.

But as time had worn on, it was becoming abundantly clear that, Rebecca had been right after all in her conjecture as to what the motivation behind the thefts had been. Simone was curious not whether either she or Gavin would have thought of it, but why they hadn't sooner. They were what were called by their contemporaries in the field 'The voices of authority,' and although that was a terrible thing to live down, and it was beginning to visibly wear on Gavin just enough to be noticed by those close to him. Such things were dangerous. It made one lean towards being unfocused, this evening may have been proof of this more than anything else.

There were several books that could be combined in order to form what Simone had called a 'Supernatural cocktail,' but there could be at least seven different books with the properties that could be meshed together to form any form of destructive or constructive capability. It was possible that the *O'Barr Manuscript* had some real value, after all.

It was over dinner of delivered Chinese that they went into their version of brainstorming over the subject. They'd done it several times in the past, usually during a period of time when one was writing a book, or preparing a lecture for a class. Simone always found herself in the same place during these times; the recliner at the end of the couch, munching on the crispy chow mein noodles Gavin only liked a pinch of and Rebecca didn't care for at all. Shoes off, socks on, toes tapping out a rhythm only she could hear in the air. It was a nice mode to be in, comfortable.

To an outsider, Simone realized, their conversation would have appeared quite counter-productive. It didn't stay on one particular subject, and would occasional veer wildly off into the direction of music or movies with absolutely no reason whatsoever. Even the living room would have seemed the wrong venue for a conversation of this sort. Rebecca would wander about barefoot, long since kicking her black leather boots off, meaning she intended to stay at a given place in an informal capacity with the proverbial shields down for a while. She would pick around the house, picking up CDs, flipping through a magazine, or just staring at one of the Harbor Lights miniatures Simone kept on the natural rock mantle. Gavin would take this time to talk with his hands and go into that tone of voice he used that could lull Simone to sleep if she let it; smooth and remarkably articulate. Her passion for well-spoken words would come to the for and she would find herself staring at the man she loved like she did when they first spent an evening together, first having a dinner of salmon cooked by Gavin followed by – of all things – a viewing of the Marx Brother's *Horse Feathers*. After that, they talked until three in the morning about everything they could think of, neither wanting to say goodnight. And so they didn't.

Simone was broken out of her reverie by the two pairs of eyes staring at her. Rebecca still at the mantle, Gavin watching Simone patiently, waiting for an answer.

Rebecca spoke into a cupped hand, mimicking Mission Control, complete with bursts of static: "Earth to Simone. Earth to Simone. Can you read us?"

"Um, could you repeat the question?"

"We were just discussing the fact that we have no idea where to do to from here," replied Gavin. "And what to do about it."

Simone found herself nodding. "Yeah, we've kind of gone as far as we can." Her legs curled up under herself as she brought the recliner back up straight. Her eyes flicked to the clock sharing time on the mantle with her miniatures. Well past midnight. The session had gone on longer than she'd thought. And they'd hit the wall. Forcing the issue further would just send the work that was already done crashing into bits. Forcing things to happen rarely made them do what you wanted them to do.

"Well," she said, to no one in particular. "Are we all in agreement that we're looking for the next book that is going to be stolen?"

Rebecca nodded her chin. "I think I could get the Second to help hide it if we could get to it first."

"Might not be a bad idea, if they're going to ground like you say," said Gavin.

"It'll keep the focus off us," Simone agreed. "Just in case this person has done his homework and knows we're going to notice this."

"I think every sensitive in the world has a good idea of the fact that something's going to happen," added Simone, pushing away from the mantle. "But yeah, this guy's smart enough to know he's not going to have to look over his shoulder all the time. He's going to know who he needs to look out for. Namely, you guys. You're the only ones I can think of who would be this far in the know." And so began the casual ceremony of sitting down on the floor and putting the boots back on the feet.

Simone watched Gavin rub his chin. It was a manner she knew well; he was turning something over in his head that he did not want to be there in the first place.

She had a pretty good idea as to what, but decided to verbally nudge him anyway.

"There *is* someone we can talk to about this."

Gavin's eye immediately came up to her. "No, absolutely not."

Rebecca, now standing, tapped her heel into the floor, securing her boot. "Who, if I may dare ask?"

Gavin shot Simone a dark look, but she rebuffed it. She had a point. She was standing her ground. He could growl at her with his eyes all he wanted.

"Come on, Gavin. It might be the only way."

"*Who?*" Queried Rebecca again.

Gavin shook his head. "No. Absolutely no way am I speaking to him."

"Okay, then let's turn off the lights in every room of the house, because if we're going to be bumping into walls for however long, I want to have a decent reason."

"I'm not asking again," muttered the witch. "No matter how hard you beg me."

Gavin's back sank into the cushions of his chair. "I don't think we need his help."

Simone jutted her hip out, placed her hands atop them.

"You can look like the cocky gunfighter all you want," Gavin said. "I'm not in a million years talking to Markab about this."

Simone nodded. "Good. You shouldn't have to."

Rebecca stood, face turning from participant to participant.

"Thank you for understanding, dear." Gavin's face broke out in a smile and he lifted his weight free from the chair, a slight spring in his step.

"Markab the Finder?" Asked Rebecca.

"The very same," said Gavin. "I have no reason to speak with him. Finders are an odd lot, to say the least, and I'm not especially fond of them. Markab will find anything for anybody, and the cost doesn't matter."

"Well, I understand honey. That's why we're going to talk to Lucas Brady, and not the handsome Mr. Markab."

Simone had braced for the look Gavin turned on her, but was still taken aback by the darkness that was now clouding the features of the man she shared a bed and her body with. This was the true Fox family trait, she knew. A terrible, impenetrable glare sent into the person in front of them. Looking through them, barely perceiving them. It was only by the grace of her being the most important person in his life and knowing it was she spared whatever daggers could all too easily be spit at her in the form of words from between her man's teeth.

"I am not," Gavin stated, words perfectly weighted. "Under any circumstances, going to consult Lucas on *anything*, much less this."

Simone felt Rebecca's eyes on the both of them, considering either an exit or an intervention. Neither were necessary, Simone knew. "You once considered him your peer."

"Once, yes. Not any more. Not for a long time."

"Not even to find out his – "

"I said no," Gavin snapped.

Simone's eyebrow arched and her feet carried her toward him in two even steps. "Under no circumstances will I accept you speaking to me in this fashion. I love you to the extent that it scares me, and I freely admit that in front of anybody because you mean the world to me, but that does not mean that I will accept that sort of crap coming from your mouth." At this, Gavin's eyes dropped. "I am making a point, and a damn good one, in my humble opinion. Now, if you want to let all of whatever unravel because you can bear to talk to an old college friend you once considered a colleague, that's all well and good. I'll go see him myself. But there's too much going on to allow for your foot stomping."

Rebecca studied the insteps of her boots, and Gavin finally brought his eyes back up to bear on Simone, whose own eyes met him halfway.

"I'm sorry," he said.

"I know." Her hand reached out and squeezed his shoulder. She willed her voice to soften. "I think we both know talking to Lucas would be the next logical step. You two aren't at war."

At this, Gavin made a sound closing related to a chuckle. Classic Fox family mode still intact, Simone noted. Just lurking beneath a polished surface. "No," he admitted. "Just short of one."

"Fine then, you can be Kennedy, and Lucas can be Castro. But we're talking to him."

"Right, Jackie."

Simone smiled, broad and slow. "Jackie, hell. I'm the Missiles of October, baby."

CHAPTER TWELVE

In spellcraft, there are things called 'Casting costs' and 'Components.' In layman's terms, this means a price to pay to balance out the universe as best as can be done and what can only be called a 'Sacrifice.'

The word 'Sacrifice' does not neccisarily mean the dark terms it is most often equated with, as it can be anything from a pinch of ashes to the core of an apple. But these things are reserved for the most banal of spells.

Among the highest component is that for the ability of teleportation. In all grimores of any validity whatsoever, it is to done each time teleportation is to be used, and the terms of the components are, without fail, maddeningly vague, usually along the lines of being phrased as 'Things belonging to the most innocent among us,' allowing for the interpretation that this means a body part from a child or in fact a sacrifice.

The abomination that calls itself 'Human' and falls to this kind of ambition is best left to the universe to be dealt with, as it is this author's opinion mortal wrath is simply not enough to punish those responsible.

That said, teleportation is often referred to as the highest price in terms of casting cost as well as universal repercussion. Truth be told, it is one of three; the other two with greater cost being, in order, that of invisibility, and the ability to raise the dead, the latter of which involves the forfeiture of ones sanity.

Lucas Brady, THOUGHTS ON THE OCCULT

They weren't compatible with each other.

It wasn't the first time Rebecca Scott would come to think such a thing about Gavin and Simone, but now more than ever was the time she felt it ring the most within her as she drove the Mustang she had purchased from the man known as Markab down the winding road away from the Manor and into the ugly sprawl of Hollywood street.

She'd been surprised at that little display of Gavin's back at the house. Not because he'd finally done what she'd expected to do for quite some time now, but that it came up to the surface now, with Rebecca as witness. The darkness with The Fox family was something well-known amongst their closest friends, with one biographer actually going so far as to actually say so in print. It was this faceless something just lurking around in there, the same something that came with the inborn know-ledge and intuition required to work things of magick in the real world, a world that would always insist it could see the strings.

It was a thing of contempt, Rebecca realized in that moment at the manor. Of ego and supposed intellect that comes with it. Of things razor-sharp. Being a Fox, she could expect Gavin to be nothing else.

But still, she couldn't help but feel a little pull of disappointment at him for declaring such a thing in the face of Simone, who was able to stand face-to-face with it, but ultimately, never understand the nature of it. Not fully, anyway.

Rebecca pulled a Marlboro Light from the pack waiting for her on the passenger seat and thumbed the dashboard lighter in.

And Lucas Brady... she groaned inwardly. The only voice in the field of parapsychology that Rebecca might actually take instead of Gavin's. Together, Lucas and Gavin were a wonderful force full of knowledge and approachability.

They were authoritative voices that deserved more of a chance to collaborate than they actually did.

The lighter popped, allowing her to remove it and press the glowing coils to her cigarette. She exhaled blue smoke, watching it curl against the inside of the windshield glass before lowering the window on her side to let the smoke escape and rest her elbow atop the door before tapping the barrel of the lighter against the lip of the ashtray a few times before replacing it into the dash.

She read everything Lucas Brady had committed to paper. Perhaps *devoured* would have been the better word for it. The man's passion for the art came through every sentence, and his ability to communicate ideas while retaining an obvious love for the language was intoxicating.

More than Gavin's, she'd daresay.

But she would never make the mistake that several others had in regards to the two men's approach to their work, and their results; that one was jealous of the other. Nothing could be further from the truth. The two men respected one another, and although their writing and overall communication styles varied, it was clear that they were equals, and gave each other considerable respect.

At least they *used* to.

Maybe they still did, Rebecca mused, and took another long, contemplative drag on her cigarette. They never actually declared war on each other, at least as far as she knew, and while they hadn't spoken in many years, she would hazard a guess that they both (if questioned, and if pressed for an answer) would admit to a constant in their respect for one another, if not for their handling of it and approach to it, which had become more and more different as time went on.

She spied a couple of the girls on foot from the Shadow Haven, a Coven in the loosest sense of the word composed of anywhere from five to ten witches. She felt the compulsion to wave as it was clear they saw her from their own waves and smiles as they saw her pulling away from a stoplight. It wasn't that she felt a certain resentment towards those who practiced the art for the sake of wearing black and being fashionable.

Shadow Haven wasn't quite like that. Just this side of, lending it a bit more legitimacy to it. Gavin, and to a lesser extent, Simone had that resentment without much regard for finding out exactly how much commitment such people had, or didn't have, to their particular brand of spirituality. Their reaction to the occurrence with Dawn's Eclipse was indicative of this. Not unexpected, just not helpful, given the circumstances. The girls in question walked right past the featureless *façade* of a business that seemed to have no name, past the new graffiti there, paying it no mind; A pair of crudely made wings with a halo over a question mark making the body of what Rebecca understood to be an angel, indicated by its simple outline of plumage.

Maybe the girls knew something she didn't, but Rebecca doubted it. She'd seen it once before without giving it heed, on the way back from the lighthouse. She hadn't given it a second thought then. But now, it was something she felt needed attention, and would try to meditate on it later that night.

The Mustang's headlights pushed into the darkness as she turned the wheel left, up the incline of Starfall Lane, where despite all the lights Hollywood had to offer, few were to be seen here. It wasn't much of a bother, just a curiosity. It was an old, forgotten part of the city, winding up away from everything past The Hotel Monaco. The lane would lead into an area of Hollywood Rebecca could go to without driving very far that seemed positively devoid of any supernatural activity. There were no lines of power here, especially as one climbed further and further. It wasn't like they were cut off, it was more like they just stopped for a time before continuing about a mile further west. It was one of the few places Rebecca could think of that offered such a thing without the smothering feeling of being cut off from whatever personal power one brought into a place such as this. Such a feeling was akin to claustrophobia, from what she understood of it.

While many would probably be threatened by the presence of such a place and avoid going into it at all costs, Rebecca wasn't. In fact, she reveled in the reality of the fact that she was gracious that it existed at all; it allowed her to feel safe enough to put the shields down completely – probably because of the presence of whatever nature happened to survive the push of development – and relax for a time, recharge the batteries, and clear her mind without all the residual psychic crap floating through her world. Not even her own home had been able to offer that.

It was, she'd decided, because of the combination of her home being located amongst paranormal powerlines pretty much like everything else everywhere and the fact that there was nothing especially unique about its location. Isolated areas like up on Starfall Lane were given to random circumstances, she believed, rather than the more popular belief that areas were like that because of a great expenditure of energy, namely a battle of large proportions, and quite possibly many deaths. The area is so greatly affected by the trauma that it loses all of its natural ability to retain and compose energy. An interesting concept, to be sure. But she wasn't convinced of it. Not because of some grand revelation, just an inclination.

After about a three and-a-half mile climb, she turned the wheels of the Mustang over the soft gravel of a turnout she had come to frequent, the tires crunching into the loose stones and earth. There were no lights in this remote part of Starfall. One could actually see them slowly decreasing in numbers, then stopping completely if one paid found their respective end down the unguarded embankment, not much more than dirt spotted with exclamations of scrub brush and yucca.

But in the darkness, mused Rebecca, you could find the darndest things.

Using her thumb, she extinguished the headlights, staying in the driver's seat as her eyes re-adjusted to the darkness around her. After one final drag, she crushed out her cigarette in the Mustang's pop-out ashtray, exhaled deeply and opened the door, swinging her legs out onto the gravel, carefully, methodically pulling off her boots, then her long black socks, allowing her bare feet to press into the gravel as she made her way to the hood of her car, where she perched, legs folded in a half-lotus position. Her hands rested palms up upon her knees.

Again she exhaled, deeper this time, forcing the unseen heaviness from her lungs, her chest, her body. She felt her eyes close almost of their own accord, lulled by the sound of the crickets chirping in the night. Occasionally, a lone animal, either a wolf or a coyote, she couldn't tell which, would lend its cry to the air.

Rebecca became in tune with her surroundings in the blackness behind her lids, coming to almost a thrum within her.

It was familiar. It was friendly.

It was home.

"By the forces respected, I summon, stir, and call you up in my own name."

It was an old incantation she had altered just so to identify herself to the powers she believed in and perpetuated in her own writings, which differed greatly from Gavin's as well as Lucas Brady's, let alone other witches.

Even here on Starfall, where there was no discernable power to be respected, or recognized by, it was important for her to make the effort and not respect what was outside of the immediate reach of her senses. She also wished to make a point in letting them know she was not under any guises. She was coming to them as is, whether they could see her or not.

There was none of the residual noise in her head that had been creeping into her everyday thoughts. It came with being sensitive, she knew. Not like Gavin or Simone, who seemed to be able to block out the distractions with a minimum of effort. It certainly wasn't physically taxing on them, at least not that she could discern. She was beginning to fear it was on her. But that was the price one paid for being a lone practitioner, she knew. When you decided to just let your own understanding of your own given spiritual path be your guide, and let instinct and intuition fuel your way to wherever it was you were going, you tend to bump into walls that, had a trail been blazed before, you probably wouldn't have bumped into.

But then, as a lone practitioner, you also didn't have someone over your shoulder, telling you what not to do, and not always telling you why. You found that out years later, although not always through the act of a mistake. Pretty much like when a parent would say 'You'll understand when you're older.' The only thing more infuriating about that was when you realized they were right.

As her consciousness slipped away, her thoughts and concentration became glassine and focused, and she was still aware of the fact that she was not as widely respected as she'd wanted to be. Those who practiced her line of thinking were often shunned as loose cannons or elitists who thought they knew better.

But Rebecca wasn't under any of those self-delusions, of that she was sure. She tried to think of herself as self-aware enough to know that she didn't know *better*, she knew *different*. Spiritual belief systems, by definition it seemed to Rebecca, were deeply personal things, and if one wished to be alone with their thoughts and his or her own god, gods, or goddesses, to each his (or her) own.

The city lights dotting the Valley before her left not altogether unpleasant afterimages behind her eyelids, glowing there for a time until she could visualize four wall around her lowering away soundlessly, leaving behind a perfect blankness that always made her lips curl up into the bow of the slightest of smiles.

She was disconnected.

The now-familiar and welcome sensation of weightlessness came over her then. Many mistook this as the starting point for astral projection, and maybe in their own individual cases, it was. But for Rebecca, it was merely the aftereffect of letting the walls slip away into nothingness. For her to relax and calm the immediate world around her, just for a little bit. She had no delusions that she could control or alter things to the point of being able to harbor absolute stillness within her as she had seen other people, one of them a witch, the other a Buddhist but she just wasn't built that way, and going against the capabilities of one's innate self was to invite chaos. You had to learn about yourself in order to know whether or not you could make such a journey, then you actually had to take it to see if you were able to achieve the person you wanted to be. Sometimes that involved more work than most wanted to put out. That was fine with Rebecca, as it made the path less crowded with soul insisting that they were something that they were not. Sometimes the effort of just making the attempt was sufficient to let the person discover enough about themselves.

She tried to relax further and let come what would come to her. Sometimes, she would receive a brief vision of a future event to tell her that things in the now would work out. But not now. The world was too awake for that, even if its occupants weren't.

Rebecca rested within herself, conscious of her shoulders relaxing far more than she'd figured she'd needed. Not a good sign. She was usually more in tune with herself than this. The distractions of the now were pulling her away from herself. It happened to the best of us. She felt grateful she was able to catch herself now rather than when it became too late to steer back to shore, so to speak. To center and relax and regroup. It was important to get this time to do some mental and spiritual preventive maintenance, because she wasn't sure when she'd get the chance again. It worried her that she had gone so far away from herself and harbored more tension than she'd expected in such a short amount of time. It wasn't that the past few days hadn't been filled with the kind of excitement you wish to have, but she prided herself at being able to tell when things were getting to crazy and that she needed time to regain her perspective.

And so she tried to find it, without walls, without invasive light or thought. But in the stillness of herself. The deep kind of meditation she found positively addictive. She'd wondered more than once what might happen if one simply refused to come out of the meditative state. She'd heard it was possible to lose yourself once inside a deep state, but had never heard anything concrete about it. It was something Rebecca could understand, though. It was peaceful there in the deep.

If Gavin couldn't see enough of the big picture to get Lucas Brady's help, Simone would, Rebecca knew. If Simone was unable to for some reason, Rebecca would find him herself.

Hours later, Rebecca was able to rouse herself from the depths of herself and the peace she found there. She rolled her neck, finding some odd enjoyment in the way it popped in response. A small groan escaped her lips as she unfolded her legs, but not one prompted by protesting joints and a suddenly unrestricted blood supply. It was just a matter of bringing herself back to her body fully so when she got behind the wheel, she was fully herself and not still trying to shake the remnants of her meditation, which had been getting deeper and deeper each time she did it, a fact she tried not to think too much about.

The Mustang's headlights flared into the darkness as she keyed the engine. She kept the stereo turned off, enjoying the crunch of the gravel beneath the tires. The night air sank into the interior, and she breathed deeply, regretting the loss of clarity the crickets would have from here compared to her own house.

As the ribbon of blacktop before winded and wove its way further down the sloping road, she could feel her fingers tensing at the wheel again just moments before the city lights grew in the glass of her windshield. Rebecca didn't sigh, or roll her eyes at the multicolored riot of light and activity unfurling before her, she just kept her foot poised on the accelerator and continued on her way. The last of the houses that dotted the first mile of Starfall Lane was coming up, then she would be lost in the throng of people milling about in the Hollywood night.

A song she couldn't remember the name of came to her then, not much more than the melody of the chorus, distracting her for a time until she was just past the final house when the blur landed heavy on her hood.

Rebecca swore, but remained in control of the vehicle, swerving to the side of the road, fist over fist thudding onto the wheel.

In one motion, she unbelted herself and pushed free from the car, turning back in a defensive posture, fingers poised for the short but effective confusion spell of popping lights when she was finally able to get a better look at what had landed on the hood of her car.

What at first she thought was an animal of some sort was still crouching on the hood of the Mustang's still-running engine. In the streetlight dappled through the white oaks, it was obviously a woman, nude and feral staring back at her.

The barely perceptible thrum between the two of them, and the wild-eyed stare from the woman was unmistakable. She was completely out of any semblance of control, and would rip to shreds anyone she felt posed even the slightest of threats.

The woman did not growl, but fell into a sort of crouch, toenails scratching at the Mustang's paint, searching for purchase.

Instinctively, Rebecca felt the fingers of her right hand bend into a simple sygil of protection. She held her them palm up to face the woman. A breath before the woman leapt at her, Rebecca said, "Rest," whereupon the woman's body immediately fell limp onto her side upon the hood of the car.

Rebecca did not wait before her feet took up the space between her and the woman's form. The woman's ribs rose and fell in fast, shallow breaths, her lips parted slightly. Her skin sported a few spots of bruises, some older than others, which very well may have been made that very night. There were exclamations of scratches on her extremities, and dirt and mud and grime had gotten smeared across her skin during her travels.

Rebecca pressed the palm of her hand across the woman's sweat-slicked forehead.

It was going to be a long night.

CHAPTER THIRTEEN

Despite the fact that we as humans have decided to aggressively do away with much of our instincts and animal inclinations with great effect, there are times when those very things insist on being noticed, in spite of our wishing them gone, instinct, and other things we have eschewed let us know they are indeed real, and will be noticed, whether we like it or not.

Gavin Fox with Lucas Brady, from TECHNOLOGY AND EVOLUTION ON MAGICK.

Smoke.

The first smell that burned itself into her nose, down her throat, and into her lungs, was smoke.

Diana Adair's stomach rebelled, retched once, and was still.

She was not at home. She was not outside. Senses rushing information to her too fast, and reducing too soon for her to get a grip on what it was they were trying to rely. But her eyes snapped open. She was not in her familiar territory. And that smell was not only smoke, it was the domesticated smoke of a cigarette; false and noxious.

The light invaded her head as her lids opened, but it was not as difficult as it had been in the past to confront.

Perhaps she was getting more used to this than she'd figured.

Her head snapped up. It made her vision swim, but she forced her eyes to remain open. A living room. A pillow and wad of blanket beneath her. Her visions sharpened by degrees, allowing her to see the woman sitting on the couch a few feet away, legs curled up beneath her, magazine on her lap, and a cigarette burning in one hand. She didn't seem the least bit alarmed.

"Well, look who's up," the woman said, looking up from her magazine.

Diana pushed herself away from where she had awakened, clutching the blanket to herself. The pounding in her ears wasn't as bad as it had been, although her body protested as she found her way to her knees, shooting fresh threads of burning heat through them. The biggest problem was that cigarette, the steady plume of blue smoke curling away from the glowing coal at the tip seemingly multiplying the ache in her head.

As if reading her mind, the woman crushed out her cigarette in a nearby ashtray with an apologetic expression on her face.

"Sorry, this probably isn't helping you," she said. "Been trying to quit."

Diana realized the room wasn't spinning quite as badly. Her head, while in less than perfect shape, was far from exploding from the effort of sitting upright so soon after waking. Her eyes followed the woman's progress as she stepped towards her.

Diana tried to move away, but any movement involving speed and judgment were completely out of the question. Her motions gave the other woman pause. She came to a halt and spread her hands before her.

"Don't panic. I don't want to hurt you. I just thought you might need a safe place to hang out at for a bit. If I wanted to harm you, I would've already."

Diana found herself nodding despite not wanting to communicate until she truly got her bearings. There was a feeling of peacefulness here, true, but at the same time, that didn't settle her, either. It only contradicted the confusion, not solve it.

The woman hunkered down before her.

The shivers were hitting now. It wasn't an every time occurrence, but when it did, it only served to make Diana feel worse. Like catching a cold and having it run through you in about five minutes, leaving you dazed and shaking. "I don't know you."

A half-smile touched the woman's face. It looked oddly natural. "My name's Rebecca Scott." When Diana didn't respond, Rebecca continued. "See? Now we're not strangers." Again, Diana was unwilling to speak.

The woman named Rebecca rose to her feet and shrugged. "You know, I could have just left you there on the street."

Diana shook her head, as if to clear it. The joints of her body were still aching. She'd need something to bear down the rest of the pain before she could function better, But she was feeling better than she ever had when waking after one of her nights.

"What happened?" She asked finally.

"You attacked my car when you were wilding," came the reply. "Landed on the hood. Gave it a good dent, by the by. On a nineteen and sixty-eight Ford Mustang, no less."

Diana stared at a spot on the carpet. "Sorry." Her eyes came up. "When I was what?"

"Wilding. You've never heard of it?"

Diana shook her head.

"It's what you've been doing..." Rebecca's head tilted, like a curious child's. "You *do* know what you do at night isn't normal."

Diana's fingers held the blanket tighter around herself, eyes continuing their study of the carpet. "For me it is."

"I'm sure."

"What business is it of yours?" Diana's chin snapped up, her eyes on Rebecca. "Why do you care?"

"Because someone has to."

A laugh escaped her, and Diana found she could hold the woman's gaze. "And what might you be, Rebecca? A humanitarian?"

"Witch."

Another laugh. Stronger this time. "Yes, of course."

Rebecca's eyebrows furrowed, and she closed the space between them. "Hard to believe? Yeah, fine. But your current condition is a lot harder to swallow, dearie. I put you down to sleep last night and I'd wager you're feeling a lot better than you normally would when you wake up after a night like last night, and I'll take credit for that, too. I didn't have to do those things, and don't make me regret them. You're as more of fantasy than I am, Woman Laying Naked On Floor."

"Okay, okay." Again, Diana's eyes dropped. She could hear her Dad's voice piping up. She could stand her ground. Half of that was meeting the other person's eyes. Don't drop your eyes. Giving them that edge was one too many.

She couldn't help it. Part of her, the part that was grateful for not waking up wishing she were dead, was too put at ease to care. A million terrible things could have befallen her at any time she was outside in the dark like the way she was last night. She knew that, and didn't need anyone to remind her of that.

"Diana."

Rebecca seemed sincerely confused for a moment. "What?"

"Diana. My name's Diana."

The smile returned to her host's face. She nodded. "Good. Now we're getting somewhere."

In short order, Rebecca had offered a glass of ice water, which was gratefully accepted. While Diana sipped, Rebecca left the room to retrieve a blue silk kimono robe with the illustration of a crane woven into it and turned her back so Diana could slip into it.

The pain had receded sufficiently enough for Diana to make her way to the front of the couch, happy to lean against it while sitting on the floor away from the mess of blanket and pillow Rebecca soon removed, somehow knowing not to offer assistance to the cushions of the couch. Diana would be able to get up on her own soon enough, but for now, the water and a place to rest her back would do.

Rebecca came back from the bathroom with a shallow white porcelain bowl filled with steaming water, another quick trip brought with her a sponge, bottle of alcohol, and a towel. In her confusion Diana realized that she was sporting a variety of new scratches, some fairly deep, on her skin.

Diana made a request for any number of painkillers, not the grand sum of what she was used to when waking in a condition similar, to which Rebecca wrinkled her face and said she had only Motrin, which was gladly accepted.

"I'm sure it must be difficult to hear me ask for so much, judging by your reaction." Diana said, swallowing a few less of the caplets than she really wanted to. "You witches are into natural stuff, right?"

"That's not why I made a face. I've just never been in *that* much pain before. It must be difficult."

Diana washed down more water. "It's pretty bad, but whatever you did helped lots. Thanks."

"I fell out of the tree in my front yard when I was a little kid," Rebecca offered. "Broke my arm but good."

"Not the same thing."

"No, I don't imagine it is. Trying a little humor."

"I know."

96

Diana watched as Rebecca cleansed her skin of dried blood and dirt and dabbed at the scratches with a swab dabbed in alcohol. The damage that was being done to her while she was in a different kind of consciousness was increasing, which probably meant that she was becoming more comfortable in that new sense of being, a thought that simultaneously interested her and scared her. It allowed a vent to the anger that a burgundy dress and love songs only seemed to invalidate.

Her eyes swept the room as Rebecca went about wringing out the sponge and giving the wounds the once-over now that they had been cleaned. Neo-Pagan was the best way to describe the settings she found herself in, and even that felt inaccurate. On the coffee table a few inches from where she set her water glass was a crystal ball set on a highly polished hardwood base. A three-stemmed flat black candelabra stood in a corner away from them, white taper candles burned down about halfway, a blood-red feather boa wrapped around the stems for nothing more than dramatic effect, it would seem.

"Want something to eat?"

"Maybe a little dry toast?"

Her host quickly went about making the toast as Diana's eyes flicked across the titles on the nearby bookshelf. Judging by the titles, most, if not all, of them were concerning witchcraft, the occult, and all the sundry aspects of it.

She sipped at her water, placed it on the coffee table, and pulled a trade paperback off the shelf. *Magick, After Dark* and others near it had a familiar name as it's author.

"Did you write all these?" Diana asked, counting no less than ten books boasting Rebecca's name.

"Yep," came the response from the kitchen. Soon after, Rebecca emerged from the kitchen with a plate of two pieces of toast. "Didn't know if you liked them cut."

Diana smiled and accepted the plate. "Whole is fine."

She examined the back cover where a black and white author's photo was positioned over a short synopsis of the book's contents while its author returned to her seat on the couch.

"'Acclaimed author Rebecca Scott examines in whole and in part, the facts and fallacies of the practice known as night magick,'" Diana read aloud, as if to herself to eliminate any mockery that may be detected. "'The effects it has on its practioners, and how technology and other aspects of the modern world have affected the rituals and spells.'"

Her eyes skipped down to the bio, again she read out loud; "'Rebecca Scott is among the most respected voices of the study and practice of magick in contemporary times, the author of seven previous non-fiction books on various subjects found within the belief of witchcraft and Wicca.'" Diana looked up from the blurbs and quotes from others in the field, as well as various publications that followed. "I am in the presence of a respected author."

Rebecca made a theatrical gesture of straightening in place. "Indeed."

Diana replaced the book, eyed the others while speaking. "Would it offend you to say I don't believe in this stuff?"

"Not at all."

Another book was pulled down, its cover scanned. "Most folks would make an argument out of that."

"That's true, they would."

Diana turned to her. "But you're not one of them, right?"

"Oh, no. I can be one of them. I'm pretty secure in my balance, is all. I don't have to make someone wrong. Sometimes I fail. I can be pretty petty."

"Can't we all?"

Diana helped herself to the toast, feeling the uneasiness and remnants of pain still leaving her body, although the fatigue was still there. After she had finished her food, she turned to Rebecca once more. "So I landed on your car, huh?"

Rebecca nodded, sipped some coffee from a plain black mug.

Diana winced. "So, big dent?"

Again the nod from her host.

"I'll pay for it."

"I believe you."

Diana scribbled her information down on a nearby tablet. "Just call me when you know how much it'll be."

"Okay."

Then came one of those pauses that Quentin Tarantino's characters talk about until Rebecca set down her coffee. "Mind if I ask you a question?"

"Not at all."

"How is it that someone in your situation doesn't believe in magick?"

Diana's shoulders hunched. "I don't know. I was just raised that way. If you can't touch it, it's questionable. My mom was sort of religious, my dad wasn't. I guess I just gravitated towards him. Genetics or whatever."

"Then how do you explain what's happening to you?"

"I can't. I just don't think it's magickal."

"Then what is it?"

Diana's eyes studied the floor. "Primal."

"Okay. Good answer."

"What?"

"Good answer. Pretty accurate, too."

"You know why this is happening?" Diana tried to keep her eyes from widening too far.

Rebecca didn't answer for a long time. "Yes, in a way. You do, too. There's a magickal way of making it happen, and there's a natural way."

"How do you know mine is the natural one?"

"Because if it wasn't, my spells wouldn't have worked on you."

"Ah." Denoting interest level drop. "I thought you said you didn't need to make someone wrong."

"I don't."

"Then why do I feel like I've been given a cosmic lesson as to why God's universe has done something to me in that kind of circular logic those who are better than me use?"

"I'm sorry, that wasn't my intention."

"Do something magickal."

"Excuse me?"

"Cast a spell, or show me how you did what you did to me last night."

"That's not how it works."

"Why not?"

"It's not intended to be used to prove something, let alone it's own existence."

"Uh-huh."

"Do you really want me to rescind the spell so you can feel like you normally would after a night like last night?"

"No, I don't think I would."

"There could be, and probably are, several reasons for why you might feel better than usual. Accept that my doing might be one of them."

Diana's hand went up, palms showing. "Okay, look, I'm sorry. I didn't mean to offend you."

"You didn't."

"You sure?"

"Yeah, I'm just trying to help out."

"Even if you don't know me?"

"Right. That's the whole point. We're supposed to be kind to each other, and we aren't always. I just try to do what I can when I can."

Diana's attention gravitated back to the books. Picking one at random, she idly flipped through the pages. "So are these spellbooks, or what?"

Rebecca parted her hair onto one side, a gesture Diana took to mean that her hostess may be trying to find out if someone was being sincere in their interest. "Mmm. Some have spells, but none of the ones I've written are strictly like that. A couple, like my first two, are just me rambling on, trying to clarify my belief system to myself."

"And what might that be, in a nutshell?"

"We're all connected to each other, that we're all better than ourselves, and that I believe there is an ultimate good and an ultimate evil, and we perpetuate one or the other, or one of the myriad shades of grey that come in between."

"Is God a woman or a man?"

"As a maker of world, I believe He's a She, but I don't believe in there being a wrong answer. There are many ways of seeing many things, a higher power is one of them."

Diana closed the book, set it down on the coffee table next to her water and rubbed at her temples. There was an ache there that she could not rub away. "I think this is too heavy a subject for me right now."

"It's too heavy a subject most times, I think. Don't worry. Just rest up."

"I'm glad I don't have to work tonight."

"What do you do?"

"Lounge singer at the Hotel McFarlane," she said with theatrical prestige. "All the jazz standards that made the greats great."

"Is that where you were coming from last night?"

"I don't remember. I think I usually start from home."

Rebecca nodded, looking like she wished she could say more.

"Can I ask you something, Rebecca?"

"Sure."

"If I'm such a guest in your house, how come I woke up on the floor?"

A wide smile broke across Rebecca's face. "I dragged you to bed, but after a couple minutes, you crawled out and went to where you woke up. I tried to get you back onto the bed, but you were like a sleeping cat, and I wasn't sure what might happen if you woke up and thought I was trying to hurt you. So I made with the blanket and the pillow to at least make the effort for your comfort. But now that you're awake, you can make the conscious decision to sleep wherever you want, so feel free to crash on the bed."

"You sure you don't mind?"

Rebecca made little shooing gestures with her hand.

Easing her way up to her feet, Diana thanked her and after being told which way to go, headed into the hallway, where she paused for just a moment.

"Rebecca, do you really know what's happening to me?"

I think I have an idea, yes."

"I'd like to talk about it when I get up."

"Surely."

Diana nodded, turned away, and went into the bedroom, grinning inwardly at the sight of the sumptuousness. Rebecca Scott was obviously a woman who took great pleasure in spoiling herself in given areas of her life; the king-sized four-poster bed that was covered in some kind of dark, soft-to-the-touch comforter, and an array of various-sized pillows, everything from Sobakawa to cylander-esque varieties. Diana was fairly certain the one she picked to rest on was genuine duck down.

Sprays of great ferns kept time with black lacquered cabinet and matching bureau. Candles and oil lamps everywhere, even on the small stereo system, and a single Teddy bear atop her nightstand were the orders here, and not a thing felt out of place. It was a place of peace and solace here, a dynamic that a part of Diana found unwanted, but the side of her that was tired beyond the telling and simply wanted shelter and blessed silence for as long as it could manage was stronger. Perhaps it was the room and its settings. Maybe it was simple exhaustion. In the end, it hardly mattered.

She slept without dreams.

CHAPTER FOURTEEN

If I were to have a halo, I would think it would be of some bent, corrupted metal.

Stefan O'Barr, NOTES FROM THE OCCULT,
Edited by Fred Frazier, John Freise, *et. al.*

That particular morning was one spent awkwardly in the Manor, Gavin reflected, staring into the blackness of his coffee. They had been civil following his display of sharp temperament that, although he would never admit it to anyone, surprised him with the ease it came to the fore. But civility is only that, and it becomes tension if not cured. Which it hadn't been.

It was evident in her morning kiss, as well as their goodnights. The fact that neither one of them had brought up the issue was enough to make the stillness more still until Simone had put on a Platters album. The sounds of 'My Prayer,' and 'Twilight Time' being familiar things to their courtship and romance, being the album Simone had listed as being her 'Number One Desert Island Pick' for music. The only thing more popular in her admitted soundtrack to them was the Flamingos' recording of 'I Only Have Eyes For You," a song that was not unfamiliar to Gavin for her to remind him that despite his self-admitted grumpiness, she actually still loved him, which was a miracle in and of itself.

In his past relationships, while not numerous, had always ended badly, and always in a fit of temper, and in the fullness of time, Gavin Fox had come to blame himself fully for each failure.

But Simone had given him something he had not been able to give himself; a sense of forgiveness. And, if that failed, a sense that she supplied a new path for him to go. It was cliché, and he'd never admit it to anyone in his family, let alone anyone in the handful of friends he'd entertained at any point in his life, but he actually felt like a completely different person once she had entered his life. All the past relationships and all their faults fell away to reveal this new person he came to recognize as himself.

But this was the stuff of Hallmark cards and the like. In the reality of his own world, Gavin Fox understood the grimness of the human condition, and how fleeting happiness could been, especially when one entertained pursuits such as his own. Magick and all its shiny trappings had a nasty habit of swallowing every nanosecond of your time, and by the time you had achieved what you had eventually set out to achieve, you found that all that you had gained had come at the cost of failed romance and friends that you could not speak to anymore because you were no longer yourself.

That in itself was Made for TV movie melodrama, but it was also one of the truest things Gavin could find to cling to as an ultimate truth. He had known enough about himself and others (a trait shared by all the Fox men) to understand this. It wasn't the brightest of truths, but it was his world and, after all, that is all one has; the world you have created in conjunction along with the one others have created for you.

He had seen it in his own family long before he had even known it was there; none of his relatives had any close friends that Gavin ever knew of; the occasional colleague perhaps, but that was about it. Family functions were fairly common during his parents' reign, as was it during the more romanticized era of his grandparents and beyond.

Not so during his own time with Simone.

No children, no extended relations. He was the end of his line, and that did not make him utterly unhappy.

Practicioners such as he were by his definition, solitary beings. It was just what was dictated by the lifestyle and the inner drive. There were friends along the way, certainly, and even a few of them that he missed, but he was on another wavelength now, and they would not recognize him now, and he would most likely not want to be recognized.

Simone was the closest friend he had ever had, and one that genuinely didn't give a damn about the wealth. He could tell by the way she had suffered the snide remarks from her own well-to-do family in order to be with him. She had sacrificed a great deal to be with him, and he had never thanked her for it for fear that she would realize what a mistake she had made. A bit melodramatic again, but he gave himself some slack regardless. What could one expect from a line of practitioners who had at a couple points in their rather distinguished lineage, actually had to reduce themselves to stage magickians in order to not only explain their earnings, but also to perpetuate the hoodwink on unsuspecting crowds. Their considerable fame was just something else to live down.

But there it was again. The Fox ego. Taunting the crowd with itself and developing a deep resentment towards them for their ignorance. A resentment that Gavin found natural enough.

Something that Lucas Brady had been able to wrench him away from, he remembered.

But that was Lucas, and that was one of the reasons to not see him. Simone knew that. Lucas had seen him at his deeper levels and pulled him free of it. And that was in the good and bad days at Washington State University, where he had met Lucas just days before he was to meet Simone.

But Lucas had that way about him. He knew how to help certain people in the best way. Others he had to leave by the wayside.

Ultimately, Gavin was convinced that that was part of Lucas's problem. The weight of the ones he had not been able to help in whatever way bending him down, derailing the thoughts of a good man into what Gavin felt were the ramblings of a disorganized mind corrupted only by the fact that it constantly reminded him that he had indeed failed a few times.

Which wasn't to say Lucas was utterly insane, left to is own ranting voice. No, the worst part of Lucas Brady was the sad fact that he had once been a much better man, and not the slightest bit tilted by the world around him that insisted that he hadn't the first clue in how random and chaotic the cosmos was, and was hell-bent on proving it to him every single chance it got.

But his old friend and college roommate never admitted defeat.

That was, in the considered opinion of Gavin Fox; author, grump, and magician, the core of Lucas's problem. The man simply didn't know when to stay down.

But on the other side of that very coin lay the thing Gavin saw in himself; the man who did not know when to get up.

The headaches were coming in greater frequency now. All the Fox men had to deal with them. It was the family tradition, it was believed. The Fox men were so attuned to this great ability that the universe seemed to have nodded its assent and say, 'Fine, you can have that, buy you have to take *this*, too.'

Balance, at least in theory.

It was also a crock of the universe, when one considered the Fox tradition of brain-splitting migraines beginning at the age of two or three. And there wasn't a lick of a spell that would touch it, which seemed to affirm to Gavin that it was indeed the universe thumbing its nose to those things on Earth that were just this too far out of its control. One of his grandfathers, his great-great-great, had done considerable research in spells and holistic remedies for the headaches. He had used specific handwritten journals away from his usual day-to-day books, all of which were still stored away in the library upstairs. Elias Fox had spent a good portion of his life on the research, oftentimes using himself as a Guinea pig for a variety of experiments, and would continue until the day he died with a good amount of ideas that amounted to anything.

And then Simone's arms wreathed his shoulders, pressing her forehead to where his neck met his body. Everything else became ashes as he indulged in her.

"You okay?" She asked.

He reached for her wrist, held it. "Yeah, you?" He could feel the tick of her pulse, warm under her skin.

She nodded. "I don't want to fight about Lucas, though. Okay?"

"Understood." It had been so since the evening before, but why bring that up now?

"Are you going to call him, or just show up?" She separated from him then, taking a seat on the floor next to the desk on his left, folding her legs crossways. She was wearing her wire-rimmed reading glasses and had her hair parted on the side of her head, more than a little rumpled.

"I'm thinking that telling him that I'm coming over would only serve as a warning."

"Right," came the mock-serious response. "Can't have that now, can we?"

Gavin pushed his chair away from the table where several reference volumes lay out before him, open to whichever given page was either marginally helpful, or at a passage that sparked some offhanded thought that at least started to help him before it too, sputtered out. "I've gotta tell you, honey. I'm not sure how this is going to go over. I haven't actually spoken to Lucas for what, five years?"

"Six, but who's counting?"

"Right. The last time I even communicated to him was I think four years ago, and that was via email regarding his getting permission to reprint a part of my work, which I remind you, was used out of context."

"Yes, I remember the rant. I also seem to remember something about his saying publicly that it had been out of context, and that it was a slant his editor put on it without his okay."

"He would have seen the galleys before it went out to print."

"You're right. He must've gone and done something rash like become human and made an error in reviewing his book. How long did that error in your own book about the *Davis Manuscript* last? Five printings? Six?"

"That was minutiae, and was based on a mistake I made reading a *handwritten* manuscript that had been gnawed on by bookworms over a hundred years ago."

"And did you catch it?"

"On the second edition, yes."

"And how long did it take to get corrected?"

"Too long. But that was in part to the editor-of-the-week program the publishing house was supporting at the time."

"And partly because it was a minor note."

"Yes, that too."

Simone's eyebrows arched and she tilted her head just so. The beginnings of a smile at her lips.

"To answer your question, I think I'll just show up."

"And what will you do if he's no longer living there?"

"I guess I'll cross that bridge when I come to it."

Simone nodded, then unfurled herself at the sound of the cordless phone ringing on its cradle.

Gavin made a show of sipping his coffee and reviewing the same words in the same books, hoping that at some point they would form a cohesive notion. Nothing was forthcoming, and it seemed to Gavin like one going to the refrigerator to look for a snack, finding none, then returning shortly thereafter, as if something may have suddenly appeared. Although whether he would have eaten something that had just shown up in his fridge was another matter. Simone returned, holding the phone out to him. He could see her thumb resting on the receiver's mute button.

"It's that Finder from the Valley," she said.

Gavin's eyes returned to the futility before him. "I'm not talking to Markab."

"Not that one, the other one."

There were entirely too many Finders cropping up in the world, Gavin thought. Something that couldn't possibly be good. They usually only came three or four at a time, maximum, and that was worldwide. This latest one,

Karac, was the third Gavin had counted in America alone, and there were others in Geneva, Wales, Switzerland, and two more rumored to be in Italy.

Finders had the ability, and – worse still – the drive, to find things regarding matters of the occult. Markab had the unfortunate talent of finding things that shouldn't exist, but do. This Karac could find things, usually manuscripts, that it could be debated actually existed at all. It was if the simple desire for whatever it was was enough to make it happen, and Karac was able to get it for you.

They were parasites of a kind. The worst kind; the ones that can occasionally come in handy.

But Karac was one of the few Finders he had ever come into contact with that didn't immediately hackle Gavin's nerves. When he had told the younger man this, Karac gave a kind of chuckle and said, 'Give it time.'

It had only made Gavin like him more.

All Finders knew they were less than perfect people on the ethical scale, but at least Karac made no pretense. Markab could argue with you until the end of time about the validity of his vocation, but Gavin suspected that was because he would be able to find something that would enable him to do so rather than any real conviction about himself and his aims. There was an emptiness about Finders, Gavin realized some time ago, and it was as if that fact only made them that much more dangerous in the darker aspect of themselves they wouldn't talk about to anyone.

He accepted the receiver and spoke Karac's name.

"Hi, Gavin. Look, I know I'm bugging you, but I have this situation, and I can't come up with any help."

Gavin straightened in his chair, and the word 'Help.' It wasn't said very lightly around Finders, and when it was, it was to another finder, not someone who made it no secret how little he thought of them. "What's going on?"

Karac had a habit of detailing an even a little too much. This was no exception. In short order, the highlights regarded a man stricken with the ability to see spirits, now to the point that he was having difficulty determining real from spirit.

"And he's out of his twenties?" Gavin asked as Simone made gestures to ask if he wanted a warm-up to his coffee, to which he readily agreed with a couple of nods. "Man, he's lucky to have made it that far. The last one I heard of – "

"Put a gun to his head, yeah."

"And you can't find anything?"

"There's nothing regarding this in terms of getting rid of it."

"Right, stuff like 'A terrible gift bestowed…'"

"Blah, blah, blah."

"Not going to help the man."

"No, and he's fraying."

"I almost hate to ask, but have you talked to Markab?"

A long pause. Gavin was about to call his name again when the Finder finally responded. "I was hoping you might have something to tell me."

"Not off the top of my head, no."

Karac swore. "All right. Is there any way you'd be able to look into it at all?" He knew better than to ask to peruse the Fox library.

"No," Gavin said. "I'm up to my armpits in research on another subject right now." It wasn't that Finders couldn't sense things like Gavin and Simone; they were just as attuned to it as they were. But the fact was Finders tended to have a bad case of tunnel vision, with very few exceptions. Gavin wished for a welcome distraction such as this one, but there was no going to it.

"Okay, Gavin. Thank you. If you come up with anything…"

"I'll be sure to call," finished Gavin and hung up. He gave a brief explanation off Simone's questioning look.

"That's too bad," Simone said. "I don't know how people live as long as they do when they can see that sort of stuff."

"I don't know if I'd call it 'Living' as much as I'd call it 'Existing.'"

"Right." Simone sipped at her coffee.

Gavin's hand closed a pair of books shut with an air of finality. He would probably have better luck finding something to help Karac with. He actually toyed with the idea before responding. "As hard as we try, I don't think we're going to catch a break with this one."

"What makes you say that?"

"Well, part of me says that because we're not going to be that lucky."

"And the inevitable other part?"

"That one says we're not smart enough."

CHAPTER FIFTEEN

Is it odd to anyone else that Milton and Dante were the only ones who seemed to have a decent grasp of the devil and his surroundings?

Simone Perfect, from the foreward of Fox and Lucas'
MAGICK AND RELIGION

The unknown, whether it be magick, or some quiet corner of the human mind that could tell you how to be better than yourself or somesuch notion or activity had no place in the sun. It was left reserved for the darker times, namely late evening, or very early morning. It had always been that way, Karac mused as he made his way past Bobby and Tony, the bouncers he had come to know at the Wash, even before humans had realized it was there for the taking.

Magick worked its own rules on its own turf. It only allowed mortals to think they were harnessing it and controlling it.

And it was doing a damn fine job of it.

It knew human nature and behavior better than humans themselves did. Oh, they could natter on about the subject *ad nauseum*, and often did. But that only served to reinforce the hold the unknown had on them. They understood that there were ways to be better, but in the currents they found themselves in, they all too often found themselves reacting to things instead of acting.

Which he supposed was probably why he found himself at the Wash.

It wasn't the physical need for a drink, or the mental one, for that matter. It was the simple act of being around people who under the way the 'real' world operated, could be considered by others, if not themselves, more or less normal, a state of being Karac felt less and less connected to.

The stage was empty, and he hadn't thought to check the board outside to see if any entertainment was being offered that night outside of your usual garden-variety Wash crowd, and during a weeknight such as this one was, it could be anything or absolutely nothing, which was what made the Wash the Wash.

The new pretty face with the shoulder-length dishwater hair behind the bar nodded and smiled at the order of a whiskey sour he had no intention of drinking. It was a prop, nothing more. Just one more thing to make him appear normal outside of his bag, which was never off his shoulder as he stood at the bar, waiting for the drink.

It was something one usually saw at the Wash; new faces, although that seemed to be more on his side of the bar than the other. Folks came and went, but even those whose names Karac never knew would show up again, sometimes years later, just for one drink. It was the draw of the place. You either fit in, or you didn't. And if you did, it may be a good idea to keep your distance for a while so you didn't burn out. Or if you were so inclined, come in every night just to hang out with people likeminded enough to realize this was a rare place, and to just enjoy it enough to not put too much of yourself into it.

There weren't enough places like that on Earth, Karac thought as he was handed the glass.

"Where's Deke?" He asked. The shift's usual bartender was a longtime fixture, and a favorite of the regulars.

"Took some time off," the woman said, smiling. "I'm just filling in."

Karac nodded. "A friend of his?"

"Of Evan's," she replied, tossing her head in the direction of where the owner stood talking with a couple shooting a game of nine-ball.

"I'm Karac," he said, extending his hand. "Welcome to the Wash."

"Rose," came the reply and a firm shake over the highly polished bar. "Thanks."

A familiar voice came at his shoulder, giving his skin a start. It was Markab.

Dressed in a black work shirt decorated with what appeared to be tribal lines in white embroidery on the back was untucked from jeans with the distressed look of a pair that had earned every minor tear and fade. Capped off with what Karac supposed was a pork pie hat and a lopsided grin, Markab's ensemble was complete.

Karac regarded him with a curious tilt to his head, taking him in from foot to head once more. "Looks like Markab, sound like Markab, but..."

The man opposite raised his hands. "I know, I know. Someone got on me about wearing too much black, so I thought I'd go in the opposite direction for a night and see what people thought."

"And what's been the consensus so far?"

A shrug. "Dunno. No one will talk to me."

Karac laughed and turned to Rose, who was partly listening, partly mixing drinks. "Pay this one no mind, Rose. He lost his mind loooong ago."

"Oh, so you must be a regular," said Rose.

Markab tilted his hat like a grateful balladeer and widened his grin.

"Okay," Karac said. "Now that the costume party's over, what can I do you for?"

Markab beckoned him with a chuck off his chin away from the bar. Business, then, Karac figured. It was the only time Markab got away from a crowd. There was a recently vacated Brunswick pool table with blue felt a few feet away. Markab headed there, thumbing quarters into the table and bending down to rack a game of straight pool.

Markab used things like his surroundings like props. Not just for visual effect – he was notoriously poor at the game of pool. Cards were more his game – but to seemingly distract himself away from the business of being a finder, as if he didn't want to think about it too closely. Most finders acted that way, Karac realized. At least the ones he'd come across. It was a kind of internal safety mechanism; treat it like an offhand conversation, and the ethical part of you won't wake up and make you realize that what you're good at, or more to the point, the only one who can do a given thing, often comes at a great cost from the source. In other words, sure, you could find a heart that would never stop beating, and it was rumored that Markab had done such a things, as his finding abilities came in the form of things that shouldn't exist but do, but chances were it was already being used by somebody. Somebody who would have to be relieved of it.

And it was the passion that each finder had that made them go forward and do whatever it was they were asked to do. Money, while the end result, was never the real issue. It was the doing of something no one else could do that was the satisfaction.

So someone with a lot of money got what they wanted, as usual. Someone got screwed, and the finder got to bask in that darkness only they knew, and made themselves busy so they didn't have to think about what they did while sharing space on planet Earth.

That included amongst themselves.

There was no written history about finders so far as Karac knew, even for their own use. They knew how to keep a secret, so that wasn't the issue. It was almost as if they knew a part of themselves regretted the fact they did what they did, and writing things down would only galvanize this fact. Their history was primarily part oral, part intuitive. Their abilities seemed to come from instinct, so that made sense to Karac. The one thing that was known by this instinct was something that none of them ever spoke about for some reason none of them could put a finger on; There had never been more Finders in existence than there were today. And while Karac had not the slightest notion that this could possibly be a bad thing, he wouldn't bet money on it if asked.

The one thing that stayed in the back of Karac's mind was that no one knew if finders died of natural causes. The very nature of their business made them popular among every sect of people. Young and old, rich and poor alike all had an interest in their abilities, and if wanted badly enough, could always find some way to pay the finder whatever fee he (or she – Karac had never met a female Finder, but had no reason to doubt they existed) commanded. This also meant they were also the subject of making enemies, usually easier than expected, and rarely from the source one would ordinarily expect, given whichever set of circumstances a finder found themselves in.

Markab edged a house cue from the rack on the nearby wall. He didn't roll it across the felt to see if it was warped or check it for weight, he simply took it and scrubbed a bit of the cube of blue chalk found on the long rail of the table without looking at Karac.

So it would be a casual, spontaneous game, Karac knew. Otherwise, Markab would have produced his own cue custom-made from some sort of undisclosed wood from a gentleman in England Karac could never remember the name of.

At least it just appeared to be a casual game. Markab could be putting up some kind of front… Karac wasn't buying the shirt, either.

Karac almost shook his head to break him free of the tangent. Stop over-thinking everything, he thought. That's why you keep grabbing for the bottle; it quiets things down just enough. Softens the edges *just so*.

But by doing so, it also made him something he wasn't. He didn't know who or what that was, but it wasn't who he really was. Or, more to the point, maybe it brought out the real him, and that wasn't acceptable, either. Something that tended to be a trait in Finders, he noticed. They were so good at doing what they did, they looked for distractions; for Markab, it was that '71 Plymouth Hemi 'Cuda he could never bring himself to finish. For himself, Karac selected something that divorced him from the life that part of him was so very proud of.

As if reading his mind, Markab smiled at him and nodded. If it had been anyone else, Karac would've figured the person had allowed his talents of perception and intuition to develop to the point of being nearly psychic. But with Markab, it was though the man could pick out stray thoughts from the air.

Which, Karac reflected, made him a very dangerous man.

Markab invited him to break, which he did to little luck save giving Markab the run of the table. They discussed the things they usually discussed; women of classic beauty, whether they were on the screen, or lived next door as was the case of a certain neighbor of Karac's, Lily of the Unpronounceable Italian Last Name. Names like Monroe were rarely brought up during such times. Nothing against the great beauty, but it was just too patently obvious to discuss the famed Marilyn when there were others made impeccable simply because they eased in among the mortals and appeared to be just like them.

Music and film would come up just as often. Karac had been concerned on more than one occasion that he and Markab only had three topics to discuss, but when parties are like-minded, you could talk about three different shades of blue and come up with something compelling, even though it would bore most folks to tears or give them the impression that you thought you were in a movie, and they were the extras. And even though extras were little more than dressing to sell a story, they were nevertheless integral elements to a given world. But nobody was ever happy being an extra, and Karac couldn't blame them. To be ordinary is too dark a fate to consider for many, even those who actually are.

Karac tried to bring up the case of one Solmon Archer as casually as he could, but Markab was too sharp for subtlety of that kind. He gave a baleful glance to his fellow Finder for bringing up work, but listened to the case as closely as he could.

Markab nodded, planning his next two moves on the table. "Yeah, your man's screwed."

Karac racked another round, despite the fact that it was clear he was a league behind Markab. He was already down two racks. "Don't sugar coat it. Give it to me straight."

Markab shrugged. "What do you want me to say? There's nothing the poor guy can do. Maybe in time it'll get better. These things are the type of stuff that requires the person suffering to come up with the solution to his suffering. It's messed up, sure. But that's the way it goes."

"Yeah, that's pretty much what Fox said."

Markab's face stiffened at the name. "Gavin or Simone?"

"Gavin."

"Figures. If the man was a rock, he'd be the kind that grumbles to the other rocks about not being stony enough."

"I'm not sure that's fair."

"It may be the voice of experience," Markab shot back. "He thinks very little of us, Karac. Thinks we're pretty much scum." He went about chalking his cue.

"Sometimes we can be. We know it, and we do it anyway."

The small block of blue chalk stopped moving. Very purposefully, Markab replaced it on the rail of the table. "Why are you here, Karac?"

The business side of Markab had just officially opened, and now it was up to the patron to walk in or not. Karac had hoped it didn't need to be like this, but with age came liability, especially with a Finder with the reputation of Markab.

"I'm just looking for help."

"Aren't we all?"

"That's not what I mean."

"Then speak plainly. The birds are ready to come cover me with leaves."

The two men stared at each other for a long, uncomfortable silence. Karac didn't need to look behind him to know that on instinct, Rose had been keeping track of the conversation's dark turn.

Karac forced his face to relax. "I'm looking for a book or a talisman or a scrap of paper to actually help this poor guy who wants nothing more than to be normal."

To his credit, Markab matched tone. "I know, Karac. Look, I want nothing more than to provide you with an answer. To me, the worst three words in the English language are 'I don't know.'" He shook his head not as a dismissal, but rather meant of empathy. "There's nothing out there, man. Nothing. If there was, I'd know it. You'd know it. If we didn't, I'm sure a guy like Gavin Fox would actually own it or Simone would have written a comprehensive article about it. But it just doesn't exist. I'm sorry."

Karac nodded, stuck out his hand. Markab took it in his usually viselike grip and pumped it twice before moving to the rack and replacing his cue. "Listen, man. Just don't be satisfied with the answer when it's no, okay?"

"What, you're not going to finish kicking my ass?"

Markab's face broke into a smile. "Nah, I think that's what she's come in here for." His chin chucked in the vicinity of the front door, where the vision of the street regal Mia Baudino was now entering, taking stock of her surroundings, an action that at once made one aware that she knew exactly where she was at all times, but wasn't quite savvy enough to know what she was doing was a kind of tell, checking the location of every exit door and checking those who sat with their backs against the wall. It wasn't the kind of place where such a thing was necessarily indicative of someone wanting to stay on is toes, but she didn't know that. Not intuitively. She listened to the room before judging its occupants, who in turn watched her move into their space. This last she was aware of. Karac could tell by the way the corners of her lips curled in an almost snide grin.

Karac was pinned to where he stood by her eyes, and that casual walk that would have killed him where he stood if it didn't look so *practiced.*

But that was Mia. And Karac found he cared not at all. The men watched her, and the women watched who she walked to.

"I don't know if I'm the mongoose," Karac said to Markab. "Or the cobra." When no answer was forthcoming, he discovered Markab had disappeared. He swore under his breath as Mia ended her approach within arms distance.

"I'm sorry," she said. "I didn't mean to interrupt. Please, continue talking to yourself."

"No, it's good that you interrupted. I was about to start an argument with myself."

Mia tugged a cue out of the wall rack. "Then do you mind if I play?"

"I'm not very good," Karac admitted.

"Neither am I."

And as the first game progressed, Karac couldn't help but think about what else Mia Baudino was lying about.

Karac knew better than to look at his watch when the two of them finally closed the Wash, saying good night to the last bouncer who walked Rose to her car. It wasn't within reason to think daylight was around the corner, but it was early enough that he could dread it coming sooner or later.

He had had a drink, just one, a whiskey sour, and that was just because Mia had bought him one without asking, and there was no way he was going to say no to her because when he could see just below the surface of her every once in a while, he saw a young lady who knew enough about trying to be polite and have manners to at least try to emulate what she thought was appropriate when she thought it was wise. There was no guile in that face at times like that, and that was what made Karac want to see more of that smile that reminded him of a lady that had seen a bit too much too soon in her life but knew to be happy that she had done something right.

Karac was no master of comprehending body language by any stretch of the imagination, but it didn't take a master at it to understand her stance during most of their conversations during their games that she was trying to be open with him. And while he was by far no a challenge to her at the game of pool, he could tell when someone was throwing a game. And there was something so sweet about the gesture when it came from her in this slightly altered personality that it prevented him from being angry at her for doing such a thing.

She wasn't a brilliant conversationalist, but she knew what she was talking about when she opened her mouth to speak an opinion about whatever topic was being thrown about between them. She also was smart enough to know she could be smarter, and that asking questions was not a sign of weakness.

Mia was pursuing him, and trying to impress him by relaying the information to him that she had been paying attention to him and noting little personality quirks like how he looked like he was squinting when he asked someone to repeat what they had just said. She was a woman who would never use the word 'cute' in a sentence, but had no problem conveying the fact that his thought that she thought someone was attractive.

What struck Karac so off about this woman was the fact that his entire life he had pursued women who were the absolute embodiment of the girl next door. If nothing else, Mia was the furthest from that. Mia Baudino was the girl-next-door's evil twin, and made no apologies about it.

She drank the occasional whiskey sour, but obviously preferred beer – Guinness, thank you very much, Harp if you don't have it – she was Rock and Roll, but only the 'good stuff', in her own words, Zeppelin, The Who… the 'groups who devoured the cities they toured in.'

It was in searching her face that Karac noticed something for the first time. And while he chastised himself for not noting it sooner, he was able to push the voice away with a certain degree of ease and instead ask aloud, "What happened there?"

For the briefest of moments, Mia's confidence faltered. When she recovered, it was tempered with careful defensiveness. "What? What happened where?"

Karac smiled the smile he had acknowledged long ago that made people feel at ease. "There, that little scar on your chin." He was becoming more and more convinced it was the only flaw on her face.

Her eyes kept him pinned while she briefly touched the pale sliver that curled just under the chinbone. "Oh. I got picked on at school. I was kind of a tomboy." She shrugged.

"Was it a boy or one of the girls?"

"Oh, a boy. I beat him at a footrace, he cracked me good with his fist, and I landed in the gravel." Her fingers once again went to the scar; this time intentionally. "Six stitches," she smiled.

"And what happened to the kid?"

Mia blinked, holding his eyes. She was not looking past him, not through him, but within him, a feeling Karac was not entirely sure how he felt about.

She's sizing me up, he thought. Here's where she first tests someone, to see if they can get close enough to lie to. She can open the door to her world or slam it shut right here, right now.

The trick, he realized, was to decide whether it was worth the risk to shove his foot between the door and the jamb if the door swung the wrong way.

"I hurt him."

Karac remained quiet and attentive.

"There I was, all of sixteen, flat as a board and shy as all get out, and this boy who I thought I could impress by winning a race with him actually clocks me with a closed fist." The corners of her mouth twitched upward.

"And I stand up, straighten my back, act like it's not really my own blood dripping on my brand new Motley Crue t-shirt, and I deck him."

Karac felt himself nodding. Had this been anyone else telling the story, he would have nodded and said something that let the person know he was on their side.

"And he hits the ground, and his friends kind of laugh at him just like they did at me when I went down, and it's like something just got flipped in my head. This is how it is, I figured. Doesn't matter who goes down or how hard. The audience wants their gods to bleed.

"And I got on top of him and started hitting him in the face. This sweet, beautiful face I had such a crush on. I kept going, and all his friends were cheering me on, and I just couldn't think straight. Next thing I know, I'm getting dragged off him and told to run for it. And I did.

"No one ever said anything to the adults that came over, no one said anything to my parents, and the boy who ended up spending the night in the hospital never said anything to anybody.

"And that's when I understood."

"Understood what, exactly?"

The grin spread across her face. "That I could get away with it."

At this, she broke away and swallowed the rest of her third beer.

She's never told this story before, Karac thought. No one's gotten past the doorstep until now.

"And did you ever talk to the boy again?"

With a mouthful of beer crowding her cheeks, Mia looked at him as if a pair of wings had just sprouted from his back. She swallowed and belched.

Right, thought Karac. Moment over. Probably for the best.

"Now why would I ever want to do a thing like that?" She asked, obviously not one to deliver a rhetorical question often enough, much less entertain one.

"So what about you?" She asked

"What about me?"

Again the twitch at the corners of her mouth. "Impressed?" Then she actually let out a chuckle.

The night air was colder than expected, and Karac felt his cheeks immediately flush with the chill. Mia closed hereyes and walked into it.

"What time is it" she asked, not being able to be bothered to look at her own watch, too enveloped in the breeze to care about such things as lifting her wrist to her eyes. "About two?"

Karac looked at the Timex on his wrist. "Five past, actually."

"Your watch is fast," she said, only now opening her eyes and looking at him from their corners, a good-natured dare to contradict her.

He made a show of pulling the stem on the Timex and setting the minute hand back by five. "This look all right?" He inquired, showing her the face.

114

She made a perfunctory inspection of the watch, holding his wrist at eye level, then popping the stem back into place, letting the sweep hand resume its orbit. "Perfect."

"Can I walk you to your car?" Karac offered, regretfully taking ownership of his arm back.

Mia grinned. "Nah, I'm right over there." Her finger pointed over to a black Challenger. "Nice of you to ask, though."

"Chivalry is not dead," he noted. "It just takes long naps once in a while."

"Right. Well, thanks for the company. We should be careful, though." Her boots made sounds too loud for a mostly deserted parking lot behind a bar.

"Why's that?"

She turned her head, but not enough to actually look back at him. "People will start to talk," she said, then slid behind the wheel of the muscle car. Karac watched her drive away, standing there until he could no longer see her tail lights. He smiled.

CHAPTER SIXTEEN

There was a time when actions spoke louder than words, and might was more than able to come from mere eloquence. Such things are gone now, and no one seems to miss them.

Lucas Brady, from 'An Untitled Essay' from THE
COLLECTED LUCAS BRADY, VOL. I

The Nedry home had always felt to be a welcome place to Alec Copeman. David and Alice had welcomed his arrival, acting as what would pass as official town spokespeople, explaining that while their family wasn't terribly religious, they both recognized a certain importance in having some sort of spiritual belief, and when Alec had made a point to try not to convert the entire town or resort to the expected scare tactics during sermons, he had won not only them and their now ten year-old daughter Josie, but earned a given amount of respect amongst the natives, for which David was clearly thankful for.

The two had struck up a friendship over the past few years when Alec had offered to help with a few repairs around the Nedry home, having a love, and best of all a talent, for basic carpentry and was able to learn a few tricks from David as well as pass on a few of his own. Such things resulted in regular invitations to dinner, which he accepted more and more as the page in the drawer weighed on him, provided he be able to help prepare, which endeared him to no end to Alice, who took joy in ribbing her husband over his complete lack of skill in the galley.

And there was Josie, who when her hamster Domino died, had invited Alec to the funeral and asked him to say a few words over the shoebox before her dad had lowered it solemnly into the ground dug in the backyard, had forever held a place in his heart he had reserved for innocence that he would go to his grave defending against even the grayest of evils. The innocence and outright trust in a child's eyes could mend you while it tore you in half, and while he understood that to overprotect a child was to render it to innate vulnerability, it still made him want to preserve the beauty of it as best he could. The little ones would come to inherit what their elders left behind, and Alec couldn't help but feel that just wasn't enough.

'Susie Donovan at school says I shouldn't be sad,' Josie confided in him a couple days after the funeral. And as would become the norm, would be brought up at the dinner table. "Because animals don't have souls.'

Her parents both told her that maybe that wasn't the best subject to be brought up at, but Alec had given her parents his *No, it's okay with me if it's okay with you* look, to which they nodded their agreement and Alec looked at Josie and replied, 'And yet Saint Francis was able to reason with a wolf that had been terrorizing a village and insisted he commune with nature. Seems to me he had a good idea of the bigger picture God had in mind, man and animal living together.'

Josie didn't look at him. She wasn't buying it. He was watering it down a tad, and she knew it and took it to mean he was acting the grown-up to the child, which was something she never entertained.

'Okay,' he said. 'You've seen on TV those programs that show how the presence of cats and dogs can help the morale of the elderly?'

'Uh-huh.'

'And that sometimes the interaction with an animal will cause great healing in the human mind, maybe because of the feeling of companionship?'

'Like that little boy on the news who started talking after petting the dolphin,' replied Josie, now brightening.

'Right.' He smiled at her for a time, then said. 'And Domino could always make you feel good just by looking at you?'

Now a smile. 'Yeah.'

'Now, I don't think something without a soul would be able to do that, do you?'

Josie shook her head and giggled.

'Thank you,' Alice had whispered.

'Just don't report me to my bishop,' he smiled.

And dinner resumed as usual, with Alec quietly thankful that she hadn't asked him if maybe Scripture was wrong about the animals. There were some things, others more important that the animal-soul issue that he hadn't ever been able to reconcile. But then, he supposed, he might not continue the journey he saw himself on if he had all the answers.

And now, with years behind them, Alec was glad that the family had not seen him as an interloper looking to convert them, in fact, they had a few occasions when questions of a larger issue would arise, as they have a habit of doing in everyday life, and took comfort in Alec's word as he took comfort in their trust, and Alec was more than happy to partake in everyday life. Books were fine, and studying Scripture was not only a necessary part of his vocation but also something that flowed through him, making his blood and mind and spirit sing, but actual interaction with other humans was something he got only enough of to want more.

He had helped Alice prepare a dinner of smoked salmon, which Josie turned her nose up at but agreed to try. David was a self-confessed meat-and-potatoes man before he met Alice, he confessed, but was enjoying the fact his wife liked playing the role of Doctor Frankenstein only without the corpses.

"Ewwww!" Came from the repulsed Josie, despite the fact she couldn't help giggling.

A long wooden spoon Alice was then rinsing was turned on David and shaken with considerable skill, droplets of water hitting her husband square in the face.

"Honey," David said. "There's a priest in the house."

Alec raised his hands in an attitude of helplessness. "Hey, I'm just here for the food."

Dinner itself passed in a cheerful clatter of silverware and glass, punctuated by Josie stories from school and Alice's dry wit. When it was over,

Josie cleared the table while the adults gathered in the kitchen, accepting plates and the like to place in the dishwasher and generally discuss topics adults who are comfortable enough with each other to dare to disagree on occasion care to indulge in from time to time.

When the dinner plates had been cleared and Josie had taken a bath, she said goodnight to all and placed a special request to her mother to sing her a few songs before she went to bed. Alice tried to decline, asking halfheartedly if her daughter wasn't getting a bit too old for such things when David reminded her that Alice would only really begin to have valid complaints when her daughter *was* past things. Nodding, Alice and Josie went off, leaving Alec and David to venture outside for the latter to have a rare after dinner cigarette. With the strains of Alice's contralto version of 'Across the Universe' soft in the background, Alec declined the offer of a cigarette as he always did whenever David offered one.

"What was it that made you believe in God, Alec?"

The question was so sudden and unlike David that Alec could not begin to hide his surprise or how he had somehow found himself at a loss for words. When he replied, it was with choosing his response as carefully as possible.

"There was a time that I wasn't sure myself, so I went on a bit of a mission to find out."

"A seeker, huh?"

"Of sorts. I tried to find answers for myself, not just a blanket statement for faith to simply be believed in and don't look at it too closely, or you'll make God blink kind of thinking. That's what got me there, but it wasn't going to hold my attention. So I did everything I could think of that indicated to me a getting closer to God, or 'Getting to Know the Universe As You See It 101.' My search was a personal one for my own questions, not everybody else's."

"How did you do it?"

"It was a matter of immersing myself in all the things that made me get a better understanding of myself and the world around me and above all, trying to figure out how to cope with the whole overwhelming thing. I listened to the great composers, not just Mozart and Beethoven and the like, but of delta blues and of jazz and even a little classic rock. I read as much as I could about philosophy, especially the material that came into direct conflict with the church. I tried to study science, but failed simply because I couldn't get my head around it. It was like they were speaking a completely different language from my own. But some kinds of philosophy can come from scientists as well, and that helped me find my center. Einstein helped when he said, 'God is subtle, but not malicious. I cannot believe that God plays dice with the universe.' Then came the 'The Watch and the Watchmaker'."

"How was that?"

Alec smiled. "William Paley, *Natural Theology*."

"Go on."

"He simply proposed that a universe as complex as this must have been done by design, not some cosmic accident. When I thought about it, I found I could not argue it. You could say that the universe is itself chaos, but that doesn't disprove the argument, it only shows it's deceptively simple to answer in such a way as saying 'God moves in mysterious ways.' Which is to say, 'I have no idea why certain things happen.' Both science and religion have that catch-all for the unanswered."

David looked into the night, dragged on his cigarette, and for a long time, said nothing. Then; "And why do you suppose that is?"

"What, why are there unanswered questions?"

"Yeah."

"I suppose because if there weren't, there'd be no faith."

"What about in science, then?"

"Then it would be without a primary component; curiosity."

David nodded.

"Do you mind my asking what brought all this on?" Asked Alec.

"Having a child brings lots of things to the forefront. One of them for me is why I became a cop, which was to protect people and to make a difference. Nice and simple.

"But then, you realize one day that things aren't as simple as that; other things are happening because people set them in motion. Things you cannot control. Some of these things are terrible things that I cannot believe could come from." Alec nodded for the man to go on.

"When I became a parent, I also became very aware of some of the horrible things that can happen to children because of adults and their actions, and while I've never not believed in any kind of God, I've never believed in one either. Because of stuff like that. I just don't understand how innocence can just be completely disregarded by someone who is like God, and if there is fear of Him, why people carry on acting that way."

"I asked a similar question to a class I once taught before coming here."

"Was there a right answer?"

"I think there *is* a right answer, but whether the one I was looking for them to respond with is the right one, I don't know. I only know that it helped *me*. The same thing that gets me up in the morning isn't going to be the same thing that gets a scientist studying dark matter or whatever up and at 'em."

"And what was the answer?"

"I put to them that mankind does, as you say, terrible things to one another. On a small scale as well as the large. The question is always, 'What kind of a father would allow such things to happen to his children?' The question, which is also the answer I was hoping for, might very well be, keeping free will in mind, 'What kind of children do such things to their brothers and sisters in the eyes of their parent?'"

David looked at him, dragged on his cigarette and crushed it out against his heel. "And has that answer rung true for you?"

Alec shrugged. "Would you have preferred, 'The Lord moves in mysterious ways?' Me neither. This was the one that got me out of bed."

After a time, David's face broke out in a smile. Alec couldn't make out the tune at first, but was soon able to identify 'The Long and Winding Road.'

"Funny how questions like that just come up when you're not expecting them to," David said. "Even after they've been cooking in your head for longer than you'd care to remember."

"Everything okay, David?"

David pulled at his beer and stared into the neck. "I just can't help shaking this feeling that all the faith someone might have won't be enough to get them through."

"Are we talking about anyone in particular?"

"Just worried, that's all."

"I had no idea Alice was such a Beatles fan."

"She sang lead in an all-girl band back in high school through college."

"You a Beatles fan, David?"

"More of an Al DiMeola or John McLaughlin kind of guy. Drives Josie nuts." He smiled. "You?"

"Yeah. I liked the *White Album*. There are songs they did that still raise the hairs on my arms. Listening to their stuff feels to me like stepping into a giant's footprint. Music's a force of nature, don't you think?"

David's brow showed he'd never quite thought of it that way. If he disagreed, he showed no signs of wanted to discuss it. Then, "Does God answer all prayers?"

"Funny thing; lots of people ask me that, thinking that the old saying means they'll always get a 'Yes.' It seems to me the hardest thing a child needs to learn is that parents have to say 'No' sometimes." Alec stuffed his hands in his pockets, fingers touching the rosary. "Sometimes we don't need all the answers, just a few of them so we can move on to the next ones."

David nodded, and led them back inside. They would never discuss anything close to the subject again.

CHAPTER SEVENTEEN

There is a popular misconception that to believe in the occult is to indicate those who practice believe in a deity of some kind or another. This is not the case. In fact, there are a great deal of contemporary practitioners who seem trouble with believeing that they themselves are channeling the energies around them. They may not be the creator of the current, but they are the tamer, and weilder, of it.

Gavin Fox, MEDITATIONS ON THE OCCULT

The fact the he was the first Finder ever to proverbially darken the door of Fox Manor was not lost on Karac in the least. Karac understood that Gavin seemed to actually like him, God knows why, and Karac was eternally grateful to whatever force in the universe that decides who likes whom decided to smile on him, at least for a little while, as the universe had been known to be fickle at the very least.

The morning phone call that had roused him at the crack of dawn from Fox himself was enough to send the message, even if Gavin's offer to meet with him on Fox turf didn't; Gavin needed help of a kind he was reluctant to ask for, and he was willing to see if he could help Karac in his quest to help Solomon Archer.

Solomon Archer. There was a vase ready to fall off the end table. After looking into the man's eyes for longer than five seconds, Karac understood Solomon was not the type to have the bravery – or cowardice – to put a gun to his head, or swallow a bottle of sleeping pills with however much whiskey he could stand. No, here was a man who understood his misery in a special way; to bear it as best he could without giving up. But therein lay the trick; Karac was not at all sure if Solomon had given up well before he'd come to him or not. The fact the man came to him looking for help, indicated by nothing more than instinct, a trick most humans couldn't pull off simply because they'd talked themselves out of listening to such a thing since they couldn't put their hands around it, showed Karac the man was still indeed serious about ridding himself of his trouble.

And if Gavin Fox couldn't help him, Karac didn't know what to say. Thus far, Solomon seemed to be able to be satisfied with half-answers and nebulous replies to well thought out questions. Worse, Karac had not the slightest inclination as to what Solomon Archer may do when confronted with the very real possibility that there was nothing to be done and that he would simply have to understand that.

But he wouldn't. No one would.

He was shaken from his reverie by the door opening. Before him stood what could only have been Simone Perfect. In his opinion, far too radiant to be with a grouch like Gavin, even with no makeup and her hair pulled back in a simple ponytail and looking like she'd been up longer than Gavin had in their research and weathering it because she needed to, not just for herself or for the greater good, but because her man was counting on her, and she'd have it no other way.

"Karac," she said. "Simone. Hi." She stuck out her hand and shook his with a firmness that only made him like her more. "Thank you for coming." She moved aside, allowing him entry into the foyer.

The smell of the place was what hit him first; coffee, well-loved books, and a kind of magick that came with two people in love and in balance with one another. It felt to him like what a home should feel like. The furnishings and artwork were things that could be easily distracting to the point of it almost being spellbound. The Foxes were not known to be flashy about the wealth that they had, but behind closed doors, they were more than able to appreciate the finer material things life had to offer.

"Thanks for having me," he heard himself say, reminding himself not to touch anything.

Simone's eyes flicked across the room to a closed sliding glass door, then back to Karac. "I hope you know how much trust Gavin's putting in you. I can count how many guests he invites up here on one hand, and that includes me."

Karac nodded. "I understand, and I'm honored someone of both your statures would have me here. I don't know how you feel about Finders..."

"I tolerate them," Simone answered. "I don't approve of what your ilk does, but I admit your ability's worth."

Karac nodded. So much for the friendship thing, then. But then, allies had their own value.

She guided him through the living room, past the ticking grandfather clock that had probably come over from whatever country the Foxes had originated from, and operated just as well as it had the day it was made because of the legendary Fox magick. He was walking through history here, he knew. Those with names he dared not utter simply out of respect for a craft he did not practice had walked across these floors, their breath still lingered in the walls, and he knew, a part of them still remained here, because being who and what they were, it was unreasonable if not outright impossible for them to move on anywhere else. Their home was here, in the Manor, and not even death itself could stop them.

Given the choice, Karac realized he would rather be anywhere else but here now.

Simone held the glass door aside for him to gain access to the lush backyard where museum replicas of statues depicting angels stood, keeping time with manmade waterfalls and other the statues collected at poolside of Neptune and a court of sundry mermaids.

And there, seated at a veranda covered with an awning to protect from the glare of the sun rising in the too-clear southern California sky sat Gavin Fox, barefoot and dressed in cream-colored cotton slacks and shirt. He looked more like a businessman on holiday rather than the most powerful person Karac had ever stood in front of. A copy of the *Los Angeles Times* was hoisted in front of his face.

"Hon?" Simone called, too loud in the stillness.

Gavin Fox turned his attention to their guest, smiled, and put the paper down before standing and meeting them halfway. His viselike grip was simultaneously as intimidating as it was reassuring. Here was a man whose personality if it had been inside anyone else would have appeared to be well-rehearsed and bottled, and even though one may not agree with everything Gavin Fox said or did, the man was true to himself, as was the woman he'd chosen to spend his life with.

The three sat down at the stone table where bowls of fruits had been laid out along with an icebucket full of sparkling water and a carafe of coffee. He was invited to partake in however much he wanted of whatever he wanted, and as Karac was a firm believer in discretion being the much better part of valor, accepted their offer in a conservative manner, mindful of his manners. For the first time, he could notice the soft strains of a doo-wop band coming from somewhere behind his host. Hidden speakers were strategically placed on the veranda.

"I hope you don't mind meeting out here," Gavin said. "We've both been cooped up in the house with our noses in books for too long."

"Oh, no problem. I don't mind the outdoors at all. It isn't every day I see the sun." It was Finder humor, and misplaced just a bit, But the couple seemed to weather it with smiles and nods.

"Besides," added Gavin. "We're just talking. Not negotiating."

"I have no problem with that."

"Great," Gavin smiled and leaned back in his chair as Simone outlined what they had discovered during their investigation about the robberies.

"Right, I'd heard tell about some of that stuff," Karac replied. "Some of the Finders were grumbling that it might be someone taking over their turf."

"I thought all Finders were specialized," Simone put in. "Only one per specialty…"

"Until they die," Karac finished. "That's right."

"So is it possible that someone is nosing around on Finder turf?"

"Not according to the legend as we understand it. It's never happened before, that's why some of us are more than a bit nervous. They think it's a calling card from someone telling them that their ability is no longer what is was."

"Which is?" Asked Gavin.

"Unique."

"You don't seem too worried," this came from Simone.

A shrug. "I'm not."

"How come?"

"It's not about an invasion of turf, or who specializes in what. Half of that comes from the fact that if a Finder were hired on to find this stuff, he or she'd be more than able to do it. This person wants to do it for themselves."

"Exactly," said Gavin. "They want to keep a tight rein on who knows."

"And it's very likely," Simone added. "That no one else does."

"What makes you say that?" Karac asked.

Simone and Gavin exchanged glances before Simone replied. "There has been evidence that this person has the ability to teleport."

Karac regarded the two of them carefully, then chewed on a grape as he considered this. Strictly speaking, teleportation was not a gift that was shared. Those who had a desire for that sort of knowledge tended to keep to themselves because such knowledge was indicative of a certain personality type some in overly polite circles might call 'Unsavory' others still, 'Unnatural.' While the ability was a mystery that could be sought after for a lifetime to no good ends and no true definition as to how one actually obtained it, the actions some took in their quest for it as well as other equally dangerous powers had led to nothing more than insanity and the heartbreak of murder of the innocent for absolutely nothing. Or, that was what saner heads believed.

"Okay," Karac said at last. "So you're in search for a solo practitioner, which can be a danger anyway, and now this person has the ability to teleport, which doesn't put him high on the social order either and therefore more difficult to find."

The two just stared at him for stating the obvious.

"What were the articles stolen again?" Karac asked, and turned the list over in his head when it had been recited in order of the theft.

"Those are all things mentioned in the *O'Barr Manuscript*," he said. "Just not in any particular order."

"Right," said Gavin. "We don't know if he's picking these things off out of order on purpose or because he has specific targets that need to be built up to. Do you have an opinion of what the *Manuscript* lists off?"

"Not really. I haven't put much thought into it until now. It could be anything. I've heard it was just a list of things to be found by a Finder to prove he could do it, but there's never been a challenge in finding them because nobody needs them. I read once that O'Barr was really just some eccentric old man who liked to affect that he was insane and just scribbled stuff like that down to confound people."

"Do you believe that?"

"No."

"What's your opinion?"

"Maybe he was just a guy who had a talent for a kind of magick, but not the type he wanted, but that didn't stop him from making notes that made sense only to him. Although there's no proof of it, I'm a believer he was a solo practitioner simply because he kind of fits the MO and there's no account of him being in any sort of group. Also, he never published anything, even privately, which is odd. Most folks like to keep their thoughts and studies pressed into binding for the vanity and the romance of it. I also think that they like to think what they have to say is so important that only one book of their wisdom will command a respect after their death."

Simone leaned forward. "Why would they care? They're dead."

"Doesn't matter to them," Karac answered. "A half-assed legacy is better than having to admit you had nothing significant to say."

"If it's a half-assed legacy, why hasn't anyone figured it out and just produced copies of it and take in the one-sided joke. The same personality would enjoy that just as much."

"Because no one wants to be wrong. Maybe it's nothing, maybe it is."

Gavin leaned in. "And what do you think?"

Karac drew in a deep breath. "I feel that our Mr. O'Barr had a great deal on his mind and was playing with things he didn't understand."

"You just described ninety-eight per cent of the human race, Karac." This came from Simone.

Karac nodded. "So lies the problem."

"Go on," said Gavin.

"I've never seen it, which to a Finder, is odd. Even if someone doesn't want a specific thing, sometimes you find it just because it so happened to be sitting near the object you were originally after."

"There are only two in existence," said Simone. "It's considered rare even amongst Finders."

"That's my point. Whoever has it knows what it is, otherwise, in my humble opinion, they wouldn't have it."

Gavin waved that away. "No, Calarco didn't know what he had, only that it was worth money and was reputed to be something spectacular. He didn't care whether it was a spectacular fraud."

"*Tony* Calarco?"

"That's right."

"That makes sense; He's the type of guy who would pour money into a good practical joke. Maybe even buy it to make the value appreciate so he could sell it and have a good laugh." The others concurred. "Wait, if Calarco's involved, why aren't you talking to Markab? Wasn't he the one who authenticated it?"

"We authenticated it," noted Gavin. "Markab signed a piece of paper."

"I don't want to tread on anyone else's turf."

"It's not Markab's turf to tread on. It's Calarco's. And besides, Finders specialize. Markab finds things that should not be. You find things that are, but aren't. I think you're just as, if not more, qualified for your opinion."

Karac spread his hands and smiled. There was nothing else to do.

"Do you think you could find the second copy?"

"If I were hired to. That's how the dynamic is created."

Gavin Fox reached over the right side of his seat. When he straightened, he held the briefcase, a Halliburton, Karac noticed, out to Karac. "I hope this will be enough."

Karac's thumbs unsnapped the locks and prised the lid of the Halliburton open and tried not to look shocked. He realized that if he had to remind himself not to look that way, he probably already was. He closed the case with no ceremony and waited until both latches were in placed before he raised his eyes once more to Gavin and Simone Fox.

"Yes," he said. "This will do."

When he had placed the Halliburton was to the side of his own chair, Karac smiled again. "And what about my own problem?"

"Archer's his name?" Asked Simone.

"Solomon Archer, yeah."

"Couldn't find anything about his family history regarding it. So mostly likely he isn't being made to pay for something an ancestor did, and since there's no evidence of it manifesting in anyone in his family before him, it's odds-on that if it was, it would be recent, say a parent or grandparent."

"I hadn't thought of that," said Karac.

"It's an odd thing," said Gavin. "There's not much to go on. Stuff like seeing the dead is usually reserved for vengeance. Occasionally it's used as a gift, but it never lasts long. Or more to the point, the user doesn't."

To Karac's surprise, they would speak a great deal more about Solomon's problem than the *O'Barr Manuscript*. They were saying they knew he could do the job without having to say it, and coming from Gavin Fox specifically, that was no shallow praise.

"You should bring Solomon over to see us," said Simone. "Let us talk to him for ourselves. Sometimes just getting someone inside your own sphere of influence can do wonders and set them on a different course."

"Do you think he'd be game?" Gavin asked.

"I think he's close to doing anything to get rid of the visions."

Gavin nodded curtly. "Then call us when he's ready, and we'll be waiting for that manuscript."

Karac rose, hoping there would be an offer to see him to the door so he could turn it down. There wasn't, and so with polite goodbyes, they parted company. It wasn't a flat-out promise of a cure, but hopefully it was enough to provide Solomon with at least a pinpoint of light at the end of the long darkness ahead of him.

CHAPTER EIGHTEEN

The first step on any path of any spiritual belief is almost always borne of a desire for power. Illumination comes much, much later, after the follower has seen fit to become pentitent.

Simone Perfect, A STUDY OF OCCULT ART

Diana Adair was not was not a woman with nothing to live for, Rebecca Scott reminded herself. She was in all actuality a pretty together person with absolutely zero grasp on her own reality and that she indeed could very well affect others, provided she could bring some sort of balance to herself and her head. Because Diana Adair was not as uncommon as she or others may have first thought. She was merely a person who had a heightened sense of the primal.

The fact she was actually looking for help was the kicker.

As she understood it, Rebecca knew that such a manifestation was rarely genuine. Mostly it came across as unreasonable anger or repressed rage. Yes, there were classes one could take to become a better person and try to put a lid on whatever was really bugging you, there were even medications one could take in order to be a more productive and less confrontational human being, and those human beings knew it. And didn't take their meds. And forgot their classes, and thought it better to just blow up and cause dangerous situations they couldn't brings themselves to contain because nobody knew what it was like to be them…

But Adair was different in that her manifestations were the truest form Rebecca had ever heard of in the modern era. It was very nearly a complete reversal into the animal form. Diana would not actually change into a beast of some kind or another, but her body would withstand greater degrees of pain and be more in tune with the wordless things of the world like the innate understanding that there is great goodness, but there is also a terrific awfulness and that things born from chaos, as she believed mankind and it world was going to lean toward that selfsame chaos that created it, maybe because it meant to, in spite of the fact that they could be greater than themselves if they tried and they refused in the name of whatever it was they preferred to see in the chaos that was not possibility.

People like Diana could see goodness, but feel the chaos and bad flowing through everything like a channel, pulling at various limbs until something fell in and could not be bothered to fight back. Call it the Dark Side, evil, absolute chaos, it didn't matter, because Diana was attuned to it, and as such, had become a part of it, and was physically manifesting it.

In its truest form; something humankind could never talk itself into believing it was possible of becoming; of regressing to; it's most pure base.

And Diana needed to decide whether to be free of it, or embrace it.

Rebecca knew this had been a long time in coming for Diana, anger rising up to power, and her comfort with it growing with it without her knowing because power is what we all want whether we talk about it or not.

But a part of Diana had remained quiet enough for the beast beneath her skin to stop noticing. A part that was greater than it, and knew it and knew to keep its big mouth shut until the time was right.

This part, it could have been argued, was the component of self-preservation.

It also could have been referred to as her soul.

But Diana denied that to the best of her ability as there was no belief in God for her. None. It wasn't with malice, Rebecca noted, it was out of her choice of considered thought. A soul more than implied belief in a higher power, a greater plan, and Diana simply did not have that within her.

The difference with Rebecca hearing this was that she didn't see the need to pass judgment on someone because of this belief system. It was unlike hers, but then again the way she used the word soul could have meant one of two things; the immortal soul that we hope will see Heaven, and the second definition being that of 'spirit'. That part of you that told you to get up. That keeps you going, no matter how mundane your life is. The part that makes you greater than that coffee table, whether you believe in it or not.

Diana wanted help. That set her apart enough for Rebecca to believe her and trust in her intent. She wasn't looking to magnify her anger, and therefore whatever power came with it, usually brute strength, she wasn't even looking to find her center, so to speak.

She didn't want her faith in God restored, but she wanted her faith in *humanity* restored and learn how to bolster it so she could look beyond what she could already see. She wanted to be happy, and she knew she could be happy being happy.

And despite, no, *in* spite of, the fact that the world wasn't a perfect place, Rebecca was going to do whatever she could to pull Diana into it. Not because Rebecca felt it was the right thing to do, but because Diana wanted someone to.

Bonding with Diana was easier than Rebecca could have hoped or expected, given Diana's cynical way of looking at everything. The woman wasn't inherently negative, but approached her cynicism with as wide an understanding as possible; expect what you get. If it's better than you'd hoped, so much the better, but don't set yourself up.

And if there was one phrase that came up more frequently than any other in Diana's speech, albeit in various forms, it was 'Depend only on yourself.'

But Rebecca picked up on something she did not let on about; Diana said it with the air of someone who wished that she had at some point trusted someone further than she had, and wanted to in the future. But to do so was going against her nature, or whatever part of herself that now referred to itself as such.

Staying within the walls of Rebecca's house was something that Diana clearly wanted nothing to do with for any length of time. She had surveyed the place for as much as she cared to, didn't feel comfortable with all the trappings, whether they be Wiccan or not, and just wanted to get out, something Rebecca recognized as something someone becoming more in tune with a different, older part of themselves would wish to do; smell the air, feel the wind. The San Fernando Valley was not known for its clean air or its natural experiences, but the hills around it were old, and would be there when the concrete and glass and famous people crumbled away, and that gave comfort enough to some.

Pleasurable sensory experiences were also something that people in Diana's mindset enjoyed on a level separate from others. Diana led her into Brook's Coffee and Books and sat down at a table seemingly chosen from at random, ordering for both her and Rebecca a coffee and biscotti. Although Rebecca sniffed at bit at the biscotti, as well as not being able to choose for herself, she let Diana do as she wished. The woman had been subjected to Rebecca's world for long enough. And trust needed to be built on both sides, lest Rebecca fall into the trap that was always under the feet of those who only mean well; a deep pit with smooth sides and floored with two-foot long sharpened stakes. The camouflage was friendship.

Rebecca watched with this in mind, as Diana would hold her coffee gingerly in both hands and bring it to her lips, eyes closing as she sipped and inhaled the steam that curled off the surface of the coffee. Hers was an unenviable life, but anyone in their right mind would kill to be able to experience the simple everyday things like coffee like she did. There was darkness and suspicion in Diana's world, as there was in any animal, but there were also experiences behind her eyes that no one else would have a right to.

Perhaps that was the price; the thing that put her in balance within the big picture. She felt things other people couldn't, but to deal with those people outside of her sphere if influence was something that was difficult, even to much to ask for. But that didn't keep the universe from asking. Every day. A little louder each time.

When Diana's voice broke her out of her reverie, for a moment, Rebecca didn't recognize the other woman's voice for a moment. When she did, she asked for the woman across from her to repeat what she had just said.

Diana gestured with her biscotti, a bite already removed and still being chewed. "I asked why you don't like biscotti."

"Oh. I don't know. I guess it's just that I don't like to impose on my food to eat it. You know, the dunking of it and everything. It's like you have to convince it to be eaten."

Diana's hand was already across the table. "Then you don't mind if I eat it?"

Rebecca pushed toward her fingers. "Feel free, please."

After another munch and silence, Diana spoke again:

"So what's up with all this graffiti, anyway? I've been seeing it more and more these days."

Rebecca's snapped away from the nearby shelf of New Age books she was criticizing vividly in her mind. Some of the names these 'authors' wrote under. She tried to sound offhand, "I noticed that myself. I meditated on it, and I came up with something like 'Are there angels among you?' or 'Who are the angels among you?'"

"What makes you think that?" Diana seemed genuinely interested, rather than someone merely trying to stall for time as they tried to come up with a snappy one-liner.

"When I meditate on stuff like that, sometimes it works, other times it doesn't. Sometimes it tells me what I don't want to hear."

"We all have that in our lives."

"Can't argue with that."

"So what do you think it means?"

"Well, I think artists in general are sensitive creatures, and maybe that translates into their art. Some one sense something they cannot put into words, so therefore, it comes out some other way that at least the artist understands."

"Like music says what the lyrics can't."

"Right. I'm not artistically inclined, so I can't say for sure, but that's about where I'm at on it, yeah."

"Why do you think someone's so concerned with angels that they have to spread the word like that?"

"Maybe the afterlife is on concern to them. Lots of people react to things in different ways."

"It's not one of those crackpots you see yelling about the Bible or walking around wearing a sandwich board with Bible verses on them."

"Why do you suppose that is?"

Diana seemed to consider that for a time, staring off into nothingness, munching on her latest bite of dark biscotti. "I think it's because they've gone back to do their homework. It's fine and well to shoot your mouth off about something, but the second you realize you'll have to back it up, it begins to be a different animal."

"I thought you don't believe in God."

"I don't. What I believe has nothing to do with what other people believe. I don't believe in something purely because someone tells me it believes in me, and that I should be afraid of it."

"And what about this consciousness of yours?" Rebecca asked. "What do you think it means? Why do you have it?"

"I honestly don't know. Maybe it's more a case of why *not* me. I'd actually be enjoying this if something in me wasn't so damn scared."

"What's that something saying?"

"'You're way over your head, and you have no choice in the matter.'"

"And what do you say back?"

"Nothing." This came with a slight shrug. "What do you say to something like that? I don't know why I do what I do, and I'm caring less and less."

"I can't imagine what that must be like."

Rebecca sank into the fashionable wood chair and stirred at her coffee with a small plastic straw. Of all the things she understood, and had come to and understanding with regarding the universe, it was things like this that ran her battery down faster than anything.

"So," Diana said at last. "Tell me about this meditation stuff."

The interior of Rebecca Scott's home wasn't to the taste of Karac, but he could appreciate the vibe that was cooler than the one he had managed to cobble together at his own home only a scant handful of miles away.

Such things that dotted the landscape of Rebecca's home were there for two reasons, Karac believed; one was to project a given idea about her and her lifestyle, and therefore misdirected, and therefore indirectly confuse the visitor. Second, to provide her with a bit of cover as to the general location of things.

It was indeed well thought out. But she had neglected one thing: That there was the slim chance that someone like Karac would be looking around. People like Gavin and Simone Foxes were smart enough not to be tricked into such things, but they were a couple who understood all to well the powers of aesthetics, and as such may very well be subject to confusion by someone who might very well know them better than they knew her.

It worked, as far as Karac was concerned, as Rebecca's vivid sense of darkness and color pulled at him from every pillow fabric, or the imposing candelabra and other like things about the house.

But he was a Finder, and while a Finder can admit to the pull of certain things, the thrill of the hunt of that which did not belong to him was what made his senses lay on a keener edge than others. That included Gavin and Simone. Mostly it indicated Rebecca herself, but Karac reminded himself not to get too cocky, and resumed his sweep of the house.

He kept his eyes closed, and held his head in a slight tilt, listening to the room.

When some people leave a room or their home, they take every last vestige of themselves along with them. You can feel the dynamic change when they leave. Rebecca, however, was still in the walls, her feet still on the carpet, her still body laying still in the bed. If he tried, Karac could hear her breathing.

There were things, not-quite there things that clung to the vaulted beams of her fine living room ceiling and meandered at the curtains of her bedroom. He was reasonably certain that Rebecca didn't know they were there. It was not the witch herself that was causing the presence of the watchful glances of the unseen, but more her promise of what she could offer should she fall to their way of thinking.

He had never actually met Rebecca Scott, but knew of her. Indeed, one was hard pressed to not find her works on the same shelves as such respected authors as the Fox and the like. But Karac himself felt that she was the worst kind of something he referred to as Big Power, which was someone or something so naturally inclined to something in the world of the wonderous that it was akin to a gun that could fire itself. She didn't impart dangerous knowledge as such, but she did do her best job at provoking thought, and in the untrained, which in his opinion most witches were, that was just as bad as supplying novices to the arts with ancient grimores no one had a right to get their hands on at any time in their life.

And in the matters of religion, newcomers rarely admitted themselves to a belief system for spiritual guidance. No, most of the time, they applied their learnings to be better than their neighbors, and in the study of belief that involved one taking an active role in the destiny of others, that move was usually motivated by power. The first step was usually books.

It was no small grace many of them were written by fools.

But he had read some of Rebecca Scott's work, more out of curiosity than anything else, and Karac hadn't liked it one bit.

She wasn't supplying a dangerous commodity to the public, but it was potential. Oftentimes, that was enough. And in the hands of an angry heart, scorned by an unrequited love or a sensitive soul bent on a deep-seated kind of revenge, she could make one think, and not in a calming way.

Karac liked to think he wasn't talking himself into the justification of lifting the manuscript from a house belonging to a powerful person. In fact, up until he'd arrived, he wasn't entirely sure she was a viable option; rumors had it that she hadn't written for a year, and that she had gone clinically insane. Another report noted her as being bumped off by a group of witches who despite their own social differences had banned together to rid themselves of a terrible potential, worst of all, one that refused any such activities in an organized coven situation.

But Rebecca Scott was indeed alive and well and living quite nicely, gathering power and trying to maintain what seemed to be a focused balance in herself, although the power base of the balance was unknown to Karac, and his abilities didn't reach that far. They served him only enough to gain an idea about his surroundings in how they would help discern the exact location of the object. Instinct gave him the general idea, then once at a target area, he would listen to its finer points to discover more about the item's owner.

It took two minutes to come to focus on the antique maple teacart Rebecca apparently used as a writing desk and phone cradle. And there, tucked into the letter organizer between the gas and electric bills, was a folded and torn square of linen-soft parchment.

It was no decoy. None had been created by anyone, not so far as Karac knew or had heard of. The exact nature of the *O'Barr Manuscript* was so uncertain that either no one wanted to visit an odd bit of luck from forging one or if it actually did contain nothing but the ramblings of an eccentric, take the time to actually create one.

The folded paper came away from its resting place, tucked between Karac's index finger and thumb. His other hand freed it from its creases gently as he lay it on the teacart's top. A quick scan of the titles present there and the confirmation that a good part of the handwritten notes within the margins seemed to be Aramaic, a language that eluded him in the written form. He couldn't always read the language he was seeing in a book or somesuch that he was seeking, but he could always tell it was what he had been looking for.

Gavin could probably decipher it. Failing that, Simone would be able to.

He took his leave of the house after giving it one more good look, just making sure of something he wasn't entirely certain of himself.

CHAPTER NINETEEN

Everyone gets the devil or angel they come to deserve.

Simone Perfect, REAL OR IMAGINED?

Of all the expressions Karac would have expected to see on Gavin Fox's face as he scanned the Manuscript, the aspect of the slightest bit of puzzlement wasn't one of them. In fact, Karac found his own reaction to it to border on alarm. His natural instinct to ask Gavin what was wrong was overridden only by his trepidation of what could actually be worse. It was bad enough that they had gotten off the wrong foot when Karac revealed he would actually have to return the manuscript. Soon. There were consequences to a late arrival.

"Well, it certainly *appears* genuine," Gavin said at last.

"Why is there a doubt?" This came from Karac, who wasn't sure whether Gavin was just muttering or actually attacking his credibility.

A shrug from Gavin Fox. "Parts of it look like they're written in the Atbash cipher in a coded hand. I think it's mostly in Aramaic. It's hard to tell what it actually says."

Karac blinked. Something he may have been able to find a small amount of humor in if it wasn't for the thud his stomach had just made around his feet. "You can't read Aramaic?"

The brows of Gavin Fox furrowed further. "No. Can't you?"

Karac felt himself take a step back. "No. What gave you that idea?"

"You're a Finder."

"Right. We know what it is when we see it. That doesn't necessarily mean we can read dead languages. Our instinct is what makes us valuable. No finder has ever handed over a forgery of anything. I though you were an expert on stuff like that."

"I can read a little Aramaic, sure. Not much of it, though." Gavin handed the manuscript to Simone's waiting hands. "Simone's better at languages than I am."

Simone made no secret of rolling her eyes upon hearing this, but inspected the page anyway. "Well, I can read *some* of it, but not with any confidence."

"How do you mean?"

Simone's nose wrinkled, as she read off a short passage in Aramaic verbatim off the page still held gingerly on the tops of her fingertips. "Now, that either means something like 'From the book of Bryant, or 'Tread lightly upon the reading.' The context is unclear, and with these archaic texts it's best not to speculate. I think that if it is in the Atbash, we need to be even more careful, since scholars are still finding meanings in the language in manuscripts like the Dead Sea Scrolls."

"So we have what we want," Karac said carefully. "But we have no idea what it means."

"Exactly," said Gavin. "Let's call Markab. Since he's the one who found one in the first place, maybe he can help translate it."

A headshake from Karac. "He's even worse than me at Aramaic."

"I thought you couldn't read it at all," this came from Simone.

"Right, which means he probably wouldn't even be able to identify what language it's written in, even if he is a Finder."

"Lucas can help us," said Simone, more to Gavin than Karac.

"I know," replied Gavin. "And I'd go at this point, but there's this feeling to not tip my hand so soon."

Simone gave him a look that he had most likely been the recipient of more times than either would care to count. "Uh-huh. You and your feelings."

"Maybe someone I know could help," Karac put in. He's great at translating old texts like these. I'm sure he's translated older."

"Who's this?" asked Simone.

Karac shrugged. "I know a guy."

"You're not leaving this house with the *O'Barr* with an answer like that. In fact, I'm not at all convinced you're going to leave at all with it."

"Okay, okay. He lives in Benjamin. Alec Copeman. He's a priest, so he's okay."

Both Gavin and Simone regarded him warily. "Since when have you considered clergy to be okay?" Asked Gavin.

Karac shrugged. "I don't, usually. But I know this guy, and even though I'm not thrilled with his vocation, and we don't have the greatest history of getting along, I *do* know that he can be trusted, and that if there's anyone outside of our sphere who thinks something's going on and wants to make sure it doesn't, it's him."

Simone held out the manuscript. When he reached for it, she pulled it back as carefully as she could, obviously knowing that he wouldn't dare lunge for it.

"It comes back by evening," she said, pinning his eyes with hers. "That mean closer to dusk than dawn, do we a have a happy fun understanding?"

Karac was careful to keep his eyes on hers as he replied. "We have a happy fun understanding."

"Do I want to know who you stole this from?"

"Smart money would be on 'No.'"

Karac shifted his weight from foot to foot as he watched the smirk on Simone's face try to define itself. At last she finally broke her gaze away from him. "Go on, then. It's a two-hour drive to Benjamin. If you're in as much trouble as I think you are, the sooner you get that things back to its owner, the better."

"And," said Gavin. "Don't forget; A full translation. Anything less will be useless."

"But no pressure," said Karac. "Right?'

The couple only smiled at him.

Two hours, he thought. Right, if traffic wasn't bad.

Alec Copeman would never be sure as to what it was exactly that told him to go to the sanctuary, but he'd learned to listened to the inner voice, whether it be the whispers of God, or the universe pulling at him, or simple instinct that always seemed to lead him in the direction best suited for him to go.

From the west entrance, he was able to take stock of the church. Edna and Lucille, the two eldest women of his congregation, had finished their volunteer weekly cleaning and had done their usual best, and the pleasant scent of wood polish still hung heavy in the air. He glanced at the crucifix behind the altar and crossed himself as he passed it.

Something in the church pews made his step come slower. Something still and used to being seldom seen. His turn to the pews was careful and steady.

A man was nearly at the last row, center to the crucifix. He sat on the backrest, hunched over with his hands carefully folded in from of him, his forearms resting on his thighs. Unkempt dark hair hung over his face, obscuring his features. When the priest made no further motion, the man raised his face to him, an unreadable expression there.

Alec made a show of moving a few steps closer and shading his eyes. His eyes squinted as if peering through some sudden cache of blue smoke.

"It's Karac, right?" He asked.

The man did not acknowledge the name, simply continued staring at him for a time. Alec smiled inwardly. The pose was meant to look casually intimidating, he knew, but still...

"You know, in this light, you look like Snoopy pretending to be a vulture, sitting on his doghouse and glaring."

At that, the man known as Karac set a booted foot down upon the floor. The other boot followed suit, and with practiced ease, allowed him to bend and pick up the satchel that had been resting in the aisle and sling it over his shoulder. Keeping Alec in his sight, never dropping his eyes, Karac slowly made his way up the aisle.

"Father Copeman," Karac said.

Alec inclined his head just so. "Dare I ask what brings an illustrious Finder such as yourself to my humble parish?"

"I'm in need of a translation."

"Of what?"

Karac's finger gingerly removed the paper from its resting place and held it up to him. When Alec reached for it, he found it not snatched away by the Finder, but held at a careful distance. He was able to read a few words, and blinked at the jump in his chest. It was in Aramaic, and while he could not be completely certain, he thought he saw the words used for 'gate' and 'open.'

Alec nodded, his expression dropping all pretense. "Perhaps we should move to my office."

Karac offered no alternative.

Alec had made a point to tell Edna and Lucille to not clean in his office for more than one reason. Not the least of which was the sporadic pile of papers that tended to flock to his desk. Handwritten notes, calendar entries and the like all kept time on his desk. He had been a man to have taken no small degree of pride in his ability to keep his workplace clean, but as the years faded into one another with alarming speed, he was having difficulty fighting the battle with as much zeal as he used to.

He picked up the reading glasses he'd picked up in the Benjamin drugstore two weeks before to replace the others that didn't work as well as they used to and perched them on the end of his nose, taking his seat behind the desk. He made no motion to the Finder across from him, knowing Karac would take it upon himself to simply sit down and hand over the paper, staring at Alec until he got what he came for.

The page was set before him with practiced care. It was of vellum, yellowed and darkened at spots too random for even the best of forgers to duplicate. Clearly written in hand in red ink still vivid despite what seemed to be genuine age from a hand belonging to a master scribe who seemed to be more than able to give illustrations of illuminations but for reasons of brevity decided to not go that route.

None of it was written in any of the standard ancients; Greek, Latin, the Romances. Several forgeries had cropped up in those languages, usually painted with great illuminations, and on one occasion Alec had heard of, gold leaf was used, and most of the forgeries he knew to look for were most often composed on parchment, possibly made from that of a sheep, giving the appearance of a slight dabbled pattern.

The titles of the volumes were composed entirely in Aramaic. There were accurate, and in the correct order of appearance.

He willed his hands to be steady as he read the short two-verse series of words that lay beneath it, finishing the document in the Atbash cipher:

One word to call and unmake,
To Know.

Give me a gate to open,
And one word,
Spoken by mortal coil.

It was, without a doubt, the *O'Barr Manuscript*. If he could be positive about what Karac would do, he would have burned it to ash right then and there, then flushed the blackened bits of it down the toilet. And despite his uncertainty, that was very nearly what he did.

But instead, he eased back in his leather chair, steepled his fingers and regarded the figure of Karac over them and the edges of his reading glasses. The pose would be purely for effect, but he felt confident Karac wouldn't be looking at how he was selling, but *what* he was selling.

"First, may I ask where you got this?"

"Nope."

"What do you think this is?"

Karac's eyes flicked away for a moment, then returned. "The *O'Barr*."

Alec nodded. "And why do you want it translated?"

"Because somebody else does, too."

Again the nod. An idea formed in Alec's mind. Karac was a sharp man, and although he didn't know who else wanted the translation, he felt certain whoever they were happened to be on the opposite side of whichever one Karac was on. And regardless of what the man had done in the name of being a Finder, Karac was not a completely corrupt soul.

Alec could still see the light of the man's better angels flashing behind his eyes as he spoke.

"And what makes you think I'll give you the accurate translation?"

At this, Karac's eyes lowered and did not come back up. "Because you know I trust you."

The smile at Alec's lips was wan, but it was welcome by its host nonetheless. "Can you read the list?"

Karac nodded. "But I'd still like a complete translation."

Alec open the drawer to his left open, two fingers catching in the pulls. He pulled out the pad of church stationary with a calm he didn't feel, careful not to upset the gun in its space there. The glossy black Mont Blanc he'd had since graduating seminary was taken in hand, and on the pad, the list was written, as was the pair of verses. When he was done, he capped the pen and freed the page from its pad before pushing it across the desk to Karac. The *O'Barr Manuscript* was left where it was. Let Karac stow it away in whatever fashion he saw as best.

The Mont Blanc swept at the paper, leaving behind as close a translation in English as Alec could manage. The Atbash Cipher was, after all, known for being difficult to the English manner.

"May I ask how you came about possessing this?" Alec asked, still leaving ink on paper while Karac paced around the office, touching the grain of bookshelves or staring at the spines of the volumes there.

"Nope," Karac responded, not bothering at all to look up at his host. His attention seemed to be fixed on an aged volume bound in cracked but still complete black leather. The book's gold lettering at the top third of the spine had long since been worn away; The Bible, a Latin translation. The copy Alec's mother had kept in her house until he'd received his assignment to go to Benjamin. It was her best present to him. In exchange, he'd managed to find a similar volume and sent it to her.

Now Karac looked at Alec. "May I?" Alec waved at the query. Karac probably wasn't going to wait for a response, anyway.

"I was only being polite," Alec said as the other man opened up the hefty tome and turned to the passages marked with the colored ribbons of its markers. "I'm actually insisting in my mannerly way."

Alec gave Karac a full five seconds. He stopped his writing and set down the Mont Blanc. At this, Karac's eyes came up.

"A rival," was all he said.

"Still living?"

Karac returned to his reading. "So far as you know."

It was typical Karac. Alec leaned back in his chair, a full half of the translation left unfinished. While he knew that Karac knew what the *O'Barr Manuscript* was, and what legend belonged to it, and how many versions of the truth, Alec very much doubted he fully comprehended exactly what was in the list, much less would have been able to figure out the two verses, which were mercifully vague.

Karac stared at the older man for several long moments over the cracked uppermost edge of the Bible's cover. "Look, I'm just here for the translation."

"And thus far," Alec said. "I've yet to hear what's in it for me."

The expression on Karac's face was genuine. To have provoke actual shock on the man's face was a moment Alec would come to savor. It made for a difficult time not to smile.

"That's not very priestly of you."

Alec shrugged. "How about my eternal gratitude?"

Karac's fingers closed the Bible carefully, and returned it to its place of honor on the shelf next to some of the oldest texts Alec could find regarding matters of the soul and the Catholic church and its books of missals and manuals of prayers. "How about the truth?"

Alec eased up to the edge of his desk and placed the tips of his fingers atop his pad, still holding the partial translation, and the other pinning the parchment firmly to the desktop. Karac eyed the fingers pressing into the *O'Barr* and leveled his eyes into Alec's.

"Please get your fingers off that."

Now Alec grinned. "No."

A chuckle from Karac. "Listen *Padre*, what you're doing is leaving microscopic deposits of oil behind on that manuscript which is worth more than you'd care to admit while you're sitting behind that desk of yours."

"I know that. And you'll do what about it, precisely? Please tell me, I'd very much like to know. Perhaps rip my heart out of my chest or pluck my eyes out? I understand that's what Finders have been known to do in the name of their pay?"

"I understand you have no respect for me, but try to understand the position I'm in. My intention is not to devalue that paper, or to cause harm to someone."

Alec held his eyes.

"Do you mean that you wish to harm me by course of action?" Karac asked, genuine concern thickening his words.

Alec's fingers lifted away from the *O'Barr*, but his gaze remained fixed on Karac. "Sit down."

The Finder did as he was told.

"Understand this, Karac. I can give you a partial translation. I can even mess it up, and no one knows for sure what would happen if I were to do that, do they?"

The Finder had to admit that was not a single person who could.

"Then tell me where you got this. It's nothing unreasonable."

"I stole it."

"Well, imagine my surprise."

"No, it's not like that. I have to return it."

"Why? Who did you steal it from?"

"A witch."

"A bit more specific, please."

"Rebecca Scott."

The name hung in the air between them. Karac was unable to continue Alec's stare.

"Who?" Asked Alec.

Karac gaped at the man. "Rebecca Scott. Haven't you heard of her?"

Alec shook his head. "Any reason why I should?"

"She the author of some of the most authoritative texts regarding the phenomenon of Wicca and witchcraft in the contemporary belief system of urban America."

"Oh."

Karac made an effort of composure. "It's just important that I get it back to her."

"Before she knows it's missing."

"Right."

"Then I should stop talking and get writing."

"It would help, yes."

Alec made a few more translated words before stopping again and looking up and the exasperated face of Karac, who no doubt had recently come to the understanding of himself that it would be a good idea to become well-versed in the Atbash.

"But I thought you didn't put much stock into those who wielded their faith for the sake of power?"

"I don't."

"Why the cause for concern for this Rebecca character, then?"

"Well, because while I don't share her belief, I don't think she was one who came into her faith looking for power. But once she found it…"

Alec nodded. "I understand."

"There's nothing scarier to me than someone who used to be a good person," Karac said.

Alec regarded the man who had by now slumped into the high-backed black leather chair opposite him. The Finder who had made his entrance like a bird of prey (or more likely, that of carrion) now sat there, staring at his pack he held in his lap, letting his fingers trace the lines of stitching he found there, over and over.

Alec asked softly, "Who are you getting this for?"

The Finder didn't look up. "Gavin and Simone Fox."

Alec sighed at the names. After a moment, he rubbed his eyes and returned the pen to his hand.

"Well, then. We shouldn't keep them waiting, should we?"

CHAPTER TWENTY

Beware beautiful lost angels, as true angels always know the way home.

Unknown

The witch was clearly out of her everloving tree.

Diana Adair sat across from her in the dirt of the hills overlooking the basin of Hollywood. It was a place Diana had seen numerous times as she drove across the boulevards but never paid much attention to. As Rebecca described it, as a kind of 'Neutral zone,' it seemed pretty attractive; free from all sorts of outside irritants such as random thoughts or energies that just didn't do one's body and mind any sort of good at all. And, since the topic of meditation had come up, Rebecca thought this a better place than any to start for the curious.

And having sat in her own version of the lotus position for what she guessed was for the better part of twenty minutes and all she had to show for it were a pair of legs that had long since given up the warnings of going to sleep on her and were currently totally useless.

It wasn't for Rebecca's lack of trying, or her obvious gift for being able to calm and instruct people how to allow themselves to do a given thing, it was just that Diana didn't feel it. It just wasn't there.

Worse still, she had wanted it to be. Just lurking beneath the surface of whatever that Rebecca knew how to uncover better than she did.

"Let yourself relax. Allow it to happen," Rebecca had said at the start. "Don't force it. The more you force it, the further away it'll get."

But the emptying of her mind and the balancing of her spirit or whatever you wanted to call it simply wasn't happening, and she tried to force it, to make it come over her. And, true to form, it got further and further from her, until mediation was well removed from her ability to grasp it.

At last, she screwed her courage up enough to let one eye open. It was only then that she realized that she had been concentrating so hard she'd been squeezing her eyes shut.

Across from her sat Rebecca, grinning at her, eyes open.

"What?" Diana asked, brow furrowing as she began to understand the feeling she had was that of someone caught exposed and unarmed.

"Nothing, I've just been waiting for you."

"Waiting for me to what?"

"See if it was safe to open your eyes."

"Oh." Then, "Is it?"

The grin widened. "Of course. I've said before, you can't make it happen."

"Wish I could. Maybe then I'd be able to not let my legs fall asleep so damn easily."

"That comes with practice. And if your body just doesn't cooperate, go with another position. You can lay down, sit up in whichever way suits you best. The thing about meditation is to let it flow like water, not trying to restrict it in a kind of discipline. It doesn't work like that. It's not a pupil; You can't expect it to act like one."

"I'm afraid I'll fall asleep if I lay down," smiled Diana.

"So you fall asleep. That's what you're body needs. And if by disconnecting through meditation is the only way your body can make you shut up long enough for it to talk to you, it'll show you what you need. Which is better than running yourself down until your body just gets pissed and shuts down on you."

"Has that ever happened to you?"

"What, the shut down? Yeah, pretty much. It's just that I'm an ambitious person, and because of that, I'd learned bad habits like how to shut out signals your body's giving you, like 'Sleep.'"

"What did you do?"

"You mean after I was hospitalized with exhaustion? I wised right up. It's amazing what can motivate you when you wake up in the hospital with tubes sticking out of you and your mom and dad standing over you wringing their hands."

The wind picked up just enough to toss Diana's hair about her face. She closed her eyes and let it wash around her. "Yeah, my dad would've kicked my ass. But in a nice way."

"Pretty much what my parents did. Then the doctor came in after they'd left and told me that unless I could pull myself together and realize I wasn't immortal and that I wasn't unstoppable, I was going to end up dead before long, which really wasn't a goal of mine."

"But can't you use magick to keep yourself going?" It was delivered with a lopsided sense of tone, but Rebecca's eyes darkened for just a moment.

"Yep, you can. The problem is, it ends up making you its bitch and sending you to the hospital."

"Sorry."

A shrug from the witch. It was over, forgotten. The meditative Rebecca Scott was back. "No worries. See, magick doesn't work like that. If you don't treat both you and it with a huge amount of respect, it'll take over your life and start effecting your judgment and health. It's like eating nothing but potato chips for every meal of the day. It rots you out, mentally, and physically. It makes you soul-sick."

"I think I understand. Kind of like carrying anger around."

Rebecca nodded. "Yeah, in it's way. But if you're referring to yourself, that's something a little different."

"Primal, like you said."

"Uh-huh."

"Something to be afraid of, you think?"

"What, anger? Definitely. The primal side? Yes, if you don't know what it is and what good it can do."

Diana managed to will her legs out from under her and pushed her hand palm flat against the gravel to get a push up to her now tingling feet.

"And what good can it do?"

"When it's controlled, it can allow your senses to be much sharper than the rest of us."

"You mean like smell and taste?"

"Sometimes, but those are literal advantages. If you were relying on those senses to maintain your well-being, you would be noticing those advances over others. But that would be more present in animals like dogs and the like. As a human, an animal – albeit an advanced one, you represent different needs, like the need to trust and such."

A snort from Diana. "Yeah, I'm real good at that."

"The man you had the affair with?"

"Yup."

"Didn't you know what was going to happen? Did his final reaction come as that big a surprise?"

"I acted like it was."

"See?"

"Not really. I thought I was just being cynical."

"You were, but there's more to it."

"Like how?"

"What did your instinct tell you about him?"

Diana's eyes trained to the ground, the laces of her shoes.

"Diana?"

"That it wouldn't work and that it was the dumbest thing I could do."

"And what part of you pushed that aside?"

Her eyes came back up to meet Rebecca's "What?"

"I said, 'What part of you pushed that aside?'"

"I heard what you said."

"Then why don't you answer the question?"

"I don't understand it! Tell me what you mean by it."

At some point during the exchange, Rebecca had found her footing and while Diana could not remember seeing her get up and move, was now inches away from her face. "Don't think," Rebecca said, unblinking. "Just answer the question; what part of you pushed it away, Diana?"

Diana held the other woman's eyes for several heartbeats until, "My rational side."

"Your what?"

"My civilized side." It was barely a whisper.

"And you shouted down your instincts."

"Yes."

"Why?"

"Because I couldn't listen to it anymore."

"Listen to what anymore?"

Diana muttered something throwaway, couldn't hear her own voice anymore anyway. Her chin was suddenly in the witch's hand and those points of light within Rebecca's head burned at her. "Again, " Rebecca said. "Say it again so we both can hear it." Her voice eased and her eyes softened just a bit. "What couldn't you listen to anymore, Diana?"

"The animal," she said in a husky breeze. She was dimly aware of her cheek being wet and a clink in her throat. "I couldn't listen to it anymore, I had to shout it down."

"And what happened?" There was no cruelty in Rebecca's query.

"I made a mistake. A big one."

"Do you understand why, exactly?"

"Yes."

"Tell me."

Now Diana brought her eyes up to bear on Rebecca's. "You know why."

A tilt from Rebecca's head was her only reply.

"Because I didn't listen to my instinct," Diana said. "Because I didn't listen to the animal."

Tears then, hard sobs aching from her chest and burning into the soft tissue of her throat. Rebecca's arms were around her and she said no words, just held her until the sobs ceased wracking Diana's body.

After a few quiet moments, Diana was able to burst away from the embrace and circle Rebecca. "You bitch! Why'd you do that to me? Why'd you cut me down like that just to make me cry like that?"

"Because I had to. *You* had to."

Diana noticed that despite her rage, it did not give Rebecca cause to step back or raise her hands in a placating gesture. "Had to what, have a nervous breakdown?"

"When was the last time you cried?"

"What? I don't know!"

"Sure you do. When?"

"I don't know! Maybe when I was ten."

"Long time ago."

"So what?"

"Even animals cry, Diana. Some of them bay at night, others seek solitude. Some mate for life and become hermits if their mates die. Young animals cry out for food, for the comfort of their mother. It's the way to get it out of your system."

"Get what out of my system?"

"The part of the animal that knows it's better than it is."

Diana sat down in the dirt. Her hands still trembled, but the click in her throat was gone. "So what do I do now?"

"The only thing you can do. You can't be rid of the animal, so you have to learn how to live with it."

"You mean give in to it and just accept it as part of 'Who I am?'"

"No," Rebecca smiled. "I mean be able to control it."

Diana nodded, and eased back into her pose of legs crossed and back straight. Her eyes shut, and this time she allowed herself to not fear the blackness, but to find in it a balance, a blessed quiet.

"Better," Rebecca said, and the lesson continued.

CHAPTER TWENTY-ONE

Lucifer has no need of telling the story himself. The ones others come up with for him are much more effective, even if they are mistaken, and he knows this.

Simone Perfect, from the foreward of Fox and Lucas'
MAGICK AND RELIGION

By the time Karac pulled the Tucker Torpedo against the curb in front of Fox Manor, the early evening was already turning the sky from a deep blue to the dark bruise that comes just before the darkness.

Even with traffic being with him, it would have been a three and half hour trip. As it happened, his detour to the Copy Palace to run off a few copies of the *O'Barr Manuscript* before returning the original to its rightful sitting place in the home of someone who might very well not be able to turn himself into something unseemly, it had been nearly half an hour past that. There was a theory amongst some, and Finders particularly, that witches with high powers seemed to fall into the habit of hanging out with people less intelligent than they themselves were, sort of like Tolkien's Gandalf, in Karac's humble opinion.

But magick did exist, a part of Karac argued. It's only who one's perception of it that colors it, and whether Rebecca Scott was a complete charlatan was academic, at best. The fact remained that Scott made a habit of either being a loner, or working the lecture circuit with the likes of the Foxes, who like it or not, were certainly no fools. Her books also sang the praises of exactly where this woman was coming from, and while Karac may not have publicly bought in to Rebecca's public persona, he was reasonably sure that even if it turned out that she *couldn't* turn him or others into toads and the like, she could still do considerable damage some other way that had yet to reveal itself to him.

He saw a shape at the porch of the Manor, backlit by the light pouring through the now open front door. Karac could tell by the cut of the figure for it to be Simone, standing with one hip cocked against the porch wall, arms crossed over her chest. Another figure, obviously Gavin, followed soon after, standing still in the doorway. By the way Simone's torso moved, Karac figured for them to be having a conversation.

As he pulled the bag to his shoulder and exited the suicide door of the Tucker, he smiled. He was certain that the translation Alec provided was more than spot-on. It could have come with footnotes, had Karac asked nicely enough.

But now it was time to find out if his visit to either Alec's church or Rebecca's home hadn't all been a great waste of time, and at too great a risk.

No words of greeting were shared before he gained the door, just stillness around his hosts, the house, the leaves on the trees flanking the west and east sides of the house. Karac met their eyes as the pair became defined in the cool glow thrown by the porch light over Simone's left shoulder. He stopped before them, each of them waiting for the other to speak. When no one could come up with anything, because they knew what news Karac carried, the Finder took it upon himself:

"Well, you gonna let me in, or are we waiting for Johnny Depp to pull up and let this get *really* weird?"

Simone pushed away from the wall and walked into the Manor, Gavin stepping aside for Karac to go next, before following suit himself.

The snap and hiss of the fireplace burning genuine wood against the growing chill in the California hills came first to him, then the homey smells of the smoke and the fire itself. These things seemed too far out of place in a home like Fox Manor, which while had indeed actually been a home, simply did not feel that way to a man like Karac. It was too steeped in its own mythology to have more footsteps running through it, which seemed a shame, in a way. Those banisters would look better with kids sliding down them, and the laughter would ease away the gloom hanging about like it owned the place. But looking at Gavin Fox, perhaps it did have a home here, after all. The last of a breed that garnered more fear and respect than Karac could think of. It was a kind of sacred bloodline, the Fox line was. In a way, it was good that it would end here with Gavin in the care of someone like Simone, the only person Karac sensed he could trust inherently, if only because he was certain she didn't trust him as far as she could throw this house.

What did you find? Was the priest of any help?" Asked Gavin.

Karac crouched in the middle of the living room floor, shrugging off his bag. Opening it, he produced the folded piece of paper and handed it to Gavin. "I don't know how much help it'll be, but he was able to translate the entire thing."

Simone looked at the paper over Gavin's shoulder as he unfolded it. "Even the Aramaic?"

"He didn't seem to even slow down in his writing."

Seemingly finished, Gavin nodded and held the paper out to Simone, who accepted it. "Did he ask what this was about?"

Karac smiled. "We have an understanding, he and I do."

Gavin grunted something before moving off into the kitchen. "Want some tea or something?"

"If you're making some, please. But don't go to any bother on my account."

Simone's eyes raised from the paper to Karac. "Did you read this?"

"Yup."

"And what did you make of it?"

"Made more sense to me when it was in Aramaic and Atbash."

"You really have no opinion?"

"To be honest with you Simone, it looks to me a lot like something people shouldn't screw with. Outside of that, I'm in the dark."

Simone waited until Gavin returned from the kitchen. "What do you think?"

"It's an incantation," Gavin said. "And I don't like a single word of it."

"Why's that?" Asked Karac.

"Because it's phrased in a way that makes me believe that the person who wrote it knew what they were talking about."

"Well, doesn't it make some kind of sense that it was written by someone sane?"

"No," Simone answered. "Because if it were written by a madman, only people who didn't understand what they were looking at would take it seriously. In this case..."

"Those in the know would... know." Karac finished.

"And," added Gavin. "The fact that it was written in the Atbash means to me that it was important to write down word for word that it worked in the face of numerous failures, and that it was not meant to be read by just anyone."

Simone rubbed at her eyes with the balls of her fists. "Remind me of how O'Barr died?"

"He committed suicide," Karac answered.

"How?"

"I have no idea."

"I think the only record considered anywhere near genuine just says that he took his own life," said Gavin, now opening an amber prescription bottle.

Karac asked, "You okay?"

"Migraines. This is just the latest attempt at stemming them." Gavin returned to the kitchen and the sound of the whistling kettle, prompting Karac to rise and follow.

"Need any help?"

"Nah, the tea is pretty domesticated, even for Chinese Gunpowder."

"Don't swallow that pill with tea," Simone reminded from the living room. "The bottle says to swallow it with a full glass of water."

"Yes, mother."

Karac led the way back into the living room, where Simone now sat on the couch, the paper spread before her on the knurled walnut face of the coffee table that was most likely older than the three of them combined. He took his seat in the leather recliner and accepted a mugful of tea from the passing Gavin. While Karac had half-expected a fairly chintzy teacup, he found an odd comfort zone in being handed a mug instead of a teacup that was older than the coffee table. Knowing Gavin, it was probably done for just those ends. Here was some discussion whether as to ask Rebecca Scott to join the discussion, but as Karac was readying his excuses to leave, it was discovered that she was not at home, and an attempt at her cell phone gave the same results.

"Probably meditating," Simone figured after leaving her respective messages.

Karac nodded, all the better with it. "So what do we do now?"

Gavin didn't bother looking up from the piece of paper Simone now handed to him. "'We?' Your involvement with this ends here."

"Well okay, but there is your side of the bargain."

Now Gavin's storm colored eyes flicked up over the page. "Karac, right now I have something in my hands that has words on it that I don't dare speak aloud, just to be on the safe side. My concentration is elsewhere."

Karac rose, shouldered the bag. "Right. I'll be sure to let you know when Solomon goes and blows his own head off. Shouldn't be too long of a wait."

"Karac."

The Finder spun on his host. "What? You want pictures? Someone in forensics owes me one big time, but I'm not sure I can guarantee anything."

"If we don't figure out what our friend is up to out there, it won't matter what Solomon's condition is."

"It will to Solomon."

"You're not seeing the bigger picture here."

"Outside of photographs, would you accept being invited to the autopsy? I *know* I can swing that."

"Karac!"

A blur and Simone was between them, taking turn locking eyes with each of them as she spoke; "Shut up, the two of you. Dammit, you sound like my mother and my aunts, arguing about how to cook Thanksgiving dinner as it burns. Karac, let's get Solomon over here, we can at least begin some kind of counseling for him, even if we can't find him a cure, which just for the record doesn't exist."

"Yet," said Karac.

Simone wet her index finger and made a tally mark in the air. "Point goes to Karac for being the optimistic Finder." Now she turned to Gavin. "And yes Gavin, the world will surely fall apart should we not decipher this little poem, but we made Karac a deal, and I'm not going to go back on it. If we couldn't have managed it, we shouldn't have promised it."

While Gavin towered over her frame, and was obviously easygoing with shutting people down, he help his hands palms facing her and nodded.

A glance from Simone to Karac. "You going to put your two cents in with a brainstorming session?"

"I'm not sure what help I'd be," admitted Karac.

"Doesn't matter. Another brain is another brain. We're all in the same world. Besides that, look at it this way; the more help you give us, the more indebted we'll be."

Karac spared a look at Gavin, who did not raise his eyes from the paper he now resumed his interest in. He nodded.

"Yeah okay, I'm in."

Karac sat in stony silence at the dining room table that Gavin and Simone had suggested as their brainstorming place. They never, Simone told him, used the same place twice in a row, and their library was irrelevant, because in light of their situation, there was no starting point in them.

They'd started hours ago. Long enough for dawn to be approaching and Karac's eyes to be aching for rest. The only forward progress they'd made was that O'Barr's suicide probably had something to do with the incantation rather than any indication of insanity, as the list as well as the cipher used would indicate thought with a purpose, not the erratic ramblings of the truly insane, and that the poem was most likely stemmed from several attempts at an incantation that hadn't worked, although the inspiration that supplied the words remained questionable.

Karac hadn't been aware of his dropping off until Gavin spoke up.

"Is it just me, or is it just too damn obvious that this is an incantation to open the gate to hell?"

Simone groaned. "Please, honey."

Gavin straightened, "No, I'm serious. What if some loser like O'Barr actually came up with a way to do it?"

"If he came up with a way to do that, he wouldn't be a loser."

"No," said Karac. "He'd still be a loser, just one smart enough to figure out something that's been a cliché since forever."

"But would it be a cliché for someone mad enough to try it?"

Karac shook his head. "I don't get it."

"What he means," Simone put in. "Is that every clichéd horror movie or story has someone threatening to open the gateway to hell itself, so that it can spill over into our world."

Karac yawned behind a fist. "Sounds pretty crazy to me, yeah."

"It is," answered Gavin. "Which is precisely why no one with a brain in his, her, or its head would try it. Anyone intelligent enough to figure out a way to let hell run roughshod over Earth would be smart enough to realize that it would be his own unmaking, as well. Nothing would be gained. And the only explanation given to us is that they would do it because they are insane."

"Do you believe the truly insane would be completely incapable of doing something like this?"

"This organized, this intentional, yes. The way the brain works would require a patience only the sane, in my opinion, would be able to possess."

"I agree," Simone said.

"So it's what," Karac asked of no one in particular. "Someone with a grudge who wants to go postal in a whole new way?"

Gavin shook his head and rubbed at his eyes. "That's where the contradiction comes in. Only the insane would try it."

"And I have no better suggestions," replied Karac.

"I do," said Simone, rising from the table. "Sleep. A nice session of it. This staying up late is doing none of us any good."

The men agreed, rising. After Karac had pushed in his chair, he asked when they were to expect to work on Solomon's problem. Gavin and Simone exchanged a glance that Karac was not at all sure he liked before Gavin replied that they would call him when they woke up in a few hours, and would plan their course of action then. Karac grumbled, but accepted it given the circumstances.

They parted ways, the front door to the Manor closing before Karac had gained his car. He rolled the windows down to let in the chill that would keep him awake before he drove home in silence, not watching anything but the horizon.

CHAPTER TWENTY-TWO

It is a common misconception that the devil is ugly or somehow misshapen. That may be how some wish to see him, but it is folly, as it is clear he was indeed the most beautiful angel of them all.

Simone Perfect, from an unauthorized recording of a
lecture given at an unidentified university

Sleep had not come easy the night before for Gavin Fox considering the ache behind his eyes and their weighty lids. From the moment his head touched the pillow, the thoughts came, as they usually did; crashing into one another before dissolving in the face of the much-needed sleep, only to find themselves to be reconstituted as mutated logic and borderline paranoia.

Simone, on the other hand, was the absolute vision of restful sleep, curling onto her side with her face to his side of the bed. Taunting him, no doubt, in her own sweet way. She knew all too well that when his mind raced at bedtime, she was the one actually able to find solace at the pillow.

With the translation now in the library on the grounds that it felt safest there, Gavin stared at the ceiling. He'd sooner have a loaded gun in the house than that single piece of table paper. Worse, both Karac and Simone knew it.

He couldn't remember the last time he'd seen words that he wouldn't speak aloud. Years, possibly. The memory of such an event was foggy, prompting to figure that if it had been such an important thing, he would have remembered it. He decided not to push the issue and just let it go. He was happy to think it hadn't actually happened.

The books in the library or elsewhere were going to be of no further help. He thought of this not as a fatalist, but as a realist with more than his share of experience in this given field. The *O'Barr Manuscript* was simply not a subject written much on because what more was there to write, outside of the definitive answer as to what was actually hidden in its words.

Gavin wasn't sure as to what the priest Karac confided in had thought about the Atbash, but tried to keep it in the back of his mind because the priest was the x-factor along with whoever it was who was trying to open the door described in the invocation. Karac's priest may very well have made himself a target should the information regarding his assistance become known to the other party.

But, Gavin tried to reason, that wasn't his concern.

He was going to have to contact Lucas.

That, it seemed, was the reason his was not going to find much rest. He knew eventually his body would assume control and knock him out whether he liked it or not, but the thought of reestablishing contact with Lucas was something that just didn't lend itself to ease of mind.

People change, friendships take on different paths. That he could accept. But it was different with someone like Lucas Brady who lived with his abilities only as gifts and actually took a kind of joy Gavin himself could only approach when it came to the topic of debates on matters of spirituality, magick, and the perception of faith.

Worse, Lucas was better at expressing it than he was, both on the page and off.

They didn't have to agree on every topic. They'd had discussions and arguments and fights – one of them nearly coming to blows toward the end of their working relationship regarding the disposition of given sets of spirits and their perception of physical reality – this was one thing that they understood. They both thrived on it, made them better writers and better thinkers.

Dissention came when Lucas became even further outspoken regarding the elements of evil, and how disseminating same was just as bad as being the embodiment of it and that led Lucas down a road Gavin didn't care to follow. Things became black or white for Lucas rather than the shades of grey they both agreed upon when they met in their freshmen year at the University of Washington.

It seemed to Gavin that in the years to follow, his friend's tolerance threshold for the ignorant went from moderate to absolute zero over the course of maybe what came to a cumulative total of one year. There was no great catalyst for this, just the elements of thoughts and years going by and the experience they brought with them that saw his friend's change.

And Gavin understood now, in between the bedsheets and the ambience of Simone's metered breathing that the main reason for their spilt was because Gavin himself simply wouldn't accept it.

His feet swung free of the sheets and mattress at 9:05. He couldn't remember when he'd slept as late as this. Simone had been getting up before him as of late, but his usual hour was around six in the morning. Six-thirty at the latest. Even still, he felt as if he'd just fallen asleep, and realized that he hadn't even checked the time before he'd fallen asleep simply because he was too tired.

He'd ask Simone. She would have checked.

His feet shod in the soft suede moccasin slippers he'd purchased on their last vacation to Laguna Beach, Gavin padded his way downstairs and made his way to the writing desk in the hall to retrieve his old, battered address book. The leather that had once covered its entire face was now mostly gone, flaked away and folding and peeling away at the edges. Still, when he pressed it to his nose in the subconscious habit he'd carried since he was a boy and was awarded the book as a birthday present from his grandpa, the leather retained all the scent and sense memory of itself as if it was the first day he got it.

He made a pot of strong coffee and sat on the couch, the address now before him on the coffee table and open to the page that featured in faded blue ballpoint pen ink:

Lucas Brady
2642 Auxillary St.
Chevron, WA 98119

The phone number was largely unreadable due to what appeared to be a sizable coffee stain. It hardly mattered, Gavin had memorized it over a decade ago.

Newer ink, red rollerpoint had crossed this out, and in hastily written pencil strokes, the following had been noted down:

Lucas Brady (Marie)
1702 Starfall Ln.
Oswald, AZ 86336
(928) 555-6749

Arizona was a couple hours ahead, Gavin thought. But he was pretty sure Lucas was up one way or another, whether just because he was like Gavin and an early riser, but also because of his care for his mother, Marie following the stroke that had led to Lucas' decision to move to her home in Arizona a few years before.

But even still, he waited until he'd poured his first cup of coffee of the day and had it set firmly on the grey stoneware coaster in front of him before he punched in the number. As he listened to the line click over and start to ring on the other end, he was slightly curious as to whether Simone would be cross with him upon finding that he'd called Brady without her. This thought was pushed away as a familiar voice picked up the line on the fourth ring.

Gavin couldn't help but smile a bit at the sound. "Lucas?"

"Yes." A pause. *"Gavin?"*

The smile grew. This was the real test. Either he would get hung up on following a creative string of epithets and oaths, or they might actually speak civilly. "Yeah, Lucas. It's me."

The pause returned. "What's happened to Simone? Is she okay?"

"Yeah Lucas, she's fine. Why do you ask?"

He could almost hear the shrug through the phone. "I just always figured that after our last conversation that the only time I'd hear from you is if something happened to Simone."

"No, no. She's fine. As a matter of fact, it could be that she's the reason I'm calling."

"Really?"

"Yeah, kind of a long story."

"I've got time."

"I'm sorry. I completely forgot my manners... how's Marie?"

"Mom passed away last year."

Gavin swore softly. "I'm sorry."

"No, it's okay. It was a really long battle. She's not suffering anymore."

"She was a good woman." Gavin swallowed something thick and sudden in his throat.

"I know it."

"Right. Of course."

"But why the call, Gavin?"

"Wait. How come you didn't call me?"

"When my Mom died? Well, I have to say you and I weren't exactly on speaking terms then."

"We're not supposed to be now, either."

"True. I'm sorry, Gavin. I didn't mean to not include you, but it's not like there was much family to lean on. I was just in my own little headspace and I wasn't the same person I was even then. By the time I thought about it, it had been months, and I felt bad enough. Then it was just too late."

"I understand," Gavin said. Brady's father had passed away shortly after he'd begun college, and neither side of the family had any close relatives to speak of.

"So what do I owe this auspicious occasion?" Brady asked.

"I was hoping you could help me with something."

"Okay. What's got you bothered?"

Gavin squeezed the bridge of his nose and squeezed his eyes shut. Brady was the right person to go to with this sort of thing, but after all this time, it just felt too odd.

"Have you had any feelings of serious foreboding lately?"

"No more so than usual. Why? Do you sense a great disturbance in the Force?"

"I'm not the only one."

"Simone, too?"

"And others. Like Rebecca Scott and apparently any number of the sensitive."

A sigh from Arizona. "I'm really out of touch with everything not inside these four walls. Sorry."

"No, it's okay. Are you not practicing at all anymore, then?"

"Not much. I'm researching a book that's outside of that realm, and after Mom died, I just focused on other things, I guess."

"Understandable." Gavin watched as a familiar shadow made its way down the stairs. In a moment, Simone finally made her appearance, dressed in the light blue kimono festooned with white cranes he so adored on her. "Should I go on, or stop here, then?"

"Nah, go ahead. Let's see what kind of memory I have for this kind of thing."

Gavin smiled at Simone as she sat on the couch beside him, folding her legs underneath herself and leaning against him to show her support. "Well, it has to do with the *O'Barr Manuscript*."

Now it was Brady's turn to swear. "That thing? What, is Calarco insisting his is the only legitimate copy around again?"

"Actually, his was stolen."

"When?"

"A few days ago."

"Huh. Okay, so what about the *Manuscript?*"

156

"It seems as we've cracked it."

"Really? How?"

"A Finder by the name of Karac supplied the aid of a priest who could decipher Atbash."

"So it *is* the Atbash Cypher."

"Yeah."

"Can this priest be trusted?"

"As far as a Finder can throw him."

"Okay, and the translation is ominous?"

"Well, that and the fact that there have been robberies of occult antiquities, namely books."

"What's the translation say? Wait, just give me the highlights."

"Well, something about opening the Gate of hell."

"Oh jeez, Gavin…"

"I'm serious!"

"*The O'Barr Manuscript*, in all it's mysterious glory has revealed itself to be a guide to something only the insane would embrace and never be able to find?"

"That's sort of where we're at, yes."

"What books have been stolen?"

Gavin named them, causing a long pause on the other end.

"I don't get it," Lucas said at last. "There's no reason for those books to be of significant value together."

"But do you feel they could be tied into *The O'Barr Manuscript?*"

"They're mentioned in it, sure. But honestly, the *gate of hell?*"

"I'm only able to go by what we have."

"And all the items listed are now stolen?"

"All but one, yes."

A sigh across the phone line. "How's the weather out there, Gavin?"

"Seriously, Luc."

"Okay, okay. Just trying to prolong the inevitable."

Gavin heard himself say, "Why don't Simone and I make a trip over to AZ and see if we can't find out more through picking your brain?"

"You two are both welcome, Gavin. I'm not much company, but I'd love to lower the drawbridge between us and see what's there."

"This may be the best way."

A chuckle from the other end. "Yes, I suppose it is. Whenever you're ready, Gavin."

Oswald was located several miles from Sedona, but Gavin was at a loss to actually find any road signs, instead going by the directions he'd written down during his conversation with Lucas and now related to him by Simone, the fine hairs at her temples swirling in the air conditioning in the rented Dodge Magnum in defense of the heat bearing down upon them. The CD was what had long since become a usual of their travels by car, a mix of Michael Buble. The desert stretching in every direction the eye cared to see played delicate counterpoint to the music.

The view of the Red Rocks and the surrounding area they saw whipping by on the sides of what he hoped was still the strip of 89A was punctuated by the stunning clarity of the huge azure sky overhead. It served to underline the unhesitating beauty of the natural the legendary rock formations. There was what Simone would later describe as a 'Beautiful stillness' to itself.

Simone hadn't said anything regarding direction for a couple songs now, so he had figured that all was well, her sense of direction, or what was occasionally referred to her as her 'Uncanny ability to read roadsigns' was considerably more acute than that of Gavin's.

Miles later, as the CD was coming to the midway point of it's ending track, 'Save the Last Dance for Me,' Simone spoke up and indicated a turn that he would have otherwise missed.

The stretch of paved road sent them to a kind of side community where the architecture of the houses bore proof of the affluent community despite the actual sparseness of the number of houses.

Most of the houses were of the expected Southwestern flavor with their red tile roofing and mock-adobe finishes and the like, and despite the street addresses were clearly marked, Gavin found he had no need of them or Simone's direction as to when to slow down; the home looked as if it had to have somewhere in the neighborhood of 2,800 square feet with no visible garage stalls. The exterior looked like half temple, half southwestern home and in spite of its grayish paint conveyed a sense of serenity that a man like Lucas Brady would certainly seek out, knowing it when he found it. Gavin found himself wondering whatever had happened to Marie's place once she passed away, only seeing an aspect of its west side in a picture Lucas had kept on his dresser in the dorm room they had shared the shot featuring a very young Lucas and his mother and father. Gavin seemed to remember the snapshot had been taken before the family had attended a church service.

Gavin pulled the car to the curb where the landscaping was free of the tall cacti and various other succulents dotting what constituted the front yard, which was punctuated by a stepped concrete walkway.

The couple groaned in tandem as they pulled themselves from the car, legs complaining. The ride from the airport had taken longer than either would have liked, but there had been a tacit agreement not to stop until they reached their destination.

"Well, " said Gavin, shielding his eyes from the glare of the sun with the edge of his hand. "We're here."

"And not a second too soon," replied Simone, already on the pavement walkway. "My bladder's no longer politely asking, and those cactus plants on the side of the road were looking mighty good for that last mile there."

Gavin followed. Moments later, he realized the figure of Lucas Brady stood in the threshold of the house, watching them approach. A small smile was at the man's lips. Careful not to look to happy to see them, or at least

Gavin, but not appearing as if to be on his guard now that they had arrived. It was then Gavin spied what appeared to be a Victorian-Era cane made of blown deep blue glass and twisted from the pointed tip to its curved handle. It was a piece of art in itself. Carried by anyone else, it would have looked patently ridiculous, but Lucas Brady who carried himself well enough to be a man who could be afforded the currency of eccentric whimsy without compromise.

The smile at Lucas' face as Gavin and Simone grew closer to him put Gavin at ease, although it was more than a little off-putting to see his friend growing as they say 'Distinguished' with graying at the temples. The pang of regret seeing the cane and not knowing of the injury at all, let alone when it had actually happened because of their estrangement, and the amount of weight Lucas rested on the glass cane indicated to Gavin that its presence was indeed due to necessity rather than some degree of vanity. Lucas had never been the sort to have to require such trappings of ego, even one as eccentric as his.

Simone's steps hurried and her arms spread wide open in anticipation of a hug as they made their way to the covered entryway where Lucas waited. They exchanged kisses on the cheek as Lucas gave the beginning of one of his trademark bearhugs, at which Simone made little time-out gestures.

"Don't squeeze too hard, otherwise I'll be cleaning up instead of catching up."

Lucas laughed the same easy, sincere chuckle he'd always had and eased off. "Sorry, didn't realize the ride had been that long. Go through the foyer and hang a left until you come to a door."

Simone nodded, now nearly trotting inside while shooting a thank-you over her shoulder.

And after five wordless years, the ex-collaborators and confidants looked at each Other across the years, one still smiling, the other just beginning to.

"You make an honest woman out of her yet?"

"Nope."

"Chicken."

"Critic."

A chuckle from one of them. It didn't matter which. It came easy, and that was what counted to both of them. Gavin held out his hand only to be rewarded with a jerk on his arm and a hug from Lucas.

"So the truce is still on?"

"Until you've stopped having a use for me, Lucas."

The other pulled away, nodding. "Someday, I'll have to actually see the interior of the Great Fox Manor. You know, it's not on any of those star maps I hear about."

"Am I a star?" Gavin felt his face screw up. "Wait, what? You've been there."

"I haven't."

"No, during the collaboration for our second book…"

"Which was not unlike our other collaborations, with either you traveling to my first home, or trading emails, faxes or phone calls."

Gavin shook his head. "Isn't that the weirdest thing? I never even thought about that."

Lucas nodded.

"Okay," said Gavin. "Okay, we'll have to change that."

"Deal. Now come on it and make yourself comfortable. It sounds to me as if there's a great deal to discuss."

Drinks were offered in what Lucas referred to as 'The Great Room,' quickly adding that it was merely the title afforded to it by the architect, not their host. The room itself was grand yet simple, sunken with antique cream couches and loveseats. A tall oak library took up a good section of the west wall, and was lined with what Gavin estimated to be about three hundred books, both hardcover and paperbound., including the editions co-written by Lucas and Gavin as well as the five volumes that were written solely by Lucas. A fireplace, now cold by a season, stood in the northeast corner, its mantle decorated with small fossils of indeterminate origin and species. Scattered about the room were tables of dark polished wood upon which sat various chessboards, many of which were for display only (this included the antique marble and glass set Gavin recognized from college), while others were already in play, which included a tri-dimensional board, and one Gavin thought was called Chess Empire, which allowed a total of three players taking up the colors of black, white, or red for a total of 28 playing pieces. It turned out that Lucas had continued his games by mail with many of his previous acquaintances the college Chess Club had afforded him before the days of email, which he revealed to Gavin as Simone returned to the room.

"I love email don't get me wrong," said Lucas. "It just takes the romance out of correspondence, especially to a game such as chess."

As the preliminaries continued, it was revealed that when Lucas first had the house built, he did it of the grand size that it was simply because he could, and now because of that folly, he had a house he had little need for outside of a few rooms.

"After Mom died, I just kind of reeled around my head for a couple years. I thought about staying at her house, but I just didn't have the stones to do that."

"It's not always the best thing to do," said Simone, sipping the iced tea provided them by their host.

"True. And I didn't feel at all comfortable moving back into my own house because after staying with Mom for a year and a half, it simply wasn't mine anymore because I wasn't the man I was when I had *that* one built." A look came over him. He was no longer in the room with them. "Isn't it strange how much we can invest in a single man-made thing?"

"One that we build around ourselves, no less," Gavin said. It was almost like they were back in their dorm room, 3:00 in the morning and following a thread of a discussion that was far removed from whatever topic that had started them talking in the first place instead of studying for midterms.

As if aware of the slip in time, Lucas blinked and smiled self-consciously. "Look at me, all melancholy."

"You always were the poetic one," noted Simone.

A wry smile from Gavin. "Gee, thanks."

Simone snuggled close. "Love ya, honey."

"I know you think you do."

"Oh, now you two're getting all mushy, and I just had the carpet cleaned." Lucas waved the scene away. "Is there something we can all talk about?"

"The occult?" Suggested Simone, eyes batting.

"See?" Said Gavin. "The Yin to my Yang."

"I'll let that one go," said Lucas, rising with the aid of his cane to the portable silver and crystal bar service a few feet away.

"What happened to your leg, Lucas?" Gavin had been meaning to ask ever since he'd spied the cane, but hadn't felt the conversation had had an opening up until now.

"Oh that. Well, it was during that spot where I was building a house I could never fill because I could, and I figured that in my infinite Celtic wisdom that I should very well start rock climbing. After all, there's no shortage of them here, and if I were to do it, I might as well have a vista to enjoy looking at."

"So you taught yourself." Gavin figured.

"I continue to be transparent." Lucas used a long pair of ice tongs to remove a few cubes from the gleaming bowl and let them drop in a carved crystal tumbler. Foregoing the other spirits already decanted, he handled a wooden presentation case with brass fittings and produced a bottle of whisky from it as he continued to speak. "So, I found myself going up a modest rock face called the Matheson. A good starting point, I figured; not too short, not too dangerous."

"And?" The prompting came from Simone.

"Well, about halfway to the top, I misjudged a step, a rock crumbled out from underneath me, and I turned a long fall with a messy end into a series of short ones, which involved the all but shattering of my knee only to be discovered a couple hours later by a Boy Scout Troop."

Simone covered her laughter with her palm, making apologetic gestures as Lucas returned to his seat.

"That must have been humbling," said Gavin, grinning happily.

"It was indeed. The Great and Powerful Lucas Brady laying there broken on the desert floor, expecting to be worthy of... I don't know, perhaps a medicine man to happen by because he had had a vision I'd be there and help me. Instead, I end up helping kids earn their merit badges. And by the way, it's a walking stick, not a cane." He took another swallow. "Please help me drink this. Consider the Dalmore 62 whiskey as an indulgence that will take the sting out of the hundred thousand dollar price tag."

161

Gavin nearly choked. He didn't need his friend to tell him that this was one more expense thrown during his bout with mournful insanity. But perhaps it was something he needed to do in order to carry on in some way, maybe the most poetic way he could come up with; sharing the spoils of temporary insanity with a friend he was now mending fences with. Gavin had heard a bit regarding vintage whiskeys from Calarco during of the occult collector's conversations with Simone. Calarco was a man who made a habit of looking down his nose at such things as whiskey, which he considered far too vulgar of a drink to be taken seriously, all the while paying close attention to market values of European whiskeys and the like. The only thing the man could tolerate outside of wine was brandy. Gavin couldn't remember much more about the Dalmore than an overly extravagant price tag and that something like only twelve bottles still peppered a few collections.

Gavin sipped at the amber liquid, enjoying the manner the warmth spread through him despite the fact the liquor tasted pretty much the same as any Crown Royal XR or Johnny Walker Blue Label he'd ever tried.

"What have you been up to?"

"I know that we can catch up," Lucas said, taking his seat while paying close attention to the highball balanced in his hand as set his body down. but you sounded more concerned about the *O'Barr* than I'd like to remember."

"The biggest problem," said Simone. "Is that whoever's going by it is serious. This is no college frat trying to tap into their dark sides."

Lucas hunched forward, stifling a laugh. "I'm sorry, but that was spot-on. Do you have it with you?"

Gavin answered in the negative and produced the folded sheet he'd placed in his breast pocket. With a flick of the wrist, he shook it to let it fall from its creases and handed it to Lucas, who accepted it and leaned back as he read.

After a time, Lucas' fingertips pressed to his temples for a moment, regarding the slip of paper left in his lap. He closed his eyes. "And the original this came from, you two personally saw it and consider it genuine?"

"Yes," Gavin and Simone both answered.

"Well, then, I guess we'd better talk."

Gavin tried to lower his eyebrow. "What's your take on this whole thing?"

"It's real, it's dangerous, and someone's been able to crack an ancient cipher that so far as I know, is pretty damn difficult. But there's something worse."

"What might that be?"

"Someone is indeed about to open the gates of hell, and worse, they know what they're doing and obviously smart. Have they killed anyone in order to get to any of the items on this list?"

"Not that we know of."

"Okay, good. Although that means they've probably performed enough sacrifices to provide sufficient power."

Simone leaned forward. "I believe this person has been able to teleport at least once."

At this, Lucas' face gave up any pretense of appearing anything but darkened. He handed the paper back to Gavin, who now regarded it as a live cobra. "Then I wish you luck."

After a few heartbeats, Gavin found his voice. "But we're going to need you for this. That's why we're here."

Lucas nodded. "I know that. But I'm just not up for something like this. I've been distancing myself from all this for years now. I don't have it in me anymore. Further, I don't *want* to have it in me. Frankly, I'm surprised that you're willing to get involved in this."

Gavin kept his voice steady. "Someone has to."

Lucas' pale green eyes stared at him. It was not accusation or rebuke. It was simply the way things were in his world, and his eyes now pinned Gavin to it.

"I have made my mark in the occult, and am happy with my body of work. I have nothing else left to say regarding the subject. If I had, I would have published yet *another* book on it. Now, I'd just as soon do what I wanted to do at the start; write what I want. I'm working on what I'm hoping will be an exhaustive biography of Pilate."

"How is that going?" Asked Simone.

Lucas' smile was self-conscious. "Not as well as I'd hoped. It's three years in the making now."

"Surely you can take a break for something of this magnitude."

Lucas regarded Simone through a gentle expression. "I could, yes. But I won't."

"Why?" Asked Gavin. "Are you actually afraid of something?"

"Actually, as a matter of fact, yes."

"And what might that be, exactly?"

"Gavin… Simone, I really didn't want to actually have to say the words, but since I'm obviously not going to get that kind of grace today, I will; I'm no longer strong enough to handle such a burden. Pithy wordplay regarding my philosophy of the occult won't bail me out of something like this. I'll give you my advice, but at this point in my life, I'm afraid I've become more of a liability rather than much of an asset to something like this." As they continued to stare at him and this confession, he continued; "I… just… *don't… have… it… in… me,*" in little more than a harsh whisper forced between clenched teeth.

Gavin eased back into the cushions of the couch and tried to smile at his old friend. It felt more like a wince, which truth be told, it really was. "I'm sorry you feel that way, Lucas. I really am. Not just because it puts me in a more difficult position than I felt I was when I first walked through that door of yours, but because I'm watching a great voice in the world growing quiet."

Lucas turned once more toward Simone. "And you said *I* was the poet?"

Simone shrugged, having no problem meeting Lucas' gaze. "He does have his moments."

"Is there anything I can do to help?" Lucas asked of neither in particular.

Gavin said, "Tell us what we can do?" It was half-question, half-demand.

"I've been called many things in my life because of the things I've said and written, Gavin. You know that. Because some of them have been extreme, I don't feel that my opinion is one you're going to want to hear."

"Try me."

Lucas' hand tightened at the curve of his glass cane as he leaned toward the couple with a conspiratorial air. "The only way to stop this is to actually prevent it. If whoever it is succeeds, then it'll already be too late. You cannot contain this.

"So must stop it before it starts. Anything less is going to mean failure on your part, as such people will never stop so long as they have breath.

"Gavin, you must kill whomever is responsible and destroy whatever components they have. *Destroy* them, not put them away in your library for safe keeping and reference. That's what allowed them to fall into the wrong hands in the first place, as if there *are* any right hands."

"But who would actually try to do this?" Interjected Simone. " It's insanity."

Lucas nodded. "It is, isn't it? Unlocking the gate to hell itself? Utterly mad." He eased his weight against the backrest of the chair. "But how many villains really consider themselves villains? And for that matter – "

"If the insane were to question what they were doing," Simone finished. "They would have enough aspect of sanity to identify an action as wrong."

The hands of Lucas Brady spread wide before him, a crooked smile on his face. After a moment, he piped up again, "Both of you identified a valid threat, but neither wanted to confront the solution."

"It's not that," Gavin said, bristling.

"Then what is it?"

"We were hoping for some kind of alternative to your rather permanent suggestion." Gavin felt the sudden presence of Simone's reassuring hand on his knee, but gave no outward sign of it. This was just Lucas Getting warmed up. It wasn't so far in the past that Lucas could actually be reasoned with, but he had intentionally and aggressively gone in this direction, one that Gavin could not follow, although was understanding enough when it came to the act of preserving his own life, or that of Simone's.

"Gavin, what were you planning to do? Lecture him to death? Simone's already stated that your man is able to teleport. In my book, that makes him a monster for even considering the costs."

"Doesn't mean he needs to be killed."

"What *does* it mean, Gavin?" Lucas' voice was gaining volume now. "Hmm? Rehabilitation? Please. Someone greedy for that kind of power needs to be put down."

Gavin just stared. Words, it seemed, had utterly failed him in the face of Lucas Brady. The worst possible time one's mind could pick in turning itself off. If you don't have it in you, Gavin, then perhaps you should get the hell out of the way for someone else who can."

"Like who?"

"I have no idea. This isn't my problem."

"The hell it isn't! It's everybody's problem."

"Then why don't you broadcast it? Send the three people who will actually believe you into such a state of panic, they can't be held responsible for their own actions?"

"Somebody has to do it."

"*Credat Iudaeus Apella, non ego.*"

"*Iventus stultorum magister,*" Gavin hissed from behind clenched teeth and rose, bringing Simone somewhat regretfully to her feet.

They moved to the car without further comment to each other or coming from their host, who remained seated as they took their leave. It was Simone who spoke first, but only after the had been in the sudden quiet of the now-traveling car for five minutes.

"Well, that went better than I'd hoped."

Gavin kept his eyes on the blacktop growing smaller in the distance.

"You going to actually speak to me, or are you going to keep trying to melt the road with your Kryptonian glare?"

His eyes snapped to her in an instant, but returned to the road. His hands held the wheel tighter in an attempt to keep his hands from shaking visibly.

"Is now really the time for one of your pithy comments?"

"Is now the time to blow the head off of the one person who might actually be able to *help* us?"

"Help? You call that help?" Gavin was laughing, but if called, could not come up with a single reason why.

Now it was Simone who turned her eyes to the road. "More than we have elsewhere."

"Are you saying he has a point?"

"A point. Yes. One. And frankly, I don't have a better one."

"What about justice?"

"What about it? What exactly are you going to do, honey? Handcuff the guy and take him to jail?"

Gavin just drove.

"There has to be a better way," he muttered at last.

"Okay," said Simone. "Fine. Come up with a better way."

"Have you actually considered who'd have to do it?" Gavin asked, making no effort to hide his doubt. "Would I? Would you?"

"I hadn't given it much thought," grumbled Simone.

"Well, I have. Not much of it, but enough." He turned to her, hoping her face would be turned to him, open and reassuring. Instead, he got the closed door of her profile. "I don't know if I could bring myself to do it, Simone. Could you?"

"They say everybody has the capacity to kill."

"Given the right circumstances, I suppose that would be right."

"And what might be the right circumstances?"

"I've got no idea."

"You mean to tell me that if someone were to threaten me, you wouldn't be able to dig down and find the place in yourself where you could kill them before they killed me?"

"That's not what I meant. Further, that's not the case."

"Then what is?"

"What do we know about this person? Is he really so far removed from reality that he can't see the mistake he's making?"

"So out of pity, you'd not kill him?"

"I don't think I could walk up behind somebody and slit their throat, no. I really don't. Could you?"

"With the fate of the whole world at stake?"

"The whole world doesn't give a shit."

"What?"

"Everybody says life is worth living and all that, but how many people are going through life happily addicted to painkillers or alcohol or drugs?"

"Oh good *Lord*, Gavin!"

"What?"

"Can you for a second open a drape in that head of yours and let in a sliver of the sun? Yes, the world has a population that maybe isn't the brightest, but wouldn't you want to do the right thing for the benefit of the greater good?"

Gavin grumbled something. If she'd had asked him to repeat it, he wouldn't have been able to.

"What about the aspect of hope?" Simone prodded.

"What about it?"

"For the benefit of hope, wouldn't nearly any sacrifice be worth it?"

"Not my life." He turned again to her. "Or yours."

"What was your plan, then?"

"Either get the last edition on the list and keep it – "

"Instantly turning the both of us into targets," she retorted.

"Or intercept him and keep him from saying the incantation long enough to steal or destroy whatever we can."

"Odd how you never cleared this little idea with me."

"I didn't think I had to. I wasn't aware you'd consider murder so quickly."

"I'm sorry, I'd rather kill this cobra rather than try to put it in some zoo."

"I'm not talking about a zoo or whatever."

Simone made the sound of a half-growl. "I'm using hyperbole to make a point. Why do you choose to take me literally at the worst possible point?

166

"Gav, Lucas had a point. What *did* you plan on doing with this guy once we catch him, whether he has the last component or not? He's willing to kill children in the name of his cause."

"Is this someone we can afford to leave alive?"

Gavin tried to answer, came up with nothing, and ended up just shaking his head more in frustration rather than trying to provide a real answer.

"With the lives already sacrificed," Simone said, her voice softening. "Can you honestly tell me you don't want to spend five minutes alone with this guy?" She waited for him to answer, but when he couldn't, she continued. "You're not a bad person, Gavin. You're one of the good guys. Just because you don't wear a halo doesn't mean you're not worthy of some grace. Listen, don't worry about lowering yourself to this monster's level. You're not. Just the fact your questioning it tells me that." Now she waited until he turned his eyes to her, if just for a moment before watching the road yet again. "This is a war, Gav. If you stop to think about whether this is murder or just something that has to happen, which is *not* your fault, in order to save not only your skin, but others as well, you're already dead."

There was nowhere else left to go, Gavin knew. He let her touch his cheek and silently reveled in her soft touch.

"And you're not dead," asked Simone. "Are you?"

"No," said Gavin, taking her hand and holding it in his own. "I'm as alive as you make me which, at this point, is startling."

CHAPTER TWENTY-THREE

We don't need God to tell us how we're supposed to act. We already know. We just don't bother.

Gavin Fox, THE SHADOW GALLERY

Because there is an awful certainty that comes over one's voice when faced with having to deal with something one is utterly at sea with, Karac keyed the Torpedo's engine to life not two minutes following the beginning of the conversation with Solomon Archer.

Karac's foot pressed the accelerator as far down as he dared along the twisting routes leading to the outskirts of the Valley. It was an unfamiliar stretch of blacktop for the Finder, and so he wasn't sure where the cops may be hiding, waiting for some poor soul in some kind of great rush to happen along. Still, he couldn't let Solomon waiting.

The man had called him at half-past eleven that night, full of apologies and a near monotone in his voice that was tempered only by his words stumbling over one another as he tried to find the words. Karac had tried to console the man and mellow him enough for him to know he wasn't being a bother, and to just slow down and talk. The ghosts, Solomon explained after he had calmed, had come to him again. Worse, they seemed to be prepared for a long stay.

Karac knew he could not turn back the clock, and saving whatever was left of Solomon Archer's mind or soul would not bring back the dead, but it could prevent Solomon's untimely demise and maybe staunch the withering inside his own soul.

With the address that Solomon had given him, he drove to just past the incorporated city and into the outskirts; it was neither a bad or good neighborhood the Archer duplex was located in. Just a bit of urban neutrality. The supernatural didn't care which sector of status it struck; it by and large seemed unconcerned with the trappings of wealth. It was equal in its opportunity to give someone a cross that most couldn't bear.

The door opened as Karac raised his fist to rap at its face. Solomon stood behind it and gave the Finder a curt nod.

"Thanks for coming, man."

Karac started to say he was welcome, but the words were stuck, and Solomon, who then stepped aside, didn't appear to need them anyway.

While Karac looked this way and that when he entered the living room, he had no idea why. Exactly was he expecting to find? He was unable to see anything outside the real world, and from visiting Solomon's eyes, he was all the grateful for it. The only life Karac could see would be that of Solomon and himself. Karac turned to him, who took his place at the end of the couch.

"Please sit," Solomon said.

"Where is there an opening? I thought you had a pretty full house."

A small smile looked uncomfortable on Solomon's face. "I do. But the chair over there has an opening." He gestured to a battered recliner that must have belonged to his family for quite a while before Solomon got it. "Some spirits seem to still have manners."

Karac sat, sinking into the worn cushions, eyes riveted on the man across from him.

"How many are there, Solomon?"

"Five. There were eight when I called you."

"My reputation precedes me."

"No, I don't think that's it. I think it's because they just figured out a better place to go."

"What are they doing?"

"Nothing. They're just sitting there looking at me like I'm supposed to help them."

"And they've said nothing."

"Right. None of them."

That was encouraging. Usually, when spirits chose to speak to someone like Solomon, they were either out to hurt the sensitive or had some message to pass on. When they were still, like these were, it might be because they were lost, or unwilling to move on, and were attracted to Solomon through means only spirits could understand, if some only barely. Such spirits did not seek to harm their hosts, although there had been cases where inadvertent damage had occurred. The biggest risk at this point was that other spirits were seeing more and more like them gather around Solomon and would gravitate towards him and stay for as long as they could manage. It was reasonable to expect enough spirits to come in to the house over the next few days to make the place look like Grand Central Station. Not as many souls were as enlightened and wise as their physical bodies liked to believe.

"Is there anything you can do?" Asked Solomon.

"No. I'm not sure there's anything that can be done. That's why I'm here."

Solomon nodded, far from placated. "Would an exorcist work?"

"Well, I don't know, but there would have to be research done by a priest, then the buck would get passed to the line to the Vatican, at any time during which it can get knocked down." He'd thought of approaching Father Copeman, but knew the man would simply shrug his way out of it. He understood that laypeople could find their way through the Roman Ritual, but no one he knew of, except possibly Simone could be considered strong enough to face off against the otherworldly forces, and he wasn't convinced that such a strong remedy was needed against what was by and large something non-threatening, except to Solomon's sanity.

The spiritual and physical could exist, Karac thought. But when one was stronger at least in representation than the other, understanding went out the window and took balance with it.

"What did they do when I walked in?" asked Karac.

"They just looked at you, then went back to looking at me, or just looking around like they were waiting for something."

"Are they threatening in any way?"

"No."

"Have you asked them to leave?"

"A couple times."

"And what happened?"

"Some of them left, but they were replaced with more. I asked again, but they just looked at me like they didn't understand."

"They may have no where else to go."

Solomon stared at him. Not in shock, just distance. "Is there a Heaven?"

"I'd like to think so."

"Then these are the ones who are going to hell and don't want to go."

"No, I don't think so. They may not want to go to either place, or are just too confused. They see others here, and figure misery loves company, so…"

Solomon nodded. "Lucky me."

"I know it's not much help, Solomon. I'll stay for as long as I can."

"I know you have a life, Karac. I'm sorry I called."

"No, don't worry about it."

"It's not fair of me to just keep you here."

"You're not. I'm offering."

"So what do we do, just sit here listening to each other breathe?"

"Does that sound like big fun to you?"

"Nope." "Then why do it?"

"Because I'm depressed?"

"Then let's watch some TV or listen to some music, show some signs of life."

"Will that make them go away?"

"It might make some leave, yeah."

"Will it cause more to come and stay?"

"I'm not sure."

"But I can't live like this, just staring at these things."

"No you can't. You have to have a life of your own."

"Even if they're wandering around me?"

"Think of them as your groupies."

"Please."

"Well, then don't think of them at all. If they have something to say, they'll say it. You can't come up with things for them to say." Karac turned to the room, addressing all. "You can't help those who don't know what to ask for."

"Well, that made two of them leave. Just don't make them angry, okay?"

"They're not here to be angry. They most likely are here just to try to make some sense."

"What if they get impatient and get pissed off at me for not knowing what to do?"

"Then get mad back. They don't have the monopoly here. This is your house, this is your life. If they see fit to just sit there and not do anything, then get pissed. Well, as host, you have every right to kick them out."

Solomon seemed to brighten, albeit carefully. "That got their attention."

"Maybe you all can co-exist peacefully. They act mannerly while they sort their baggage out, and you can accommodate them until they act like a bunch of ingrates."

"And I can tell them to leave."

"Provided the parameters are set and understood, sure. " Karac grinned, not bothering trying to hide it. The energy level in the room had just spiked in favor of Solomon, and as long as Solomon stayed with it and didn't get drunk with it, things would be fine. For a while.

It was only a matter of time until the spirits figured out who had the upper hand, even if they had no idea as to what to do with themselves. They could externalize it in physical manifestations. There would be no where safe for Solomon Archer to hide.

And from time to time, Karac wondered if that meant him, too.

Without a doubt, Simone knew the young, slightly disheveled man before her introduced to her only a handful of minutes ago, was not going to end well. There wasn't a thing on earth that could keep him from seeing the things he had been seeing, but there was that familiar voice inside her head that she could make a difference in the life of Solomon Archer, even if that meant just trying to stem the flow of his vision to somewhat lessen the impact. But Solomon had been suffering from this peculiar problem for longer than she would have liked; his life had fallen into given ruts, and worse still, a kind of belief system that somehow did not include him as a player, much less a key one.

"Do you see any ghosts here, Solomon?" She asked.

Solomon was seated across from her in a recliner he was unable to relax in. Gavin, arms folded across his chest, sat on the arm of the sofa that Simone was sitting in, and Karac was cross-legged at the floor a few feet from where Solomon was. She shot Gavin a brief look, whereupon he relaxed his arms as is suddenly remembering the basics of body language when performing a consultation. But he'd never been much for those, and so in the situations like these, she was defaulted into the position. "No."

"You don't seem very relieved."

"I'm not sure if it's a good thing."

"Why?"

"Well, I mean they're dead, and they won't set foot in here. It makes me more nervous than if they were around."

"Fair enough. Do you trust us?"

"I guess."

"No, I need a yes or a no answer. There is no wrong answer, and you won't hurt anybody's feelings if you say no."

Solomon seemed to think about it anyway. "Well, then. Okay, no."

"Why?"

"I thought you just said it was okay to answer no."

"It is, but I'd want to know why even if you'd said yes."

"I don't know you, and I don't know if the ghosts not following me in here has to do with the two of you, or just the house."

"When did you notice they left?"

"They don't follow me if I'm in a car, although I can still see them. But as we got closer, they just stopped being there."

"Okay. Now that's what you wanted, right?"

"Yeah."

"But now that you have it, it makes you nervous."

"Because if the scary stuff leaves, I wonder why."

"Did Karac tell you about us, Solomon?"

"Yeah, that's why I'm here. He said the two of you were really experienced in the paranormal and he showed me some of your books."

"Did you read anything we've written?"

"No."

"All right. Let me give a basic reason for why the ghosts might not be up here; the history of the Fox family is strong in the occult and the paranormal. Just the name makes others in the field nod knowingly whether they agree with us or not. Now, have you ever heard of the only time you should feel in trouble with the spirit world is if you should do something that makes them notice you, a mortal?"

"Nope."

Simone grinned. "I thought not, but that's not a problem."

"I haven't read that saying in any of the books I've read."

"Everybody has their own opinions regarding the supernatural, Solomon. It's all in the point of view and sometimes intent. Anyway, with the spirit world, that saying can also go for the forces of the supernatural. Fox is one of those names they don't want to be noticed by."

"Why?"

"For the same reasons mortals fear the other side; it's the unknown. They don't know how to fathom new things."

"But they're ghosts, that means they once were human."

"Right."

"So how come this is so unknown to them?"

"Just because one becomes a ghost doesn't mean they're going to automatically become enlightened."

"Okay."

"So let's try to work through this trust issue as we go. Deal?"

"Sure." "Are you able to manage seeing how others will pass on?"

"I guess. I try not to think about it, but I think it rotting at me anyway."

"Can you control any aspect of this ability at all?"

"Not that I know of. I've tried."

"What methods have you used?"

"Everything from denial to the power of positive thought."

"What about meditation?"

"Nope, doesn't work. In fact, it sort of amplified the effect when I started getting used to it."

"Right, you were allowing yourself to get comfortable."

"Yeah, I think that's why, too. But I thought it might lead to y'know, being balanced about it."

"Nothing unreasonable about that."

"But I guess it had the opposite effect."

"The meditation was working, but it just didn't have the desired effect." Solomon nodded.

"Have you used drugs or alcohol to see what that would do?"

"No, I figured that would be a really bad idea."

"It is. It would also promote dependency." Considering for how long the man had been under such misfortunes, he seemed remarkably balanced. That might come from someone who had simply accepted their fate and wanted to be done with it as soon as possible. Whatever had left Solomon Archer's eyes had done so long ago, and it seemed that since he was still looking for help in the face of what must at least seem to be hopelessness, he was remaining careful but hopeful. But for how long, she could not be sure.

The interview which Simone sincerely hoped seemed completely unlike an actual questioning lasted until noon, when even Gavin suggested they take a break for lunch. Karac volunteered to go to Carter's Deli a few blocks away for Italian subs, and Gavin went along for a quick getaway. Simone could tell he was feeling more than a little claustrophobic, and didn't blame him, although not for the first time she had concerns about how his metaphorical legs were going to handle more inactivity about the *O'Barr Manuscript*. There was one book left on the list, and while Simone wasn't sure at all about how they were going to find it without asking for further assistance from Karac, she had a feeling that Gavin thought they could bypass working with a Finder at all.

So she was either going to have to wait until Gavin's misgivings or prejudices towards Finders gave out sufficiently enough for him to come to the conclusion himself , which could take quite a while.

In the meantime, she had to keep company with the tattered soul before her.

"I'm surprised I'm actually hungry," Solomon said.

"You're listening to your body. That's good. Most people in your position would most likely not have that in them."

A shrug. "I've been doing this a while. You get used to it."

"What do you like to do when you're not researching your condition?"

Solomon seemed almost surprised by the question, but perked. "Well, I don't do it very much anymore, but I collect baseball cards."

"I did too," admitted Simone. "Back in the day."

"Yeah? I don't think I can remember any women I met who were into it. The few girls I've dated kinda considered it trivial, I think."

"Well, there's no accounting for taste. I liked watching the games, but there was something about completing a set out of millions of wax packages."

"I wasn't able to complete many sets until specialty stores started opening up."

"I miss doing that. I should get back into it."

"To take your mind off headier matters?" Smiled Solomon.

"Well, that. But just to have something to complete again, I guess."

"Let me guess; your mom threw them all out."

"Oh, no, no. Mom knew better than that. I have a bigger collection than my brothers. She has them all."

The conversation steered itself into which cards they have they were the most proud of, but Simone broke away from it and asked, "You mind if I ask another question about what's happening to you?"

Solomon, who had been visibly relaxing, now tensed once more. "Sure. Okay."

"You said that the girls you dated considered your collection trivial."

"I'd like to recant and say 'Childish,' if I may."

"Okay. How has your situation effected your relationship with the opposite sex?"

"Oh I don't have a relationship anymore with women."

"Why is that?"

"My choice."

"But why?"

"This is something that gets worse as time goes on, not better. So, I'd have to find someone who would be a bit more open that your average girl-next-door."

"What else?"

"What do you mean?"

"What is the other reason?"

"What makes you think there's another reason?"

"Because you'd keep trying if it were as simple as what you're saying."

Solomon's eyes narrowed. "Is that so?"

Simone held his gaze. "Uh-huh."

Solomon eased back against the cushions, his eyes flitting away. "Because I can see how they're going to die."

"Every time? Every girl?" "Every last one of them, even though I've only gone out with three." He chuckled. "Hell, I didn't even lose my virginity until I was twenty-six!"

"Did you have a vision of that girl before or after?"

"After. Why?"

"Just curious."

Then nothing between them. The soft tick of the antique clock on the mantle.

"Solomon."

"Hmm." Still not looking at her.

"Can you see how I'll die?"

His half-lidded gaze considered her now, just for a moment before slinking away.

"No."

"Don't lie."

"Yes."

"Have you ever told anyone how they're going to die?"

"No. How could I?"

"Could you tell me?"

The front door burst open from one of Gavin's too-hard kicks as he had his hands full of brown paper bags filled with eight-inch subs. Rebecca followed close behind, carrying the cardboard travel container holding the soft drinks that no one to the best of Simone's recollection actually ordered. Karac brought up the rear, the limp body of a woman in his arms, and although she was wrapped loosely in the blanket Simone remembered buying with Simone for the witch's earthquake kit for her car, Simone could tell she was nude beneath it.

"What, you could only find one nude woman at Carter's?" Simone asked.

Rebecca set the drinks down. "Simone, this is Unconscious Diana. Unconscious Diana, this is Simone."

Gavin told Karac to help Simone open the hide-a-bed in the couch and placed the woman gingerly upon the mattress. Simone observed Diana for a few moments before picking the errant twigs from the woman's hair. "Gavin, be a dear and get a washcloth for me."

Introductions, such as they were, were made between the strangers. Seemingly glad to be out of the limelight of Simone's last question, Solomon tried to busy himself by helping wherever needed.

"I take it this is our lycanthrope," Simone said while mopping slashes of dirt away from Diana's cheekbones.

"She went completely berserk this morning," Rebecca supplied. "She took off into the hills. Took me three hours to find her." Still and all, the witch did not appear disheveled. If Simone didn't know better, she'd have thought Rebecca had stopped home to tidy before delivering her charge. But it was the way Rebecca was; she never once looked like she worked. Even after cleaning out her garage with Gavin and Simone's help years ago, it was as if dust simply couldn't bring itself to land on her shoulder.

Karac tried to explain what a lycanthrope was to Solomon, who cut him off with the air of one so insulted that he may not know of such things. Given the amount of research Solomon admitted to have given the paranormal, Simone wasn't surprised at all that he knew exactly what they were talking about, although he did seem a bit baffled as to why she didn't look more, in his own words, 'Wolfen.'

"She wouldn't respond to my first castings," Rebecca went on. "She's getting stronger."

Gavin nodded. "Getting more comfortable with this version of herself."

"I don't understand it. I thought we were making such great progress."

"What were you doing?" Asked Karac.

"I was teaching her deep meditative states."

"Kind of a gamble," noted Simone.

"Well, I wasn't sure what I was supposed to do. I thought trying to teach her how to tap into some kind of inner calm might help."

"Looks like you tapped into something deeper," this came from Solomon. If it wasn't for the marveling tone in his voice, Simone knew Rebecca would have verbally assassinated the man.

"I knew the risk," Rebecca admitted. *Mea culpa.*"

"That's all you could have done," said Solomon.

Simone moved to the kitchen to wring out the cloth before moving on to inspect the rest of the woman's body. Thankfully enough, none of the men needed to be told to turn their head before the blanket was folded away from Diana's body. "What spell did you use?" "I tried two different angles of bliss before she was in line-of-sight, but I don't think that didn't even slowed her down. Once I could see her, I tried sleep, but that only aggravated her more." Rebecca rubbed at her forehead at the memory. "I finally tried an old bringback I learned, and that finally brought her down."

Simone looked up from Diana's bruised body. "My God, Rebecca. You could have killed her." The witch's head cocked. "She was going back down into the residential area, Simone. What would you have done, pray tell?"

Simone didn't answer, and that was answer enough for Rebecca who backed out of her pose and helped clean away some of the dirt out of the scratches now marking her charge's legs.

Soon, the wounds were cleansed and bandaged where needed. Both Simone and Rebecca stopped to sip from their take-out cups. "The wounds aren't that bad," Simone said. "A couple are pretty deep, both on her legs, but they'll heal. She's lucky she didn't need hospitalization. By this point, it's a miracle she isn't in the morgue."

"Or someone else," said Gavin as he unwrapped his sandwich. "Oh, don't look at me like that, folks. It's not like it's unheard of that a lycanthrope kills."

"Out of fear," said Rebecca.

"Not always. Sometimes they eat their kill. Sometimes it seems to be for sport."

"Or out of fear," Rebecca repeated.

Simone stood between the two and held her hands away from her sides. "Shut up, please." She removed the sub from Gavin's hands, took a bite and handed it back. "Eyes on the present, people. We have what amounts to Wolverine on our couch. Can we discuss the possibility of restraints?"

As if on cue, a moan came from the blankets.

Diana sat up, rubbing her biceps. Her eyes were mere slits.

"I can hear you, you know," she said.

Rebecca sat at her bedside. "Are you okay?"

Diana nodded. "Not nearly as messed-up as I normally feel." Simone shared a look at Gavin, who nodded. The change in her behavior was now no longer a realistic concern for pain. This usually meant, in the limited amount of study that had been given to genuine lycanthropy studies, that the subject was now ready to begin the final stage; complete ferality.

Diane's eyes scanned the room and went to Rebecca. Not out of fear, just the quickest reference point.

"Dare I ask?"

Rebecca smiled. "Diana Adair, may I present to you Fox Manor. Our hosts today are none other than Gavin and Simone. The gentleman off to your right there is known as Karac, and the man with him has been introduced to me as Solomon."

"Thanks for the hospitality, folks. I hope I haven't been too much trouble."

"Not at all," said Simone.

"We are a little concerned about your erratic behavior though," added Rebecca.

Diana's expression was one Simone liked not in the least. The woman appeared to be surprised at the notion.

"Really? I thought I was doing pretty well."

"Do you remember anything?" Asked Simone.

"Almost everything. I stayed conscious throughout the change, and I think I can remember leaving the house." Then a cloud fell over her features.

"I didn't hurt anybody, did I?"

"No," replied Rebecca. "But you were harder to stop this time."

"Which isn't a good sign I take by all the concerned looks."

"There could be better," Gavin admitted.

"And so here I am, naked and battered."

"I'm afraid so."

"Are you the good people who are going to stop whatever it is that's happening to from happening to me?"

A grin from Simone despite her misgivings. "That's what we're hoping."

"So you're the good guys?"

"That's what we're hoping."

PART THREE
A MATTER OF FAITH

CHAPTER TWENTY-FOUR

I am the brother to dragons,

And friend of bird of prey.

My skin becomes a husk,

And my bones bemoan my soul.

THE VERSES OF NON, Author Unknown

All things considered, Diana was open to restraints, provided Karac, or as she had come to refer to him, 'The cute one', was the one doing the job. To his credit, Karac tried his best to keep from grinning at the various sexual innuendoes flung at him by Diana as she lay, now clothed in some of Simone's flannel pajamas on the bed in the first guest bedroom in the upstairs on the Manor.

And he only made eye contact with her once.

Solomon Archer had been more than accommodating, as well. Letting those in the know speak about matters he clearly had not the slightest understanding of, nor pretended to have much of an interest in them, up until it became clear that those who he assumed were in charge were talking about a crisis that would effect everything he could imagine.

Gavin, Simone, Karac, and Rebecca made no bones about their sudden position, and decided without discussion that since everything had hit the proverbial fan, there was no point trying to speak in code and answer whatever questions came up later provided, Rebecca noted, that there was such a things as a later.

The 'Civilians' as they were called, Diana and Solomon, made it clear that whatever help that was needed would be provided, although there was a great deal of suspicion on the part of Gavin and Simone regarding the validity of her being able to do anything but go out of control at any given moment. This was handled by Diana herself, who said:

"Look, at some point, you're going to have to let me up. I'm not so uncivilized that I'm not going to ask to use the bathroom at some point. Second, I'm not sure what you're all talking about with gates opening and what have you, but I do know that it scares the bejeezus out of me, and if something scares you guys, I'm going to be scared too and on your side. And frankly, I'm surprised none of you have seen the protective advantage that I could provide."

178

"What are you saying?" Asked Gavin, clearly already knowing and dreading the need to hear it out loud. "Well, I'm a curious sort of gal," said Diana. "And to be quite honest, I was wondering this morning if I could go wild at will." At this, she struck a cheesy grin and rocked her head from side to side.

"You mean you meant to freak out at my house?" Asked Rebecca.

"I didn't mean to freak out, I just wanted to see if I could do it." Amid the silence that followed, she smiled and added, "It wasn't as hard as I thought."

"But you didn't mean to go as far as you did," Simone noted.

"Well, no."

"Still leaves us in a pretty dangerous position."

"No dangerous than the one Solomon and I are in." The smile was gone. "So far, none of you have been able to help either one of us."

"Not really the time to be pointing fingers, Diana."

"Okay," said Gavin. "Let's all take a mental step back for a second. What's the world at large looking like? We've lost perspective on that."

Rebecca crossed her arms across her chest and blew a stray forelock of hair from her eyes. "The serious covens have all gone to ground. There are a few left, but they're either not aware what's going on, and if they are, they're so far out of the orbit of reality that they'd rather stay and watch the fireworks."

"Lucas Brady is not getting involved," Gavin added, allowing time for Rebecca to say to the uninitiated that the topic of Brady was a long story and that she'd fill them in later. "The rest of the occult community seem to have just slipped off the face of the earth."

"So we're alone," said Solomon.

"What about the churches?" Queried Rebecca.

"Only one I'm aware of that seems even the slightest bit aware of it is up in Benjamin, and I can't say that much is going to come of that one. The only source I'd even consider would be the Vatican, and somehow I don't think they'll take our calls."

"So now what?" Asked Solomon.

"We find the last book," said Karac.

Five sets of eyes turned to him. He raised his chin to face them.

"Can you do that, cute stuff?" asked Diana.

"I'm a Finder. It's what I do."

Gavin snorted. "I thought that was out of your bailiwick or jurisdiction or whatever the hell you people call it."

"It is. It's a professional courtesy. The gift extends past that, we're just not supposed to do it."

"Something that would have been helpful to know several days ago, Karac. What else aren't you telling us?"

"The winning lottery numbers for the next two years, where Jimmy Hoffa is really buried and where you can go and do when you get there, Mr. Fox."

Gavin said nothing but took great pains to glower at the Finder.

"I thought another Finder would have either stepped forward by now. The proper one. Instead, I think he or she has been otherwise employed or compelled in some way to help find the books."

"Who in their right mind would help such a person?"

"That's just it," said Karac. "I honestly don't think the Finder knows they're helping the wrong side. They probably just think they're helping an eccentric collector round out his or her collection."

"*His*," put in Simone. The person looking for; It's a him."

"And," added Gavin. "He's a teleporter."

"Okay," said Simone. "Let's keep level heads, shall we? He may not even have a Finder doing this. If he's as in tune with mystical things as he seems, he could very well have a series of spells that could allow him to see where these things are. He could have actually created a dynamic that allowed him to become a half-assed Finder."

The decision was soon made among Gavin, Simone and Karac to continue the conversation elsewhere while Solomon kept watch over Diana in the guest bedroom.

"Do they really think you're going to break those handcuffs if you change or whatever?" Solomon asked the bound woman after the door had clicked shut behind the leaving party.

Diana shrugged. The man before her didn't seem as twitchy as someone with the ability that he said he had. His eyes had that sort-of bedroom quality to them she liked to look at, but knew that was probably from the lack of sleep he was suffering as evidenced by the dark circles beneath his eyes. The only thing she wasn't at ease with was the way he kept staring at her body, eyes flicker here and there, then back up to her eyes for a moment, then back to the swell of her chest or the curve of her hip. His eyes were wide enough to indicate at least to her the distinct possibility that he'd never actually touched a woman in an intimate way during his life, maybe touched one at all. "I've never been restrained, so I can't say for sure," she said. "But they're the experts."

Solomon was about to respond when the door opened again and Solomon found himself holding what appeared to be a simple, business-only rifle. Maybe a .32 caliber, if Diane's knowledge of standard weapons – courtesy of Dad – stood after a few years off the US Marine Corps firing range.

The Finder held a hand palm up in Diane's direction. "It's just a tranquilizer rifle."

"What for?"

Karac gaped at her before coming to grips. It was actually kind of cute. "In case you change."

Diane nodded. "Right. Just in case." Karac ducked back out then reappeared. "You know how to use one of those things, right Solomon?"

"I hold the hollow end at the target, pull the trigger."

"Right." Karac glanced at Solomon's trigger finger, reached, and unlatched something next to it. "Safety's off. Be careful." Then he was gone.

"Interesting fellow," muttered Solomon. The gunbarrel came down to the floor.

"Think I should be concerned about why he keeps a trank rifle around?"

"I don't know him all that well, but I can say that I'd be more afraid of what *else* might be in there."

"He seems nice enough, though."

"Yeah, he is."

"Has he been able to help you at all?"

Solomon shook his head. "That's why we came here."

"And we're left at the kid's table while the grown-ups talk about serious issues."

"I don't think it's that. I figure it's more like not scaring the hell out of us while they talk, and how we might interrupt."

"Like how, asking questions?"

"Well, yeah."

"How are we supposed to know anything if we don't ask?" "It does seem like they've got a bigger issue at hand."

"Sure, I know. But..." She waved the rest away. "How long have you known Karac?"

"Oh, not very long. Three weeks, tops."

"Nice guy, though?"

"Yeah. He's helping a total stranger."

"He married?"

"Not that I know of. He probably wouldn't volunteer that information with a client."

"Didn't see a ring. But that doesn't mean anything."

"What about you?"

"What about me?"

"You married?"

Diane's laugh surprised her. "No, no. If I'm to believe the true state of my condition, that's for the best. Lycanthropes as a rule go through life single."

"That's too bad."

"Why? Sometimes a little alone time's not that bad."

"I guess the grass is always greener on the other side."

"That's what they say, but I wouldn't mind a nicer lawn now and again."

"I'm just not a fan of being alone."

"Yeah, I get that." A pause. "Can you see ghosts right now?"

"No, that's why I like it here. They didn't follow me."

"Maybe Rebecca can cast a spell to get rid of them or something."

"Karac said there's not much on the books about this kind of condition. Plus, the complication I have doesn't help much, either."

"Complication?"

"Yeah, I guess that was sort of glossed over in the introductions. I can sometimes see how someone will die."

"Wow. That must be tough."

"You have no idea." Solomon sat heavily on the champagne carpeted floor. "And no, I cant."

"Can't what?"

"See how you're going to die."

"How did you know I was going to ask that?"

"Eveybody does."

"Even Karac?"

"Well, no. Not Karac. I don't think he wants to know."

"Do you think being at the Manor has to do with that?"

"I'm pretty sure of that, yeah." This was the true face of Solomon Archer, then. Soft-spoken, gloomy. Defeated, but still trying to find a reason to wake up tomorrow and drag his bones into the day. There was something too genuine, too pure to even consider suicide. Unlike herself, who simply didn't see the point. A nice man, overall, but far too lost, and had been lost too long to be of much use to anyone. He didn't live in everybody else's world, and so therefore, could never find a place to live comfortably within it. Diane doubted very much that even if his abilities were suddenly gone, it would make no difference. He'd be even more at sea with the world around him than ever before. He'd have to start again, and that distance behind his eyes was just too great for him to bother. He'd rather sit down and read quietly, and enjoy the silence and find his own solace in some other way.

Diane was sure he wouldn't find the slightest peace within himself because of this. His was a position she would not wish upon anyone.

"Why don't you sit up here with me," she offered. "I won't bite. Promise."

His expression registered suspicion, then ran through the gamut of trying to find some ulterior motive for him to be on the bed with her.

"Solomon, the floor is hard, the bed is comfy, and I'm not changing, am I?"

"No."

"Then relax, allow yourself to have some small comfort in life, and come sit down."

Without appearing too resigned, Solomon lifted himself and went to the bed. When he sat, it was with the air of waiting for something to explode.

"I'm going to take a wild guess," Diane said. "And say that you're not seeing anybody, either."

"How do you mean?"

"I mean socially."

"Oh. Uh. Well, no."

"Because of your condition."

"Yeah."

"Well, it appears as though we have some common ground."

His eyes now returned to her. He even smiled a bit. "I guess so."

This time, it was her time to smile. "So, tell me what else you know about Karac."

CHAPTER TWENTY-FIVE

There are so many things to find joy over in this life. Then why can we not see them? Because we do not sit when we are happy and think about how happy we are.

Lucas Brady, ON THE ABYSS

"I am not going to lower myself to the level of this maniac and consider murder as an acceptable means of handling this." Gavin tried to keep his hands from shaking, but it was a futile effort as he only clenched them into fists that would turn his knuckles white. It would have been easier to control himself if the topic had not been brought up by Simone. Karac had seen fit to cross his arms, lean into the corner of the library, and glower at the tops of his beat-up motorcycle boots. The witch was satisfied to just sit knees up in the center of the floor, staring at the patterns only she could see in the carpet.

"Then we only have one choice," said Simone. "Get the element first."

Karac raised his palm about midway up his ribcage. "I don't mean to be the one who pees in the Weetabix - "

"Then don't," snapped Gavin, who couldn't find the bother enough to look at him.

"We're still going to have one hell of a liability out there."

"We can cross that bridge when we find it."

"Why not burn it?" responded Karac.

"You don't burn bridges," Gavin said as calmly as he could bear. "Because you might need them yourself."

"I think," said Rebecca. "We're in this situation because someone took that thought a little too literally."

"So we kill someone solely on the thought that they might do wrong again?"

"In military terms, it's called a pre-emptive strike."

"If we commit murder on the basis of what someone *might* do, what's the next step?"

"You're thinking way outside the box, Gavin. I'm just saying in this instance, the greater good could be served by a less than envious task."

"In *Patton*, George C. Scott would have said 'Let's waste the bastard.'"

Gavin found a bit of himself was actually pleased Rebecca's eyes shut and the lids became tight at his taunt.

The witch's eyes opened and never left his. "Let's waste the bastard."

"This is a no-win situation," Karac put in. "I think we can all stop pretending there's a correct way of handling this."

"Karac's right," Rebecca said, standing and glaring up at Gavin, who stood at least a head and a half taller than she, even with her in her highest heels. "I'll do it."

"Do what, kill someone?"

"If I have to."

"Then you do it without our help." Gavin turned to the library door, but was brought up short by Simone's voice.

"Gavin."

He turned slowly to face her.

"I'm not trying to advocate violence," she said. "But I can't act like things will go better if we take the higher path. Whoever this is who is going to the bother of finding all these books and is willing to commit himself to the road that allows teleportation is not one to be trifled with. We cannot send him on to the police, we cannot arrest him because where are we going to put him?"

The words came quickly for Gavin, "A binding spell. Something of that nature. With the four of us we it might be enough to cast a strong enough spell."

"And if we're not, we won't find out except for the hard way." This came from Karac.

"Can a Finder help us get the next book?"

A shrug from Karac. "Hard to say. This character's probably already using one. If that's so, we'll have no luck pulling him to our side just out of fear."

"What about you?"

"I'm not that kind of Finder. I'm not sure which you'd need. You two," he indicated Gavin and Simone with a toss of his chin. "Would be just as suited for it. These days, all I can say is that I can't find anything that can help."

Gavin stepped toward him. "We know the next book exists because the culprit wouldn't be going around collecting the other volumes if he wasn't sure his ambitions would fail because of a technicality of something like a good, old-fashioned17th-century book-burning."

"Which means he's knowledgeable enough to find things on his own."

"But he hasn't gotten the last book," said Rebecca. "Why? Why wait? Because he doesn't know where it is."

"The second I start looking," Karac said, his voice now couched in uncharacteristic softness. "Someone or something will feel the shift. This kind of energy just works that way."

Gavin nodded, a small smile rewarding his features. "Like ripples in a pond, of course. But it won't reveal who's looking, and it won't show where the book is."

"Until we get it," said Simone. "We could very well lead someone straight to our house." "Or to the delightful soul who's helping you find, whereupon all sorts of fun things like torture and death can be looked forward to."

Gavin nodded. "Okay, let's agree on this; I only want the book out of the bad guy's hands. What you three want to do about cleanup is between the three of you."

Rebecca laughed. "And the role of Pontius Pilate will be played by..."

Simone took over the space between them. "Shut up, the both of you. First priority is the book, I think we're all in agreement about that. Without the book, our actions won't mean a damn thing, because who's to say this won't happen twenty years down the line because we never got rid of the damned book?"

The others nodded.

Karac stepped forward. "Okay, so I try to find... which book is it?"

"*To Pick Stars From the Sky*," Gavin and Simone both responded by rote.

"So it's entirely possible I might die because of some musty old book that nobody can find only because it has the reputation to hold nothing of value except its rarity."

"Right," said Gavin.

"Well, let me get right on that, then. Tell Solomon I'm out doing something noble instead of something promised." The Finder edged past Simone then Gavin as he exited. Rebecca called to him, but the only response coming was the decisive shutting of the Manor front door.

The room was still for a time, then Gavin spoke again:

"He'll be okay."

The women didn't respond.

"What about Solomon and Diana?" Said Rebecca at last.

"We can deal with Solomon a little quicker,"said Gavin. "Maybe a casting from *The Book of Allot* could help him."

"A book of illusions?" Replied Rebecca. "You going to try to help him with that?"

Simone held up a placating hand. "Hold on. Rebecca, you know that's about all we can do for him. His ability is beyond what anyone can do for him."

"So he's a hopeless case?"

"No," said Gavin. "But there's no cure."

"And we treat him like a dying patient," Rebecca nodded. "Just keep the poor thing comfortable until the end." "What else is there, Rebecca?" ask Simone. "What is it we've missed?"

The witch hid her features behind the fan of her fingers and hand, shunted her head violently. "Nothing. There's nothing. I know that. There's nothing."

Gavin and Simone exchanged a look as Rebecca regained her composure, bringing her chin up and letting the tears pooled in her eyes to lend a kind of brightness. "And Diana? What of her?"

"If she's open to some experimentation, we might be able to slow the ability. This comes from the core animal, we have to find some way of quieting it, the key is in her wanting it quieted, which I don't think she does."

At this, Rebecca nodded. "I think she's beyond that. There's that carefree existence that she sees as if she can reach out and possess it, rather than it possessing her."

"Does she understand that?"

"No. But she seems to think she does."

"Can we somehow make her?" Simone asked.

"No. She's beyond stubborn. And she likes the animal too much to let it go."

"We can handle her after we handle the situation with Solomon. It's the least we can do for Karac," said Gavin, who glowered at the faces of the women when it was apparent they were taken aback by this softening of heart. "He's helping us. We can help him, and Solomon's a person we would have helped without anyone telling us to."

"Odd that he went to Karac, though." Muttered Simone.

"I can't account for instinct," replied Gavin. "He did what he did, end of story."

Rebecca rubbed at her eyes. "So what do we do now?"

"We start on Solomon," Gavin said.

"I'll talk to Diana," Rebecca said. "See where her head's at. If we can, we should go into a holding pattern with her until we can see if she'll actually accept help."

"So we wait for Karac?"

Gavin nodded and opened the library door. "For now. Maybe we can actually do something besides argue with one another until he gets back."

CHAPTER TWENTY-SIX

I am not sure that there are any right hands for power of any significance to be in.

Leland Fell, THE FELL BEASTS

The first ripple in the water of the pond:
Initial interest bearing weight of sudden value.

To Pick Stars From the Sky, as a book, was not collectable in the slightest. What usually gave a thing its worth was that somebody wanted it, and then a book such as *Stars* would find its intrinsic value by proxy, by simple want and desire. It was a semi legend at best in the occult field only because of the vagaries mentioned in its pages which contained short, simple poems of a decidedly dark nature. Occultists such as Gavin Fox gave small notice to it, only noting in forwards of collector's reference books such as *Marquand's True and Unusual Volumes* or in The Globe Antiquities Society annual auction book, the latest edition of which spanned well over five hundred color glossy pages.

The true beauty of the book was twofold to collectors, and by course of action, resulting in a lack of interest to actual occultists because on the grounds of it popularity; the fact that only one copy was every made, and that its hand-binding was of a painstaking variety even for the 13th century. The (allegedly) supple brain-tanned leather thin enough to be of questionable quality, yet resilient enough to withstand the centuries. It had been heard by Karac on more than one occasion that the leather was actually either human skin (unlikely) or the hide of a proto-demon of some kind.

Karac couldn't have cared less in regards to which skin it may or not be, but could appreciate the art of a well-made book, especially one that had supposedly lasted as long as this one had. The pages were thick, apparently made of a hybrid of perhaps papyrus and elements of animal hide, but swung easily on the sinew rings holding them in place. The hardcover volume contained a rumor of no more than fourteen pages, each holding poetry on the left leaf, while on the right would be an illustration inspired by the poem on the opposite page, first drawn in ink on a thin 3 X 3 inch square of nondescript paper, then pasted onto the desired page with an adhesive that apparently did not degrade the paper. One article speculated that animal fat may have been a component to the paste, but Karac never figured how that would have mattered in the degradation or non-degradation of the paper it was applied to.

Whomever had it was being quiet about it and was unconcerned about the wealth it could bring. Most likely, this could indicate a man of status, such as a world leader. Following World War II, most, if not all of the mysterious antiquities that were even so much as rumored to have existed were scattered nearly beyond reach. This did not only include such high-profile items such as the Spear of Longinus, or the Ark of the Covenant, but also books, some mentioned in Scripture, others recorded by men with motives to keep the things that found their way home to them. And although it had never been outright said, Karac would have wagered a good amount on *To Pick Stars From the Sky* to be among them, although even as great of a body on texts as the Vatican's library, the Vatican itself denied any existence of the book, saying such a thing was merely created from heresy and innuendo that the Holy See had no interest in.

But then, basic logic as well as established science flew in the face of the reality of certain things Karac had seen, all of which were created by Man himself. This included things that were officially not in any library, especially the Vatican's. And everybody lied. Everybody.

The second ripple:

Activity of interest. This became a ring on the face the still water the moment Karac's booted feet crossed the threshold of The Wash. He barely nodded at Gregor but began almost instantly scanning the thin mid-week crowd of hard-core Wash-goers, of which were fewer and fewer each season.

The part of him that held little love for human beings and their love for power and one-upsmanship in the face of what quite possibly could be something greater than themselves winced.

Everybody had the capacity to achieve great things, simple things. Everybody.

Some, Karac figured, simply couldn't be bothered to reach for the remote, and on occasion, there were better things to do than try to get drunk and laid, not necessarily in that order.

With a flick of his wrists, Karac's collar of his beaten leather jacket plumed around his neckline and he made his way to where Markab was holding court with his latest pool hustle, a newbie to the Wash who was now getting his own proverbial head handed to him on a platter gleaming cold in the overhead lamplight.

Markab took short note of his arrival and gave a slight move of his hand, which translated roughly to 'Be right with you' to Karac.

Markab's mark eyed Karac as if trying to gauge whether he could consider himself tough enough to take Karac if a fight should ever occur, or most likely, bully after losing what appeared to be a large sum of money to someone not only better at the game, but also about a foot taller and with the natural born air of someone who never had to prove anything to anybody.

The eight ball rolled across its green felt almost hesitatingly.

Karac hid a grin behind his fingers. Markab did that on purpose; to allow the mark to hold out hope just long enough for it to build interest only for it to be paid out in a dash and, after the eight had hung on to the lip on the corner pocket, the thunk of it falling home. It was these things that Finders did when all else resembling joy at a well-played game had fallen from their lives into the shadow of living in a world whose occupants knew little of.

It was one of the prices to being a Finder, Karac knew. That little dark streak of sadism running up the spine. Entertainment such as this was one way of dealing with it. They were no different than those like Solomon or the psychic from any number of movies who eventually screams through tears that they 'Didn't ask to be this way.'

The mark didn't bother trying to hide a wad of bills from his hand to Markab's, who then pocketed the money and gave the man a jaunty two-fingered salute before the man slinked away, unscrewing his cue.

"That must have been exciting," Karac said. "Sorry I missed it."

"Got boring after the guy tried to win back the money the second time. I was expecting him to say 'Double or nothing' any time." Markab ordered a drink for the both of them, then turned to Karac as he leaned against the close bumper. Karac could now see how drawn the man looked, the dark crescents under his eyes lending gravity to his features. Markab had let his stubble grow out past what could be considered fashionable and looked as if he were contemplating a beard.

"You doing okay, man?"

Markab nodded. "Just tired. Impending doom has that effect on me."

"I'm surprised you're still around."

"Well, Finders will always be where they're most needed."

"Or wanted," Karac corrected. "We don't deal in the needed."

"Sure we do. Just not all the time."

Karac nodded, studied the cues in the dark wood rack on the wall facing him.

"What's up, man?" "I need a starting point for something off the radar."

"Business, then."

"'fraid so."

"Okay, fair enough. What's the thing?"

"To Pick Stars From the Sky."

"Wow. Tall order. Who wants it?"

"I think the question is 'Who doesn't?'"

Markab nodded, unscrewed his cue and placed it into its carrying case.

"Karac, I'm not sure what to tell you. I don't find stuff like that."

"You do the stuff that shouldn't exist but does."

"Mmm-hmm."

"I'm starting to think I find the stuff that people should know better than to have a need for, and create them anyway."

"Ninety-eight per cent of the stuff we find is man-made."

"I have no instinct on this one. It's weird."

"It's also pivotal, from what you're telling me."

"What, you're saying I'm trying to defeat myself?"

Markab accepted the drink and paid the server, who mad a point of smiling at Karac before pulling away. Karac had never seen her before. "Yep."

"Well, then, any bright ideas?"

"Run away?"

"From what Fox says, that's not going to help."

"The end of the world again?"

"So it would seem, yes."

"Must be a day that ends in 'y'."

"Right, but this is a serious guy trying to unmake a helluva lot of stuff. Gavin says even Lucas Brady's taken himself out of the game."

Markab's forehead creased, then relaxed with visible effort. "Okay, Fox is looking for a worthless book of poetry and Lucas Brady is noncombative. Well, just so long as people are acting accordingly."

"What can you do to help?"

Markab stared at the same bit of green felt for what seemed to be ages.

"You can talk to Fade, he may be able to help."

"He's still around?"

"Just quiet. You know, the Finder who is trying to retire is the one who tries to just keep his mouth shut."

Karac had heard of the occasional Finder who denied their ability. Most simply withered and died as they tried to seem normal and lead everyday lives, all the time wondering why they couldn't shake that feeling of void within a place in themselves a little to the left and behind of the soul.

"Know where I can find him?"

"Lives off Daylight, 2625 Allyson Court Avenue. Can't miss it. Looks just like the Brady Bunch house."

But for all the credibility Markab otherwise had, the closest the home on Allyson Court Avenue, named after the daughter of the land's developer, Stephen Court, had on the Brady house was that this one was a split-level, as well and there was a wood-paneled station wagon in the driveway on the west side of the house. The neighborhood itself did resemble where a family such as the Bradys would fit in quite well and quite easily.

A man like Fade, on the other hand, would spend the better part of his time insisting to himself his neighbors accepted him, while knowing all the while that on some level none of them could explore, there was something about him that just didn't fit.

They would keep their distance. Fade would be ostracized and he'd never be able to go back, because he would feel he couldn't. The water would be considered too deep to get back into.

So Karac would bring the ocean to him.

After the second chime of the doorbell, the porchlight snapped on before Karac's left shoulder and a man no more than twenty-three dressed in a rumpled button-down Oxford and well-worn jeans that might have been s shade of dark blue at some point in their life answered the door. No query, no check through the peephole in the door.

"Fade?"

The man was taken aback, but somehow didn't appear surprised to be called by that name.

"Hey, I'm Karac. I understand we're in the same business."

"I'm sure we're not."

The door began its silent swing shut, blocked by Karac's boot. Fade appeared perturbed, but not actually angry.

"I really need to talk to you," Karac said.

"About what?"

"Business."

The man's lips pressed to a thin, bloodless line. Then, "Listen, Karac I'm not interested in this."

The door began its closing once more, but this time, Karac pulled his boot away.

"I know what it's like," said Karac. "To not want to do this."

The door was still closing, slowly.

"To stay awake nights until morning, and you still can't fall asleep even though your body's screaming at you to. To feel something gnawing at you and you can't figure out what it is until you finally figure it out; emptiness. Only one thing will fill it for a while."

The shadow of the door halted.

"What is it?" The voice behind the dark oak door asked.

"The location of a book."

A pause, perhaps from the drag of a cigarette. Then, "What sort of book?"

Karac told him.

The door swung open.

"What's in it for me?"

"For Gavin Fox to know your name."

Now Fade appeared, his head cocked in a childlike way.

"I thought Fox wasn't a friend of Finders."

"He's not, but this is a personal favor."

"*The* Gavin Fox."

"Indeed."

Fade eyed the spot on the ground between them. Karac could almost hear the thought of the book being turned over in Fade's mind.

"Come back tomorrow."

With that, the front door clicked back into its frame. There was no sound of any locks being turned.

The deal was done, but still, Karac stared at the door for a time before starting back to his car.

The third ripple:

Obtaining the help of others without benefit or concern for them.

Karac keyed the engine of the Torpedo back to life, and started homeward. He didn't care how long it took. He was on Fade's time now.

It was the least he could do.

191

Even the greatest dragon has need of the smallest mouse, because it knows how many pay it no mind.

Angus Hyde, THE PHILOSOPHY OF THE OCCULT

In the considered opinion of Diana Adair, people like Gavin and Simone and perhaps most of all Rebecca had no idea what they were talking about because they could only see on one side of the looking glass. She didn't fault them, really. She almost pitied them.

But she couldn't understand them, just as they couldn't understand her. They were very different animals. From her and from one another.

The difference was, she was right. They may have had an illuminated way of looking at things, but being who and what they were, they were unsure of what someone could do given the abilities that her beliefs had given her, of that she was certain. These things were not simply the stuff of opinion, they were fact. You could dress things up as pretty as you could possibly want, but on the inside, things would always rot.

It had nothing to do with God or money or envy. Those things led to war, which proved her point to a degree, but it was not as complex as even that was. No, it was the nature of things. Everything tended towards chaos, and as long as there was that condition perpetuation itself through its manifestation of humanity, nothing would change.

Diana saw this, the others didn't. She could spend her time trying to explain it, but to what end? There was no point. The only one who might understand would be the rather googly-eyed Solomon, who couldn't hide his attraction for her if he tried. He probably wasn't even aware of who obvious he was being. It was nice to think of such genuine innocence, but it was always either short-lived or became a nuisance.

And she just didn't have the patience for either anymore. It was enough for her to try to be herself. Act as she felt was her right, and allows those around her to sniff at the decision and be in charge of the keys.

And to tell her it was wrong.

They all explored the dark, but not the ugly. The recognized it, disagreed with it, then sought fit to argue about it like civilized people do in the stead of actually doing something about it, weighing every single point, for the good and bad.

Meanwhile, plans contrary to theirs were hatched and acted upon. The bad guys did not while their time by twisting their handlebar moustache.

And they never considered themselves bad.

She grinned and looked at Solomon, who had run out of things to say regarding Karac, the only soul among them who seemed to understand darkness and ugliness, if only to wait until there was a time to act rather than speak. A very unusual man, that one. And that as just fine with her. Maybe when the dust cleared, they could actually talk about things the two of them could understand and agree with. But for now, her time was occupied with thoughts of wondering whether she could actually break the cuffs that held her to the bed and what sort of fight Solomon might give her if she did.

His eyes gave away far more than he could ever believe. He was twitchy enough, she decided, that his reactions could very well be better than hers, if only in the act of surprise.

She'd lose.

And instead of getting upset, she allowed it to instead spread its own kind of patience through her bones and the pit of her stomach. Solomon was a good sort, just hopeless. That didn't mean he had to be an enemy, and he was gifted, too. Just in a way that had driven him insane, far further than the lot of them were willing to admit. They had lost the Battle of Solomon before it had began, and were acting on it anyway, and although that was certainly noble, in the case of Solomon Archer, Diana didn't see the point. But she had no solution, and speaking in regards to it would only make it worse for Solomon, and he really was a sweet soul.

If Diana could have helped, she realized she would have, just as Gavin, Simone, and Rebecca were doing. But she understood her place in the scheme of things here, even if she didn't much like it.

Rebecca entered the room, leaving the door open to allow Gavin and Simone entrance.

"How are you doing?" Asked Rebecca.

"My wrists are getting a bit achy," Diana appeared to admit. "Any chance I can get a reprieve?"

"I think so," said Simone. "But we would like to try to help you get a grip on your power."

"No. *I* can help *you*," she said, and told them how.

The Bic lighter's flame flicked to life in Simone's fist. She touched the flame to the tip of her cigarette and watched the tip glow. After a moment, she passed it to Rebecca, who dragged at it. She closed her eyes and exhaled into the rays of the new morning falling across the two of them.

"I don't like it," Simone said at last.

"It may be the lack of sleep," Rebecca said. "But neither do I."

"I mean, she's basically volunteering to become an assassin."

The witch nodded.

"You don't seem too torn up over this."

"Neither do you. You act like you're testing the waters before you say you think it's a good idea."

"She's resigned herself to being this way."

"I've lost her, yeah."

"Can she be trusted?"

"At least to what she's talking about, yeah I think so."

"It's like she's looking forward to it." Another drag. Their words were falling flat in the garden she and Gavin had created, as if all the statuary and plants and water refused to allow it here.

But still here they were, forcing it out there just the same.

Rebecca took the cigarette from her fingertips again and dragged, the coal glowing pale in the growing sunlight.

"She's the perfect assassin," Simone heard herself saying. "Willing, mostly likely to pull it off, and not give a whit about the guilt." She took the cigarette from Rebecca, touched it to her lips, thought better of it, and crushed it under her heel before sending it into the Bradbury-green grass of the garden. "And, ultimately, she's disposable, and doesn't care about that, either."

"Nope. She's pretty happy to be a self-destructing entity."

"Don't try to follow her wherever she's going, Rebecca. Don't try to save her twice."

Rebecca wouldn't look at her, but shook her head. "I don't have that in me."

"I'm sorry for that."

"Don't be. I'm glad I can recognize when I've done my best and that's all I can expect to do. If nothing else, this mess has shown me that I can accept that and still wake up in the morning."

The days closer to October were drawing colder now, but the mornings and evenings still held that odd warmth that Simone could continue to draw solace from in along with the sound of the leaves blowing across the street on a warm breeze that felt just as good on her face now as it did when she was a child. Looking at Rebecca's profile, she wondered if she had ever felt such comfort.

Light spread evenly across the air now, and Rebecca's eyes narrowed into it, almost suspicious of what daylight could bring.

Simone couldn't fault her for that, but in her experience, walking into a situation with suspicion often created trouble in a self-fulfilling prophecy of disappointment.

It was an expression Simone had seen on the face of the woman she no longer knew far too often as of late, even before all the trouble. Sun was no longer a glow, it was a glare. It no longer warmed, it simply annoyed. It wasn't fatigue or whatever you wanted to call it, it was soul-weariness. Rebecca knew enough about the world and life and herself to have recognized it from very nearly the start. It was something that one usually had to deal with and muddle through. It may be lifted at some point, but looking forward to that only seemed to lend any sort of relief wings and speed.

Not long ago, they had been able to gossip and drink coffee and spend hours in bookstores and picking through whatever clothing stores that had cropped up wherever their travels had seen fit to take them. They laughed, and gave good-natured ribbing towards one another's viewpoints, and it never mattered because they had always been on the same level ground despite the legendary Fox ability to go the opposite direction than the one they should.

But now that Rebecca had gone her own way in the manner ordinary people can be able to do in their own everyday lives, he had seen fit to break away from it. At least, that's how it seemed. Gavin himself had fallen back into a place his forebears would not have expected or probably approved of; that of an intentional pacifist.

It was Simone who wasn't agreeing with it.

It was fine and well to allow oneself to gain higher ground and see no good in dealing death to somebody, but in Simone's opinion, Gavin had picked a less appropriate time to do it.

But now, there was Diana.

There was also now that part of herself that Simone hadn't expected to find in herself, or if she did, for it to rise to the surface so easily, full of a distressing and casual nature.

The room Gavin found Diana Adair in was one that he had realized he had actually forgotten about. It was perhaps twenty feet by twenty feet, and served no outward or point outside of being yet another room in the Manor. His great-grandfather may have used it to try out given illusions or something like that, or it could have been used as storage. He really didn't know, and could only remember it as it was right now; a self-serving sitting room with a matching couch and loveseat of indeterminate origin and age set before a picture window sporting a view of the valley beneath.

The decision to release Diana wasn't easily come by, but once she had volunteered to do something Gavin himself had been loathe to consider, he Simone and Rebecca had agreed to let her go ion the grounds she stay inside, letting her know there were ways to stop her should she try to make a break for it.

But these things were not her concern. She wanted to help and find her place among them, something most lycanthropes wanted to do. They felt themselves to be social outcasts, and rightfully so.

She was also mostly a stranger, and while she was one needing help, she was also one who didn't want it, and that was what ultimately had changed Gavin's mind. Once he had decided that Diana Adair was on a path all her own and could not be called back from it. She was a woman fueled by passion in its raw state of belief and couldn't refine it. She saw things as she did, and would do things as she liked.

It was the animal, convincing her she was less than she was, and she had been worn down by it through ignorance and physical exhaustion that she now listened to it, learned from it.

Soon, she would become it.

Welcome it. No one would follow her, and she would not come back.

Gavin was fine with that, provided the ends justified the means.

Even still:

"You sure you understand what it is we're talking about?"

Diana regarded him, eyes half-lidded. "What?"

"I'm just trying to make sure you understand."

"Death. Got it. Do you want me to start singing 'The Circle of Life?'"

"You're being asked to be a blunt instrument."

"Gavin, I'm a big girl. I understand what it is we're talking about, and you're forgetting that I told you I wanted to do it."

His gaze remained on her. In her eyes. The humanity was slipping, not falling away. Who was to say what would happen when she gave up all pretense of being human?

No one. There were no formal writings of any kind regarding the abandonment of the human self by a lycanthrope. The term 'Feral' came to mind, but one thing Gavin couldn't shake was the certainty that those who did it didn't miss it.

"Gavin," she said, shaking him from his reverie.

"Hmm? Sorry, I guess I'm not as awake as I thought."

"It's okay. Listen, it's okay. You guys keep acting like this is something terrible, and I'm flattered that you have your concerns for the consequence of my actions, but their my actions, and I'm in tune with them. The fact of it is that this person needs to be taken out… it's not the ideal, but a reality we have to face. I'm past the point of caring, and if all of your expressions are any indication, I'm well on my way to becoming whatever it is we lycanthropes become." Her eyes widened for emphasis while she finished: "*It doesn't bother me.*"

"And what will you do after?"

"After?"

She was making him say it. So be it. "After you kill him."

"I have no idea. Maybe I'll be finished with this life and start a new one. Maybe I'll stop being anything. There's too much out there for me to know."

Gavin nodded, and neither of them spoke for a long time.

"And what about you, Gavin?'

"What about me?"

"What are you going to do after you save the world?"

"Continue living in it."

"Even though no one will know about your deeds?"

"I think there's something to be said for that, yeah."

"And what makes you so sure that it will go unnoticed?"

He moved to the window, watched the fog burning off amongst the buildings and cars already moving.

"Because people have better things to do than be amazed when it doesn't suit them."

The man known as Solomon Archer would have been considered quite attractive in a mussy sort of way had his face sported a bit of color and his eyes didn't have that half-dead glaze about them that indicated to Rebecca that he knew far too much about most of the world he saw around him.

But the oddest thing about him was that he hadn't given up. No matter how many ghosts he had seen, or how many deaths he had been able to know, he always kept trying to rid himself of the pain, and in a way that didn't harm others or himself.

To the witch, that was most extraordinary in the face of modern life.

He kept the rifle close to hand, although now it was leaning against the west wall in the breakfast nook no one was using. She expected things to turn in the afternoon, when hunger would get the best of them. That was fine for her. As it was, she was ready to make a huge bowl of oatmeal for herself. All this moping around waiting for Karac to return was more than she could enjoy.

And while the distraction from her own thoughts was attractive, at least for a little while, she most sincerely hoped Solomon would stop asking questions about Diana, a woman she clearly did not know the first thing about anymore. The poor man had a severe crush on someone who most likely didn't know he drew breath. That in itself was bad, but throw in the added complication that he would probably see her death before his eyes, and things got too unsavory for her to even entertain for the point of distraction.

But Solomon was also the type of person she was trying to do her best for. Someone who didn't ant to know about the big picture not because he couldn't deal with it, but because he was of the mind that it was beyond him and he'd rather just get out of the way and let others handle the problem, which was a pity, because the man had a brain in his head and knew how to use it. He only wanted a normal life in the face of abject abnormality and willing to actually appreciate what he had once he got it, which in his case, would just be peaceful days and evenings where he could visit sleep and know when he was dreaming and enjoy the wakeful day.

He would only find solace in the illusions Gavin and Simone would cast over him, which after awhile would no longer suffice. And, he was bright enough to know when he had been under the wrong impression for too long, and therein would lie absolute resentment, even in a soul such as his.

But she still tried to hold out for the hope that it would be enough for him to only think he was cured. Maybe the spirits would get the hint that they were only causing pain and leave. Half of the time they didn't know why they were wandering around anyway. Maybe this would be sufficient proof their his not wanting them around and it would allow them to get their heads together enough to realize they should leave.

Or they would try harder, trying to pass on messages to loved ones or just being so miserable in life that they had to tie down the living even in the stillness of death.

Karac didn't feel the slightest bit guilty about stopping home after his visit with Fade to catch a few hours of sleep with not so much as a phone call to the Manor to give them an update. Let them work and concentrate on Solomon and Diana instead of what was now his problem.

He wasn't terribly surprised that little more than inroads had been made on the subjects, although he was glad to see they had let Diana have the run of the house rather than chaining her down. The rifle was now in Gavin's possession as lunch – delivered Chinese – was scarfed down.

"So has Fox Manor become the stronghold for us?" Asked Karac as he helped himself to a helping of broccoli beef. In the breakfast nook, Diana patted the spot beside her and scooted to the side to allow him room.

"It would look that way, yes." Gavin picked at his steamed rice.

"You feeling okay?"

"Yeah, more headaches is all."

"So what did you find out?" Asked Simone.

"I was informed to try back tomorrow."

While Karac continued to eat, he was very aware that three others; Gavin, Simone, and Rebecca, had all but frozen in various positions of chopstick-to-mouth.

"Is this Finder," Gavin muttered. "In fact, a Magic 8-Ball?"

"No, he's a Finder, which means we play by his rules. If you want him to get results, you have to realize you're on someone else's turf when you're doing it."

"So does that mean we'll see the book tomorrow?" Asked Simone. "I mean, how specific does this get?"

Karac's chopsticks lowered and he laid his hands palm flat on the surface of the table. He could feel Diana's eyes searching him for amount of tension and gauging his reaction. "I am a professional asking specific location on an item. You can either trust me to do this the right way, without bringing utter chaos upon you and your house by actually bringing the book in here or you can do this yourself."

Simone's hand came up. "Okay, Karac, it was just a question." She resumed eating. Rebecca followed. After a time, Karac did as well. A sound made him turn to where Gavin was now walking to the trash can to drop in him mostly uneaten food. He notified all that he was going to lie down, and not to wake him unless the world ended,

"Which will give you about ten minutes," Rebecca countered.

Whatever Gavin said in return was lost to grumbling and the growing distance between him and the group as he gained the stairs.

The fact that night arrived without further incident did little to quell the tension in the house. Simone made sure everybody had either a place to sleep or some kind of distraction to keep the peace amongst the obvious fact that they were all trying to act normal.

Except for Solomon, who seemed to have little to no trouble actually adapting into the new circumstances now that what he understood as trust among his surroundings and those who shared space with him were not out to harm him. He helped load the dishwasher, made the coffee and did whatever else might have been needed to make things go down a little easier. When one job was done, he'd turn to Simone and ask 'Okay, what else needs to be done?'

She could admire the work ethic, but after a point, it got to be where there really was nothing left to do except rest and try to keep your head from turning itself inside out.

But it was during that time of rest when she felt it best to give an illusion a shot. A simple one, just to ease him into the mindset. Regardless of what he might have said, he was not in the mindset to have a spell cast over him and have him wade hip-deep into the real world while she held out hope that it would be enough.

When he was asked to join her in the sitting room at the front of the house, he seemed to understand this was the business part of the situation. The only sign of distress he showed was a quick look over his shoulder at where Diana was watching television with Karac.

Simone moved a matched pair of Canterbury chairs to face one another in front of the bay window. Solomon sat and seemed relaxed as he smiled at her.

"I know you can't make any promises," he said. "But I feel better staying here, even if it's just for a little bit."

"Do you understand what's going on?"

"As much as I care to. There's something somebody wants for the sake of destruction, some people might call it hell. Karac might know where to get it, and you and Gavin are the ones to know these types of things."

"Okay, and what about you, Rebecca, and Diana?"

"I think me and Diana are just in the wrong place at the wrong time, if you get my meaning."

"I think I do."

"And Rebecca's just trying to help."

"Are you scared?"

Solomon's head tilted and his eyes stared at a spot somewhere past Simone's head. "I don't think I've considered that. I guess that means I feel pretty safe."

"Fair enough."

"Simone? Sorry to interrupt." She turned to Karac, who had appeared in the doorway, Diana now behind him.

"Would you mind if we stepped out for a bit?"

Simone made a show of raising her eyebrows. "You sure that's wise, Karac?"

"I think we're safe, yeah."

"Taking the rifle?"

"I *am* in the room," noted Diana.

"I know," replied Simone. "Karac, are you taking the rifle?"

The Finder looked sheepish, but produced the rifle.

"It's your call, Karac. I'm okay with it, but if something happens, it's your responsibility, and you get to tell Rebecca."

"I am not Rebecca's ward," said Diana, no longer looking into the room.

"No, but you're here because of her, and you owe a bit of gratitude for that."

Diana nodded, but would not turn her head to face her.

Simone could feel a throbbing at her temples and her shoulders beginning a soft burn. Tension headache, she knew. Otherwise known as a 'Do I really have to take this crap?' headaches. She waved the pair away. "Karac, you know the risks."

"I won't lose her."

"Woof, woof," said Diana. "Still in the room."

"Actually, I was referring to the glaring fact that if she kills you, we'll never find that book."

"Ah. And on that touching note..." The Finder led the way to the foyer. Simone kept her eyes on the doorway until the front door closed. When her gaze returned to Solomon, he was trying to find the Torpedo through the window.

"You okay with this?" She asked.

Solomon snapped back to her. "Huh? Yes, that's why I'm here."

"Not what I meant." She shunted her head to indicate the engine keying to life.

Solomon looked at his lap, his foot pulled up across his thigh. Foot tapping at the air in a tune only he could hear. "I owe Karac a lot."

"He hasn't done anything for you yet."

"He's led me to you."

"We haven't done much, either."

"Do you guys not like Karac? Seems like a nice guy to me."

"He's a Finder. They tend to be real cool, but then you get to know what they'll do in order to make something happen in their line of work, and it kinda ruins the whole effect."

Solomon looked up at a spot on her face, then looked away. He was trying to decide whether he wanted to know the specifics. Simone decided to make the decision for him.

"What say we concentrate on you for a bit?"

Now Solomon's eyes stayed on hers. "Okay."

"May I hold your hands?"

"Excuse me?"

"For the benefit of contact and knowing I'm here. Sometimes it's best that way until we do this a couple of times."

"What are we going to do?"

"Trust each other."

"Oh."

Solomon held out his hands for Simone to accept. They were dry and warm with some slight fall chapping on the knuckles. Her eyes held his.

"This won't hurt a bit, but try not to jump."

"Why?"

And she was in.

It was a state of being not outside of oneself and not inside another, but somewhere in between, where it was not intrusive to the person it was being done to, nor destructive to the person performing it. To the best of Simone's knowledge it had no name, and she had never heard of anyone doing anything quite like this before.

It was a technique she tried solely on imagination and inspiration, spurred on by Gavin's incessant migraines. It had taken the edge off them, but hadn't alleviated them completely. But it was a means to an end, and something she'd never experienced before, but since it didn't appear dangerous, she figured she could try to at least find the edges before she tried to push them.
Unless, a part of her warned, she'd already jumped well past that point.

It was peaceful there between them, and to his credit, Solomon jumped not a whit. He even smiled at her in a way that didn't seem like he was trying to just appear normal.

"You're safe here, Solomon. Do you know this?"

"Yes."

"Do you believe this?"

"Yes."

"Is this house worthy of your trust?"

"Yes."

"Then let's start small. Let me show you something you want to see."

And he did. The sound of pattering just outside the window began almost immediately. It grew in intensity and frequency until it resembled a sizzle.

She separated then, and looked at him. But his attention was diverted outside at the falling rain he had wished to see, and with her help, he was. His smile spread and he couldn't take his eyes from the pane.

"Is that real?"

"Certainly seems real, doesn't it?" Don't lie, but don't reveal the truth.

He chuckled and went to the window, where rainwater was now leaving blurry rivers flowing down the pane, causing shadows to fall down his face, lit and thrown by the exterior garden lights.

"Is this how it starts?"

"In a way, yeah."

"But how did you make it rain?"

"It's all in being in control of balance." Not a complete lie. She was in control of his balance of perception. His own imagination was doing the rest. This would include the smell that created the smile in the first place. "So yeah, this is how we start down the road. We start small and nice, just like this."

"So the change isn't shocking."

"Right. You may be comfortable within our house and the rest it provides from your ability." Be careful not to call it a 'Gift,' she reminded herself. "But there may be a point that the absence of the presence you're used to may cause an odd kind of withdrawl."

"That would suck. I don't want that."

"And you might now suffer from it. It's just a possibility."

"How long will it last?"

"Hard to say. Maybe a couple hours, tops."

Solomon nodded as she returned to her seat.

"In the meantime, just enjoy something you *want* to see for a change."

Solomon smiled and touched the pane. For once while he was awake, he appeared to be somewhere he sincerely wished to be.

Imagine, she thought. And watched.

Diana was the first one out of the Torpedo when they had reached the right turnout at Crest Heights, well above the hoi and polloi of Hollywood and its trappings of light and fame that didn't seem quite so important or nearly so blinding these days.

There were things behind her own eyes that were far brighter and larger, not the least of which was herself.

Her palms rubbed at the backs of her thighs to re-stimulate the blood the Torpedo's seats had taken from her, skin whispering against the denim of Simone's jeans.

Karac seemed completely at ease as he emerged from the driver's side, staring into the horizon as the door shut with a swing of his arm more like an afterthought rather than an actual action. Diana lowered herself on the cooling hood of the Torpedo, watching Karac's expression carefully. If he gave a care about someone sitting on his car, he gave no outward sign, and went so far as to lean against the front end of it himself, arms crossed, eyes strictly on the stars overhead.

"Come out here a lot?" She asked.

"Not often enough. I keep forgetting to come out here to get the old bearings back."

"Seems to be a popular way to do it. Rebecca tried to turn me on to it herself."

"How are you getting along with her?"

"She's sweet in a strict 'I'm gonna fix you' sort of a way."

"Something you don't care much for." "Not as a rule, no."

"Why?"

"Because I'm a big girl and I can think for myself. I was always taught that you need to rely on yourself more than others."

"Sound advice, knowing yourself."

"I don't see how you can let others know you if you don't know what's in you."

"And do you like what's in you?"

She regarded him, pursed her lips. "You mean the animal?"

Now he turned to face her. Here eyes dropped for a moment, probably just enough for him to notice. "I mean what makes you you. There's more than the animal."

"Did Rebecca tell you to bring me out here?"

"What? No. Actually, the idea for company was me being polite."

Diana made a point of narrowing her eyes. "Well, aren't you the chivalrous one."

"No, just honest. I didn't think it would be such a bad idea for either one of us."

"Neither one of us fit much with the rest."

"I'm not sure any of us fit."

"Meaning?"

"It's just uncomfortable."

"There's no comfort for any of us?"

"Not much, no. I'd just as soon wait for this whole mess to blow over. It's effecting more lives than it has to."

"It's just how it worked out."

"With Rebecca and I relying on others to solve problems."

"Well, it's noble to help."

"Two people have been dragged into something they are not prepared to deal with, and Gavin and Simone seem to be just fine with that."

"They have something that needs to be done. You know, the greater good, and all that."

"And now, life for the two of you will never be the same."

"It was already changing, Karac." Her fingers traced his shoulder through the faded denim of his tattered jacket. She rested her palm on him for a moment, then returned her hand back to her lap. Her gaze remained fixed on his profile. He hadn't shaved for at least a day, and his upper lip was showing the first sign of chap. "Nothing would've changed that."

"That's what I'm upset about."

Simone's shoulders angled toward the brooding man next to her. "Has this whole thing been *all* bad?"

"It's hard to see the forest for the trees right now, I'd say."

Her hand reached out to him then, fingertips curling at his chin, turning his face to her. "It hasn't been all bad." The corners of her lips were still curled upwards as she drew his lips to hers. Her lips parted and sought his again even as he pulled away.

"I don't think this is what we need to be doing."

Diane's palm rested flat against her lap and her upper teeth worried her lower lip.

"I thought this was why you wanted me to come along."

"I thought we could both benefit from getting out of the house."

"I misread the signals. I thought there was some mutual attraction there."

"It's just not the right time to get into something like that." Then, as if a thought had occurred to him, "What about Solomon?"

"What about Solomon?"

"I got the idea he thought you were attractive."

"Not really my type. I'm trying to get around the guys I think need help."

"I don't need help? Who doesn't need help?"

"You seem to have a good understanding of your surroundings."

"And zero control of them."

"No one has absolute control over their surroundings."

"I just react to them."

"You're not saying it's not me, it's you, are you?"

"No. Not at all."

"Okay." She rubbed at the side of her face contemplatively. "I just got out of a bad relationship, so maybe my scope's just not working."

"What went wrong?"

"He had a terminal case of marriage."

"And did we know this?"

"If you mean 'We' in the queenly sense of the word, yes."

"And you pursued him anyway?"

"No lectures."

"No, honest."

"Yes, I pursued him. Who wants to be alone? I thought. For some reason, I didn't want to be the woman sitting at home wondering what could have been."

"Nobody wants that."

"Yeah, but the perspective changes when it's you, doesn't it?"

"Usually."

"So I pursued something that was doomed from the start with a man that was unworthy of my attentions because a part of me was afraid of being alone."

"And what has all this taught you about that?"

Now she faced him. The smile had returned. It felt good. Strong. "That I'm not afraid anymore."

"Is that the animal talking?"

"I think so. I'm all right with it."

"What do you find in it?"

"Excuse me?"

"What do you find in the voice of the animal?"

"Me."

"Weren't you in there all the time anyway?"

"A bit of me was, looking."

"And this is your true voice?"

"The animal doesn't have a voice, *per se.*"

"Your true self, then?"

"Well, a self that I'm comfortable with anyway."

"Aren't you concerned about the safety of others or yourself?"

"Myself? I'll be fine."

"And anybody else?"

Her gaze returned to her lap. A cricket chirped alone in the dark. "Diana?"

"I heard you."

"And do you have an answer?"

"Not especially, no."

"Are you still satisfied with your decision?"

"What decision is that? To be myself?"

"Well, it's pretty clear you feel comfortable with going feral."

"Is that what it's called?"

"Charming, isn't it?"

"Not really."

"Hmm."

"There are places I can go where I won't hurt anyone."

"Why don't you allow the others to help?"

Diana held his eyes. She reached out to him, stroking his face as if the tips of her fingers had need to remember the curve of his jaw. "Because I'm not broken."

Karac's eyes were the first to lower.

The two of them sat on the hood of the Tucker, and after a awhile, just enjoyed the silence and the pinpricks of starlight pushing their way to Earth.

Gavin was awake, but stayed still on the bed as he heard the click of the bedroom door pulling away from its frame just enough to let in the silhouette of his Simone, who moved otherwise soundlessly across the floor. The headache was gone, but it had left the familiar soft-headedness that was not entirely unwelcome and allowed him to focus on the digital clock which was busy burning 2:25 in red numerals into the darkness of the bedroom.

He watched as she paused before the window on her side of the bed, her form illuminated by moonlight and shadow. She pulled her shirt from over her head and let it drop to the floor. Her hands disappeared behind her back to unclasp her bra and let it join her shirt. The jeans whispered against her skin as she hunched to pull first one leg, then the other free of them. He eased herself onto her side of the bed, swinging her legs in as she raised the sheets to accommodate her in that one smooth motion she had. A soft sound escaped her as he curled close to him, mindful of keeping the cold skin feet from him. She'd wait until she knew he was feeling better before subjecting his calves to such terror. No matter how often he'd told her to sleep with socks on, she simply didn't like them, except for those little red ones she wore, but she only seemed to put those on when she was feeling like being the amorous side of herself he referred to in his mind as 'The Cute Smart Ass.'

Gavin rolled to face her, took her smooth body in his arms and held her warmth close to him. "Feel better?" She asked, her breath warm against his chest.

"Mmm-hmm." Her hair still held to slight scent of her shampoo. "How are things?"

"Well, the house is settled." Simone replied, nudging him onto his back so she could rest the side of her face against his chest. "Karac and Diana just got back."

"Beer run?"

Simone told him about the conversation she had with them before they left, and Gavin was glad she couldn't see him rolling his eyes.

"Well, I suppose we should be thankful they both returned."

"Yes, I suppose."

"How's Solomon."

"Not bad. Maybe this whole thing can serve some small good for him. He trusts us, and we've got some progress going with a bit of perception changing."

"Straight illusions?"

"So far. I'm starting with rain."

"How'd that end up?"

"By the end of the session, he was adding lightning and thunder all by himself."

"So he's receptive."

"Aggressively so, it seems. He's on the couch, sleeping."

"Guest rooms for the others?" "Rebecca and Diana are sharing the one to the west, Karac was supposed to be sharing with Solomon to the east, but Solomon wanted to be alone. For that matter, I have no idea where Rebecca's actually going to sleep, because the last I saw her, she was meditating at the kitchen table."

"She wasn't burning the incense, was she?"

"I'm afraid I said she could."

"Not that god-awful patchuli."

"Sandalwood. I made sure of that."

"Another reason I love you."

"Hey, I like the smell of patchuli."

"And I like the smell of you." He pulled her closer, the softness of her breasts pressing into him.

"That's not quite what I had in mind."

"Ireland? I'm sure Shannon Airport's forgotten that whole thing with the Tabla Box."

"Actually, I was thinking about maybe staying here and adding something to the house."

A groan. "Oh, good, like a third story or developing the south wing for some reason?" A yawn.

"I thought we might add the sound of some extra feet."

The yawn stopped. "What kind of extra feet. We got extra feet now."

"Small ones."

At this, she raised her face away from his chest and looked at him. "Small ones?"

"Teensy."

He wasn't sure, but Gavin thought Simone may be smiling.

She chuckled and kissed his chest and curled herself closer to him. "Just hold me tonight, huh, baby?"

Gavin smiled and kissed the top of her head. "Anything you say, killer."

He stroked her hair and felt the rise and fall of her shoulders. He let his eyes close and enjoy the sensation of the woman he loved held tight in his arms and still feeling comfortable there.

After a time, he kissed the crown of her head again. "Awake?"

She made a sound into his chest. "Mostly. Why?"

"I was just thinking about what we were planning to do when this whole thing blows over."

"Actually looking at the light at the end of the tunnel as something other than an oncoming train, are you?"

"Mayyyyyybe."

"My, my. Gavin Fox, whatever has come over you?"

"You, probably."

"*Pffft.*"

"I'm serious."

"Then double *pffft.*"

"Maybe I just want something to look forward to."

"Doesn't sound too unreasonable," she said, words blurred by a yawn. "Maybe we can actually go to Italy and be normal people." "You ready for that?" She asked. "Big step, something we thought we weren't going to do."

"The world needs more of your light," he replied, stroking her face. "And I would love to see that. What about you, are you ready for that?"

"More than you know, honey." Her mouth pressed down to his and held him there for long enough for he couldn't remember when they'd kissed for as long. When they broke away, her fingers played at the hair on his chest. "Does this mean you're going to make me an honest woman, too?"

He chuckled into the darkness and held her. "Now why ever would I want to make a big step like that?"

He could feel her smile pressing into his chest.

"Bastard," she said, and gave his stomach a slap.

CHAPTER TWENTY-EIGHT

What you fear becomes your leader.

Lucas Brady, IF IT CAN BE

He was running out of words.

Alec Copeman made his way back to the familiar confines of the sanctuary as the last of the mourners pulled away. No matter how many times he had performed a graveside committal service, it never seemed enough to remember someone with. And, more often than not as years went by, he was burying more and more strangers; most of them had followed God, according to their loved ones, but never kept a church home.

He did better at the memorial services before the burial, but he had no idea why.

Alisha Hazard was eighty-eighty years of age when she passed away due to the term 'Natural causes,' which had always seemed a bit more nebulous for its own good, in Alec's opinion. Similar to 'Heart failure.' It gave a reason, but not the cause. In Alec's opinion, it allowed too much room for someone to believe somebody somewhere couldn't be bothered. He'd had the pleasure of meeting the departed a few years back, at his church, during her daughter's wedding, over which Alec had presided. She was one of those people who you could just look at and know they had a greater understanding about the world than most of those among them, and had no need to prove it to themselves or others. She'd complimented him on his ceremony, and thanked him for its brevity. He had a voice built more for the radio than the pulpit, she told him. Later, as he was departing the reception after he'd said a few words in prayer for the couple, she had stopped him, and quite matter-of-factly stated that while she thought most organized religion was bullshit, he seemed to represent the God she believed in well enough, and said that he 'Didn't seem like such a bad egg.'

And somehow, coming from her, whom he didn't know and had her own understanding of – no, perhaps 'Agreement with' was better put – the universe, it had meant a great deal.

But it never seemed enough. A life had left the world, whether he or anybody else hade known them. A presence had left, and Alec was of the mind that everyone had an impact on everyone else, in some way. A kind of spiritual domino effect most seemed to discount at an alarming rate.

He didn't write it off to distractions. More to the need of them just to get through a day. Everyone needed to disconnect, to be with themselves once in a while. It was only healthy to center oneself. But when it went beyond that, it became distraction, and when it went past *that*, it became a liability. It became status.

But these were things that people had to come to grips with themselves, and then agree with one another about them. But even that shattered as the 'My way is better' came into play.

And even as distanced as Alec felt, he was glad he was where he was. It was an advantage that he felt quietly proud of. Bono had nothing on him; Alec *had* found what he was looking for.

He went into his office, sat down behind his desk and began going through his schedule, mostly correspondence that needed to be kept up on. Mostly email, and of a more casual nature than anything official. For that, he was grateful.

The knock on his door brought him away from his thoughts. It opened as he acknowledged it. Mrs. Carrey poked her head in.

"David's here."

Alec thanked her and pushed away from his desk and made his way to the entrance of the sanctuary. David was still walking up the smooth stone pathway from the unpaved parking lot to the north of the church. He tipped the brim of an imaginary hat as he gained closer to Alec.

"To what do I owe this visit, Sheriff?"

David shook his head. "Wish I could say it was social. I'm trying to follow-up on the death of Bishop Ashe. Everybody's hit a dead end with it, and while the Vatican has acknowledged it and has made arrangements to have his body flown back to Vatican City, something doesn't fit right, and I wanted to get your two cents."

"You have no suspects?"

"None. The State's fine with counting it as a 'Roadside fatality,' regardless of the proof in my mind that it was murder. The damage to that car was just too great to be figured as a simple tumble off the side of the highway."

"Road rage?"

"Thought of that myself. Road rage can involve running another driver off the road, but not like this. There are paint markings along the guardrail, primer left behind on the deceased's car that's obviously from the other car. There didn't appear to be anything missing from the car or the body, either. It was like somebody found a target, and hit it. The motive is beyond me."

"So the case goes cold."

"So it seems. And without sufficient evidence, I can't open the file once it's closed."

"I'm sorry, David."

"I know, Father. But that's not why I'm here."

"Why, then?"

"It seems odd to me that out of all the travelers on the road, a Bishop was the one to push the buttons of this guy."

Alec nodded.

"His briefcase was opened, and while it could have popped open in the fall, and there's no sign of tampering, I can't shake the feeling the perp was looking for something."

"I can't think of anything of value he would have had."

"All this just make me believe that the person or persons responsible were out to get him because of his association with the church."

"Someone killed him because his was a Bishop?"

"It's happened before. Not often, and never around here, but I've heard of people who misplace a given kind of anger toward God toward his representatives."

Alec agreed. Such stories never seemed to make the news unless it was Christmas or especially heinous. "Sometimes they have been dealt a trauma personally."

"Molestation?"

"Sadly, yes."

"Have you received any threats?"

"None."

"Okay. Keep an eye out, though. It may be anyone. A stranger, someone you know as a regular in your congregation."

"I'll do my best. Business isn't exactly booming, so I should be able to keep a fresh perspective."

David nodded, looked out to the horizon. "Those are some nasty-looking clouds coming over."

Alec hadn't noticed the sky for days, just nodded along with the Sheriff.

"Bad storm coming," David said, eyes squinting as if trying to focus on the deep pewter clouds.

"Looks like. Maybe it'll pass us."

"We've been lucky for as long as I can remember. The last case of flooding we had was in 1962. There's a store on Main that still has the watermark they made that day. Nearly six feet of water."

Grant's Collectables. Alec had seen the line drawn in the door jamb with a note written about what it was from, noting the water level at five and a half feet.

"No way it can be as bad as that one was," said Alec.

"There's all sorts of damage that can be visited, not just from flooding." Now he turned to Alec. The wind kicked up a scud of his hair across his eyes. "You may not know it by the size of your congregation, Father, but you are a loved member of this community."

"Thank you, David. It's always good to know these things."

"People haven't forgotten how to look out for others around here. Well, most people."

"And I'm proud to be among them."

Once again, David's eyes went to the sky. "There are few things I can believe in anymore, Father. I have my family and my job, but it's the job that shakes me most."

"But you stay with it."

"That's right."

"And why is that?"

"Because I feel that I need to do it. Someone has to keep trying in the face of all the quitters and corruption."

"Right there with you."

His eyes returned to Alec. "I know. That's why I'm here."

"Pardon?"

"Because, for once, I know who the good guys are."

David once again tilted the chapeau only he could see, and made his way back to the car.

That was good, Alec reflected as his own eyes took in the clouds that even now looked darker than they were mere moments ago, because judging by the looks of things, the bad guys could be anywhere.

He was becoming a regular again at The Wash, and the one thing Karac knew that meant for sure was that he was going to have at least more than one drink, which he found curious as the flask of Bols was still in his bag untouched since he'd fallen in with Gavin and Simone.

He was the only one who seemed to have any trepidation as to the use of the Manor as a stronghold. It was telling the enemy that there were others who were afraid, and it happened with enough speed that it would appear a genuine action, something, if the enemy did indeed have spies of some kind lurking about, would be able to use to their advantage.

But none of this seemed to worry anyone. Surely, Karac would lead them to wherever it was they needed to be going and Gavin would be able to browbeat their enemy into submission.

But that wasn't going to be enough. This person would have to die.

Enter Diana Adair, the Not-Quite-Reluctant Assassin. She had found her place, and herself by the sound of it. Others would try to tame her, but there was no point. She'd been on the civilized side of the fence, and didn't much acre for it. Cared so little for the experience, in fact, that she seemed able to break away from everything and everyone she could have possibly held dear.

And not look back.

That, perhaps, was where her humanity ended.

And as long as Gavin could keep his hands clean, she could do as she wished with whoever it was who they now considered an enemy. Convenient. It was what made the world go 'round. At least for now. At least for them.

He had tried his best to allow instinct to hit him and lead him to the book, but nothing was coming. Not because he was trying too hard, but because it wasn't working for him then. The older he got, the less often it worked when he was on a schedule.

And there was always a schedule.

He ordered a whiskey sour from the waitress whose name he knew but could not dredge up at the moment and watched the patrons going about what they knew as a regular routine; escaping the workweek by going to the Wash. Dancing. Hooking up. Flirting. Drinking. Doing things people did when they didn't know how close to the edge of the knife they on, and never would.

Karac watched as he made short work of the drink.

He hated them. Every last one.

The touch at his shoulder made him leave his chair, but he eased down as Mia Baudino came into view from behind him, dressed in what appeared to be a black Lycra bodysuit with only a pyramid-studded belt to top it off, her hands raised in surrender.

"Jeez, mister, calm down." She took the seat opposite him. This time, she used the chairback to actually lean against.

"Julie Newmar know you've got her clothes?"

Mia laughed, a loud sincere thing that made Karac smile. "Catwoman ain't got nothing on me, honey. Hey, did you ever think she and ol' Batman knocked boots?"

"I got that impression when I older, yeah."

"Think they kept their masks on?"

"Oh, I'm sure of it."

"Kinda distant," she mused. "But kinda kinky in a mask-wearing sort of way."

Karac nodded.

"I see you've seen the light I've been trying to show you."

"How's that?"

She chucked her chin at the empty glass still in his hand. "The whiskey sour." She waved to someone behind him. It turned out to be his server, who took Mia's order for two new drinks.

"What brings you here tonight?" She asked. "You don't look too happy."

"Just got a lot on my mind."

"Penny for your thoughts?"

"Is that all they're worth?" He grinned.

"Hey, you should feel lucky. I usually only offer my ear. I charge extra for concerned nods."

"Ever feel so out of place you have nowhere to go?"

"I have. I'm familiar with the feeling."

"What do you do?"

"Whatever I can to remind myself of who I am and to let myself be different."

"You don't want to be like them?" He glanced at the dance floor.

"I don't know. I used to think so, but I'm my own person. If I were out there trying to act like them, I'd make an ass out of myself. And if I'm going to do that, I might as well be in on the joke and have a good laugh my own self."

The drinks arrived and he regarded her over the edge of his glass as he now sipped the amber liquid, allowing to spread and warm instead of burn on its way down.

"What's that expression on your face doing there?" Mia asked.

"What? I'm smiling."

"Right. Looks out of place on such a hangdog face."

"Sorry, I'll get rid of it." He made his best Charles Bronson face.

"Naw, I like it the other way. You don't look so damn shut off."

"I'll do my best."

"Yes, you will." She smiled, and they drank.

The evening wasn't the total loss and embittered thing Karac had been bent on making it for himself. They shot pool, proving that Mia was better at Eight-Ball where Karac dominated in straight pool, exchanged blue jokes, which Mia won hands down, with her uncanny ability to use mouth-generated sound effects, facial expressions and hip motions to further augment her tales. Karac found that even in light of her use of various sexual terms, he was unable to form certain words in front of a woman, something that seemed to endear him to Mia.

The only thing Karac couldn't bring himself to do was dance. The music was too upbeat, he claimed to her. Not really his thing. He had no natural rhythm. She smiled, and continued to ask through the night anyway. When the Cowboy Junkies' version of 'Sweet Jane' began to smolder through the house speakers, she all but dragged his protesting self onto the dance floor. She stopped when they were parked at dead center of the hardwood and looked at him. She was not an angel, but there was light behind her eyes just the same.

"You don't have to dance with me to this," she explained. "Just hold me."

He just held her.

As soon as her head rested on his shoulder, he understood where he needed to be. The answer to what Gavin and Simone wanted was in Mexico City.

His eyes opened partway, and he watched the colors and shapes of the other dancers sway in and out of his line of vision. Mia's body was warm against his, and the flat of her thumb was stroking his collarbone through his shirt.

"Mia."

"Mmm?"

"I've got to go."

Her face turned up to him, her brows creased. "Why? Did I do something? Did I not do something?"

"It's business, Mia. I'm sorry. I just remembered I need to be somewhere." He couldn't look at her as he pulled away and slalomed his way through the forms of the dancers.

He made a quick wave to Gregor in an effort to seem normal as he moved past the main bar and through the back way after seeing the front entrance was blocked by a throng of club-goers who were in a snit with the management about something.

The only light the rear entrance of the Wash gained was the light that bled through was from sodium lights of the parking lot behind it. He palmed his car keys, only now remembering he'd taken the beaten-up Mazda, and headed west for the parking lot's closest of the two entrances.

And he was certain he was going to die.

Shadows moved from the right and to the left as he jammed his hand back into his bag, coming up with the switchblade. The *snick* of its opening rebounded off the alley walls and off into the night.

He smelled rain.

The shadows became form; hooded sweatshirt. About as tall as he was. Then came the hiss of the Bowie knife, at least nine inches long, leaving its sheath to flash in the sporadic light.

The man wasn't here for his wallet. He were here for what they thought he had. And, having nothing, kill him. Knives were quiet, and when handled correctly, they were fast. The figure stepped in and spun, giving a quick swipe that hissed in the air. He lunged in, then recoiled as Karac dodged, his feet slipping in a pool of vomit. The only hope Karac had was to run and make it back to the door. He turned into something of a blur. Wind and motioned whipped across his face as the clicking of another kind of knife came into play.

Mia stood to his left, facing the attacker. She gained the ground between them and was nearly cut by a diagonal slash from her target. Her arm blurred as the knife whipped across the attacker's hood. The grunt from within the hood told Karac she had struck flesh.

Mia's free hand came and slammed into the attacker's face, she spun and readied a roundhouse kick when her target decided to run. Karac knew if he had actually appeared to have been able to take the attacker, Mia would have chased them down instead of turning back to Karac himself.

He stared at Mia then, maybe three feet away. There was the clicking sound again. It was from the butterfly knife she now flipped closed.

Karac turned on rubbery knees and made his way back to the parking lot. He was dimly aware of Mia following him. Blessedly, she did not speak until they were in the lot and Karac had slumped behind the wheel.

"That can't possibly be what you meant by business."

"I can't do this right now, Mia."

"What, talk or drive? Your hands are shaking. You've done this before, but you still don't like it."

He tried to swallow the ball of cotton in his throat. "I was being mugged."

"Of course you were."

She leaned into him, pulling him close by the collar of his jacket. Her lips found his. They were warm and soft and full of life. Their kiss deepened, and she held him by the back of his head, fingers curling into his hair. She broke the kiss, lingering at his lips as long as she could before rising and moving to the passenger side and getting in. She took his hand and pressed it to her lips, eyes boring softly, steadily into his.

"Home," she said, and smiled as he keyed the car.

It began to rain.

Karac awoke on his belly, face profiled across a pillow. He was dimly aware that he was naked, and the evening returned to him, gleaming and sure.

She had the capacity to be so gentle that it startled him. She had smiled, touched his face just so, and made a reality for him, as momentary as it may be, that was he was instantly at home in.

214

He turned to the side of the bed where he had last seen her, chest rising and falling in sleep, one corner of her mouth still curled. But she was not there. He pushed himself up to where he could sit and rubbed his face with his hands. The warm smell of freshly brewed coffee wafted its way into the room and he smiled, swinging his legs free of the bed and pulling on the crumpled pair of Levis that had been discarded in the night. His steps were heavy and lazy as he made his way down the hall. The voice from last night yammering about Mexico City was still on its train, riding around his head. Mia had driven it from him last night and, despite what he knew to be better, he allowed it.

She sat on the floor with her back to him, sifting through his CD collection, sipping a mugful of what had to be the strongest coffee he'd ever smelled. She wore the white button-down shirt he wore the night before, nothing else. Her hair had been pulled back into a half-completed bun, tendrils of hair still free around her face. Karac knew she heard his approach, and she only turned her head enough for part of her profile to be seen by him. Her eyes still lowered to the CD booklet she had laid out on her lap.

He pressed his face into her neck. Her hair still smelled of the rain that had fallen into it the night before. "Morning."

"Morning."

She spun in place and turned to plant a kiss on his lips, then on his nose. "Sleep well?"

"Yes, ma'am."

"Good."

He straightened, went to the kitchen where the smell was even heavier.

"How long have you been up?"

"Mmm. Dunno. Haven't paid much attention. Maybe twenty minutes. You looked so peaceful I didn't dare wake you." "Thank you. I needed the rest."

Most of Mia's chuckle was lost in her mug.

Karac poured his first cup of the day into a nondescript black mug and joined Mia on the floor.

"Should we talk about last night?" He asked.

She peered at him through her bangs. "I don't think we need to."

"I do."

"Okay."

"I don't normally do this."

"Are you talking about having sex with a strange woman, or what happened in the alleyway?"

"Both, actually."

The tip of her tongue flicked to the middle of her upper lip and her head cocked slightly. "Karac, look. What happened last night was self-defense, and no matter if we'd slept together or not, I consider you a friend, and I helped protect you."

"And thanks for that. Without you, I'd have – "

"Found your way out. I know you, Karac. You're not one to die in an alley. You're too dynamic for that."

"Not the word I would use."

"And you're smart enough to know they weren't after your wallet."

"Yeah."

"Any idea as to what would make someone try to kill you?"

"I lead an eccentric lifestyle."

"I can tell."

"How so?"

She stretched her body across the floor to the nearest shelf holding various DVDs. A part of him somewhere near his stomach warmed and sank.

"Let's see: *Captain Blood* starring Robert Donat; *Batman*, directed by Orson Welles; and a copy of *Butch Cassidy and the Sundance Kid* starring Paul Newman and Steve McQueen… shall I go on?"

"What are you trying to say?"

"None of these movies were made with these exact lineups. I mean, I'm not for old movies, but I know Paul Newman was with Robert Redford when they bust out of that shack at the end of the picture, and Errol Flynn was the only Captain Blood I know of."

"They're just rarities, is all."

"Uh-huh." She stretched out once more, this time to where a stack of CDs stood on the floor. "This is Led Zeppelin's first album."

"Right."

"With Steve Winwood singing."

Karac snatched the CD case away and glared.

"What, you're pissed off at me for looking at stuff that's left in plain sight?"

"Been a while since I've had company who'd have a care about what's on my shelves."

"So I figured." "What's your take on all this?"

"You're involved with some weird shit."

"Indeed," was all Karac could think of to say.

Mia grinned. "I like weird shit."

"Don't you want me to explain?"

"No. I'm afraid that if you do, they'll all disappear. I don't pretend to be the smartest cookie in the world, but I know there's things I don't understand. These things are among the stuff that can't kill you." Her expression tightened. "They won't kill you, will they?"

"No. They're meant to be enjoyed. They should exist, even if for curiosity's sake, but don't."

"I think I understand," Mia said, rising. After a soft kiss, she held up the copy of *Butch Cassidy and the Sundance Kid*. "I want to watch this one first."

He drew her close and held her. "I can't stay long."

"Business, right. I know. I promise to leave right after the movie, and I won't take anything home with me."

"And?"

She beamed dutifully, only a pinch of sarcasm with her hands folded beneath her chin. "And I promise I won't tell anyone what I saw here."

216

But for the grace of believing her in the continuing afterglow and his being grateful for it, he let her have her way, and true to his word, stayed for a few minutes before leaving for the Manor.

CHAPTER TWENTY-NINE

We are all attuned to one another. It is up to us to decide whether we want *to be.*

Rebecca Scott, THE THIRD AGE

Rebecca stood barefoot on tiptoe upon the balcony belonging to the west guest bedroom, eye lidded and drawing in the rain-soaked air deep into her chest, holding it there, and letting the breath do slowly through pursed lips. She repeated the process until she felt the time was right open her eyes and look upon the world, which she did.

It was too still. Fox Manor was located far enough away from the beaten path to allow for sounds of nature to be a regular attraction, yet there was none. No amount of meditation had helped her drift off to sleep, she had to resort to an antihistamine offered by Simone in order to feel drowsy enough to drop off to sleep. She now shared a bed with Diana, but the two had little to speak of these days as it became clear that Gavin was discovering how much power Diana had over her lycanthropy, and that degree of control was considerable, as was Diana's growing interest in becoming something less than human and with a dire mission. Most of all, she was not considered expendable, when in point of fact she very much was. Who would mourn this woman should things go wrong? Her parents, surely, but how would they be notified?

Rebecca herself would mourn, but she had already done a bit of that for Diana ever since it became obvious the woman had little to no interest in pulling free of the wild.

But this was Diana's choice; to not be cured, and to give over to a side that did not readily accept or understand consequences.

In his training and observance of Diana, Gavin had also felt it was high time to give her the run of the house. After all, Rebecca mused, it certainly didn't seem right to let the one person you were counting on to do your dirty work for you not have certain freedoms or liberties, even though Rebecca was sure that given the chance, Diana would bolt.

Then there was the case of Solomon Archer. Yes, that sweet man whose life had changed dramatically since arriving at a place where the ghosts would not follow. He was a kind man, and seemed to easily slip into the comfortable persona of someone who belonged and felt safe, even if they knew that was to be short-lived at best.

But exactly how long this would last for him was anyone's guess; Simone simply couldn't let go of the fact that keeping illusions before his eyes and teaching him in a way that masqueraded as not teaching to reinforce these things instead of solving the problem.

But there was the rub, there was no cure.

Only illusion.

She envied the possibility.

The knock at the door made her turn and gather the robe borrowed from Simone around herself.

"Yes?"

"It's Solomon, Rebecca."

"Come in."

Solomon peered into the bedroom, apparently on the pretense of seeing something he shouldn't. "I just wanted to invite you downstairs. I made breakfast."

She smiled and stepped toward the door. "Really?"

"Yeah. It's not bad, if I do say so myself."

"Well, that sounds lovely, Solomon, I'll be right down."

At the table were everyone save Karac, who had called earlier to tell Gavin he would be on his way shortly.

Playing the part of proud cook was Solomon, who provided the assembled eggs Benedict with Hollandaise sauce, bacon and orange juice. "Solomon," said Simone. "This is fresh squeezed juice."

"Uh-huh."

"Where did you find the time to do this?"

"Well, I'm an early riser, and haven't had the fresh orange juice in I don't know how long, and since I can't provide much in the way of help around here, I thought I'd at least try to earn my keep."

Gavin raised his glass. "Here's to Solomon, a good man if ever there was one, and an even better cook."

Diana raised her own glass. "Hear! Hear!"

Despite his darkening cheeks, Solomon was one who looked the happiest of them all. His spirits continued high even when Karac joined them and said those two fateful words, 'Mexico City,' assuring a division of attention in the needs of Solomon's condition, and that of Diana, although that last had been already decided upon by Diana herself, and Gavin seemed quite happy about that.

The Finder declared that he was sure they were ahead of their enemy by at least a day, but each second they took became a liability. Such information was coming at him at a blinding speed, and they needed to keep up with it.

The good Mr. Archer volunteered to keep track of the Manor and enjoy its protection while they were away. The 'They,' Rebecca was soon to learn, was comprised of Gavin, Simone, Diana, and Karac. Rebecca would stay back, in case something went wrong and someone needed to finish the job. Solomon blanched at this prospect, and Rebecca genuinely believed it was because Solomon felt he was going to lose some friends from this venture. His own investment in them, particularly Simone, was secondary in his concerns, if he even considered them at all.

Rebecca simply listened and watched the reactions of the chosen Away Team; Gavin took a brief counsel with Karac and Diana while Simone called in a favor of a friend whose named sounded a lot like 'Snog' to get a private plane to Mexico City ASAP. When she'd hung up, the following course of actions assured Rebecca that all was going well, and that the plane would be gassed up and ready for them by the time they got to Burbank Airport.

Simone took time to talk with Solomon about reinforcing his new reality and 'The power you have over it,' going so far as to give him a small spiral-bound notebook to lead him on three new things he should try next, and to note down his thoughts and ideas regarding his success for her to talk with him about upon her return. She also as able to pull Rebecca herself aside long enough to tell her to help tutor Solomon while she was away and to help him as much as she could. Rebecca's answer was a grumbled, noncommittal something Simone was in too much of a hurry to acknowledge.

The door closed behind the away team before the dishes were in the washer, which ended up being loaded by Rebecca as Solomon rinsed the plates and utensils.

"You okay?" Solomon asked after a time.

"Hmm? Me? Sure, of course."

"You're a rotten liar."

A grin and a shrug. "Guess I just don't feel like trying all that damn hard."

"So you're not okay?"

"Definitely not okay." Rebecca nodded.

"Anything I can help with?"

"No, Solomon. I'm afraid not."

"Want to talk? I like to think of myself as a better than average listener."

"Nah, that's okay. I think everything's just getting to me."

"I'm sorry about that. Must be hard."

"Yeah, you seem to be doing better. At least there's that."

"Well, I hope so."

"Have you gone outside the house yet?"

A shake of his head, tight-lipped.

"Scared?"

"Yeah."

The loading ended, and Rebecca switched the wash cycle on, a bit grateful for the added noise.

"Solomon?"

"Yes?"

She approached him and took his face into her hand. She was slightly surprised to find that he did not flinch away from her touch.

"I want you to look into my eyes when I ask you this."

The man's eyes widened, but remained on hers.

"You can still see death, can't you?"

"I think so."

"Tell me the truth."

His eyes fought hers. "Yes."

"Solomon, can you tell me how any of this will end?"

His face went from side in her hands. "No. I've tried, but I can't see a damned thing."

She nodded, and made to break away, maybe go into the living room, turn on the TV, and watch *Passions*, anything to feel like an ordinary human being, but something made her pull a slip of folded paper from the front pocket of her heavily embroidered denim jeans, and turn back to back to Solomon, holding it out to him.

"What's that?"

"Please just take it."

His hand reached out and accepted it, regarding it as if it may very well go up in flames between his fingers.

"What is it?" Solomon asked, not looking at it.

"It's the phone number of a man named Lucas Brady. If the worst happens and Gavin and Simone are no longer able to help, that's the man you're going to need to go to."

Solomon nodded, and slipped it into his pocket.

She is at the University of Notre Dame. It is just after Mass. She is buoyant, happy. She and her schoolmates follow after a kilty band made up of six bagpipers and three drummers in Notre Dame tartan, down through the main quad, past the statue of Father Sorin and O'Shaughnessy Hall to the stadium, where she finds herself alone on the field, a lone spotlight bathing her in pale warmth. In the stands, some of the Alumni are laughing, others are pointing. She spots her mother, burying her face into her father's chest, weeping. Her father is giving that steely-eyed glare at her, lips a fine, wrinkled, bloodless line, his face darkening with contempt.

She is alone, afraid. Nude on the fifty yard line.

Simone woke with a start as the private plane touched down at the airfield her mind struggled to recall and was shoved from her mind completely when Gavin touched her arm. He looked watchful and loving.

"You okay?"

She nodded quickly, wishing for a glass of water. She looked behind her to where Karac and Diana were seated to see the Finder giving her an effeminate little wave and Diana sound asleep and snoring beside him, her head resting on his shoulder.

"We're all going to hell," she muttered, and waited for the plane to finish its approach to the gate.

At the hotel, her mood was no better. The rate that had been promised on the phone was not owned up to, as was their request for a suite. There was a room with two beds available, which Diana seemed to be just fine with, but that was all. Gavin seemed to be the most balanced among them all about the situation. He kept reminding her that mistake happen, and the hotel had been otherwise spotless in their performance in their past journeys here. For a change, the manager of an establishment was glad that Gavin was doing the talking and leading away his wife, who suffered from a case of the dark mumbles.

It all played out to the certainty that this was the worst possible course of action they could be taking. It had started when they landed and darkened on the rental car trek here. She went about ordering a couple of bananas and milk from room service to try and balance herself out, but to no avail. The birds cartwheeling against the color of blue which they only made in Mexico City sky outside their balcony cried out repeatedly, an omen.

The touch at her shoulders made her jump.

"Hey lady," Gavin said. "You don't want your shoulders rubbed, you don't gotta."

Her smile felt tight on her face.

"What's wrong?"

Her hands went to her shoulders and she hugged herself tight, as if against a sudden breeze off the surf.

"I just want things to go right, is all."

Gavin's hands returned to her shoulders and began to knead. She willed her eyes to lid and to lean her weight against his hands slightly.

"Man," said Gavin. "When did we switch personalities?"

"I have no idea."

"Not the witty repartee I've come to expect from such a haughty vixen like yourself."

"And speaking of haughty vixens, where's our jazz singer?"

"Oh, she asked me to step out here so she could dry hump our Finder."

A glare from over her shoulder, which made Gavin smile.

"What? She said they'd be done in about five minutes."

"I don't doubt it."

"Steady."

"Sorry, I just think keeping the two of them together is a bad idea."

"Why?"

"Do you see the way she looks at him?"

"Yes I do."

"So?"

"So I'm not seeing him returning it. He looks like the old dog who just tolerates the puppy nipping at it ears."

"Okay, so where are they?"

"I told you."

"Gavin."

"Okay, okay. They're downstairs in the bar getting tacos and enchiladas for dinner. I thought we could eat up here tonight."

"Gavin?"

"Yes, dear?"

"Stop that. You know I hate that."

That hands at her shoulders dropped and he came to stand beside her, arms crossed. "Okay. What, Simone?"

222

"Where's Karac leading us tomorrow?"

"A place called Plaza Art."

"The museum?"

"Yeah. Small one, just about two miles from here. Karac says our man's not even in Mexico City yet."

"That's because he *teleports*."

"But Karac has a good idea as to when he'll be there, which is a few hours after the place closes."

"So what, we stake the place out?"

"From the inside."

"And did you break this to the guards?"

"Yes, all one of them."

"Security system?"

"Pretty basic, but defeatable. Remember, a lot of this stuff are nothing more than curiosities."

"Okay, so you're handling that?"

"Karac is. It's more his bailiwick."

"Of course."

"Okay, honey. What's really on your mind?"

Her hands went back to their spot on her shoulders. "Gavin, tomorrow something's going to happen. Someone may actually die at the hands of someone we have been trying to help."

"Diana doesn't want our help."

"That thought does not settle me."

"And it shouldn't. I'm not crazy about this myself. Remember I didn't want to have to have it come to this. It still doesn't."

"You became a lot more open to the possibility of not talking about it once Diana came along and the notion of using her cropped up."

"We can't force her down a road she wants nothing to do with."

"But we can have her work for us in a way."

"I don't know how we can disable this guy, honey. He's going to keep going, you know that." Simone wished she'd brought her cigarettes.

"If it weren't for the fact that Diana has basically leapt into her role."

"I know."

"And what happens if we can't stop her once she starts?"

Gavin's eyes went to the darkening sky.

"Gavin? What happens?"

"Whatever needs to," he said, and went back into the room.

That evening, after the dinner she didn't touch, Simone laid on her back next to the man she had barely accepted a goodnight kiss from and stared into the dark above their heads.

There were no answers there. But, as dawn crept into their room, Simone realized there didn't need to be.

They just needed to survive the day.

223

Diana watched the early morning sunlight trying to burn its way through the heavy curtains from the bed she'd hoped to share with Karac. Not that anything would have happened, not with Gavin and Simone in the same room with them, but it still would have been nice to have shared a bed with an attractive someone the night before she would continue far enough on the path she'd chosen to where it would just be too damn far to turn back.

Instead, Karac spent the night hunched in the wingbacked chair that looked by the pattern in its fabric weave hadn't been recovered since the Forties, snoring in a way that told her he was far more tired than he'd been letting on. But that was Karac, she realized. He had his path, and it was different than hers, even though she could still see him every once in a while in the same brush.

Robert Plant, as it turned out, had been full of it, because sometimes there was no time to change the road you were on.

Sometimes, you just had to embrace that fact in order to find your way. Even if that meant doing it alone, which was an element she was finding fewer and fewer problems with as the days went on. Donald Fagan, however, had been pretty close; Mexico City *was* like another world.

She had written off the possibility of seeing Rebecca alive again. It didn't matter. They were on two different planets, and better off outside of the others sphere of influence. But Diana had found it odd that not once did the witch who had once had such a great investment in helping her try to stop her from becoming what amounted to an assassin. An assassin that by and large could not be trusted by the rest of the group on the same basis that gave her the ability to help them.

She rolled over onto her side, pulling the blankets up to her chin, balling them in her fists.

This was far from the ideal that she had envisioned ages ago, back when she was someone else, when she was still Diana. She was sure that at some point in the near future, the name would be something unrecognizable, as would her past, and her talents, abilities, and aspirations.

She was going to miss playing the piano that was going to sit unused in her home until someone decided to try to find out why she'd gone *incommunicado* and used the spare key she'd given her parents. She was going to miss them, too.

But the person they knew was gone, and had been for longer than even Diana herself cared to admit. It wasn't just her ability at the piano that set her apart, or her innate (or as some called it, 'Spooky') instinct to know who to stay away from. It was her *beingness* that did it. She been an outsider for as long as she could remember, she just wouldn't admit to it. It was because she was different, and that small part of the human mind that knew things the civilized self had simply eschewed knew it.

And she was looking forward to finding out exactly how different she could be.

She was smiling when Simone, still curled in blankets, turned to face her, eyes open. Simone smiled back. And for a moment, Diana couldn't figure out why.

"Morning," Simone said.

"Heya," replied Diana, and swung her legs from the bed. Her arms raised high over her head as she lost herself in a stretch.

Simone gathered herself from the bed without so much as a stretch. "Need to use the bathroom?"

"Nah, you go on ahead."

Simone nodded and padded away, barefoot in her oversized flannel pajamas. They looked cozy.

Bracing herself with her arms behind her, Diana began a slow neck roll, feeling the soft pops coming from the base of her neck, lolling her head forward and enjoying the stretch under the skin in the back of her neck.

She was starving.

The honor bar was well-stocked, mostly with alcohol that she could smell even through the sealed necks. There were a few munchies like a bag of peanuts and some pretzels that probably cost a toe and two fingers if you ate them. But with little thought, her teeth tore at the bags as she made short work of the food that only allowed her to feel more hungry.

"Ah yes," Karac said, now uncoiled from his perch on the chair. "Mr. Salty and Mr. Peanut, long-standing bastions of good breakfasts."

"Morning, Karac." This came from Simone as she emerged from the bathroom. "You know, you could always call room service."

"Thought I'd wait to see if anyone else was hungry."

"Denver omelet," said Karac.

"Eggs Benedict," this came from the lump that Simone had been sleeping next to.

"What about you, Simone?"

The woman's nose wrinkled. "I'm not really all that hungry."

"Should eat something, babe," the lump's vocabulary was growing.

Simone made a dismissive gesture to what seemed to be the entire room. "Fine, toast with marmalade. Coffee, very black."

After she'd dressed, Diana made do with a breakfast streak that was better than she'd hoped and hash browns served alongside a helping of seasonal fruit. The pot of coffee didn't last long between the four of them.

"We need to get there by about seven tonight," Karac said over his omelet. He might as well have been talking about going to a ball game.

"Our man going to be there at that point, or are we beating him?"

"So far as I can tell, we'll make it a few minutes ahead of him. We just have to be careful not to be too soon."

Gavin nodded, Simone just kept nibbling at her toast.

"Wait," Diana said. "Can you repeat that for those of us who don't speak creepy?"

"If we get there too soon, " Karac explained. "Our man might sense us and take measures we're not prepared for."

Diana nodded. "And this guy can actually teleport."

"That's right."

"So what prevents him from just teleporting all over the place in one night, snatching things up as he goes?"

"Well, teleportation takes a toll on the human body. It can cause blindness, madness, any number of things. You have to do it in moderation."

"And the casting cost is too high," Simone said. "Only a mass murderer would be able to teleport in one night."

"You have to kill someone each time you teleport?"

Simone nodded. "The most innocent among us."

The fork dropped from Diana's fingers.

"How many books have there been that this guy's had to get?"

Simone told her.

Diana pulled herself up from the table. "I need to be alone for a little bit." She moved to the door.

"Stay close to the hotel," one of them said, but she scarcely cared. The door closed behind her and she walked. Eventually, she was on the street beyond the hotel's windows. She took note of every face, every smell, every sensation she could, drawing them all in; identifying them, storing them.

The real world. Harsh, and unbalanced where great power could be achieved by atrocious acts. Nothing she didn't already know, but this threw it all into sharp relief. The people around her were merely people, thinking that everything was more or less okay, and with the boundaries of what and what wasn't in their control tightly defined, even though one or two of them may try to reach past the line set before them. They might even succeed.

But in the end, not a bit of it mattered, because people like the one who was now preparing to make his appearance would always be allowed to exist amongst them. For every five or maybe even ten genuinely good and decent people were at least one that embodied enough darkness, enough evil, to unbalance the whole applecart again.

And the good people of the world would pick up the apples, and right the applecart. There would be those who stood by and watched, others to point and laugh, and still more who would ridicule the effort.

And there would be a face among them, maybe smiling, learning from his mistakes.

There would always be the argument from those who listened to their better angels that one should always take the high road. Maybe one or two of them actually understood loss and pain from more than the level of the academic.

And there would always be at least one soul who found great joy in that.

CHAPTER THIRTY

If you are afraid of dying, you never allow yourself to live.

Stefan O'Barr, GARGOYLE'S SHADOW

Mexico City was two hours ahead of the West Coast, leaving Rebecca to figure that while she and Solomon were out on an 8:00 PM constitutional that the away team were just about ready to break into Plaza Art and either meet their nemesis, or their own defeat.

It had actually been Solomon's idea for the walk, which struck Rebecca as impulsive at best from the man who she had gotten to know pretty well in her book over the past couple days, today in particular.

It was unusual for him to be as trusting with someone with the kind of personality she felt she had, that she could tell by the way he held himself around her; open but careful to keep the high cards close to his chest. He wanted companions... no, *friends* was a more appropriate word. People who could accept him for what could be called quirks, and help him through the tough spots without his having to see their ends before his eyes and force himself to act like he really didn't know, and that he was really just like everyone else.

In the case of this weird tribe who only occasionally saw eye-to-eye long enough to speak civilly, he had found it. Just as it was falling apart.

He sensed it. They all did, they just weren't talking about it.

But he was one of the rookies, and his power was beyond the scope of his being able to handle it, even if Simone and Gavin could manage to pull off whatever grand feat they felt they were capable of, which when one stripped away the veneer, was nothing more than a lie. A well-meaning one, but a false sense of reality nonetheless.

Which was why she had little apprehension when he asked her to go out for a walk with him. He sensed her strength, knew it by the way the others talked, and needed that if he were to venture outside, as if some part of himself already knew Simone and Gavin – Simone in particular – were completely full of it.

If something were to happen with Solomon, Rebecca knew she would get blamed for it. Let them. What was she supposed to do, she wondered, tell the poor man no, you can't venture outside. Why? Well, because I'm the witch, that's why!

A part of her was glad he wanted to go outside the safe confines of the Manor. It would allow some kind of real test as to what kind of faith the man was putting into his own good fortune. The spirits would eventually come whether he stayed in the Manor or not, and Simone's expectations of her experiment were a bit high. How long would it take to condition somebody to the extent Solomon would be required to take? No one knew. Simone was in uncharted waters, knew it, and was sailing on anyway, using a kind of spiritual dead reckoning to get her by.

She was a good person, that Simone, just distracted by the big game she clearly wanted no part of. It was necessary of her to be there, but she loathed the thought of it. She just wanted it to be over. The thing that Rebecca couldn't get past was why; this life had little to offer in the way of a comfy retirement, and the Fox blood ran as deep as it was dark, whether Simone cared to admit it to herself or not. There was no way in hell Gavin Fox would be able to turn away from the road the two of them were on. It was simply too deeply ingrained.

But Simone obviously had an end in mind. Perhaps a new beginning. Maybe without Gavin. Simone was gifted at least as much as Gavin. Everyone knew it, and never talked about it. It left something hanging in the air between them, something neither Gavin nor Simone could talk about, lest the thing grow legs and become mobile, and then the arms and hands that would grasp onto dreams, and even worse, aspirations.

Rebecca was sure Simone was not fooling herself into believing Gavin's ego could tolerate the competition. Especially from the woman he loved and trusted so much.

But Simone was also the one in charge of Solomon's fate. It wasn't hyperbole; it was simple fact; she was setting him up and insulting not only the man's intelligence, but his fate as well by doing so. She probably hadn't even discussed her plan of action with Gavin, who was most likely just fine with the arrangement just so long as he could save the world he felt no part of.

It was irrelevant who came back from their expedition. Evil would still abound, and morons would continue wishing for greater and greater power. A few would actually achieve it.

And there were only so many Diana Adairs out there to do the dirty work of those who wouldn't dare take on such responsibility. That might have been a good thing. Rebecca wasn't sure, and she didn't dwell on it.

There was a fine curtain of mist that clung to their hair as they made their way down the decline of blacktop that led to small arteries of streets that would branch over this way and that, most leading up into the hills around Fox Manor. Rebecca thought she caught Solomon taking a bit longer than necessary in breaking away from the way the fog landed and settled in her hair, but when her eyes met his, he merely smiled, and broke the gaze off when he was ready. He was actually kind of charming in a doomed sort of way. It was a pity he was wasting his attentions on someone like Diana, who was merely looking to devolve into something unrecognizable.

Solomon was loosening up in however many years it had been since he'd been able to do such a thing. Better still, he was enjoying it. Out of everyone Rebecca knew in this circle, he was the one who she felt deserved happiness the most, which was exactly why he wasn't going to get it. The good souls, the really solid ones like him were always tested, meaning tempered by adversity and the defining of themselves by what they cannot have. It could very well lead to a great man. Equally so, it could also send an otherwise wonderful person careening over the edge. Sometimes, such people didn't require so much as a push.

It had never occurred to her before, but on her only previous journey to Mexico City, Simone had never noticed how, even in the moonlight, unencumbered by clouds in the night sky washing everything within sight, how much brighter everything looked when compared to the States. Every brick and stone, be it set in wall or street, threw colors truer than she could recall from home behind her eyes. She was dimly aware of the grin on her face all this gave her, where it stayed until they gained the chipped red tiled stairs of Plaza Art, when a haphazard glance at her from Gavin turned to a half-glare until her lips formed a flat line across her face.

"You'll have to excuse me for taking some joy out of the evening," she grumbled, not caring whether he heard.

"What?" This came from Karac, who looked eager enough to have some break in the stony silence of the group save their muted footsteps on the deep orange cobblestones leading to the front entryway. Karac had reconnoitered the rear and side entrances earlier that day and come to the conclusion the easiest way in was also the most visible.

But Simone's concern was unfounded; the streets around and leading up to the modest gallery were all but deserted. The occasional figure was sighted, but nothing enough to alarm the party, only the soft tones of a faraway wind chime swaying.

Simone shook her head sharply and waved Karac's query aside, now eager for the quiet.

Hardly any conversation at all had occurred between any of them from when they ate breakfast until Karac asked the room if they were all ready to go. In that time, Simone had grown to dislike the fact that there was no noise outside what bled in through the windows from the street.

Karac took the lead, his feet ascending two steps at a time, although why it hardly mattered was lost on Simone, who counted a mere ten steps. It was something for Karac to do, was all. An action simply for the sake of action.

He knelt by the door and produced a small leatherette case filled with what looked to Simone like antique metal toothpicks. Lockpicks, to be sure, but they had an air about them that left her uncertain as to what being could craft something so painstaking in detail on such a minute scale and not be considered an artist of sorts. In a moment, Karac hand a tool in each hand and was prising the lock opening

The Finder's eyes flicked to the small band gathered behind him as he held his fingers steady. Taking his cue from the attentive gazes behind him, his fingers twisted just so. A soft snap from within the door followed, allowing Karac to push it open with a soft touch from his fingertips.

On the afternoon tour, such as it was for little more than a *façade* for the unusual rather than the genuinely artistic or rare, they discovered the book was on the east side, three exhibits to the left. It was then they also noticed that the highest level of security was a single guard, who while young, was surely more than capable of running down a suspect. It was through what Simone would call her own 'Feminine wiles' in talking with the young man she discovered that he was the only guard there, and that there was no need to post another at night, because even the owners of the place knew that no one would bother breaking in for the sake of a curious knick-knack. The owners, an older couple whose romance about them Simone could only hope to mimic with Gavin in their later years, knew they had little of value here, but were proud of the rich mythology their collection garnered.

The lighting now was minimal, and they had but one flashlight among them, by design of Gavin, something Simone had fought, but eventually acquiesced to. The fewer lights meant the faster it could be extinguished should they have a need to.

Gavin waited until they had made the bend in the hall that would lead them to the exhibit before the flashlight snapped on, coming to light on a carved statue of a fertility god Simone had already forgotten the name of hewn from wood pitted by woodpeckers, causing cool shadow to be thrown against the far wall.

"Um," started Karac, not another three steps towards the exhibit, now shrouded upon its pillar with a nondescript purple cloth.

Simone's lips began a word, then stopped. After a swallow, she spoke: "Why do I taste pennies?" This came from Diana.

"So it's not just me?" Asked Karac, already turning in a slow circle, as if he expected the floor to fall out from underneath them.

Simone shook her head. "Teleporter," she hissed. She pivoted to turn herself, nearly tripping over Diana, who had dropped silently into a ready crouch, something animal, but now something that looked perfectly natural for her to fall into.

There was a soft click, and Karac's switchblade was in his hand, business end angled toward the ceiling. The light provided by the flashlight winked out.

Without appearing directly amidst the group, the teleporter would have only one avenue; the darkened hall headed southward, in direct line of sight with the exhibit and just shy of being seen by the group.

Her gestures of 'What the hell do we do now?' remained largely unanswered. The only reply, if it could be called that, was from Diana as she crept towards the mouth of the hallway. Once there, her head tilted just a bit. In a moment, her hand came up, indicating the party stand their ground.

Simone's attempt to swallow again died halfway through. *"Come on,"* somebody – probably Karac – whispered.

Diana's hands fell to the floor, her fingers steepled on the cold tile. Her thighs hunched and even in the dim light Simone could see the woman's body shift just enough to be noticeable. The human known as Diana Adair was gone, at least for now. At some point, possibly at the worst time this being one of them, she would not turn back, and she would not be able to be reasoned with.

But for as long as her attention stayed toward the darkened hallway, all seemed to be as right as could have been expected.

For a moment, all was still. Simone didn't dare breathe, but could feel her eyes widening.

Then the growl.

Diana lunged into the darkness. There was a sickening thud and she emerged from the blackness, skidding across the floor on her side, the grip of a knife blade stuck up obscenely from her right bicep. Blood had already darkened the length of her arm, but she came back up on both feet, hand curled into claws, a shriek burning from her lips.

Simone wasn't sure when it happened, but Gavin was already halfway to the display when another knife sang from the darkness, this time whizzing past his cheek to bounce against the far wall. He continued his progress, but the momentary pause had given his adversary enough time to pull themselves from the darkness.

"I have to admit, I didn't think you'd get here in time," Lucas Brady said with a grin, coming closer to Gavin. He managed a slight nod to Simone.

Simone's head moved from side to side. "Lucas? Why?"

"Simone, I think you know me well enough to know that I have my reasons for wanting this book." He didn't move his eyes from Gavin, whose hand now reached for the cloth. "Gavin, I really wouldn't't."

Gavin wasted no time in reaching for the book, only to pull his hand away with a yelp, astonished at the blade now shining through the back of his hand.

Diana lunged for Lucas, but was brought up short when the latter muttered a single word. The lycanthrope tossed her head and peered at her target as if through a curtain of bright mist. Relying on her sense of smell, her closed her eyes and dashed for Lucas once more, but was rewarded with an immovable force, and she was on her back, the back of her skull bouncing off the floor. Simone's addled mind fought to remember what gesture Lucas Brady made with his hand, the fingers still wrapped around the head of the cane he genuinely seemed to need, but Diana hung static in the air. If it was what Simone thought, and Lucas Brady had actually been able to encapsulate her, the air around Diana would have disappeared, and her lungs very well had collapsed before she fell limp to the floor.

Simone dropped to her knees, and the world swam beneath her. Gavin was swearing in a language she couldn't recognize.

She tasted pennies again.

And she was gone into darkness.

The smell of a hospital never failed to make Karac's stomach turn.

He sat in the cramped waiting room, seated across from Simone in molded orange plastic chairs that seemed to have been designed solely for the design of discomfort for discomfort's sake.

Simone hadn't argued with the admitting nurse when she had been told patients only were allowed past a certain point. That had surprised him. After the retreat from the museum, he'd expected her to lift buildings if she had to in order to get some sort of sanity in her head. The ER was three blocks west, according to some instinct Diana had come into. He watched as the lycanthrope led the way, dripping blood, her wound ignored and the knife removed.

The remaining knives had been picked up by Karac himself. The blood left behind would have to remain there. He thought he had heard Simone say something about needing cover, when a soft rain began to fall, albeit briefly, obscuring the tracks left behind by the dime-sized drops of blood being left behind by Diana, who was well ahead of them.

They had let him do the talking when they arrived at the automated doors. He came up with some garbage about a group of three men with knives looking to mess up some tourists. They were drunk and unprovoked. Things became a blur, yelling, two of his friends took the worst of it... he didn't need to continue, the staff simply took over and admitted the wounded.

Simone simply sat and fled within herself.

The legendary Lucas Brady was ahead of them. By more than just a step. Of all the people he could've guessed to lose their mind, Brady's name was not anywhere near close to the top of the list. Given the set of circumstances, it was like being on the *Titanic,* rushing to the Captain and finding out it's really Groucho Marx.

But the circumstances were courtesy of Mr. Brady himself. Karac's eyes closed against the ceiling lights. A part of his brain was yammering on about how this wasn't making a damn bit of sense. Lucas Brady? Please. The only person better at what Gavin Fox did. And in Karac's book, the more authoritative.

Lucas could teleport. That indicated to Karac someone desperate, not necessarily insane, although anyone who would accept the casting cost should meet his end in an untimely fashion, and Karac mused, at his hands. After all, there ways of keeping a person alive and continue to suffer. He had once heard tell of a heart that Markab had been commissioned to find, one that refused to stop beating. Supposedly, such things could be used for less than honorable reasons.

But Lucas Brady was not known as a man who was led by sudden whims. His reputation was one of consideration. In fact, Karac could recall an interview with Lucas in print where the writer noted that his subject took a great deal of time answering those questions posed to him, regardless of how trivial the subject may have been considered. This was something that was past being out of character.

Wait.

He was concentrating on the wrong thing. His mind went back to a Miss Firestein in High School. The History teacher with the endless legs that dragged him kicking and screaming into what teenagers consider adulthood, and an expectant smile that had been known to cause him to forget there were seven continents.

And best of all, she had taught him that when he made a mistake, to try to do it wrong again. And to keep going if it still felt wrong anyway.

It never ceased to amaze him that it worked.

He was making a mistake. Something tugging at his mind ever since he'd sat down.

Try it again...

Again...

Why would someone like Lucas Brady do something as stupid as this? Make enemies of past friends?

He became aware of being on his feet as words tumbled out of his mouth.

The loveseat Rebecca sat on was the same as she could remember it, the house was the much the same in feel and smell, but the man who sat beside her in Fox Manor was not the man who had shared the house with her for a few hours, happy and dare she say it, contented.

Indeed, Simon Archer had reverted to the withdrawn husk he had been when she had first met him.

His hand were in hers, her slender fingers curling around the bony backs of his hands, her rings burning cold silver against his pale skin.

"When did it happen?" She asked, eyes searching the down-turned face.

"Just about and hour ago," he muttered. "Outside, when I was alone."

"And you saw them?"

"Yes."

"They've come back?"

"They never left. They had always been there."

Her head tilted, curious, open. "What do you mean?"

"I mean Simone's presence had something to do with how long this spell or whatever lasted. Now that she's gone..."

"So is the illusion," Rebecca finished.

"Looks like."

"How many were there?"

Now the face came up, paler than she'd expected. Eyes wide and decisive.

"Too many," he hissed, and hid his face from her.

"I'm sorry, Solomon."

"You're sorry. I'm sorry. Everybody's sorry. Who isn't sorry?"

"Solomon..."

"No, really. If I hear that from one more well meaning soul again, I swear..."

"What, Solomon?"

"Nothing. Just pretend I didn't say anything."

"Solomon, don't go thinking about how you can hurt someone because of this. I'm sure Simone can help."

His eyes came up, and Rebecca found herself fighting the intense urge to drop her eyes from them. They were daring things, taunting, cornered things

233

she could barely stand to face. In time, he stood and released her hands. She could feel his gaze as she stared into the mess of her own fingers woven together tightly on her lap.

She did not look up when he moved away from her, a single floorboard creaking in his wake.

As the front door clicked softly closed, she waited a moment.

Then smiled.

CHAPTER THIRTY-ONE

It's impossible to help the entire world. Our Mother's children are… simply too stubborn, too greedy…

Lucas Brady, HEAVEN ONLY KNOWS (Revised Edition)

The liquid Lucas Brady poured in the small stemware smelled warmer and sweeter than anything Solomon Archer had ever experienced. He raised the glass as the older man smiled and poured his own. "What did you say this was?"

"It's called sabra. It's an Israeli liquor, and quite potent. It's meant to be sipped."

Solomon nodded and did as instructed. The warmth spread quickly through his body, a welcome relief from the experience on the bus ride that had taken him from the San Fernando Valley to this removed piece of Arizona desert he couldn't help but feel at home to.

The ghosts appeared in the bus, outside of it, and wherever Solomon went. Not much different in actual numbers than he was used to, but the frequency of their appearance was what was alarming. It was almost as if whatever it was that Simone had tried to do had actually amplified the problem.

They whispered, though, instead of speaking at a typical conversational volume. There was some small comfort in that, he supposed.

But here in the desert, on the way to Lucas's home there amongst the red rocks and dry wind, even the spirits had seemed to be unsure of their footing, dropping back and keeping their distance from him as he approached the house, disappearing entirely when he knocked on the door and looked over his shoulder to check.

The ghosts, it appeared, were afraid of Mr. Brady.

Solomon took a warm comfort in that. He knew not to get to cozy with it, but he welcomed it just the same.

Lucas Brady himself seemed nice enough, considering to the degree of legend his name had been served with. Solomon had expected his house to be much bigger, maybe churchlike, with a long, curved driveway leading to a courtyard lit by torches. Shadows moving this way and that…

Instead, he found a man on a cane, inviting a complete stranger into his house for a game of chess and a glass or maybe two if he was lucky of this wonderful stuff called sabra.

The chessboard itself probably cost more than anything Solomon had owned. Brady didn't treat him any differently than he would anyone else, Solomon knew. Mr. Brady carried himself and treated others in such an easy way that Solomon felt more at home here faster than anywhere else, even the Manor. Even with Rebecca holding his hands. She was the only one he'd plan on missing.

"So Simone wasn't able to help?"

The words shook him from his reverie. Solomon blinked, realized it was his turn and moved his rook in what he hoped appeared to be an intelligent move.

"I think it actually made it worse," he responded.

A smile from Mr. Brady. "The man is nefarious. I didn't suspect his lady to be much the same. I still don't."

"So what, she just made it worse on accident? I thought she was too experienced to not think of such a thing ahead of time."

The rook disappeared in a sweep from the black bishop.

"We don't always see that far ahead," Mr. Brady said, setting the white rook off to the side, where it joined three pawn, a knight, and a bishop. "But still, I see your point. The paranormal can often veer off into paths we cannot expect, but should. If an experiment is the call of the day, best to expect the worst."

Solomon's fingertip stayed on the head of his remaining bishop. "But don't you think she would have?"

Mr. Brady smiled at him in what struck Solomon as a sad sort of a way. "I'm sure she meant well, Solomon."

"What is it they say about good intentions?"

"What, that bit about them paving the way to hell? Certainly."

Solomon moved his bishop four squares, threatening Mr. Brady's king. "Check."

"Indeed and it is," Mr. Brady smiled, moving his king out of harm's way.

"Can you help me, Mr. Brady?"

"There is one way I know of, yes."

Solomon's fingers scooted the base of a pawn forward.

"What do I have to do?"

"Well, there is always a balance to be struck when one these things. I think you've seen what happens when things are done without a leveling factor."

"Yes, sir, Mr. Brady. I sure have."

The man across from him nodded, moved a bishop into a position Solomon couldn't imagine was advantageous, therefore considered it suspicious.

"Do you have the Fox Manor address?"

"Yes."

"May I have it?"

Solomon scribbled the address down on a scrap piece of what appeared to be thin parchment using a metal pen shaped much like a small quill. "I don't know the zip code," he said.

"Not needed, Solomon. But thank you for your attention to detail."

Solomon stared past the pieces laid out on the board, into and between the squares until they simply made no sense to him any longer. There was no pattern on this battlefield for him. It was far too advanced for him to join in and hope to win.

The only possibility was to just survive.

He would have to settle with that and be happy.

It may take some work, he mused, but it would be worth it.

His middle fingertip reached out to the crown atop the white king's head, knocking it to the onyx and alabaster checks. He stated at the piece for a long time as it rocked back and forth.

"Looks like you won, Mr. Brady."

The elder man rose with the aid of his cane and extended his hand across the table.

"Call me Lucas," he smiled.

CHAPTER THIRTY-TWO

It can be said that we spend our time in two circles; one in making decisions, the other regretting them.

> Lucas Brady, THE USC LECTURES (Privately Published)

Karac didn't bother to knock, and didn't care a whit about the looks he was given when he entered Fox Manor with two books in his arms.

All was as it should be; Gavin was brooding, deeper than usual, it appeared if that were possible, Simone was nearby, but standing. She'd returned to that habit of chewing her fingernail, and when his eyes fell on Diana, hers refused to look up at him. It was only through a brief update courtesy of Simone that he came to understand that Solomon had given up and retreated for parts unknown. As something just left of rage began to form in the Finder's chest, it was also noted that Rebecca had closed herself off from the others following the revelation that one Lucas Brady had gone and lost his mind and wanted to unleash ten kinds of whatever kind of hell he could manage upon the world at large. The witch was now sitting on the back porch swing by herself, chain smoking cigarettes and licking her lips as she studied blades of grass and tapped her crossed feet in time to a hyperactive beat only she could hear. He would have called her in, but there was the now, and there was the now as Rebecca apparently wanted it, and Karac simply wanted nothing to do with that world.

The first of the two books he had been carrying landed with a too-loud thud against the deep champagne carpet of the Fox living room. It was the 1828 Baud Edition of Dante Alghieri's *The Divine Comedy*, bound in deep thick leather still supple after all these years, and with complete black and white illustrations by Strunz.

"According to Dante, there are three gates," Karac said. "One leading into Heaven, the other goes the way of hell."

"What about the third?" This came from Rebecca, now reentering the room, crushing her cigarette on the dead grey asphalt of the patio, ignoring the ashtray nearby.

"There is one leading to Purgatory itself, it has a guard in the form of an angel holding a flaming sword. But there is no gate between Purgatory and Heaven. Mythology tells us hell itself is guarded by the three-headed dog Cerberus"

"And you're taking your cue from the *Divine Comedy* why?" Asked Simone.

"Because one thing about it in particular to the Bible makes a special sense to me and indicates a deeper inspiration."

"We're captive," said Simone, cradling Gavin's still-bandaged hand in her lap.

The next book landed atop the Dante. It was a Vulgate Holy Bible, one that was considered, although never confirmed, to have been of the first run translated by St. Jerome himself. The binding was cracking, and the leather was tattered and faded, and despite its size, still remained squared off and even.

"When Christ died on the Cross, there was an earthquake that shook the very foundations of hell, causing a great deal of damage and creating the Broken Rocks of Hell. Then came the Harrowing."

Diana held up a hand. "Sorry, lost here."

"Christ descended into hell," answered Gavin. "It's even in the Apostle's Creed."

"The gate of hell was broken by holy means," Karac continued. "Whether Christ opened the door Himself or whether the rockslide caused by Christ's death made it happen. Regardless, because of that, the gate was never repaired."

"So hell can just sort of run rampant on Earth should it want to." Muttered Rebecca.

"In theory, I suppose," said Karac. "There are those who would say it already is and has been for quite some time."

"So the short end is why would anybody try to open something that isn't locked?"

Gavin nodded. "Lucas is smart enough to know all this."

"So now all we have to do is find out where he's going to next," said Simone.

Gavin nodded. "Now all we have to do is figure out how to do that."

Karac turned to Diana. "Can you maybe... you know..."

"What, act like a bloodhound and get his scent? It doesn't work that way. If it does, I haven't figured out how to make it work. I've never been on anyone's scent. You mean to tell me with all the paranormal firepower you all say you have, not a one of you can see that far into the future?"

"That kind of magick requires a long, winding road down a path even the moon won't light." Came the reply from Rebecca. "I can do it, I'm probably the most willing to try, but I know that won't be approved of by Gavin."

"Because when you walk the path, you become the path."

"And you're willing to have someone go open the gates of Heaven itself for whatever reason – he could be experiencing his Everest crisis for all we know – rather than find a way to stop him?"

"I thought it was clear that my mind had changed a bit regarding that."

"Yeah," Rebecca said. "Provided someone else is doing the dirty work for you."

Gavin rose. Rebecca matched him.

"Now wait just a damn minute Rebecca. You don't think for a second you're going to come into my house, seek refuge, and take me to task over this?"

Diane's hand raised again. "Guys?"

"I'm saying you're still unwilling to get your hands dirty."

Diane found her feet and within two steps blocked the two combatants. "Hey! You're forgetting three things." She waited for the silence to press upon them all before speaking again, ticking points off on her fingers with even vigor so as to bend her digits back into a bow-curve. "First, I'm okay with doing this. I know about what that means in terms of what kind of a person I am, or what kind I'm rejecting. It's a purpose, which I can say for the rest of you academics is a bit more real to me, if not to you. Second, we're wasting time arguing and making enemies of each other. We've already lost Solomon."

"And the third?" Asked Simone.

"That I'm strong enough to be able to take any of you lot out whenever I want. Of my own choosing, not the animal's. I can defend myself and I can keep this from happening, but if everybody just wants to fight, well then, I guess I'm not really needed here. And on Lucas' side of things, I'm not so sure he's wrong."

Rebecca blinked at her. "What?"

"Well, Heaven seems a bit more civilized to me that hell, right? So far, I haven't heard any exact reason as to why this would be such a bad thing. Hell, maybe God *should* be told to stand up an explain a thing or three."

Gavin rubbed hard at a spot between his eyes. "Because the wonder of a God and His kingdom lies in divine mystery. Without mystery there is no faith. Without faith, there is no need for any kind of given god. Some seek God for the life of their soul, insisting there must be something better than this world because there has to be. Others seek God only to prove such a thing doesn't exist, that He was something that mankind thought up to explain itself. For those who insist we are better than we are, belief if a treasure that despite being mired in chaos and mystery, allows us to feel inspired. To open these Gates is to solve every mystery, answer every question. It is to do no less than demand an audience, and I'm not sure that's a very good idea. Mortals have always carried the same kind of fault; mediocrity masquerading as ego."

"So what you're proposing is to save the world," said Diana.

"I am proposing to do what I feel to be right."

"Do you believe in God, Karac?" Asked Diana.

The Finder shook his head.

"But you believe in Him enough to be terrified at the thought." This came from Simone.

"Well, I'd hate to be left out of Heaven based on a technicality."

"If God's as powerful as He's believed to be," said Diana. "Why would He allow the creation of something that could undo his work like this?"

"Free will," answered Karac. "Something that exists whether you believe in a divine power or not. The gift of free will also includes being able to say no to God, or to doing what's right, to embrace aggressive ignorance. Even some who grasp both the belief in God and free will both refuse to take responsibility for their own actions, blaming God for everything they see fit to hang blame on. Free will at least implies that what you do is your choice."

"So how would humans have figured all this out?"

"Angels, probably." From Simone.

"Angels?"

"There are nine Choirs of angels. Among them are those called Principalities, who are now hostile to God and humans."

"Why?"

Karac picked up.

"The angels are patient in their ability to plan vengeful things, not as patient as God, obviously, but they take a special joy in watching the little things fall into place as a plan they set into motion millennia ago begins to take form."

"What sort of plans?"

"To take advantage of mankind's unerring ability to become what it despises."

CHAPTER THIRTY-THREE

It is I who come thru this Never
Of at least two roads to follow
To cast a violent shadow
Across the face of God.

> From THE COLLECTIONS OF LAST WORKS,
> attributed to O'Barr

Simone noted with a detached smile that her still-bare feet trod the carpet of Fox manor a bit lighter, a bit quicker than they had in quite some time. The house and its occupants had still not awakened, and that suit Simone still dressed in an overlong raglan just fine. Just ten or fifteen minutes of time alone with her thoughts for her head to fill with the aroma of the coffee she had just put on to brew and enjoy the feeling she woke up with. Any other day, she would have tried to enjoy the happiness of her uplifted mood, knowing that something somewhere would come along to try to cast problems upon her.

But not today. And, so far as Simone had a care to acknowledge, not ever. Hell, she may actually start frying some bacon, spatters be damned.

Lucas Brady had betrayed them and the earth and those who dwelled on it, the uncertain darkness of his selfish actions compelling her and hers into action that had no beautiful end.

But now, things would be different. There wasn't a shred of doubt in her head that the going would be less than easy, but that they were capable of doing what was right in the face of he who would just as soon destroy whatever he could get his hands on because of his cause.

And, Simone reckoned, someone with a cause was liability enough. But one with a cause and a weapon was liability turned absolute danger.

The world for Gavin and Simone would change following whatever came to happen with Lucas. She knew that, understood what it meant.

But it would also mean the beginning of something new and blessedly different in their lives. She believed she could hear the groanings of the patriarchs of the Fox clan from whichever graves they lay claim to. Such was the Fox name and reputation that she understood that some of them had been buried under assumed names.

She grinned at these phantom voices and imagined herself giving them the finger with a big, proud smile behind it.

When the door chime sounded at the front of the house, she made it to the door humming a song she could not remember the name of. It hardly mattered.

Through the peephole she saw the familiar uniform of the package carrier service that had delivered unknown amounts of creature comforts to the house, which no doubt did the aforementioned patriarchs (and some of the matriarchs) little good.

The door opened to the female driver, who stood there with a small box and a small smile framed by dishwater hair and a small row of stitches near the crook of her mouth. The smile widened as Simone's shadow filled the doorway and spilled on to the porch.

"Simone Perfect?"

"Yes."

The woman handed her the package and an electronic clipboard. "Sign at the flashing X."

Simone removed the stylus from its clip, her eyes flicking up at a motion from the driver her senses thought as odd. Her eyes came up in time to see the Taser darts launch from the gun.

She came awake under cover of the darkness of her closed eyelids. She was moving. Engine sounds. A band that sounded like Ministry playing on the stereo.

Not much pain, that she was grateful for. It felt as though she'd taken the darts square in her chest. The wounds itched where the points had penetrated her skin and she found her body had awakened in a kind of safe-mode, pre-tensed against any further shock, her nerves and muscles remembering the taste of electrical current as it twisted and turned its way through her body, knocking her soundlessly to the ground. She could not recall losing consciousness, but that could have come later by means of a drug, either inhaled or injected. Her abductor moved fast, as Simone doubted anyone in the house had a clue that anything had happened, and were mostly likely not awakened by whatever small commotion her falling body caused.

She was unhurt, moving, and had no idea where she was. She was sitting up, and so far as she could tell, secured by seatbelt and handcuffs. The longer she kept her eyes closed, the less her chances of knowing anything further, provided she could see anything from where she was seated.

Simone's eyes opened slowly, allowing sunlight to seep in slowly and letting her eyes adjust gradually.

Her head was slumped to the right side of her body, and allowed sight from the passenger's side window. She was still in the city, but if she were to tell exactly where, she'd have to move her head completely upright, which would tip her abductor off to her being awake, although she had no idea whether that would matter one way or another, as her hands were in her lap, complete with a pair of handcuffs that were attached to the door handle of this Toyota Something-or-Other. She brought her head up, and hissed at the pain striking her neck.

The woman with dirty blonde hair and the perpetual grin Simone wanted desperately to knock right the hell from her face turned to her. She was no longer wearing the uniform, instead looked overly comfortable in destroyed jeans and a t-shirt from a rock band that had disintegrated before she was born. She smelled of cigarettes.

"I tried to keep your head from falling to one side, but you seemed dead set on it."

"Where are we going?"

The woman's eyes returned to the road. "To see an old friend of yours."

Simone nodded unconsciously. "Lucas."

"I'm Rose." The younger woman stuck out her hand before retracting it. Simone couldn't tell if it was an honest mistake or the woman was just trying to remind her of her handcuffs. In return, Simone just sneered.

"Gotta admit," the woman who called herself Rose said. "I was expecting this to be a helluva lot tougher."

"Well, we all have our little disappointments today."

"Yeah, yours ain't ending up to be too hot."

"What's he paying you?"

"What?"

"He *is* paying you, isn't he?"

"Lucas? Of course he's paying me. You think I do this kind of thing for free?"

"What's he paying you?"

"Why do you care?"

"Because Lucas is a smart man, and smart men know how to save money, even if it means lying to get what they want."

"Really not your concern, Simone. I mean you're handcuffed in my car and recovering from being Tasered."

"I'll keep my own counsel on what I'll be concerned about."

Rose made a noise. "Whatever you say."

"Why won't you tell me what he's paying you? I mean, what the hell am I going to do with the information? Here I am hogtied and nonplussed. I've got to say, I'm curious as to what my life is worth."

The smile faltered. It was replaced by the slightest of frowns.

"He isn't going to kill you."

"How do you know?"

"Because I know."

"Did he tell you?" "No, but I mean you can tell when someone does this kind of thing just to kill somebody."

"So this isn't the first time you've delivered a bounty?"

"Hell, no."

Simone turned her gaze from the woman to the road in front of her. They were still in the business district, headed for what Simone guessed was the Hotel Roosevelt, where Rose's employers was no doubt a guest.

"Well I can't imagine Lucas wants me for his queen. He's never had that kind of feeling towards anyone, so far as I know."

Rose shrugged, put her smile back into place.

"Unless he plans to hold me to extract information from me."

"Wouldn't know about that?"

"Ever torture someone, Rose?"

"I've made people beg." The smile grew once more.

Simone shook her head. "Not what I mean. Have you ever hurt someone so profoundly for so long a time they'd do anything to stop the pain, even if they knew that meant the very death of them?"

"Not really my thing, I guess."

Now Simone nodded her head. "Gotcha. You let other people do that."

"Whatever."

"Ever hear of some of the tortures that old mystics like Lucas can come up with?"

"I can imagine they're pretty damn nasty."

"You have no idea. Man enhanced by evil becomes a machine. No longer human. Just this scary thing that does stuff that's wrong, knows it's wrong, and plunges on ahead with it anyway."

"You always chatter on like this with people who capture you?"

"You'll have to excuse me. This is my first abduction."

A small eye-roll from the driver.

"But he's not the type of person to let money get in the way of his goals," Simone said, mostly to herself. If her captor had heard, she gave no sign.

An arch of an eyebrow, and Simone continued, this time loud enough for Rose to notice:

"He isn't paying you, is he? Not in the usual sense, anyway."

"Why do you care?" Rose turned to her. "Simone, honestly, I have no idea what he's about with you. He told me to go get you, so I go get you." She shrugged. "End of story."

"Yeah, not really."

"Whatever, Simone."

Simone's eyes narrowed at the driver. "What did he offer you, Rose?"

"What?"

"You don't strike as the type of person who does this sort of thing on a whim. What's he offering you?"

"Just shut up, we're almost there."

Simone didn't have to look up to know the Hotel Roosevelt was maybe two blocks away maximum. "What's the matter, Rose?"

"You talk too damn much, that's what's wrong."

"I'm just curious, because for as long as I've know Lucas Brady, he's been able to find ways to make people do things based on promises he can't keep." She was rushing things, making room for error because of it, but the more she could do before they got in front of Lucas the better.

"This reminds me of the time he promised someone everlasting life in exchange for what could be described as 'Bizarre sexual acts.'"

"I'm sorry he did that to you, Simone."

245

Simone suppressed a grin. It was the manner of counterattack she'd been expecting. The girl was tough, but on the inside, she was a terrified kid reduced to a teenager's style of defense.

"But the capper was when he said he'd raise someone's mother from the dead if they killed someone for him."

The woman's eyes squeezed shut for a pained instant. "Shut up, Simone."

Simone changed her tone. It became something soft and comfortable. Perhaps all the worse was that it sounded trustworthy. "What did he promise you, Rose?"

Fingers drummed the steering wheel.

"Rose?"

The grin had flatlined. "Back off."

"Why are you doing this, Rose?"

The woman's eyes stared dead ahead.

"Rose, who did you lose?"

The corners of Rose's face drew up, the flattened with effort. "I swear I'll kick the crap out of you the second we're out of this car."

"You know what kind of power Lucas knows about... what he can do. You didn't align yourself with him because of money. You're a good person, I can feel it."

The knuckles at the wheel became bloodless. The speedometer climbed.

"Was it a sister? A big brother, maybe?"

The face that turned to her was nothing less than a mask of grief, loss, and absolute anger. "Shut up shut up SHUT UP!"

Then sudden fear hollowed the woman Rose's eyes. Simone had just enough time to follow them to her side of the street that had led to the middle of an intersection against the light and the freight truck that blared its horn at them, its own air horn drowning out the sound in the Toyota.

Back before she had met Gavin Fox, before magick had a hold of her life and showed her so many energy lines she couldn't see straight, Rebecca Scott would have called the current manner in which she smoked a cigarette on the back patio of the Manor 'Pulling a Ripley', a nod to Aliens and Sigourney Weaver's impossibly long cigarette ash.

She had given up watching the assembly of people who thought they knew what they were doing through the patio's glass door. The rudder – Simone – was gone, and it showed. She could tell Gavin thought he looked in control enough, but in reality, the stark quality of his expression left no doubt as to the disposition of the man. He was panicked and fearful.

A liability.

But Rebecca would never voice this to anyone. Not in this house, anyway. Come to think of it, there wasn't really anyone she could think of who she felt she could say anything to. Karac was a Finder, and one could never tell exactly what a Finder's motivations could be at any time. Diana had gone so aggressively far into the beast that Rebecca couldn't be bothered to try.

The covens she could count on had fled. The occult was led in the field by either the basket case currently pacing the living room floor, probably counting in Greek to try to calm himself, and the other was full-blown bonkers, seeing nothing wrong with demanding an audience with his god.

Not that you can do any better, she berated herself. You've spent so much time being a damn follower when you knew better that now that everyone's gone to ground or insane, you're just looking to hope whatever happens, happens fast, because it's the waiting that kills you, isn't it? Compared to that, the clean-up isn't much more because you were ready for it.

But the waiting... the waiting is what you can't stand.

A chime from inside the house, softened by the buffer of window glass and distance shook her from these thoughts, which suited her just fine. If nothing else, she knew the art of beating yourself up with your own baseball bat.

Gavin meandered to the door, in mid-sentence.

Rebecca saw the glint of a badge. By the time she was on her feet, she was able to see small flashes of blue from where Gavin wasn't standing.

The cigarette fell from her long, slender fingertips tipped with chipped black nail polish.

Her feet made the porch as Gavin's body seemed to fall in on itself. Diana and Karac blocked out any further view.

She was running to Gavin in time to hear someone –the police officer, she would later figure – that he was sorry.

Gavin's eyes turned to her then.

And she was afraid.

As she held him, his fingers clawlike into her back, she closed her eyes and wept with him.

Time within the mansion had ceased to mean a single thing since the police arrived. Very little was said, and that seemed to sit well with all assembled save Diana Adair, who could not help but think of how inane this group was; the one she considered their one actual rudder was gone, and God only knew what the hell Gavin was going to do in light of this, and He wasn't talking. Never did. Never had. Never would.

Didn't matter.

If anything, Simone's death seemed to mend, at least temporarily, the rift between Rebecca and Gavin. The two hadn't stopped holding hands on the couch since Gavin had stopped crying, something Diana considered should have been done away from the eyes of the troops.

Karac looked like someone had just torn out his spine. Whenever he had spoken, his voice barely made it above a whisper, which only made Diana want to hit him. A man like Karac cut a long shadow, and now he was just a hair away from becoming totally useless, now at the worst time.

Rebecca had softly chanted something using that weird circular breathing method she had though up until now was used exclusively by didgeridoo players. It was a kind of incantation, of that that she could be sure. But it didn't seem to do a damn thing for anyone, least of all being Gavin, who seemed to be its intended target.

Truth be told, Simone was really the only of the bunch Diana figured she could tolerate for longer than ten or fifteen minutes. Especially Solomon, who had up and disappeared some time ago, and she hadn't followed up to see if anyone knew what had happened to him.

There was a clucking sound, and everyone stared at her, as if surprised anyone dare make a sound at this point.

"I think everybody's going to be in for one hell of a disappointment."

"Meaning?" Grunted Gavin, who couldn't even be bothered to so much as look at her. Which took stones, considering the role she was supposed to have played in this little disaster.

"Meaning that but for all the tea in China I would love to see the looks on all your faces, including Lucas' when he reads from the *Forbidden Parchment* or whatever and absolutely nothing happens."

A chuckle, an actual dark thing bubbling from the chest of Karac, to whom she turned, lips cocked and surly.

"Let me guess, you're going to say something mystical like 'Don't anger the spirits' or 'Don't tempt fate, you'll make it blink and notice you.'"

"Not at all."

"What, then?"

"Just go, Diana, you've made you're point."

"No, Mr. Finder, I'm actually curious as to what kind of thought is currently bashing its way around in your head right now. By all means, share your feelings with the group."

Karac's eyes changed not a whit. This was no different a conversation for him to have than if he were talking about breaking a shoelace.

"Something will happen. That's all that I was thinking. Sorry if it got too loud for you."

"Uh-huh. And what makes you so sure something'll happen?"

A slow blink. Not from a teacher to an unwilling student, but one who had had enough of a given world and its conditions and pitfalls.

"Because," he returned. "Something always does."

Diana took a step away. There was something self-satisfied, so self-fulfilling in this man's prophecy to make her stomach roil.

"There nothing left for me then," Diana said, and rose. "See you all in hell." She was to the door by the time someone – probably Karac – tried to stop her. Without turning her head, she simply waved the person away and left them with the group as the door found its way into its jamb with a polite click.

After a time, Gavin excused himself.

248

The edges of the morgue drawer were cold and smooth even as his fingers gripped the rail tighter. The cold was uncomfortable as it insisted in invading his body beneath the skin, but he held on nonetheless. If his hands had been able to curl into the metal itself, he would have been at least a bit pleased.

He turned his head to the attendant but did not look at him.

"May I have a moment?"

The attendant inclined his head and without a sound, had left Gavin alone with his Simone.

He said three words, accented in a tongue known to maybe two other humans as Thieves' Can't. His fingers gripped the rail tighter still as Simone's lidded eyes opened and regarded him. He appeared as if she were trying to smile.

"Hi honey."

Gavin found distraction in letting his fingers trail through his beloved's hair. "Hey baby."

"This kinda sucks, huh?"

"Yeah honey, it does."

"Any idea what you can do?"

"I was hoping talking to you would give me an idea."

"I couldn't find anything out. Maybe you could talk to the woman who was with me."

"Who's that?"

"I don't remember her name. She was the one Lucas was with. Karac's friend or whatever. Don't be too mad at her. He was using her, too. "

"Right. She came to the house?"

"Yep. We have a rat, dear."

"Right."

"Shh. You can't think straight. Just carry on by yourself. You can't trust anyone."

"Is that your way of saying Lucas may actually be able to possess the dead?"

"No, honey. Even he's not that powerful."

His fingertips traced her cool cheekbone.

"I love you, Simone."

"I know you do, baby. I love you too."

"Take care, huh?"

The corners of her eyes seemed to actually wrinkle in humor a bit.

"I'll put a good word in for you."

Gavin nodded. "Hon?"

"Yeah?"

"Can you feel anything?"

"No sweetie, not a thing."

He pressed his lips to her forehead before snapping her neck.

In a moment, he eased the drawer back into place and went to summon the attendant. When the man came to him, Gavin cleared his throat.

"And the other woman, who was in the car with her?"

"Was she family? I was under the impression there were no next of kin."

Gavin shook his head, but kept his eyes on the man. "An old friend of the family. Like a sister."

The attendant's face screwed up, and in time, he looked away. "I'll have to append my sign-in sheet."

"I'll sign whatever it is you need."

The man led him to a second room a door down from the previous one. He led the way in and unlocked the drawer. "You understand I can't release this body to you, only the one you've already identified."

"Of course."

The attendant brought the drawer out, and moved to the door. "I'll give you a couple minutes. If anyone asks, I don't know you're in here."

"Thank you."

The man left, and his footsteps echoed true down the hall. But the door remained open enough to let in a wide triangle of light, thankfully away from where he was standing.

Gavin unzipped the bag quickly. The woman had suffered a massive blow to the side of her head, a grotesque bloom of red and grey over her right ear. The words were repeated over the woman, whose eyes opened without hesitation.

"Shit! Where am I? What did you just do to me?"

Gavin's palm clamped over her cold lips and he stared into her doll-like eyes.

"You're dead, you're in a morgue, and the woman I love is dead because of you and Lucas Brady. You will respond to everything I ask and I will send you back to where ever you were before I interrupted you. Clear?"

The reply was muffled but in the affirmative. He carefully removed his palm.

"Where is Lucas now?"

"I was on my way to this place in Hollywood. A hotel."

"Which one?"

The brow of the woman furrowed. "Don't remember."

"Where is he headed next?"

"He was talking about Benjamin again. My first assignment was to find the owner of the last piece and make sure his idea was right. I thought I'd found him, but I was wrong."

"Who was it?"

"I thought the head of the church there. I was wrong. Lucas thought the closer he got, they would try to move the piece. He was wrong, too."

"So what's stopping him from doing it now?"

"He's weak. That little episode in Mexico nearly did him in. He used a lot of his power. He said he was going to rest before going there."

"He'll teleport again?"

"I doubt it."

"Why?"

"Doing it as often as he has has been bad for him. Nosebleeds and headaches that won't go away."

Gavin felt himself nodding, staring into those eyes now made bottomless through the benefit of death.

"So what now," the woman asked. "Do I go on to live and see repentance because of what you've done?"

Gavin allowed his head to turn, regarding her as if in pity.

"I've done nothing but react," he said at last. "And hope against what my worst angels insist upon telling even as I tell them they're wrong. They've shouted me down, and they've done it decisively."

"I don't think I understand."

"I know," Gavin said, and sent her neck snapping against its axis hard enough for the snap to echo against the morgue walls. He began to move away from her, ready to slam her back into the dark and shut the door when he thought better of it and prised her mouth open. Lucas would come to claim the body if he had any sense at all, to see if Gavin had been there first and that any information his ally had given up in the honesty only the dead can truly convey, as they conceive of no other way within the confines of their condition.

Let Lucas Brady come, Gavin thought. It took longer than he'd have preferred, but he was able to remove most of the woman's tongue with the help of a nasty-looking bladed instrument on the stainless steel tray near an examination table. He used it to start the incision, then took the pleasure in ripping free of her mouth with his own hands before tossing it aside and moving on to the door, where the attendant now stood, protesting something in that way humans have when what they believe they are saying will actually have some burden of weight upon the person being spoken to.

There was a surge under his skin. Gavin's eyes half-lidded and a grin began to appear on his face. He wouldn't have seen fit to have blinded the attendant with a word not meant for human mouths to utter had the man not tried to block his way.

Now the grin ever widened as Gavin made his way down the exit hallway, the man's cries echoing off the smooth walls.

It didn't surprise Karac at all that Fade's front door was slightly ajar. In fact, part of him had expected it. Fade was a target. Knew it in some part of himself, but let ambition mess with him in the way it can only with a Finder, fueled by pride.

And that was the thing that blinded even the best of them to what could notice them. Not the unknown, not the beasties some of the self-proclaimed 'Mystics' Karac had encountered for years on the Sunset Strip and elsewhere, namely the places the dreamer go to expose themselves and be gutted.

No, it was far worse to face the real monsters of the world. They were quick to notice certain things and people, and they were filled with anger and contempt.

And very, very, fast.

His booted feet made no sound across the carpeted floor. The television screen flickered with images he paid no attention to. The sound had been muted, and Karac could see the white on black blocks of captions on the screen from the corner of his eye.

Part of him screamed to leave this house; it knew what he was going to find, it was just a matter of listening to another shred inside him compelling him to confirm it to himself.

And there, sprawled on the floor of the hallway leading to the bathroom, was what he had come for, the body of a man that had been known more as Fade than his real name, whatever that may have been.

He was dressed in a black cloak that fit him too well, hood up over his head. Someone had given thought to this and studied their opinion of Finders enough so that this would appear symbolic, but only those in the know would understand the traditional garb of the thief, the miscreant that would wrap night-colored robes about their body and face to obscure their identity from those curious enough to be out in the night themselves.

The knife, its blade surely poisoned, in the back of the Finder was also symbolic; there is no honor among thieves. To Karac, and those like him, the message would be clear, the actions themselves actually undoing the point of the symbols themselves because of their oak-board delivery.

The killer wouldn't have cared, because he wasn't a Finder.

After carefully picking up the phone in the living room in a shirt he had found in Fade's clothes hamper, he calmly called 911 and reported the murder no one else would have noticed for days, possibly weeks.

"How do I know?" He asked the operator in response to the half-heard question. "Because I'm the one responsible."

He keyed the phone off, threw it offhandedly on the couch and made a mental note to torch the shirt on the way home.

The mist tangling around the ivy and stones leading up to the open doors of the church was actually kind of pretty, considering the circumstances. The smell of oncoming rain always appealed to Lucas... the sound of a storm gathering and rumbling, the sizzle of the mass of rain hitting stones much like these polished ones now under his feet, the patter it would make against the serpent-green vines and glossy leaves curling away from them.

It could even make the city, no so far away, smell decent, for at time. The sky would eventually open up, the sun would glare down on the arteries of freeway and burn away the shadows cast by concrete, steel, and glass reaching higher and higher into the sky each year. The air would be crisp and clear.

Then the smog would creep back in, like it had never left. The cars and horn honking would return, and the beauty of that morning would simply be ignored as it always had been, the reach of the day shot to hell by those who couldn't lift their eyes to it without adjusting their designer eyewear.

But this was not the world of Lucas Brady. It was the world of others, and he had never cared less.

It would appear, Lucas thought as he crossed the threshold and pushed the doors closed behind him, that it was indeed true that mankind was the only beast of land or sea that could become that which it despised.

And as the echo of cane and foot made its way to the sanctuary and the man who entered from the left vestibule, Lucas tried to smile, but couldn't.

The collared priest that stood before him with hands folded more in meditation than prayer simply looked upon him and nodded.

The twist of Victorian glass twirled between Lucas' fingers. "I suppose you know who I am," he said.

A barely perceptible nod from the priest, complimented by a brief closing of eyes.

"And that means we both know I'm not going to leave until you tell me where it is."

At that, the eyes of the priest stayed closed for a moment longer. His expression did not change otherwise.

The cane swept up against the priest's chin, then rocketed across his face. The first flecks of the man's blood spattered across the floor, then the altar.

Solomon Archer's own reflection stared back into him from the window pane as he sat in the La-Z-Boy, watching the still world stand there.

Something had shifted. The ghosts had actually retreated when he felt it happen, this change that pervaded the walls, the floor of his skull, the tones of voices on radio or television. The shift had been decisive. Enough so that when the ghosts departed from his company, he could feel the loss of their presence.

A long branch, dark against the night, skidded across the blacktop bound for west. Solomon watched for as long as it stayed inside the evenly spaced pools of sodium lights that dotted his street.

The wind picked up, slamming the fine screen against the pane, giving rain to smack a short-lived smear against the glass before the fingers of rain widened further still, washing it away.

"Simone Perfect is dead."

He spun to where Rebecca Scott stood, not three feet away from where he sat in the chair that used to feel comfortable. She stood above him, all denim pants and flowing gauze sleeves, eyes wide and unblinking, her lips a thin bloodless line.

Her head tilted, an alien observing an odd life form. "Did you hear me? Simone was killed today."

He tried to rise, couldn't. His fingernail dug half-moons into his palms.

"I understand I gave you his address, and told you he was able to help you. The fact you had no idea of the feud that had gone on between Gavin and Lucas is also my doing, I committed the sin of omission.

"But there must have been some part of you that knew what you were doing. Someone as sensitive as you couldn't go into both the Manor and Brady's house and not feel some terrific power.

"A part of you knew, and you did it anyway."

His eyes were unable to drop despite his efforts. He was, as he found, able to nod. Perhaps, he would later reflect, because it was the truth.

"Simone Perfect is dead now," Rebecca said, turning away from him and moving from his shadow. It was then that Solomon noticed her feet were not touching the ground. "I just wanted to tell you that."

He blinked, and the woman was gone.

He stood then, and wept until he had brought himself to his knees.

A growing tribe of dry leaves on the low wind skittered around the ankles Gavin Fox as he gained the last step to the front porch of the Manor. He had left the door unlocked and some of the leaves gained access to the black marble floor of the foyer before a cock of Gavin's ankle found the door shutting tight behind him before he moved to the stairs, taking each step, hearing the steps that he had remembered from childhood creak as they always had for years now, and yet he had ceased to hear them.

Things were brighter now, almost too much too bear to look at. Distracting. The oak guardrail he had slid down so many time as a boy hissed beneath the skin of his cupped palm. His mother had always reprimanded him for making such sport of the house, but his father would only roll his eyes. If grandfather had ever seen him do it, the elder Fox merely would have stood there and stared at his grandson until the latter turned to see him. No words. Just the eyes. As a teenager, Gavin had called such a thing 'The Fox Stare of Death.' And in time, he discovered that he knew better than that. The glare was not one of utter harshness from an elder who had never once exhibited a sliver of humor in his tired old bones.

No, Gavin now understood that the old man who had parted ways with the Earth so many years ago had been giving him a gaze tempered with nothing more than jealousy at the young man's flight of whimsy any child would experience.

Looks such as those only coiled within the viewer and the one who harbored it. It would only threaten from a distance, and would never strike face-to-face.

And Gavin Fox doubted very much that grandfather or his own father had approved much of his lot in life.

He blinked several times as he made the second floor, eyes calmly going into a half-lidded mode as the future that once was unfurled before him and curdled time after time as he made the library door, fingering the keypad and entering.

He hoped Simone hadn't felt anything.

His feet took him to the library at the east wall, his eyes falling into the all-too familiar habit of scanning the spines he'd seen countless times before. Just out of reach was the Annhauser Edition of T.H. White's *The Once and Future King*, the dust jacket a bit tattered, but intact nevertheless. Every page hand-written with illustrations that drove the imagination joyfully mad with colors and hues only a true artist could render.

At least, that was for the real edition. The dummy copy on the bookshelf was only a fancy disguise for a lever-switch that when the book was pulled forward from the top towards the viewer, a soft click could be heard, and the section of library was able to slide with a deceptive ease inward to the depths of a room that had never seen a lightbulb or any semblance of modern wiring.

The only light here would be courtesy of any of the twenty or so taper candles made of rolled, uncolored beeswax. In the Fox Tradition, as Gavin had understood it to be called, it was not the color of the candle burning that made things happen, it was the intention behind it.

And, of course, the power that was controlling them.

He had been here more times than any of his elders were aware, discovering it somewhere around age twelve, and the blood that sang in his veins told him exactly what kind of books were stored here.

It was insisted that when this room was revealed to him at age seventeen (no reason given for that particular age being chosen) that this room was only for a means of preserving antiquities that should never again see the light of day; a collection of exactly eight books with sigils unknown to most of mankind, and only then would it be an oral tradition. Absolutely nothing could ever be written down regarding these dusty volumes. They were not to exist. They had been left behind by corruptive powers in places of desert or wilderness, buried and waiting for someone to dig at the right time.

And the Foxes would always know about such things.

Whether these books had ever seen use by anyone at all was unknown, and Gavin himself had never been one to question the authority of his elders, especially, he reflected, when he should have done precisely that.

For all he knew, they had never been used. Certainly, looked at, of course reviewed; he himself had seen fit to do that more than once since the initial discovery of this room. It was then he realized how easy it was for him to understand the languages written in these pages that had not been written in a tongue comprehendible to man, but intended for them to learn just the same.

And so again, the blood sang.

The tarnished silver box of long matchsticks stood undisturbed atop the small wormwood table, an antique before his grandpa had been born, beside the door. The match could be struck on the bottom of the box, and following a plume of acrid yet comforting sulfur, found itself touched to the burned wick of the candle in the silver stick on the study table. He inhaled the odor of burning dust as he went about the end of the table.

All of the candles in the room had been burned at some point or another, for indeterminate amounts of time. Never long, by the looks of them. Gavin judged perhaps three hours of light left in the one he currently burned.

More than enough for his needs.

He took one book at a time, starting with closing the one currently atop the table and lightly touching his fingertips to it.

Why would the Fox family have need of such things as these books?

Because this was as good as they'd ever get.

This was all the power they ever had.

The origin of that certain resonance within them all.

It took under ten minutes for Gavin to absorb them all, which, he supposed, would be enough for what he needed to do.

There was no smile remaining on his lips as he floated down the stairs. The door opened, and a whip of leaves rushed the foyer to join the others lucky enough to have made it in before. The door would remain open wide, as Gavin willed it. A flag to all who may require entry. There was nothing left to hide.

The wind felt good against his face as he made his way down the path. He closed his eyes and turned his face to the sun. The smile returned as the light touched and warmed his face, whipping his hair around his face.

This is what the Fox bloodline was meant for.

The blood within his veins no longer sang.

It burned.

The fact that Gavin Fox was floating no less than two inches off the ground was enough for Karac to realize his feet had carried him back a handful of steps, backpedaling off the stairs leading to the Manor porch before he concentrated on bringing them to a stop, now at street-level.

Gavin's eyes didn't glance at him. They stared at a spot only Gavin could see. Anything between him and his goal was at best, a momentary interruption.

And as he approached Karac, his smile widened, something that made the Finder give the man a wide berth.

Karac allowed his eyes to unfocus on the passing mystic, to allow himself to see the fuzzy outline of energy surrounding Gavin Fox.

It was not there. Gavin had become the energy surrounding him, therefore eliminating the need for it to be manifested around him.

Karac tried to swallow, couldn't.

Gavin Fox had gone dark.

Against his better judgment, Karac took two steps toward Gavin, hands raised palms up at chest level and mindful of keeping his voice calm.

"Gavin – "

Karac would never be sure of whether Gavin Fox had actually turned to him, or made any gesture at all. The blindness slammed behind Karac's eyes, causing a bright bloom of panic to grow fresh in his mind.

Gavin would care little for the results of his actions, and exhibiting an unwillingness at least for now to cause death of those who would give cause to stop him. That may or may not last.

Willing calmness to preside over his faculties, Karac took short, halting steps until his toes found the curb, where he sat, minding his breathing to deepen and remain calm. Mystical blindness was not not usually permanent, but could only be reversed when the wielder lost enough concentration, died, or willed it to be so.

This was a warning shot. He could've killed Karac if he'd wanted to.

He wanted Karac alive. To tell the others to back the hell off or be reduced to a tall pile of ash, if that. Diana was irrelevant, and Solomon could most likely be on the list that was uncoiling in Gavin's head. Rebecca might be enough of a threat, if she could gather enough covens together, and given her bent towards them, seemed unlikely to happen.

Gavin probably hadn't given any of this a thought. Someone who had essentially swallowed that degree of power didn't care who the noncombatants were; if someone got in his way, they would be handled. And the only ones who would get into his way would be the ones who wished to stop him. He would take the easiest route, which would also be the least populated way. Even though there would be little resistance, he would not want to waste his time.

This was not about savoring the taste of the chase. It was about the kill. What happened before or after were not the issue.

His fingers found his cell phone in the inside pocket of his suede jacket. He dialed Rebecca's number by touch and left a message on her voicemail about what had happened with him, and what Gavin had been up to.

Solomon wasn't the target, this was bigger game using much bigger game.

Gavin was going to find Lucas Brady, who most likely would care one way or another, and kill him in an ugly, slow way.

He rested his face in his hands and hoped that the blindness would pass soon.

It was odd, Solomon Archer thought. How he felt no jump in his body as he kicked the footstool out from underneath himself. The tug from the makeshift noose created from a braid of videotape wound around itself from what remained of a lighting fixture in the center of his living room was dramatic, but nothing compared to the sound that came from his own throat as he felt his body try to fight for its life, as if of its own volition.

His eyes squeezed shut, a warm tear expelling itself from the corner of one of them, only to die cold on his chin.

He was dimly aware of his hands scrabbling at the knot behind his head.

CHAPTER THIRTY-FOUR

Plans made after advice

    succeed;

  So with wise guidance

    Wage your war.

Proverbs 20:18

In the church, there was an uncertain stillness. Things were different in this air, Gavin knew. And continued within the double doors regardless, on foot, as to hopefully keep whatever power he could from whomever waited within the sanctuary.

Past the modest holy water font carved from what Gavin gathered to be olive wood, most likely from the Holy Land hung on the west wall as he took his first steps inside. The light emanating from within the sanctuary itself was both generous and perfectly natural – meaning from the ceiling lights rather than any sort of supernatural illumination. His soft-soled loafers made nary a sound on the tiled floor as he crossed the threshold into the sanctuary.

The parish priest, or whatever may have remained of the man lay off the altar, crumpled on the stairs leading to it. The smell of incense had instead been replaced now with the faint copper tang of blood, perhaps from the small shadow beneath the priest's body, perhaps not. It was difficult to tell, and the priest was not why he had come to this place.

No, that reason was the man standing at the altar, his handmade codex open nearly midpoint in his upturned hands. The slightest notion of a mutter came from his dry lips as he read aloud just enough to be heard by himself. Without looking up from his tome, Lucas Brady said in a considerably much louder voice; "Rene Descartes is in a bar one night. The bartender says, 'You want a drink?' Descartes thinks for a moment, then says, 'I think not,' and disappears."

Gavin continued his intentionally slow journey down the sanctuary aisle, the tips of the fingers on his right hand drifting lazily across the backrests of the polished wood pews. His left hand hung at his side, his fingers spinning the antique claddagh ring Simone had given him centuries ago on his ring finger.

"Paying your respects to Simone?" He finally said, not so much as lifting his voice one bit over a conversational tone.

"My deepest regrets for that," Brady said.

"And for your friend. Or ally. Maybe 'Sucker' would be best?"

"What are new friends beside possible allies for the future?"

"Yeah, you're real torn up. You're like that, Lucas; Always wearing that bloody heart of yours on your equally as bloody sleeve."

Now the gray eyes narrowed in concentration lifted themselves from the page to settle on him. "Simone's death is something I will never recover from, Gavin. Whether you believe that or not is irrelevant to me. She was truly your better half. Never forget that. She was everything you could have been, and more."

"Without your action, she would still be alive."

"This is true." The eyes returned to their precise place on the page.

"Were you ever the person I thought you were?"

"I very much doubt that."

"And the teleportation? You've really embraced the human monster you so despised in University that you've resorted to the sacrifice of - "

The book snapped shut with a snap louder than to be expected from a relatively diminutive book. *"Don't be an idiot!* You're second-guessing human nature and the universe itself if you think the trails of power lead only one way. Good Lord, Gavin! Look at yourself; You were good at putting the supernatural into the literary world. You were actually capable of making the belief in things unseen seem reasonable! Just because you and I stopped seeing things eye to eye didn't mean either one of us were actually wrong."

"That doesn't give you the reason to do what you're doing."

"It doesn't? Then why am I able to do it?"

"Free will?"

"Free will exists whether there's a God or not! I'm just asking Him to own up to what's going on."

"You sure about that?"

"Tell me, Gavin. What are you going to do with all that leftover power after you've killed me?"

Gavin blinked. "You didn't answer the question."

"Should I?"

"I think so. After all, you've professed to not believe in God."

"I've always couched my comments regarding that."

"That's right; in your books, you've used terms like 'Seems to' or 'May very well indicate.' You've never really addressed that fact that you really have come across as someone who believes in God just enough to try to shake your fist at Him."

A small chuckle from Lucas. It seemed to not suit him one bit. "Sort of like a mirror of yourself, then? You've admitted there is power available to all, yet you refuse to admit there may very well have been a place from where it originated with an intent."

"I have my limits. I'm still human."

"And I'm not?"

"Maybe you're even more human than either of us think, which is why you shouldn't continue reading from that book."

Lucas nodded. "And yet I disagree."

"Color me shocked."

"And you're so different. In your comfy house on the hill, overlooking all the people you're better than because of all you know and all that you *don't* do. Thank you so much. You've defined yourself by what you've denied yourself, very admirable in its way. But there are others who don't believe in the same things you do. And they will do things you don't like. This keeps you up at night. I understand. Honestly. However, it does not mean I must act in a What Would Gavin Do? Sort of way. There will always be somebody ready to piss you off, my friend." There was no change in Brady's expression. He only reopened the book and resumed him mumbled reading.

"You seemed to be the most balanced person I'd met." Gavin waited for the muttering to pause, but when it didn't, he continued on; "What happened to change that? What brings you here, Lucas?" He continued flanking the man. "'Humans in the physical sense are obviously different than the spirit. One is the reality, the other the ideal. The body is intended to be practical, and we teach it some idealized notion that it finds difficult at best to live up to. Inside such a beast, we are strangled.' You wrote that, right?"

The lips kept moving as the eyes lifted from the page once more. In a moment, Lucas spoke; "I am human, I have my common questions. I also understand that putting human limitations and reason into a deity is itself asinine and too common a mistake. No, I saw my mother suffer stroke after debilitating stroke, and all the while she was God's obedient servant. In fact, I think her faith was the last thing to go. She would cough and piss herself, she would go on rants for hours about nothing as her brain stopped working in proper order, finally parts of her simply stopped working. She couldn't speak, couldn't feed herself. I was there for all of it, watching this poor woman deteriorate in front of my very eyes. The woman who gave birth to me, raised me, and stood by me when I decided to take the path I did, which in the end, was much more similar to hers than she knew. Her body fell apart, all sense of dignity falling to the floor. Never in her life did she doubt God, herself, or the abilities either of them had. She was a woman of faith, and why I believed in God for as long as I did.

"But then, on the day of her burial, as the priest from her parish prattled on about the Lord being our shepherd, blah, blah, blah, I got to thinking… first of all, why would He let one of his humble servants… hell, any of His servants suffer the indignities of such a thing as what happened to my mother, but also, what sort of a maniac creates a kingdom of power and wonder made manifest like He did with the Earth, full of riches, then entrust it to something so inherently flawed like the human race, when He knew we'd only screw it up?"

"Because we know better than to listen to the wrong side of our angels but do it anyway."

Lucas Brady actually appeared as if he were about to explode with laughter, but soon caught himself.

"My God, Gavin. Look at you; you're pathetic; defending the God you can only be bothered to believe in enough to fear. Why are humans the only animals obsessed with the notion that they must fill up some void they can't even name within themselves?"

"I don't fear God," said Gavin, taking steps closer to Lucas. "I fear His children."

"Perhaps self-destructive behavior – including denying God – is a protest humans take up against themselves."

Lucas stepped from behind the altar, meeting Gavin as he topped the small series of steps. Lucas extended his hand palm up, the book closed and balanced upon it.

"Why do some have ambitions while others have no need of it? Why are some satisfied with having no ambition while others are absolutely consumed by it?"

"Will doing this make you happy?"

"We answer depending on how we think we propriety dictates to us. If you don't, you're an oaf. If you answer truthfully, you're a dramatic."

"Take it."

"What?"

"'One need not be Caesar to understand Caesar.'"

"'The world cannot live at the level of its great men.'"

Gavin's eyes went from the book to Lucas' steady eyes, then back to the book. The power radiated from the pages into his skin. He could feel the very possibility of anything happening leapt across the space between the book and himself and dance, electric on his skin. He closed his eyes, nearly swaying from the power before opening them. He took one step back, perhaps he lost his balance. He would never be sure.

Lucas shook his head and took his place back behind the altar. "Perfection is only possible for gods, yet it is intended for man. The body is no match for the soul."

"Spare me, Lucas. Didn't you come armed with a gun for such an occasion?"

"Never had much use for bullets," muttered Lucas, his gaze falling on the priest for nary an instant before returning to the pages spread before him. "You, my friend, have led what may be best described as a charmed life. You have experienced death, but up until recently, you've managed to keep it at arm's length. You are articulate, you are careful enough to have dreams, not ambitions, you are learned in a great number of fields, have a taste for aesthetics, and can be a downright decent person when the mood strikes you.

"But you have no time for other human life because you seem to like to think of yourself as quite the detached intellectual. Maybe even an old-fashioned mystic with an eye to the philosophic.

"But you're not. You're nothing more remarkable than a cynic. A sharp one, to be sure, but a cynic nonetheless, and this blurred perception of yourself is, in turn, your greatest liability.

"You could be happy if you could actually tolerate yourself."

Gavin's eyes once more fell on the priest, still on the floor of the altar but now watching him with an intensity that one would not expect from someone who appeared as close to death as he did. It was a gaze that said, *I'm*

262

sorry, sometimes the bad guys win. They don't wear black hats anymore. They come in faster than you expect and don't see fit to kill you in your sleep.

And there was something else in those eyes. Something just as surprising; a trust in faith.

It was too late. Men like Lucas Brady would continue to walk the Earth because that was the world we live in. It rains, the sun shines. These are things of the world. This is the way things are.

"You can't save the world, Gavin."

Gavin looked at Lucas. Blinked, unsure the man had actually spoke. As Gavin thought about it, it turned out that it didn't matter.

"That's okay," came his reply. "I'll settle for my own little part of it."

A small smile, or a tic, etched itself into the side of Lucas' mouth, then disappeared.

Raising his voice above the perpetual mumble his incantations always were sounded at, he intoned:

One word to call and unmake,
To Know.

Give me a gate to open,
And one word,
Spoken by mortal coil.

Again, that damnable smile from Lucas as he stared straight into Gavin's eyes.

"'Hope.'"

The sudden buck of the church floor brought both men painfully to their knees. Lucas was saying something burning and hating to Gavin, but the latter couldn't hear over the cacophony of rumbling earth and the terrible creaking that comes before the clod snap of the wooden beams that stretched overhead.

Whether Gavin liked it or not, Lucas Brady was going to receive his answer.

Gavin's clawed fingers pulled him toward the priest, who now stared at the roof of the very place he'd led worship in begin to collapse above the altar. Gavin managed to grab enough of the priest's jacket to lend him the power to drag him as far away as possible from the ceiling. It was less than likely it would amount to the saving of the man's life, but merely getting him away from Lucas and his sphere of rotting influence was enough.

One of the stained glass windows at the west side of the sanctuary gave inwardly. Another Gavin could see exploded outwardly and Lucas Brady's laughter could now be heard over the destruction.

The awful groaning of the south wall began as Gavin brought the priest as far as he could from Lucas and whatever audience he would actually manage to demand.

The thunder of building becoming rubble drove everything from him. He covered his head and hoped the priest was doing the same. This was the end, and it was not a whisper, it was with a shout and a strike and the destruction of brick and mortar because of one man's mission.

Deafening cracks, a rumbling from under the ground that made Gavin actually begin to cry and pray for it to just stop. Dust in his face; rubble striking his body.

And then nothing for several long seconds.

Despite the primitive cry of fear in his head that had no use for words, only meaningful sounds of panic and self-preservation, he opened his eyes.

The priest was on his feet. He appeared unsteady, but determined to keep his feet under him.

Gavin swayed to his feet, dusting himself off with slight motions he was only dimly aware of making.

The entire south wall had collapsed, exposing the hillside and cemetery behind it. The sky was cloudless and blue. The slight breeze that wound its way past the ruble actually felt tranquil, and Gavin found a child's solace in the sound of dry leaves skittering around outside.

After a time, the priest looked at him and nodded. "Thank you."

Without another word, they both began to search the rubble.

The thought that Lucas Brady may have someone to mourn him made Gavin pause in his work just long enough to realize there wasn't a whit of him that cared, and he continued to chop to body into smaller and smaller pieces. He had already pulled the teeth and severed the tips of Brady's fingers and would dispose of them separately, possibly in the desert.

He wiped away the stinging in his eyes. Come nightfall, he'd drive the rest of what remained of Lucas Brady up into the Hollywood Hills where he would burn them, and let the authorities blame the Satanists.

CHAPTER THIRTY-FIVE

Graham Greene once said, 'You can't conceive, nor can I, the appalling strangeness of the mercy of God.' I still don't know whether I agree with the man.

Gavin Fox, IN HEART AND MIND; STUDIES OF
THE OCCULT AND THEOLOGICAL BELIEF

Alec was surprised at even inside a church how much sensuality Elizabeth could pack into the handful of slow steps down the aisle toward what remained of the sanctuary. That familiar lopsided grin, the hands swaying easily at her sides. She still had that way of tilting her head just ever so slightly to her left.

"Here I am coming by to pay my respects and I find you messing the place up."

Alec moved his attention away from the cracked leg of the altar. "Well, I'm a little surprised you'd miss the party."

The witch's eyes flicked across a few random panes of stained glass. "Not really my kind of party. You understand."

Alec nodded, allowed a smile.

"It was Lucas Brady." It was not a question.

Alec nodded once more.

"What happened to him?"

"Church fell on him."

"Oh."

Elizabeth just continued looking at him as he busied himself with sweeping random bits of the fallen sanctuary away with the back of his hand from the edge of the hardwood altar, picking up some of the more interesting bits, putting them back down again.

"You okay?"

"Better after I washed up a bit."

"You look like hell."

"You should have seen me before I cleaned up."

"The book?"

He didn't look up from his work. "Gone."

"You think it's for the best?"

"I hope so, yes."

"And your wounds?" She paid careful attention to not look at him when she asked him this.

"I'll be fine."

"What do you think happened to it?"

"If that man who said he was Gavin Fox didn't take it, I'm fairly certain we'll never know."

Elizabeth puttered about the rubble, just to give herself something to do. She knew that's how it looked, kept on working in silence anyway.

"I'm sorry your church had to suffer this," she said at last. "I know how much of yourself you've put into it."

Alec caught himself nearly shrugging. "The church isn't the point. It's brick and mortar. It's the message. People have already said they'd pitch in." His eyes scanned the beams of the vaulted ceiling. "The church did as it was needed to. The page was going to lead to destruction no matter what."

Elizabeth nodded. "Everything happens for a reason."

"So it would appear." He discarded a piece of something he could no longer recognize. He went to his knees again to confirm that the floor had indeed cracked as deep as he had first thought. He raised his eyes to her. "Tell me something."

"Anything."

"Did you replace the page while I was away?"

Hands on cocked hips. Her eyes narrowing comically. "Now would I do something like that?"

"It does seem like something that either you alone or with the Coven would have done, yes."

"And what, replaced it with a forgery good enough to fool even the likes of one Mr. Lucas Brady?"

"Just so."

She reached out and touched the top of his head. Her face, first touched by self-conscious comedy, now softened and indulged him with a smile.

"Dear Alec, do you really want to know?"

Alec tried to give the appearance of one actually considering this.

"Yes," he said at last.

Elizabeth's fingers slipped from his forehead. "And that," she said. "Is why I'm not going to tell you." As she moved, she asked, "Do you think the Vatican or whomever actually believes that the book Lucas created could actually do what it's supposed to?"

"That reminds me of a story. And I love stories, don't you?"

The witch's eyes closed indulgently for a moment, her smile widening. "I love stories."

"Someone in Seminary once told me this one: In ancient times, there lived a mouse who lived in a canyon. In this canyon there also lived a golden eagle. One day, the mouse who lived in fear of the eagle decided to give the eagle warnings whenever predators were plotting to come for its eggs. Time passed, and a sidewinder came to dwell in this canyon. Every day, this sidewinder would pass the mouse, look at it, then pass it by.

"This went on for quite some time.

"Then, one day, while the sidewinder was passing by the mouse, the golden eagle swooped down from out of nowhere, grasped the snake in its talons, and dropped it over a cliff.

"'What did you do that for?' the Mouse asked the eagle. 'That sidewinder has been passing me by for years now, and never once has he struck at me.

266

"The golden eagle looked at the mouse for a long time, then answered simply, 'I could no longer accept that risk.' And flew away."

"So you don't know either, huh?"

"Not really, no."

"I heard once that during the Holocaust, Eichmann turned Dohany Synogogue in Hungary into a concentration point to send Hungarian Jews to their deaths. At some point before, several priests helped the rabbi remove the twenty-seven scrolls of the Torah and bury them in a Christian cemetery until after the war. What does this tell us?"

Alec smiled wryly, something he knew Elizabeth would be able to appreciate. "That there remains the potential for light even in the darkest of places, compassion can come from the unexpected places." He rose with a groan. "And I have two cracked ribs."

Elizabeth grinned and helped him up, her fingers light on his hand. "But you're going to live?"

"Despite the universe's apparent intent to the contrary, yes."

"You are going to the hospital before those bones start to knit, right?"

"Yes, Ma'am."

She bowed to him, her hand over her heart.

"God be with you, Elizabeth."

She smiled. "Blessed be, Alec."

As she turned, her eyes caught on the crucifix still held to the wall west of the one that had collapsed. Touching her fingertips to her forehead in a kind of casual acknowledgement, she turned and departed without another word.

When Karac's shadow fell on the sanctuary floor, Alec had made little progress and was musing about wheat toast and jam for brunch. With orange juice. With a little champagne. Something that made him feel alive and grateful for a face full of sunshine.

Instead, he got Karac.

Alec wouldn't look up, even when the Finder's shadow fell on his shoulders.

"I can't stay long," Karac said.

Alec lifted his head and stared into the other man's eyes.

"Well, don't let me keep you."

Karac's booted feet shifted. "Look, I've never been good at this sort of thing."

"And yet you continue to those around you with your attempts," Alec said, ignoring the stab in his ribs as he moved some bits of rubble to join a growing pile."

"I just wanted to see if everything was okay."

"Sorry, Karac. The church still stands."

"You're okay?"

Alec rose, failed to hide the wince. "After a fashion."

The Finder eyed him head to toe, made a face. "Doesn't look that way."

"I'm fine."

The Finder's hands rose in supplication. "Okay, okay. You won't be getting an argument out of me." He waited until Alec had turned away, casting about for something to accomplish instead of moving one mess only to replace it with another. "And, for the record, I don't hate churches. Just what they stand for."

"Yes, we're all in this racket to fleece the sheep."

"That's not what I meant. You're a good guy."

"Must kill you to say that."

"That's not very Christian of you."

"God loves everybody," Alec answered. "I am not God."

Karac picked up a part of masonry, set it aside, went on to do it again with a smaller piece. He continued to help in silence, taking his cue from Alec as best he could.

Soon, as they piled more rubble outside, Alec saw the line of six or so cars and trucks making their way up to the church road. Bars of sunlight had since broken through the stormclouds that were making their way out to sea. Light erupted in shallows of rainwater dotting the pathway to the church.

"Reinforcements?" Karac asked, deadpan.

"Yes," replied the priest, matching tone. "We're going to hose you down with holy water and tell you we're praying for because we love you."

Karac just continued to watch the line of cars belonging to the residents. "They love you, you know."

"I know. That's why I'm letting the glue a Jesus fish on the back of your Torpedo."

Karac cast him a sidelong glance. "You aren't funny."

"I told them to use Gorilla Glue."

"Still not funny."

"Then why am I smiling?"

"Because you're an idiot."

"You sure? Because I know funny, and I'm pretty sure I'm hysterical."

"No. Really. You're an idiot."

Alec nodded, dusted his hands together as he made his way back inside the church sanctuary. "That's okay, I've been called worse."

"You sure?" Karac asked, following him into the shade of the church.

"Come to think of it, not at all."

The sound of tires crunching on gravel followed by car doors opening and closing followed.

"I should split," Karac said.

"Yeah, I know."

The Finder shrugged into his cracked and faded leather jacket that, if legend held true, once belonged to Jimi Hendrix. "By the way," he said fixing the collar. "I want my copy of *The Cantebury Tales* back."

"I already gave it back to you."

Karac nodded, still moving to the door. "You're not supposed to lie, Alec. God says so."

"Hey, Karac?"

The Finder seemed surprised at the name, stopped and craned his neck to the priest. "Yeah?"

"Call Mom more often, okay?"

Karac grinned, nodded, and disappeared against the soft rush of bodies now entering the sanctuary.

In the Torpedo, Mia watched him return to the driver's side.

"Thanks for being so tolerant of me," he said.

The corners of her mouth drew up. "I told you, I like weird shit." She kissed him on the cheek and he keyed the engine to life.

Alec Copeman was surprised that it took David Nedry as long as it did to show up, almost as if waiting his turn and assuming his own role in the pecking order of the visitors. The officer didn't smile as he entered the sanctuary ahead of all the others, but instead took in the ruined wall and Alec himself, who cared not a whit for any of the attention.

"I suppose I should apologize for turning up late," Nedry said.

"Nope, you're right on time." Alec chucked his chin at the people fanning out, surveying the damage. One of them was Tom Turner, the son of the man who had helped build the towns of Benjamin and Nazareth Bay. Tom was now the unofficial worker of carpentry and construction in those parts.

Now a smile from Nedry. "That's not what I meant."

"I know."

"You okay? You look like you may need to see a doctor."

Alec found himself nodding. "I suppose. Still a little in shock."

"I can imagine."

"Was anybody in town hurt?"

Nedry appeared taken aback by the question. "It was pretty localized."

"How localized?"

"Enough so the church was the only thing taking damage that we've found. Can I ask why it took you so long to call me?"

"I really have no idea. I guess I've just been wandering around, confused."

Nedry nodded, appraised the wreckage behind Alec. "I wish I could have been here for you."

"Earthquakes are like that."

"Yeah, they beat the hell out of you, huh?" It was Nedry's not-so-subtle way of saying he noticed the damage to Alec's face, and knew he'd never get the truth about it.

Alec nodded, tried a smile, dropped it.

"Are you done now, Father?"

"Done with what?"

"With whatever it was you had to go through in order to get to *this* point?"

Alec considered this for a moment. "Yes. Yes, I think so."

Without another word, David Nedry left him to join the others.

From the rubble, something shining caught Alec's eye. He bent, his ribs complaining and swept aside crumbled mortar. His fingers curled around the object and pulled it free.

He held the twisted glass cane up to catch the sunlight now afforded to the pulpit by the fallen wall. He turned the glass this way and that, letting sun curl down its curves. Chuckling, he twirled it awkwardly between his fingers.

The sun glowed proud above Diana Adair's head as she gazed into it, admiring the glassine serenity she was able to find there, partly, she figured, because Simone's scent was still so prevalent in the clothes Diana had been lent by the woman. And now that she had left this plane, it seemed to burn all the brighter in her nostrils.

The group would do as the group would do. They would act as they would need to act, according to their own nature. Just as Diana herself was doing now.

As light expanded and increased in the sky, she was only dimly aware of her fingers undoing the buttons of the clothing she no longer needed. As her skin became exposed, it welcomed the cool wind blowing from the east, bringing with it new smells and sensations; honeysuckle, perhaps, a musk of some kind. Someone had burned their steak dinner.

Simone's clothing now in a loose wad at her bare feet, Diana closed her eyes and inhaled the night deeply through her nose, holding it in her lungs before allowing it to disappear back into itself through pursed lips.

She smiled, and ran, her feet light on the still cool grass leading to gravel finding its way to rocky terrain. There were eyes upon her, but she no longer could consider them any more animal than herself, and therefore alien to her.

She pushed into the hills. Into the wilderness.

And it did not push back, as it so often does when humans insist they belong there.

Instead, it welcomed her.

EPILOGUE

SELAH

She watched the Finder's Tucker Torpedo move down the dirt path away from the church, tires kicking up plumes of dust that wavered as the group of people moved into the church.

The church would rebuild, Gavin would move on, the others would do as the others would. Being who they were, they could do nothing else.

They had each made their decisions on their own time.

She searched for how she could feel about Solomon Archer, and all she could come up with was a kind of calm pity.

She smiled a bit at that.

Paths were already being created in these lives, carved by actions of their own. The ability to see the potential for greatness could, she supposed, be tempered by man's apparent unwillingness to actually go through with such a thing.

Imagine, she thought. Such a world that can be.

Maybe things would turn out differently next time.

Imagine, she thought.

And was gone.

Cristopher DeRose is a regular contributor to Surreal, Cemetery Dance, and FilmFax magazines and is a Staff Writer for the Sci-Fi Channel's website, scifiweekly.com. His website can be found at cristopherderose.com. *To Cast A Violent Shadow* is his second novel.

www.ingramcontent.com/pod-product-compliance
Lightning Source LLC
Chambersburg PA
CBHW020611260626
47157CB00003B/957